The Close-Up

The Close-Up

A Novel

Pip Drysdale

G

GALLERY BOOKS

New York   London   Toronto   Sydney   New Delhi

G

Gallery Books
An Imprint of Simon & Schuster, LLC
1230 Avenue of the Americas
New York, NY 10020

First Gallery Books hardcover edition December 2024

GALLERY BOOKS and colophon are registered trademarks of Simon & Schuster, LLC

Simon & Schuster: Celebrating 100 Years of Publishing in 2024

For information about special discounts for bulk purchases, please contact Simon & Schuster Special Sales at 1-866-506-1949 or business@simonandschuster.com.

The Simon & Schuster Speakers Bureau can bring authors to your live event. For more information or to book an event, contact the Simon & Schuster Speakers Bureau at 1-866-248-3049 or visit our website at www.simonspeakers.com.

Manufactured in the United States of America

10 9 8 7 6 5 4 3 2 1

Library of Congress Cataloging-in-Publication Data has been applied for.

ISBN 978-1-6680-3792-8
ISBN 978-1-6680-3794-2 (ebook)

For my mom—my first reader

One

There's a magic hour in LA, right when the sun sets, that has the whole city sparkling gold and tangerine—even the trash. It's the kind of light that makes you feel lucky to be alive, like anything is possible. The kind that has you looking out at the view and seeing the grit and poetry of Bukowski's *Hollywood* and the LA scenes from Jacqueline Susann's *Valley of the Dolls* instead of traffic, smog, and heartbreak. That whispers "Don't you dare give up, please, I beg you" in your ear.

So look, I'm not saying it was the light's fault . . . I understand that we're all grown-ups here with free will. I'm just saying it didn't help. Because much is made of the Santa Ana winds—the devil winds, they call them.

But if you ask me, it's that light, that pure, unadulterated hope, that draws us here and keeps us here, that fucks us up the most. It urges us to roll the dice, but by the time we do, the sun has gone and it is dark. And even now, knowing how this story ends, I still can't say if it was worth the gamble. But I do know what happened.

So let me tell you that instead.

I'm driving up Mulholland Drive, in a white van with a green logo on the side, on the night this story begins. It's the middle of May, the window is half-open, the sun is close to setting, and I'm frowning at street signs because the British guy in my navigation app has just said "Turn left in six hundred feet."

And honestly: *how am I meant to know how far six hundred feet is?!*

I have it set to a British voice because that's where I'm from—London—and I guess as much as I wanted to leave that little gray island, with its expensive fruit and stairwells that smelled of damp, I still miss it. Especially on days like today. The kind when gravity feels so strong your heart struggles to beat.

"Turn left," says Mr. GPS, and I do.

Trees and gates and walls blur past as I watch the numbers rise—four, six, eight—and then Mr. GPS says, "Your destination is on the right," and he's correct: there's a gold number ten sparkling from the wall.

I pull into the driveway—an iron gate in the middle of a tall stone wall—and stop at the intercom, take a deep breath, and press the call button. "Zoe from Venice Floristry, I have a delivery," I say, smiling into the camera. I smile a lot in life, and I'm not sure why because I'm sure as hell not happy. I mean, I *want* to be happy, or if I can't be happy, I at least want to be cool and jaded, but I'm neither of those. And the worst part is I'm smart enough to see that.

The crackling stops, the screen goes black, and I reach for my phone while I wait.

There is one message. Vee. She manages the florist's shop I work for. It's a picture of her swollen ankle, with a bruise poking out the top of a bandage, as it rests on a yellow velvet pillow with a large embroidered bee.

It's usually Vee who does these ultra-high-profile deliveries, the kind that double as a networking opportunity. She's a talented florist in her own right—she trained me up and helps out when needed—but mainly she's in charge of events, networking, Instagram, and everything extroverted. I, on the other hand, get to hide in the back of the shop with the flower cooler and piles of cut stems in the mornings and just do the routine day-to-day deliveries in the afternoons—birthdays, anniversaries, that sort of thing. The sorts of occasions that make people happy to see you and you can't mess up. But Vee slipped at four thirty this afternoon and sprained her ankle. So here I am instead.

And it feels like that's important—like it's proof of fate or something. Because if I hadn't been in this exact place, on this exact night, at this exact hour, I never would have run into *him*. And everything would be different right now.

Everything.

I mean, I *definitely* wouldn't be typing this . . . honestly, I probably *shouldn't* be typing this.

But I'm a writer; I can't help myself. This is the kind of story that only happens to you once in a lifetime, and that's if you're lucky. So I need to get it all down now before I forget any of the details. Before I lose my nerve.

Anyway, so there I am in the van, staring down at my phone, replying to Vee with: *Oww, that looks sore*. And pressing Send.

The intercom crackles again, the gate opens, and I drive inside.

Gravel crunches beneath tires as I head slowly up a long driveway shaded by trees that remind me of England. Ahead, there are three clean and expensive-looking cars neatly parked by a well-groomed hedge and a huge home.

I pull up to a grand circular fountain and park in front of it, then reach into the seat beside me—past my huge bag and a worn-out copy of *The Great Gatsby*—for the delivery note to check the name: Brian Rollingston.

I pop the back doors, get out, and head around to unload the flowers. The sky is burnt gold now, the sun just a sliver on the horizon. The front door of the house opens, and I turn to look as a woman with her hair in a turquoise scarf says, "You're late." And she's right. Vee was meant to be here at six. But between Vee's ankle and some crazy traffic, now it's almost 7:20 p.m. She leaves the door open and then she's gone again.

I open up the back doors and look inside. Our florist's shop specializes in "literary-inspired rustic elegance" (I'm quoting directly from our website now) in the English garden style. So that means loose, natural, and unstructured arrangements, with a mix of English garden flowers like roses, peonies, sweet peas, snapdragons, and delphiniums with foliage such as herbs, ferns, stems of pussy willow, and twigs. It really depends on what's in season, or what our supplier can source. Right now, there are four large arrangements in pristine white plum vases, together with eight matching table centerpieces in the back of the van. They're all held in place by foam blocks, straps, and a couple of empty containers to stop them moving during transit. I reach for the large arrangement closest to me. It's heavy, so I take a deep breath, grab it with both arms, and take a step backward . . . and that's when I hear them.

Low and heavy barks.

Coming from somewhere behind me.

Shit.

I freeze.

There's a voice now, a male voice; it yells: "Genius, stop! Randal!" And now there are footsteps too. *Shit shit shit.* It's all getting louder. Faster. The barking. The footsteps on gravel. Someone is running . . .

What's happening? Should I run too?

I turn quickly, just in time to see teeth and slobber and a haze of black and brown. A rottweiler. Paws hit my shoulders. I hold my breath and grab tightly on to the vase but *shit shit shit*. I fall backward, against the van. My fingers slip.

Smash.

My stomach clenches as I squint down at the ground: that pristine white vase has broken into five—no, six—pieces, and the vast arrangement of pink peonies, deep-red roses, mossy twigs, and whimsical foliage lies limp and tattered on the pale gravel, bits of chicken wire and green floral foam visible between the cracks. I kneel down quickly to tend to it, like I can salvage things. But no amount of glue and florist's tape can fix this.

"Sorry. Are you okay? They just love cars, man. I couldn't stop them," comes the male voice again. "I've only had them a year. They're still puppies."

Except . . . *Wait. That voice. I know that voice.*

I look up and my mind fills with static.

Because he's tall and rugged looking with dark hair, bright-blue eyes, and a tan . . .

And *no, baby Jesus, don't do this to me. Not today.*

Because it's *People* magazine's sexiest man alive—the one, the only, Zach Hamilton.

Two

Okay, so other places I've seen Zach Hamilton before: (1) Netflix, (2) billboards, and, well, (3) my apartment. Three years ago. He was wearing ripped blue jeans, a Nirvana T-shirt, and the same black beads around his wrist as he is right now, walking out my door and saying he'd call. He didn't call. Not even after I left a very drunk voicemail on his phone (okay, fine, two very drunk voicemails and one unhinged text) asking him whether the three days we'd spent together had meant nothing.

Yes.

It was *that* bad.

And get this: back then he wasn't even famous. No, back then I was the one with the book deal (yes, I still have a book deal; it's complicated) and he was just another good-looking guy in LA with big dreams. And now here we are and the tables have turned and why is there never an earthquake in this city when I need one?

But I have to say something and it's been three long years—there would have been a hundred other girls since then; he probably doesn't even remember me. So I go with a nonchalant, maybe-I-remember-you, maybe-I-don't "Hi . . . Is Brian around?" But my voice betrays me; it comes out flimsy. Weak. Heat moves up my neck.

And I'm intentionally looking down so he can't see my face, focusing on picking up pieces of white ceramic, but I can see him in my peripheral vision. He's watching me, his hand on his hip like Adonis. I just want him to go away.

"He's inside," he says, crouching down beside me to help, his smile broadening to a grin. "You still have the accent."

Shit. He remembers.

"I do," I say, frowning down at the floral foam, bent stalks, and bruised peonies, trying in vain to pull them back into place as that heat creeps up to my cheeks.

Because "I do"? What's wrong with me? I sound like I'm practicing wedding vows.

He picks up the larger pieces of ceramic as Genius and Randal sniff around, wagging their tails, like they've done everyone a mini-favor. And I can smell his aftershave—musk and earth; it's the same one I remember. It was on my pillowcase for five days after he was gone. I had to double wash it.

"Go play," Zach says to the dogs and points, and they run off.

"I'm really sorry about this . . ." He trails off. *He can't even remember my name.*

"Zoe," I remind him, then wish I hadn't. It would have been way cooler if I'd let it go.

"I know, I remember . . . we're both *Z* names. So what have you been doing; how did the book go? I meant to read it."

"Good," I lie, my voice jumping an octave and giving me away. I swallow hard and pray those tectonic plates will shift just a little, just a tad, and change the conversation. And then . . .

"What the fuck is going on here?" comes a booming voice from the house.

I look up and so does Zach as a short man of around fifty-five with a thick head of salt-and-pepper hair and big white teeth strides toward us, hands on his hips. I stand up and put everything I've gathered in the back of the van, my jaw clenched—I'm not good with confrontation.

"It was my fault, Brian," Zach says as he gets to us.

"I doubt that," says the man, his little red eyes trained on me now. He's been drinking, or smoking weed. Maybe both.

"We still have three," I offer, turning back to him and trying to sound upbeat.

"Well, which one did you break?" he snaps as he peers into the back of the van.

"Um . . . an Ophelia's Dream," I say.

All our arrangements have literary names like Ophelia's Dream or Mrs. Dalloway's Roses or Sylvia Plath's Tulips or Hemingway's Last Letter. That was my idea when I first started at the florist's, and I thought better of it almost immediately. But Vee loved it, she said it gave us a point of difference, and so it stayed.

Brian pulls his hands through his hair. "Of course you fucking did. That's the important one."

There are three other identical Ophelia's Dream arrangements in the back of the van right now (i.e., there is no important *one*), but I'm scared to point this out. Instead, my mind whirs, looking for a solution. These are for an event tomorrow morning. An engagement brunch for his daughter: pink peonies symbolize affection, prosperity, and a happy marriage; red roses mean romance . . . His instructions had been clear—everything was to arrive this evening to avoid overwhelm in the morning—but still, there is time. I *could* go back to the store and make another.

"Um . . . I could bring another one early tomorrow morning?" I say.

He peers into the open van and lets out a short, sharp huff, as his nostrils flare. "Fuck it," he snaps. "Just bring in what you have. I want this done." Then he calls out "Henri!" and a man with chiseled, tanned arms arrives.

Brian shoots me a hot look of hate and then storms away to the house.

And all I can do is stare at the door as my eyes prick with tears, because *of course this is how today ends*; I should have known from how it started.

"Sorry about him," says Zach from beside me as I turn back to the van. "He gets like this, but he'll calm down." Henri starts unpacking the unbroken arrangements and table centerpieces onto the ground.

"It's fine," I say, not looking at him because I might cry. Instead, I stare at the ground and pick at my nail polish, searching for something else to say. "What are you doing here, anyway? Are you friends?"

"Brian's my manager," he says as Henri grabs the last one. And with that one phrase he reminds me how different our lives are now. I have an agent, sure, but he has "people." Multiple.

"Oh," I say. "Cool. Well, it was nice seeing you again." I give a small smile, then I slam the rear doors shut and head around to the driver's door. And I expect Zach to go inside but he doesn't. He follows me. I reach for the handle, pull it open, get into the van, and pull it closed after me.

"So, flowers . . . I don't remember a day job. Is that new?" he asks, leaning against the door.

"Yeah," I say as I put on my seat belt.

I got the job at the florist's after my debut novel bombed two years ago (it was called *Fractured*, a thriller), because I'd spent most of my advance on rent, overpriced eyeshadow palettes, and books, and it turns out having glitter on your eyelids is only a short-term fix: I needed health insurance and an income too.

I put the key in the ignition.

"So what are you doing tonight?" he asks through the open window, his eyes scanning the seat beside me and seeming to land on *The Great Gatsby*.

"I have a thing," I say, glancing into the rearview mirror. My only "thing" is going home, getting under the covers, and reading until today is done.

"A thing? Well, that sounds . . . cool. But if you wanted to cancel . . . I have this party," he says. "I mean, you could come."

"What?" I ask, my eyes shifting to him.

"I have a party to go to tonight," he says, a little slower, with a big smile. "Why don't you come?"

And there is no way I'm falling for this again. He was charming last time too, and he did his voodoo on me and then I was a basket case, and I can't afford to get unbalanced right now. Although, I *did* finally manage to rewrite *Fractured* after he ghosted me last time . . . It was like my muse fed off the rejection, off the idea of what could have been, off my own descent into obsession and sadness. Those were the exact feelings I needed to understand in order to write it. But no, once is enough, thanks.

"I can't. I have plans," I say again. "But thank you."

My hands grip the steering wheel a little tighter.

"Come tonight," he fake-whines. "There's someone you need to meet. A producer friend."

And as I glance past him at the tangerine sky, I have this microglimpse of what my life was meant to be like and a surge of, I don't know, something dangerous, like "hope." Like maybe it could still be that way.

And this is what I mean about the magic hour: none of us are immune. Because if the light were stark right now, casting ugly shadows, I'd just go home. But it's not—the edges of everything are soft and blurry and there's a golden glow to his skin and he said there's someone I need to meet and I've heard stories about how just one night can change everything for someone. And I think: *Fuck it, what have I got to lose?*

That's a thought that will haunt me in time. But not yet.

My gaze snaps back to his and he sees the "yes" in my eyes. I don't even have to say it.

"Fantastic. Can you drive us?" he says before going around to the other side of the van. He opens the door, gets into the passenger side, and as he puts my things on his lap he says, "Nobody will recognize me in this van."

And then he winks at me.

And no matter what you read in the press, that's how the madness really begins.

Three

Twelve hours and twenty minutes before

Twelve hours and twenty minutes before I see Zach again, I wake to my alarm. To the sound of bells echoing off my walls. I reach for my phone, turn off the noise, and stare at the screen: a few Instagram notifications, a calendar reminder that my rent is due, and two text messages.

The first text is from my dad: *Have you thought through what we spoke about?*

(The answer to that is no, I haven't; it gave me a mild panic attack, so I've tried to block it out. Every few weeks my dad sends me a link to some recent violent crime in LA—gun violence, cult killings, serial murderers—and then follows it up with a phone call to "chat" about how maybe it's time I came home. That's what happened two days ago, except this time he was extra pushy about it, talking about helping me find a job when I got back. And I understand it—I'm all he has and I've been gone for over three years—but I don't want to go home.)

The second text is from Barb Wallace, my agent: *Got your email. Do you have anything else?*

Flashes from 3 a.m. flicker in my mind: typing . . . grinning . . . pressing Send.

Shit.

Okay, so remember I said my first book bombed? Well, it really messed with my head and I haven't written anything since. That's two long years of nothingness. I've tried, lord knows I've tried, but I'm what writers refer to in whispers as "totally fucking blocked" (a.k.a. doomed).

But sometimes late at night (it's always late at night), my muse visits for a fleeting moment and I have an idea, a golden idea. My fingers fly across the keys, desperate to get it out, until the awful moment I realize it's trash and press the Backspace button until all evidence is gone and the page is blank once more. And I'm back to looking at that little cursor blinking and blinking and blinking.

That's what happened last night between the hours of one and three.

Except *this* time I didn't have the good sense to use that Backspace button. This time, with the delusional self-confidence that only comes beyond the witching hour, I sent it to my agent . . . which brings us to: *Got your email. Do you have anything else?*

And this is bad—really bad. This is the fourth idea I've sent her that she hasn't liked. My guess is if I make it five, she'll drop me, and then I might as well douse myself in formaldehyde.

Yes, I know that sounds melodramatic, but I was one of those wunderkinds you read about and hate. Everything is supposed to be different for me right now.

You see, I've always known I was a writer, ever since I was a child—it was the one thing the world consistently agreed with me on. At school I got top marks in English, I won a scholarship to study English literature at a mid-level university, and by the time I was twenty I had a series of short stories published in various literary journals. It seemed to everyone who knew me like a foregone conclusion that I'd write novels one day, though secretly I had no idea what I wanted to write about yet. But then, just before my twenty-third birthday, I met Adam.

We started dating seriously, and around our first anniversary, I received an Instagram DM. It was from another woman claiming to be his girlfriend. Saying that there were four of us in total. I confronted him about it and he denied it, first telling me it was all in my head and then (when I showed him the message) calling her "crazy" and telling me she was dangerous and to block her. We broke up, of course, but that's how the idea for *Fractured* was born.

I would write a novel about a woman, a student, who was stalked and terrorized by a virtual stranger . . . or so it seemed. The twist, in that first draft at least, was that she was an unreliable narrator, teetering on the edge of insanity. The whole thing would happen in her mind.

It was exciting.

This was the first time I'd had a long-form story I could see all the way through until the end. And I loved the idea of a university setting.

So I started to write.

By the time I turned twenty-five, I had a solid ninety thousand words.

I submitted to at least thirty agents (who sent me back form-letter rejections) and a few international manuscript competitions, and then, out of the blue, I got a break.

I *won* one of them.

A big one.

Suddenly agents *wanted* to sign me. Everyone was super excited about how young I was, how full of promise, how far I might go. I could have signed with any number of them, but I chose Barb. I liked that she was from LA and worked across publishing and film, selling manuscripts *and* screenplays; it felt like maybe that would work in my favor one day. Maybe I could write screenplays too. Maybe I could move there, meet the right people, be in the thick of things. Who knew what life might bring?

Everything was opening up for me.

Six months later, after a heated auction, I got a two-book deal for $1 million with a US publisher. There was a *Publishers Weekly* announcement; I started finding my name on Buzzfeed and "ones to watch" lists; Barb was excited about early film and TV interest and saying things like "when you're a *New York Times* bestseller" like it was just a matter of time. It felt like I'd won the lottery.

That was back when a million dollars felt like *so much* money. I mean, look, it is. It really is (I wouldn't mind another million now). But once you deduct 15 percent for my agent, a shitload of tax, and a hefty sum for Dad to help him pay off his mortgage because *of course*, and understand that the payment doesn't come as a lump sum, once you take into account the cost of living in LA and the fact that I haven't written a second book yet, the picture skews. You begin to understand that unless I produce something great soon, I'm going to have to pay back the $250,000 I've already been paid for signing book two. Because it's been two years and I was meant to deliver after one. Which would be fine, aside from my reputation and my soul, but I don't have it. Not the book, and not the money either.

So, happy birthday to me, I guess.

Oh, yes, today is my birthday.

My thirtieth birthday, no less.

Which doesn't have quite the same ring to it as twenty-six.

I glance over at the window, the morning sun soaking through the orange curtains. This is not how I imagined thirty looking. I didn't think I'd still be alone; I didn't think I'd be renting a one bedroom in West Hollywood in varying hues of orange, cream, and brown that soon I won't be able to afford.

Still, at least it has a pretty exterior, a Spanish colonial–style building amid the glass and concrete new-build developments that take up most of the street. And it's quiet—four of the six apartments in my block are owned by wealthy investors and stand vacant much of the year while the homeless crisis soars. I mean, yes, the security light outside has been broken for months, and yes, I only have two views (the courtyard from the kitchen and the bricks of the building next door from the living room), but it's between Fountain Avenue and Sunset Boulevard, not far from the iconic Chateau Marmont.

I see that beacon of dreams every time I go to the Trader Joe's on the corner—the ghosts of Elizabeth Taylor, James Dean, and Tom Wolfe waving from the windows. There it sits, reminding me why I came to this town—to make something of myself. It felt like the one place in the world where anyone could make a dream come true if they had the talent and the drive, where nobody cared where you came from, only where you were going. There it sits, reminding me, whether I like it or not.

I get up and push through the clear plastic door beads—clitter-clatter—into the kitchen / living room and look around: a messy sink; an open bottle of red wine; a jar full of pencils on the kitchen counter; a burnt orange rug (because why deviate from orange?); a small flat-screen TV; a couple of houseplants that are somehow still holding on despite a distinct lack of watering (yes, I'm a florist, I'm full of contradictions); an acoustic guitar that hangs on the wall and is never played; a cream leather sofa (with pen marks I hide under big gold-sequined cushions); a large white bookcase full of the likes of Didion, Nabokov, Angelou, Capote, Ephron, García Márquez, Dostoyevsky, Bukowski, Poe, Stoker, Babitz, Woolf, and Plath (all secondhand; I like reading other people's notations, seeing what touched them, what I missed—which is lucky because I can tell you from this story that I miss a lot); and my laptop (still open from last night and charging on the dark wood coffee table by the sofa), an ashtray and an empty pizza box beside it (because I'm even sadder when I go low-carb). And there I am, reflected in a huge mirror on the far wall.

Me, Zoe Ann Weiss. Writer. Human. Florist. Fuckup.

Probably in reverse order.

My dark hair is messy and hangs to just below my shoulder blades, and my blue eyes have visible tear troughs beneath them that a couple of well-meaning strangers have suggested I get "fixed." But I like them; they make me look like I was up late reading or thinking deep thoughts. And as I stand here right now, looking at myself, I can't help but think: *Nothing ever changes. So maybe Dad is right.*

Maybe I *should* just go home.

Give up trying.

Buy a nice little cemetery plot by a tree.

But who would I even be if I wasn't a writer?

I head over to the kitchen, fill the kettle, and turn on the stove. And as I wait for the water to boil, I go to Instagram and read my new messages.

Happy Birthday beautiful!
Happy Birthday!
Miss you!

Something aches inside me. Mainly they're from old friends in London who now live eight hours in the future and whom I don't talk to anymore. I can almost smell the beer-stained carpets at the pubs we used to frequent, see the yellow lights atop black cabs as we'd wander down the street arm in arm, feel the freezing cold on my fingertips in the winter, back before the book deal, when it was all still in front of me. But whatever space I'd inhabited when I lived there—the shitty temp jobs while I wrote my debut; the expensive rent as I queried agents; the disappointing dating apps; the wandering through Hatchards and Waterstones on Piccadilly, imagining my name on a book spine; the constant feeling that I was meant for more, that it was London and its fascination with public schools and Oxford and Cambridge graduates that was keeping me small—has well and truly filled in now. And is my life in LA really that much different? That much better? Is there that much more opportunity here? I don't know, maybe not, but I know as much as I miss London, I certainly don't want to go back there.

Every time I even think about moving back into my childhood bedroom, having to tell everyone who believed in me that I failed, I feel sick. A part of me would die if I did that, a part I could never get back. I'd never write again; I just know it.

By the way, if it seems weird that my dad didn't mention my birthday in his text, well, that's just him and I don't mind. He'll remember later today when Facebook reminds him. Then he'll send me emergency flowers (carnations, always carnations) like I don't work in a florist's shop. As for my mum, she left when I was a baby. I probably have some deep wound around that, but I have too many other problems to worry about it right now. Besides, it's not all bad: she's American, and because of her I have the right to a green card.

But yes, it was just me and Dad growing up. Which you'd think would mean I'd want to be just like him, but the opposite is true. I love him, more than anyone, but he gave up on life a long time ago. He's scared of everything. And as guilty as I feel saying this, my deepest fear is becoming just like him.

The kettle whistles. I turn off the stove and make a cup of tea. And as I take it over to the sofa, my phone buzzes with an email. I sit down and I tap on it.

I guess I expect it to be some sort of birthday rewards email from Sephora or something lovely like that. But it's not. It's an automatically generated *Happy Birthday!* email from my university alumni group. Just another reminder of how much everyone expected me to achieve, and how little I really have.

Another reminder that I came so close to being "somebody."

Four

My phone beeps with a message as I pull closed the front door—a soft wooden arch painted green—and take the stairs down to the courtyard. As I get to the bottom, it beeps again. Beep. Beep. Beep.

Today is Wednesday, so I know what it is. My writers' group thread.

We meet once a month in person (the next one is tomorrow) and check in every Wednesday with progress reports . . . or everyone else does. I never have anything to report, which is just plain embarrassing given how much time I spend staring at my screen, so usually I just ignore this thread. But today is my birthday, so it'll be obvious if I don't reply. I reach for my phone and scan through the messages.

Tom: *two new poems this week!*

Rita: *five hundred words and three hangovers.*

Greta: *2k. Woo! But HAPPY BIRTHDAY ZOE!!!!! Xxx*

Greta is the one who introduced me to the writers' group. I met her at the book club at Small World Books in Venice a year and a half ago. Before that, it felt like I was the only novelist living in LA amid a sea of screenwriters and actors and Instagram influencers and people I'd seen on commercials and in the background of movies.

Tom: *OMG Zoe is it your birthday! Congrats!*

Rita: *HB Zoe!!*

There is only one message that is notably missing, but I'm happy about it: Sophie. She never has anything nice to say, so silence is the best birthday gift I could hope for.

I tap in *Thanks guys* and press Send as my bag swings from my shoulder, and I go past the pool—a bright-blue rectangle in the terra-cotta tiles—toward the archway that faces North Laurel Avenue. My eyes are down, watching my step, and a couple of little brown birds bouncing around in the sunshine.

And then I hear a giggle.

I look up.

The security gate is open and there are two silhouettes cut out against the morning sunshine.

And, no, *seriously*?

I stop midstep and squint a little harder at the figures, willing myself to be wrong. But of course I'm not wrong, because today is my birthday, so of course one of them is Jake. And of course I'm standing here with wet hair. And of course I'm not one of those people who looks good wet. Of course.

Jake is my downstairs neighbor. He smells like patchouli and works in a bar nearby a couple of nights a week, but mainly he's a model-slash-actor. I've seen him in an ad on Hulu for an internet company once or twice, and I slept with him three days ago. And a month before that. And three months before that. And, okay, fine, a few other times too. And every time I tell myself I won't do it again, because there are always other women, but I thought maybe this time was different. That maybe we were moving in a happy direction, that we'd had a moment, that he liked me. That maybe we'd become something in this city where true love only exists in choreographed social media posts, movie scripts, and my imagination.

But right now, he's standing with a woman I've never seen before and his leather jacket is over her shoulders and now *they're* having a moment. He leans in and kisses her and there is no way in hell I'm walking past them.

Right behind me, there's another perfectly good exit.

I rush through it and around the block, and as I turn the corner, I see my van, the roof and hood flashing in the sun, parked right by the entrance. And they're still there, under the arch, bright-pink bougainvillea on either side of them. He cups her face with his hands and shame pulses through me—*why am I never enough?* I creep toward my van, pull out my keys, and open the door, and just as I slither onto the leather seats, he looks up and sees me. Our eyes meet. And then he looks back down at her and smiles.

And me? Well, I do what I always do in life when things are bad: pretend it's not happening. I'm British, after all, raised to keep calm and carry on. So I just turn the key in the ignition and drive away.

Five

The florist's shop I work at is on Abbot Kinney, on the corner of California Avenue, right between a juice bar with fifteen-dollar vegan smoothies and a store with fake grass outside that's currently vacant.

Usually, it takes me around forty-five minutes, maybe an hour, to get here in the morning, but today there was an accident on the 10. So by the time I arrive, I'm late and I've had plenty of time to think. Time to think is rarely a good thing for me.

I turn down the alleyway behind the shop; drive past some street art, a blue dumpster, and some trash in puddles; press a button on my keys; watch the garage door slowly open; park; and rush inside through the back entrance. I'm hit with the familiar aroma of white vinegar cleaning products mingled with the sweetness of fresh flowers, the earthiness of greenery, and the slightly medicinal scent of flower preservatives.

It smells like what I'd imagine an old-school apothecary might smell like in here.

"Sorry I'm late," I call.

"Happy birthday to you!" sings Vee as I close the door behind me. "Happy birthday to you," she continues as I wander past the kitchen and bathroom. "Happy birthday, dear Zo-eee . . ." I move past my work studio to the front room. "Happy birthday to you," she finishes. She's sitting at her desk, behind a darkened computer screen, holding her phone.

"Thanks," I say, smiling a little harder. There's a question in her eyes, so I look away. I don't really want to get into all the reasons why I hate my birthday right now.

I look at the two rustic wooden tables on either side of the space, which are covered in glass vases full of tulips, a variety of roses, daisies, peonies, bells of Ireland, apple blossom branches, delphiniums, and snapdragons that look like fairies might live in them. Everything we sell is preordered and made to specification (there's very little creative freedom in my job; Vee designed them all); these are just for display, as are the rusted watering cans filled with Persian buttercups in the windows and the various potted plants of greenery draped throughout.

"You look sad. Are you freaking out?" Her brown, almost amber, eyes are wide. She moves her thick dark plait from one shoulder to the other. "I'll be freaking out when I turn thirty." Vee is twenty-six and ostensibly my boss, which tells you everything you need to know about my current life trajectory.

"Nope, just regular birthday blues," I say. "I get them every year."

And this is true. There's something about doing a full orbit of the sun that always fills me with an inconsolable sadness. It's not just to do with age. It's the inescapable realization that this is my one and only life.

And how is *this* it?

"Do you want more coffee?" I ask, nodding to her almost-empty cup.

"Fuck no, I'm wired, but I just made some. It's fresh," she says as I turn and go to the kitchen. "Look in the fridge," she calls after me.

I open the fridge door. Cool air hits my cheeks, and there on the top shelf is a big chocolate cake. Thin white cursive frosting reads: *Happy Birthday Zoe!* Beside it sits an envelope with my name on it. I tear open the top and pull out a card with a sparkly butterfly and a big *30* on the front. It reads: *Happy Thirtieth Birthday Bitch! We all have a year that changes everything for us, let this be your year. You deserve it. Vee xxx*

I close the fridge door and something aches beneath my ribs—because I want that too.

I *really* want that.

My dreams have bloodied claw marks on them, I want them so much.

But how am I going to ever achieve them when I feel ashamed to even admit them out loud anymore: that I want to be a writer, a really fucking successful one? Preferably one that writes the screenplays to her many, many screen adaptions. Maybe with a yacht and a castle if we're dreaming.

But it feels like *how dare I* even think I can do that after last time. Who do I think I am? How dare I think I'm destined for more than a life of standard survival? Which reminds me: *rent.* I'm already ten days late. I can't put it off any longer. I'll just spend it on cigarettes or something else ill-advised.

So I tap through to my banking app, pay my rent, flinch when I see my balance, reach for my favorite mug, and pour some coffee. As I take a sip, my gaze catches on the quote on the side: *Find what you love and let it kill you.* I bought this mug when I first moved to LA, back when I still believed Bukowski had said it (apparently it was actually Kinky Friedman); back when I believed that art conquered all and I was fighting the good fight, and now . . . well, now I'm just tired a lot.

Shit, am I depressed?

And then I hear: "Zoe?"

It's Vee's voice, coming from the other room.

"Just a second," I call back. I drop my phone into my bag and take my coffee back to her.

"I'm a young, attractive, energetic woman with an edge, aren't I?" she asks when I get to the door, frowning at me.

"Sure," I say. "Why?"

"I just don't get why my agent didn't send me for this," she says, pointing at some text on her phone screen. "He hasn't sent me for anything good in months." I glance down at it: it's a list of breakdowns. Casting calls for upcoming TV shows, films, commercials, etc. that are only meant for the desks of agents and managers but that Vee gets semi-illegally from someone in her acting class. One day she'll get her break and quit this job for good, and god, I hope I'm not still here when that happens.

"Maybe you should ask him?" I say, taking a sip of my coffee.

"I can't," she says, shaking her head. "I'm not even supposed to have these. Besides, how do I say, *Hey, so you never send me for anything that doesn't specify Latina—why? Are you an asshole?*" She stabs her phone and scrolls a little.

"I don't know, Vee, but maybe you *should* say something?"

"It won't change anything, so what's the point?" she says, and taps on her phone. I sip my coffee and watch over her shoulder as she opens TikTok. I'm not on TikTok myself; Barb wants me to be on there for BookTok, but I prefer to feed my self-loathing the old-fashioned way (Instagram). And honestly who the hell has time to make TikTok videos *and* not-write a novel *and* hold down a full-time job *and* maintain personal hygiene *and* doomscroll *and* do the washing *and* sometimes go to the grocery store?

There are snippets of voices as she scrolls past, then a young woman's face fills the screen and Vee stops. The woman has long, wavy chestnut-brown hair and a small gold nose ring that catches the light. She's sitting at what looks like a white kitchen counter and she's shuffling tarot cards, about to do a reading.

This is how Vee gets a lot of her life advice. But then again, she's also totally comfortable getting her drugs off Instagram via coded emojis, so . . .

"If this reading has found you, it was meant for you . . . ," says the woman on the screen as she pulls two cards and holds them up to the camera. The first reads *The Star* and the second reads *The Lovers*, and now I'm thinking about Jake and that woman from this morning, and it's not that I love-love Jake, that I think we're destined or something like that, not at all, but why am I so easy to walk away from? So invisible? So forgettable? And if this is thirty, thirty-one will probably be even worse . . . and then Vee says "Phew" and grins at me.

And I smile back and take a sip of coffee. I'm not sure I'll ever get used to drip coffee—it tastes a little like an ashtray to me.

Then she says: "Let's do you!"

"That's okay. I don't really get into tarot," I say.

And I don't. Not tarot. Not astrology. Nothing that can warn me about impending retrogrades or other things that make me not want to leave the house. Which makes me very un-LA—Vee is the norm, not me. This town may run on cocaine and hangovers, but it's also egg cleanses and sound baths and sticks of sage at every corner store by the gum. I don't even meditate.

But Vee doesn't listen; she's already tapping through to the profile. "Don't be so fucking boring. This could totally set the tone for your new birthday year." She raises her eyebrows twice, then turns the phone so I can see the screen now. "Just randomly pick one of the posts," she says.

And maybe she's right. Maybe this will perk me up. Give me a little hope. Maybe I'll get the Lovers too, or something even better . . . one of the ones with the gold coins on it.

So I study the squares and choose the one three rows down on the very left.

And as I type this right now, I can see a still frame in my mind of the exact moment before I tap on it. Except in my head, I'm in the frame too—like I'm watching myself from a distance. And I'm wondering if anything would have been different, if I'd chosen one to the right, or something from the row above it. The conversation that follows in a moment would certainly have been different . . . so it's possible I would have been in a more grounded space that night. Held on just a little tighter to that vase. Said no when Zach asked me to that party. Been a little less susceptible to the light and the hope that things might finally turn around. Made a different choice.

Or maybe *nothing* would have been different. Maybe deep down I *wanted* to blow it all up and I was just waiting for an excuse. But it doesn't matter in the end, because I don't choose one of those.

I choose *this* one.

Six

I tap on the video and it starts to play.

"No captions. No hashtags. If you're watching this, you didn't land on this reading by accident. I have a powerful message just for you," says the woman as she shuffles the cards. One falls from the pack and lands just out of frame. Her eyes move to it and open just a little wider, and then she reaches for it and flips it over for the camera.

"Hmm, interesting . . . the Five of Cups. Okay, what I'm getting from this is that you've been dealing with disappointment or even sorrow recently. Something has happened in the past that you haven't really moved on from."

My insides clench as I peer at the card.

It's a solitary figure, staring out into the distance and moping around in a long black cape. And that's *exactly* how I feel.

She continues to shuffle, and another couple of cards fall from the pack—I watch as she flips the first one over and holds it up to the camera.

This one looks like a big cement building and there are people falling out of it; there are flames.

"Wow, okay, everything is changing for you. This is the Tower card, a card of massive upheaval. Unexpected change."

And now I'm thinking about Barb's message this morning: *Got your email. Do you have anything else?* And that blinking cursor and the words that won't come and my dad and *Have you thought through what we spoke about?* And the state of my bank account and . . . *Shit.* I try to push down the panic. Tell myself it's just some woman on TikTok with an iPhone and a deck of tarot cards.

"It can mean danger or crisis, but it can also mean a positive destruction. Think phoenix rising from the ashes. But whatever it is, this is the card of change . . . and not a small change," she continues. "An entire paradigm shift . . ." She flips over the next card now.

Please be good. Please be good. Please be good.

I watch as she holds it up to the lens. Something flickers behind her eyes—*is that worry?*

My gaze snaps to the word at the bottom: *Death.*

"Okay," she says. "Now, this doesn't mean *you're* going to die . . ." She smiles at the camera. "But *something* is going to die."

My pulse speeds up and doom descends—she clearly means my writing career.

"It's a little like the Tower card: it signifies death of the way things have been, making way for a new path."

She goes to shuffle again and I swallow hard, bracing for the next assault, but then Vee says, "That's enough . . ." She takes the phone away and shuts the video down.

I throw her a smile and take a deep breath, but my lower lip quivers.

"Babe, like she said, there is always a good way to read a card . . . a good way *and* a bad way," she says.

"Well, that Tower card *did* look a bit like British architecture. And Dad wants me to go home," I offer, my stomach dropping at the thought. "Maybe it's saying I should do that?"

"What? No. That's just sad," she says. "You have talent. You have a duty to use it. You can't give up."

I take a sip of coffee and sit down. "I can't use it. I've tried. I'm blocked."

Her eyes dart to me, then to the cup in my hands and the quote, and then she sighs. "Well, maybe you wouldn't be blocked if you threw yourself into life a little more. Maybe that's what the cards are trying to tell you. Maybe you need to shake things up a bit. Like when was the last time you went on a date? You're not even on an app anymore. I can try to help you get on Raya if you want? It might give you something to write about. Or at least some fun." She shrugs.

A defensiveness rises inside me. And that's how I know she has a point—that's always how inconvenient truths feel to me at first. Like they need to be shouted down, not listened to.

"Oh, because the apps have worked out so well for you?" I say and immediately want to take it back. *I'm an awful, horrible person.*

Last year Vee broke off a four-year relationship with the love of her life—a man named Joel. They met online, and it turned out he was married to the love of *his* life. Vee had always been driven, but since then she's been so laser focused on her acting career that she ditched the regular apps, signed up to that celebrity dating app Raya, and uses it purely as a networking device. If she doesn't end up with a star on the Hollywood Walk of Fame, there's no hope for the rest of us.

"Sorry," I say. "I didn't mean that. But I *do* throw myself into life . . . sort of . . ."

She looks at me and lets out a sigh.

"All I'm saying is you can't just read old books and wear those Joan Didion sunglasses and drink out of some quotesy-assed mug and expect to have something to say. You have to be out there hustling, getting your own scars to talk about, learning shit, meeting people. Taking chances. Like me. That's the only way people like us make it, people who aren't born into the right family with the right connections. We make it through grit and effort and total fucking commitment. We have to go all in. Why do you think I work so hard? I know the odds are stacked against me, but if it doesn't work, I'll know in my soul that I gave this dream everything I had." She pauses for breath. "You need to do the same. Otherwise, yes, you might as well just give up." Then she reaches out to touch my arm and her voice softens: "I'm saying this for your own good."

A veil of realization settles over me now. I'm finding it hard to breathe. Because oh god, oh god, oh god. She's right.

I'm becoming just like my dad.

Scared of everything.

Because I *have* bundled myself up in cotton wool for the last two years. Jake is the only person aside from Vee and my writers' group I've really seen, and that's only because he lives in my building and I kept bumping into him. It wasn't intentional, but I just needed a moment to reset, to recover, before I faced the world again.

Because nobody ever talks about the grief that comes with a failed creative project, or if they do, they don't talk loud enough. It's expected that you'll just shrug and get over it. But let me tell you, when you get your big chance, when your dreams are so close that you can almost touch them, and then they just disappear . . . it plunges you into a nu-clear winter of the soul, makes you wary of any flash of light in the dis-tance. Because a near miss—an "almost"—cuts far deeper than a "never had a chance." Especially when it was all your fault. But Vee's right: I don't want to live that way.

I want to believe again. I want to take chances.

I mean, no wonder my muse deserted me—that little invisible spirit I swear exists, the one who writes the good work in between the drivel I pump out.

She probably gave up on me. Got sick of my cowardice. I don't blame her.

Still, it's my birthday. I shouldn't have to think about any of this. If there is one day a year when you can just complain about your lot and not take any accountability, surely this is it?

But now the front door creaks open, and Vee and I both look toward it. A man wearing jeans and a white polo neck steps inside.

"Hi . . . Kevin?" Vee says, flashing a smile like he's a client she's expecting. "Welcome. I'm Vee."

"Hi," he says, closing the door after him.

And I take my bag out the back, go to the fridge, get a big piece of cake, and go into my work studio.

I look around as I walk inside. Against the wall to my right stand some large white vases and a sink, the flower cooler is in the far right-hand corner, and there's a bench behind me by the door and a rectangular wooden table with a few chairs around it in front of me—that's where I make up the day's arrangements. Behind that table is a large set of shelves full of various containers, boxes, extra stationery, and a few random bits and pieces. Then there are Lomey dishes (low dishes with a one-inch lip), some floral foam in various shapes, protective gloves, chicken wire, ribbons, floral tape, and floral frogs. On my left sits a laptop and printer on another table, with a broom and rolls of plastic wrap, cellophane, and brown paper standing up against the wall next to it. We use those daily. And beside those sit some white plastic drawers labeled *Knives*, *Scissors*, and *Pruning Shears*. This all sounds far more organized that it really is—those drawers are full of a variety of tools from snips to fabric sheers to wire cutters and more, but we ran out of drawers.

I put my bag and cake on the table and pull out some tools and lay them down in a perfectly spaced neat line, like that can bring some order to my life. Then I print off today's orders and scan them. I know we have a delivery tonight for an event tomorrow morning—it's in the planner, Vee and I discussed it on Monday, and I did the pre-preparation yesterday—but I'm checking the exact specifications. That's the first time I see Brian Rollingston's name. It's third from the top. But I don't know the relevance yet.

Hours pass. Customers come and go. I prepare for the delivery this evening, put everything in the flower cooler, tidy up, and deliver a couple of small local arrangements. And at 4:30 p.m. I'm parking my van back in the garage so Vee can use it for the delivery tonight.

Because my van isn't exactly *my* van. It's the shop's van. But since I use it the most anyway, Vee said I could use it indefinitely when my old car—a vintage Mercedes I loved—was going to cost more than it was worth to repair. Eventually I'll need to buy a new car of my own, but for now we just make it work.

Unfortunately, today has not been a good day for me, and in my angst I've messed up. I've left a pile of cut stems and wet discarded greenery by the door. It's made the floor slippery. I know it's there, so I step over it, but Vee doesn't. She slips. She sprains her ankle.

And . . . well . . . now here I am doing exactly what she said I should do. What that tarot told me to do. Shaking things up.

Taking a chance on life.

Saying yes.

Driving Zach Hamilton to a house party.

He's on the phone to Brian saying: "Yes . . . fine . . . no, she's cool, I know her . . . I'll tell you later . . . I said okay . . . Zoe. Ann. Weiss." And then he turns to me and rolls his eyes as I drive. "What are your home and email addresses?" he asks me.

I give them to him, and he repeats it all to Brian, slowly, with purpose, and *why do they need those?*

"They're dogs, man. You'll figure it out. Breathe," he says into the phone again. "I'll come get them tomorrow. Anyway, I'll talk to you later." Then he hangs up.

I can see cars up ahead, the flare of red taillights disappearing into a hedge.

"It's that one," he says as he points to it. I slow down and pull into a driveway.

There's a security guy standing there, and he motions for me to put down my window. A car pulls up behind us and Zach leans across me. "Red rover, red rover," he says.

I'm guessing it's some kind of secret entry word.

The security guard nods. "You're lucky—we're almost full in there," he says. "But go on in."

The gate slides open, and as we drive inside, I glance into the rear-view mirror—I can see the car behind us parking on the road with a couple of others, but here I am, with Zach Hamilton, inside, driving up a long hill to lights and sounds and a huge house. My heart is banging in my chest. The red taillights of a Maserati turn off in front us, and as we pull up behind it, my phone pings with an email. I look around at the other cars: many of them are just regular, normal-people cars.

One of the valets comes over to us, and Zach motions to him through the van window to wait a moment.

"Okay, so I'm super sorry about this," he says to me, "but I have to get you to do something before we go in. I promised Brian; he's super strict about me getting anyone I'm seeing to sign one of these. Check your phone."

I reach for my bag and pull out my phone, and there's one new email notification.

It reads: *Brian Rollingston is requesting your signature.*

I scroll down and tap on the link.

"What is this?" I ask, but I know exactly what it is. It says it at the top. *Nondisclosure Agreement.*

"You can read it if you want, but it's all standard," he says, his hand warm on my knee.

I scroll through the pages. My eyes skip past my name and address (Party A), past Zach's information (Party B), past the bit where it tells me the agreement covers all interactions with Zach, current and future, to a list of everything I'll need to keep confidential: sex life, finances, business involvements, friendships, topics discussed in private, disappointments, infidelity, habits, insecurities, addictions, past relationship failures, opinions expressed in confidence, anything not publicly disclosed by Party B, family-related problems, anything else deemed private . . . text messages, emails, private social media correspondence, voice messages . . . the list goes on. Basically, it's a gag order.

"It's just saying that you can't tell people things about me, can't talk to the press about me or us," Zach says.

Us. He just said "us."

"It's nothing crazy. Everyone signs them," he continues.

I look up, toward the big house in front of me, then back down at my phone screen glowing in the dark as the last twelve hours flicker in my mind.

And I know I could go home right now. Tuck myself into bed. Let my thirtieth year unfold as uneventfully as my twenty-ninth. But all I can think about is that tarot reading and Jake from downstairs and Dad's text message and Vee's pep talk and *find what you love and let it kill you* and my childhood bedroom and that light. That magic-hour light that promised me everything could still be great. Better than great. Then I think about the future I'm currently hurtling toward . . . And the great chasm between that and the future I want, the one I was meant to have, is so great it could swallow me whole.

So yes, I sign it.

Of course I sign it.

Seven

I hand the valet my keys, he gives me a receipt, and I follow Zach past prying eyes to the front door. He doesn't knock, he just pushes it open, and the low thud of bass hits me in the chest. I scan the faces as we move inside. It's like walking through the pages of *Vanity Fair*, the tabloids, and *Vogue* all at once. Right ahead of us are big floor-to-ceiling windows opening out onto a blue-lit infinity pool with a spa, and just beyond that, the silhouettes of palm trees and the sparkling lights of the city below. To our left is a large pale-stone kitchen—a woman is doing a line of coke off a silver platter and a man wearing no shirt is drinking from a bottle of Moët and dancing.

"This is Zoe," Zach yells above the music, and I look away from the kitchen and back toward him. He's introducing me to someone. Someone who looks just like Lenny Kravitz but younger and taller. He's wearing sunglasses and carrying a red canvas bag. "She's a writer," Zach adds.

"Cool," says Sunglasses Guy.

"This is Kenneth," Zach continues.

Kenneth looks at me, smiles without teeth for half a second, and then leans in toward Zach and says something I don't catch. Then Zach nods, pulls out his phone, and drops it into the red bag. Then both of them look at me, and I know I'm supposed to do the same.

"You'll get it back," Zach whispers in my ear. I can feel his breath on my skin. Goose bumps.

"Sure," I say, fumbling around for my phone in my bag. There's a single email notification on the screen. It's from Brian Rollingston and reads: *Completed: Zoe Weiss NDA.* I hand it over and Kenneth drops it into the red bag.

"Come," Zach says as he grabs my hand and leads me through the crowd. I hold on tight, too tight; he looks back at me for a moment, then pulls me into a corner.

"Are you okay?" he asks.

My back is pressed against the wall and he's standing in front of me, his body slinking forward, shielding me from the room. And even though I haven't seen him in three years, it feels like just yesterday.

"There are just so many people," I say.

He grins and leans in to my ear so I can hear him. "I would have thought you'd like big parties. 'They're so intimate. At small parties there isn't any privacy.'"

He's quoting Jordan Baker from *The Great Gatsby*.

I grin up at him.

"Is that supposed to be impressive?"

"A little? Is it?"

I'm hit with flashes from our three days together: us driving to Palm Springs beneath a perfect blue sky, my hair flicking around in the wind from the open window . . . us drinking the beer then the whiskey then the rum from the minibar as we played Truth or Dare . . . then the next day, lying in bed, a view of a cactus garden out the window, my head on his chest, his fingertips tracing my arm, and me asking him about his favorite books. Him saying the only book he'd read in the last ten years was the first Harry Potter book. Me laughing, and him looking all embarrassed and saying he was going to change that . . .

"I don't know, they *did* make a movie . . ."

"I totally read the fucking book," he laughs. "You inspired me. So what happened in yours?" he asks, his eyes on mine.

"Where was I up to when we met?" I ask. Even though I know exactly where I was up to.

My protagonist, a young university student, had just walked out to her car one morning to find a bloody heart on her windshield. She was panicking about who'd left it there and whether it was a human heart. Like I said before, in the first draft, the version we sold, it turned out the heart wasn't real. I was going all Chuck Palahniuk's *Fight Club* and the whole thing had happened in her head. But Felicity, the editor who'd bought it, wanted me to come at it from a different angle and change the ending. She liked the sequence of events but wasn't keen on the protagonist being unreliable; she wanted it to be a real heart, a real stalker, for everything else to be real too. Not only that, she wanted me to insert the stalker's point of view as alternating chapters.

That was the part I was struggling with. *That* was why I was stuck at chapter 3.

Because Felicity wanted the stalker to be motivated by rejection and unrequited love, and I couldn't identify with anybody feeling so much that they'd go to those extremes. I'd never felt anything close to that myself. How could I write a character I didn't understand?

"Umm . . . the main character was getting stalked . . . She was getting creepy text messages . . . They wrote something scary on her mirror . . . Wait, didn't they leave something on her car?" Zach says.

And as I hear the words out loud, the bad reviews flicker in my mind: derivative, tropey, done before . . . even now, two years later, they make me flinch. Honestly, despite shitty sales, there were only two bad reviews; the rest were glowing. But for some reason I can't remember any of those. It was the bad ones I agreed with. The bad ones I still always come back to. The bad ones that make me not want to answer questions like this.

"What happened to her?"

"Not telling. You'll need to read it to find out." I smile.

He smiles back, and his gaze darts from my eyes to my mouth, then back up to my eyes.

"Do you want a drink?" he asks.

"Sure." I shrug.

"Okay, wait here," he says.

And then he's gone. And I feel exposed here as I watch him move through the crowd, patting people on the back, grinning, giving high fives. People pretend not to look at me, but I can feel their eyes tracing my features, my arms, my waist, and I know what they're thinking: *Why her? She's not that great.* And as I look around, at the perfect, symmetrical faces, I can't help but agree.

This room was exactly what I thought LA was all about before I got here: a blur of designer jeans, stilettos, and injectables, where everyone is either famous or almost famous. A bit like I thought the Venice boardwalk would be full of the tanned, waxed, and airbrushed, the seagulls would be . . . I don't know, a normal size . . . and that everything would exist in high definition and full saturation.

But quickly I realized the Venice boardwalk is filled with tourists, the homeless, and vendors selling bongs, dream catchers, and ski masks nobody buys; the seagulls are supersized; and everything from the street signs to the dreams is sun-bleached and fading here.

And rooms like this? Rooms full of dreams that have actually come true? Well, I started believing they only existed in my imagination and on TV.

They were something to be scorned or laughed at when people mentioned them. Fake LA, not real LA. The sort of thing people fresh off the bus, who'd bought into the version of LA they saw on the screen, believed in . . . the type who thought they could drive Uber until they hit it big with their YouTube channel or music videos because "everyone gets famous here." People who didn't yet realize that even working actors and TV writers barely get by in this town, and most of its residents don't even work in the movies.

So yes, *my* LA has always been the real people of the world—bank clerks and florists and executive assistants, people who go to Trader Joe's in sweatpants and work for a paycheck.

But here I am, in this room that definitely *does* exist and I feel like I shouldn't be here. Like I don't belong. Like I'm inferior somehow. Like I should have fixed my tear troughs.

Because now that I'm here, I *want* to belong.

I want to, but I don't.

And that's far, far worse than thinking it doesn't exist in the first place.

Zach is standing in the kitchen by the bar and I'm watching him, hoping he comes back soon, and then a hand reaches out and touches his forearm. I look to see who that hand belongs to and my stomach drops.

Because I recognize her.

I recognize *them* together. The shape of them.

I've seen them standing in exactly that pose many times on trashy magazine covers. A flash of the most recent headline: "Heartbreak— Golden Couple Splits." That was from late last year.

It's his ex.

Solange Grey.

And I think she's even prettier in person.

So why did he ask me here? And why did I come? What did I think was going to happen?

There's a lump in my throat and a dangerous ache in my chest and I don't want to be here anymore.

I push through the crowd back toward the front door. A drink is spilled down my shirt. It's cold. The fabric sticks to my chest.

But I just keep walking. Kenneth is right there with his red bag, taking someone else's phone now, so I head up to him. "Hey, I need to go," I say.

"Already?"

I nod. Kenneth opens the keypad on his phone and hands it to me. "Punch in your number."

I do, and he looks in the bag and pulls out my phone, its screen flashing blue white.

"Thanks," I say, reaching for it.

"Wait, let's see you open it," he says with suspicion.

I hold the screen so it can see my face—it opens, he nods, and I head to the door.

The air outside is cool as it hits my cheeks; it smells like gasoline fumes and bougainvillea. There are three guys ahead of me waiting for the valets to retrieve their cars, so I line up behind them, fishing around in my bag for the receipt. *Where the hell did I put it?* Then there it is, in the front pocket.

One of the valets drives up in a red car, and the guy at the front of the line takes his keys and gets in. The valet moves to the next guy in line, then heads back out into the darkness. And I just stand there, tears welling in my eyes. I don't want to cry; I don't want to be that girl; I just want to go home and let today finish.

That's when I smell cigarette smoke. I turn toward it. It's a woman—blonde, midthirties—and she's standing not far away, looking toward the gate and smoking.

She glances at me. "Sorry," she says, waving her smoke away and taking a step back. Then her eyes settle on my face. "Hey, are you okay?"

I nod and force a smile in return.

"You sure?" she asks, holding out her box of cigarettes. "Want one?"

I usually only smoke when I'm writing—it gives me an incentive—but honestly, fuck it.

"Sure, thanks," I say as she hands me the lighter. I put the cigarette between my lips, flick the lighter, and watch the end glow red. I take a deep drag, then hand the lighter back to her.

And we stand there for a bit, smoking, while I wait for a valet to come back.

"Wait, didn't I see you just get here with Zach?" she asks, and I turn to her.

"We're old friends," I lie, just a little too quickly. "I have to go home. He's still inside."

"Right." She smiles and looks down at the ground as she exhales a cloud of smoke. "Zach has a lot of old friends."

The second valet drives up now, and guy number two gets into his car. Then the valet comes over to me.

"It's the white van," I say, handing him the receipt.

He nods and grabs my keys from the valet stand, then heads over to the cars.

"So what do you do?" she asks.

"I'm a writer," I say.

"Cool," she replies.

"What about you?" I ask as I look around for the valet.

"This and that." She smiles. And then there it is, my van, driving toward us. The big green VENICE FLORISTRY sign, right there on the side of it, announcing I'm not successful enough to not have a day job.

I watch her take it in.

"Anyway, it was nice to meet you," she says, wandering off the way people always do in this town once they figure out you aren't well enough connected to help them in their careers.

"Likewise," I say, dropping my cigarette to the ground and stepping on it. But that's a lie; now I feel even worse, even less important, less visible.

The valet parks my van and gives me the keys, and I fish a twenty out of my bag for him and head around to my door.

I readjust the seat to be a little closer to the wheel, put my foot on the brake pedal and turn the key in the ignition, and then just as I release the hand brake, I hear: tap, tap, tap. There's someone at my window. I look up, expecting it to be the valet with instructions on how to get out of here. But it's not. It's Zach.

I put down the window.

"Where are you going?" he asks. "I couldn't find you."

"Home," I say. "I'm really tired. But we should catch up sometime."

Our eyes meet, something moves between us—something familiar and electric—and he pauses for a moment.

"You're mad. Why are you mad?"

"I'm just tired."

His eyes narrow a little. "Is this because Solange is here?"

"No," I say.

He glances to the side, then right back at me, his eyes looking deep into mine. "Well, this party blows. I'm coming too."

Then, before I can say anything, he goes around to the passenger side, gets in, and puts on his seat belt.

And that's just brilliant. Now I get to be a taxi for the great Zach Hamilton too. What a fantastic birthday this has turned out to be. But I've never been good at saying no, so I ease my foot off the brake and start to drive toward the gate. It opens as we get there and we move past the security guard, past roughly twenty cars that are all parked outside now, past groups of people laughing and talking as they head to the party.

"Take a left," Zach says.

I flick on the indicator and make the turn, and then he puts his hand on my leg and says, "I can't believe you were just going to leave me there. But let's go to my place. I think you'll love it." And then he squeezes my knee.

And as embarrassing as it is to admit, that's all it takes.

I forget everything else. Because this is exactly what I need to hear. That someone like Zach would choose me over Kenneth and Solange and every other face I've seen on TV and commercials and billboards. Because if he wants me, even for just the night, maybe, just maybe, I'm worth something after all. So yes, it's the first time I've seen him in three years, and yes, that last time he ghosted me, and yes, I should probably just go home right now so he doesn't get to do it again. But I don't.

Instead, I say: "Sure."

Eight

"Zach," comes a loud whisper. That's the first sound I hear. Then comes: Tap. Tap. Tap.

My eyes edge open—bright light streams in through sheer white curtains as the electric blinds lift. I squint against it. Outside are palm trees. Smog. A dissolving view.

And then I see my bra hanging off the edge of a chair. My T-shirt and skirt folded next to it. My head throbs as last night filters back.

His hands under my shirt, unclipping my bra. My arms over my head. Him lifting off my T-shirt . . . Him reaching for the edge of my underwear at each hip and peeling it down to my ankles . . . me stepping out of it and our eyes meeting. And then he was standing . . . the sound of his zipper coming down . . . him bending me over the bed, his hands on my hips as we moved together—

That was around 3 a.m. Earlier in the night, soon after we got back here, a couple of Zach's actor friends had turned up. I was pretty sure I'd seen them before in TV car chases or on low-budget comedies (they had that homogenized hot look) but wasn't sure where, and it felt rude to ask. We spent the whole night talking and drinking until they *finally* went home. Not exactly the deep-and-meaningful reunion Zach and I *could* have had after all this time. But then we came upstairs and it was just like it always was between us. Close. Right.

"Zach," comes the voice again, a little louder now. "You have a meeting, remember?"

"That's at nine." Zach's voice is croaky.

I can feel the mattress move a little, and I roll over to look as he sits up, his tan made all the more bronzed by the stark white sheets. They're so white they look like they've never been used before, so white they're giving the room a blue-white glow. And the person who must be his assistant—with a short red bob, a pair of jeans, and a black T-shirt—is hovering in the doorway.

"It *is* almost nine, Zach," she says, throwing me a quick disapproving glance, then putting a remote down on a table by the door. "And Geraldine called again."

My eyes widen: *Nine?! I start at nine thirty! Why didn't my alarm go off?*

"Shit, I'll be right there," he says.

I roll over, reach for my phone by the bed, and squint down at the screen, pressing a couple of the side buttons. My phone is dead.

"Sure," says his assistant. "Coffee is ready." I hear the door close again as I reach into my bag by the bed. I fumble around for the portable battery I keep in there, and plug it in. And great, that's almost out of charge too. I stare at the screen . . . waiting, waiting . . . then my screen blinks to life.

"Morning," Zach says from behind me, and I turn to look at him. He's glancing back at me over his well-defined shoulder, giving me a half smile, and a warmth moves through me. "How did you sleep?"

"Okay," I say, my phone and battery dropping to the bed as I take him in. And there are moments in life you can't quite fathom, blips in life's logic. Like me, right here, right now. Moments you know will pass as quickly as they came. So I'm taking mental notes of everything: the feel of his sheets on my legs, my hair falling in front of my eye, the rattle of the window in the breeze. Everything feels important. No, vital. If I can end up here, maybe anything can happen.

"Cool." A little muscle on the side of his jaw twitches. "Hey, so it's probably better you go before they get here," he says, screwing his face up a little. "I try to keep my personal life private . . ."

"Of course," I say.

He stands up, walks naked to a pile of clothes on the floor by the bathroom door, and starts pulling them on. And mine are waiting for me on the armchair on the far side of the room. I shuffle over to them, self-conscious of my nakedness.

I put on my underwear first, a pair of full-coverage briefs I might have rethought if I'd known I'd end up here. Then my bra. I fumble with the fastening and quickly reach for my shirt. There's a big dark patch down the front from whatever was spilled on me last night while I was dashing for the door, and I sniff it. It looks like Coke and it smells like brandy. I put it on, then pull on my faux leather skirt and my white sneakers and look over to Zach, who's watching me now, smiling.

"What?" I ask.

"Do you want a clean shirt?" he asks, heading to his closet and pulling out a white button-down. It's just like mine except four sizes bigger and without the Coke stain.

"Thanks," I say, undoing the top two buttons, pulling it over my head and tucking in the front. It's way too big.

"Ready?" he says.

I nod, stuff my dirty shirt into my bag, grab my jacket and phone, and follow him down a spiral staircase, quickly texting Vee as we walk.

Running late. Sorry!

I press Send, and it's right then, while I'm still looking down at my phone, that an email notification comes in. It's from Barb and it reads: *I think it's time we talk about things, Zoe. I'll call you in five.*

My throat tightens. Panic. Pure fucking panic.

Because I need to write something great and soon, and those two things don't seem to go together.

Zach and I move past the kitchen and down a hallway and now we're at the front door. He turns to me, cups my face in his hands, and kisses me softly. And I try not to breathe because I still have morning breath, and then he says, "I really wanted to talk more. I'll call you soon," and opens the door. I'm hit by bright sunshine, and I go to step outside, but my breath catches. Because we're not alone.

A man and a woman are standing there watching us. The man is maybe fifty-five. He's tall, has red hair, and is wearing circular sunglasses. The woman is in her early twenties, my height—five foot seven—with blonde hair to her shoulders, pink cheeks, and a file covered in sample pieces of fabric in her arms.

A heat creeps up my neck as they look from Zach to me and back to Zach.

"Hey, Franz, you're early, man," Zach says.

"Nope, right on time." Franz gives a tight smile, his gaze moving to me again.

"This is my architect, Franz, and his assistant, Mary," Zach says. "Super talented and hardworking team—we've been working together ever since I bought this house . . ." And then he trails off and doesn't introduce me in return.

I nod at Franz and then at Mary, and they both look at me in a way I don't want to be looked at. That morning-after-wearing-his-shirt-and-being-shepherded-out-the-door kind of way. Franz offers his hand to shake and I take it. "Nice to meet you," he says. His grip is tight. His hands are dry.

Mary struggles with the folder and fabric as she tries to do the same. Her hand flails around in politeness, trying to find mine.

"Hi." She smiles as I take her hand, and I say "Hi" back. My face must be puce by now.

My phone is still in my hand; it vibrates and flashes, and the screen reads: *Barb Wallace.*

My stomach clenches.

"I have to take this," I say as I step past them and jog to my van. And I know I should just answer, but instead I stand there for a little while, watching the screen flash with the call and the sunlight, trying to remember how to breathe. And then I do it. I answer.

"Barb, hi," I say. My voice comes out upbeat—I don't know how I pull that off.

"Zoe," she says. And I can see her there at her desk, on Wilshire Boulevard, piles of manuscripts and screenplays in front of her. She must be almost sixty now, and I like her—she's been my mentor, taught me so much, made me believe I could do this—but right now I'm scared of her, of what she's going to say.

I press the unlock button on my keys and get into the van; the sun glares off the hood. I close the door and look out onto a vista of palm trees and a smoggy Hollywood, and is this it? Where my writing career ends?

"I don't know how to say this," she starts, and I know what she's going to say and everything inside me is screaming *Do something!* Because I can't let her say it. I need her.

"I'm so glad you called. I wanted to talk to you about this new project I'm working on." My words come out quickly.

What am I doing?

"Yes . . . ," she says, trepidation in her voice. "Those pages you sent me. Did you get my email?"

"No, a different thing. I've been working on it for a while in secret, but it's kind of risky and wild. I wanted to get a bit further into it before I shared anything." I have no idea what I'm pitching here. I just know I have to do something, buy myself some time.

"What's it about?"

I swallow hard and look over at the blue BMW parked next to me, then at Zach's house, and flashes of last night flicker in my mind—the party, the drinks at his place—then flashes from three years ago, and the words just come. Like they're divinely inspired . . .

"Well, it's a high-concept thriller based on a celebrity I know. On what goes on behind the celebrity curtain," I say. "You'll love it. I just know you will."

Barb lets out a big sigh, like she's not sure about this, but she has a thing for anything "high-concept" and also she's a good person; she doesn't want to give up on me. "Okay, Zoe, get me something in two weeks. Let me see where you're up to."

"I need a month," I say. "Some of the plot points are still really messy."

"Two weeks," she repeats. Firm.

"Three?"

"Zoe, your deadline was a year ago. We need to give Felicity something soon, and it needs to be damned good after all this time."

"Please, Barb," I beg. "Just three weeks."

She lets out another big sigh. "Just remember, whenever you want to get up from the page, that there are a million others just like you who would love to do the work. None of us are irreplaceable."

I hold my breath. "I know," I say.

"Okay, fine. But we need something to work on soon. Something great. Something even better than your first book."

"You're going to really love it," I say, even though it's a big fat lie and I haven't written a single word and I don't even know what it's going to be about. But, I mean, sometimes you just have to take a leap of faith, right?

"Great," she says. "I look forward to reading it."

And then we hang up and I look back over at Zach's house and, shit, what the hell am I going to write about? And also, I like Zach and I don't want to break his trust. But I just pitched a book that I have no idea how to write, especially in three weeks—that's only twenty-one days. Not unless I can use Zach and his world and our quasi-relationship as material . . . Even then, it'll be a struggle—I may have an idea, but I don't know what the story is. And oh shit, I signed that NDA; I'll need to be super opaque . . .

But that's okay; I'll just use him as inspiration. A springboard. I mean, I'm a writer—I'll just do what writers do: blur the details and make it up . . . I can do this.

Little do I know that I won't have to make *anything* up. Life is about to do all the plotting for me.

But I'll shut up now. Nothing more annoying than a narrator who keeps spoiling the plot twists. Besides, I want you to be as shocked as I was.

Nine

I'm wearing yesterday's underwear and a shirt that's four sizes too big, and my apartment is on my way to work. So I go there first. I pull the van up to the curb, turn off the ignition, and look up at my building. I've seen it a thousand times before, but today it looks different. The beige of the walls is the color of sand today—hopeful, somehow—the bougainvillea on either side of the archway glows fluorescent pink, and the sky above isn't just blue today, no, it's *neon* blue. The blue of postcards and novel covers, a blue that says: *This is LA, anything could happen here, dare to dream. Wink.*

And I guess that makes sense. Everything looks different today because everything *is* different.

Because I finally have a book idea.

A good one.

The first *good* idea I've had in . . . well . . . ages.

And I *know* it's a good idea because Barb liked it and she hated my last four ideas.

I mean, yes, the world's rosy hue could also be my polarizing lenses, but they wouldn't account for how warm the sun feels on my face as I cross the road and punch the code into the security gate, how distant my concerns from yesterday feel to me as I pass through the archway toward the hum of the pool pump and the smell of chlorine inside.

Or how I don't even flinch when I see Jake lying there, his shirt off, on a deck chair, his perfect chest gleaming with oil in the sun, as he grins at his phone and texts somebody else. I don't give a damn. And not just because I woke up in Zach Hamilton's bed this morning (so, I won), but because I have bigger things on my mind right now, things like: *How am I going to pull this off?*

Because I *have* to pull it off.

Otherwise Barb will give up on me, I'll have to go into debt to pay back the signing advance on the second book, and no other publisher will take a chance on me after that. Bad sales are one thing, but failure to deliver is another altogether.

So if I fail this time, it's over. I'll have to go home. And what the actual fuck will I do then? Because I have no plan B.

Jake is pretending not to notice me, but I can feel his eyes on me as I rush past the pool and head up the stairs to my apartment—I hope he clocks that I'm wearing somebody else's shirt, somebody four sizes bigger than me. I hope it bruises his ego just a little bit.

As I get to the top of the stairs, there sits my obligatory bunch of flowers from Dad, the cellophane glittering in the sun. Red carnations and baby's breath—not quite roses, not quite peonies—and in this moment I see them as a symbol of mediocrity, of giving up, of (and I know I shouldn't say this, but it's true) being like him. Everything I'm terrified of; every reason I'm going to do this.

I fumble the key into the lock and take the flowers inside, and the door clicks shut behind me. I put the flowers and my bag down on the kitchen counter, kick off my sneakers, put my sunglasses on my head, and look around.

And no, I can now say it's *definitely not* just my polarizing lenses, because everything looks different in here too.

My laptop, charging on the coffee table where I left it, feels like maybe it belongs to a "serious" writer now. The pencils on the kitchen counter look like maybe they'll take important midnight notes pretty soon. Even the weird orange glow coming from the curtains gives the room a mood-board quality today.

And me? Staring back from that mirror on the wall, beneath the watchful gaze of Plath and Bukowski and Didion? Well, for the first time in a long time, it feels like maybe I'm more than just a failure. Maybe I'm a writer . . . a writer about to stage her comeback. A writer with a deadline.

Yes, it's a pretty tight deadline, but Kerouac wrote *On the Road* in three weeks, on a steady diet of caffeine, nicotine, and Benzedrine. Surely I can pull together a few chapters and a synopsis with just the first two.

And maybe if I can just write this book, if I can make it a success, I can finally forget what happened last time.

Okay, so, the official line was the book just "didn't work." But when Barb pressed, Felicity implied that it was my fault, that they'd done everything they could—poured a ton of money into marketing, put me on a book tour—but I hadn't held up my end. I'd missed all my deadlines, throwing off their calendars. This meant that by the time *Fractured* was finally released, another book about a stalker, by an already-loved bestselling author, had just come out. That was the book that ended up on the lists. I was eclipsed. Old news before I even began.

The net result being, we sold far fewer copies than we'd hoped (far, far fewer), Felicity started taking days on end to reply to my emails, and things only got worse from there.

I started having panic attacks, googling how to feel better, learning things like how breathing in-two-three-four, out-two-three-four might calm me down; I read article upon article about staying in the present moment. Not the past you fucked up. Not the future unwritten. Hell, I even downloaded a manifestation app; I even *used* it.

But none of that worked for long. All I could do was hope that when the paperback came out, things would finally turn around.

Unfortunately, by the time that happened, Felicity had signed another author just like me, and they didn't really push it. So yes, the paperback *did* do marginally better than the hardback, but not by much.

Basically, everyone just put it down to a bad experience, something to learn from, and moved on.

Everyone except me.

How could I move on when I knew I'd lost my chance at everything I'd ever wanted and it was all my own fault?

And now I have this chance to change all that.

To turn the whole sorry mess into an inspiring story I pull out in interviews to show that you can't just give up after failure, you have to try again.

I just have to . . . you know . . . write it.

I go into the kitchen, put Dad's carnations in a small glass vase, quickly text him *Thank you! Love you,* grab my dirty shirt from my bag, and rush through a whoosh of door beads to my bedroom. And as I throw the shirt in the hamper, I think: *It's a high-concept thriller based on a celebrity I know . . .*

A frisson of excitement moves through me. Because this is the one. I can feel it.

Two minutes later I've changed into dark-blue jeans, a white T-shirt, and a cardigan, and I'm tripping through to the bathroom. I dab deodorant under my arms, spray myself with perfume, and look into the mirror as I start to brush my teeth. I look tired, but it's so, so worth it.

A flash of Zach's hand on my knee in the van, then me falling asleep with my head on his chest. The sound of his heart beating.

But *stop it*—I need to be careful here. I'm nothing more than a casual hookup to him. He can't be more than that to me. Not this time. Not again. I know how that ends. Because he's on billboards and I'm . . . well . . . me. He'll end up with a Solange, not a Zoe. And that's fine, totally fine. I may not get some storybook ending out of this, but if I play my cards right, I will get a book. And maybe that's even better.

Even so, I can't wait to tell Vee about it all . . . that I took her advice and ended up in Zach Hamilton's bed.

And that's the first time I truly understand that I can't. Because: that NDA.

I need to keep everything to myself.

And how the hell am I going to do that?

Ten

I'm balancing two coffees with one hand as I open the back door to the florist's with the other and try not to let my bag slip from my shoulder. I figured Vee wouldn't be as annoyed that I'm late—she might not ask as many questions—if I distract her with an oat-milk latte, so I went to a drive-through.

"Hey," I call as the door bangs behind me, and I head to the front room. "Sorry."

She's staring down at her phone when I get there. I glance at the screen. The store's Instagram page. She presses Post on an image from an event we did last week, then looks up at me. "Where have you been?" she asks, her eyes landing on her coffee. "Is that for me?"

"Sorry, I was up really late writing and forgot to plug my phone in," I say, handing it over. "My alarm didn't go off . . ."

That's what I decided on the drive over here: Avoid the whole thing. Pretend none of it ever happened. Then I can't slip up and say the wrong thing. "How's your ankle?" I continue, keen to change the subject. "Any better?"

"No. It's so painful," she says, moving it out from under her desk so I can get a good look at the bandage. "And my Uber driver wouldn't stop telling me all about her influencing career. I hate not being able to drive. *And* I have to get to class tonight." Today is Thursday; Vee has her acting class on Thursday nights, and nothing had better get in the way. Then her expression changes.

"So how did it go last night?"

Something inside me clenches. *How the hell does she know about last night?*

"Huh?" I'm going for nonchalant, but my voice comes out like a squeak.

"Brian Rollingston?" Vee prompts.

A flash of the smashed vase. The dogs. The limp and bruised peonies on the pale gravel . . .

"Ummm . . . ," I say, my throat tightening up. "It went well . . ."

"Went well?" she replies, eyebrows raised. "You're the worst liar. How do you even survive in this town?" She reaches for the store phone. I watch as she presses a couple of digits and hands it to me, and I hold it to my ear. The voice says: "You have one new message." Beep.

"I am calling on behalf of Brian Rollingston," comes a stern voice, and my cheeks get warm. "I just wanted to let you know that we will *not* be paying the invoice you sent through. The British girl you sent to deliver the order destroyed one of the vases. Brian is still furious."

I hang up and hand her back the phone. "Sorry."

"If he puts something on Yelp, Satan will be pissed." That's her nickname for the owner—I've never met him, but Vee has worked here since she was eighteen. She thinks it's somehow his fault she hasn't made it yet—or rather, his expectations that she put the florist's shop above her auditions.

"But how did you destroy one?" she continues.

"It wasn't my fault. There were two big dogs and they jumped on me. I offered to come back and make up another one. But he said he didn't want me to."

"Entitled prick," Vee says. "Imagine if I called back and was like,

Sorry, boo-boo, you have to pay. I bet he's never experienced any push-back. These people live in a bubble."

The phone starts ringing in her hand and she rolls her eyes.

"Venice Floristry, this is Vee," she says, answering it.

I take my bag to the kitchen, cut myself a large slice of chocolate cake, and go to my work studio.

I print off today's orders, scan through them—we're not that busy today—then get out my tools: knife, scissors, pruning shears, snips, floral tape. But as I lay them down on my worktable in a neat little line, all I can think about is Barb and *high-concept* and *celebrity curtain* and *shit, what have I done?*

Am I insane?

If I haven't written anything in two years, how the hell am I going to pull this off in three weeks?

Do I even have another book in me? What if the first one was just luck?

And what about that NDA?

I need to think about this rationally. How much trouble would I be in if I broke it? Probably a lot . . .

Zach could probably sue me, maybe for millions.

But then again, right now I have no money for him to take from me anyway—all I have is a $250K debt to my publisher if I don't write this book.

And maybe there's a loophole. A workaround. Something.

I grab my phone and check my emails, looking for the last one from Brian. There it is: *Completed: Zoe Weiss NDA.* I click on it and tap the link, and up comes the signed document. It really should be harder to sign away your freedom of speech, but I did it with just a couple of clicks.

I scan past the bit where it tells me the agreement lasts in perpetuity, through the same list I saw last night—everything I'm not allowed to say or share—and down to item IV. *Exceptions.*

The following topics are not restricted:

1. any information made public by Party B (*Zach*)
2. any information that came to be in the public domain through no fault of the Parties
3. any information that Party B provided written approval of
4. any information provided by a court, government body, or law enforcement
5. any information that could be considered illegal, a threat of harm, or an emergency
6. any information that suggests or provides evidence of physical, sexual, or emotional abuse.

There are a couple more too, but the long and the short of it is I can't write a book about Zach. This is, obviously, not ideal.

But then again, I'm not writing about Zach per se; I'm just using him as inspiration for a character, his world as inspiration for the story. By the time I'm done, he won't even recognize himself.

But shit, is this bad? Am I a bad person for even considering this?

Or am I just doing exactly what he and everyone else does: looking out for myself?

I mean, he's not exactly some blameless victim here. He ghosted me last time. I was a mess. And he did that because he was doing what was right for *him*. So is it truly terrible that I might do what's right for me now? It's not like anyone will get hurt, and he owes me—but shit, it *is* bad, I know it is. No matter how I spin it, he's a good guy and he trusts me and I should just write something else. But what?

I go to the flower cooler, pull open the glass door, and fetch some peach tulips and pussy willow. They're for a Sylvia Plath's Tulips arrangement, which is pretty popular. I'm not sure anybody has actually read the poem "Tulips," but her name sells them.

I set everything up, I'm ready to start, but my eyes won't stop snapping to my phone on the table beside me. It's like there's a magnet within it. And a little voice inside me whispers: *Text me, Zach. Text me . . .*

Because the harsh truth is that if I could write something else, I would already have done it. It's this or nothing. And if I could write this idea *without* involving Zach, I absolutely would. But how? I know nothing about what happens behind the celebrity curtain. I mean, I can guess: private jets, celebrity tantrums, cocaine, and orgies. But that's so . . . obvious. I want to write something unexpected. Something true. Something human. About what it *really* means to be in the spotlight.

And I'm not in the spotlight. I'm little Miss Anonymous—even the bookshops who touted me as "the next big thing" would have forgotten my name by now in favor of the new "next big thing."

So my hands are tied.

I need access to Zach and his world, or I'll never do this.

And so, as I chew on the inside of my cheek, I pull up a message and scroll down to his contact: *Zach TOTAL DICK DO NOT CALL.*

A flash of me crying, changing his contact name in my phone three years ago so I didn't make it *three* tearful voicemails and god knows how many unhinged texts . . .

I hesitate. And it's not my conscience this time. It's self-preservation.

Am I *sure* about this? Really sure? Last time wasn't pretty.

Because it's never fun to get ghosted. Especially by someone you felt a real connection to. Someone you spent three days telling *everything* to. Someone who felt *right* in every single way. Sometimes I think that's even worse than a real breakup because you haven't seen their bad side yet; it's the thwarted potential of the thing that will kill you. But you know what's even harder? When that someone becomes a celebrity. And not just a C-lister.

When they land an action trilogy that *everybody* loves. Everybody sees. When the first film breaks box-office records and you know there are still two more to come.

When, every time you forget them, there they are on a billboard as you go to the grocery store or drive to work, or on your Netflix recommends page, or in the *Vanity Fair* issue you're reading at the hairdresser (and let's be fair, nobody needs that shit while sitting in hairdresser lighting). When you can't stop yourself from reading those articles and so now you know their favorite color is red, they always fly home for the holidays because "family comes first," and lots of other things too. Things you want to unlearn, forget. But instead, you hear every word you read in their morning voice, you can still feel their stubble against your cheek, and it doesn't matter how many times you tell yourself *It was only three fucking days, get over it*—you can't. Because life just keeps reminding you.

So eventually you give up fighting it.

You accept that they're just going to haunt you for eternity and there is not a damned thing you can do about it. You just have to grin and bear it and watch your own star plummet as theirs rises, and wonder what you did so wrong that made them never call. Why you weren't good enough. Why you're *never* good enough. But you slowly get used to it. You tell yourself *Never again*. Promise.

And then three years later there you are, about to do it all again despite everything.

So am I *sure*?

No. I am not.

But all I can think about right now is how well it made me write. The way it felt to have my fingertips fly across those keys. Like the pain seared away everything that lay between me and the work. After being blocked for months upon months, I finally managed to rewrite *Fractured* in the weeks after Zach ghosted me. Now that I understood how the sting of rejection might leave a person a little unhinged, I could do it. I mean, I'd never do what the stalker in my book did, but I could understand how it happened. Understand *her*. And that meant I could finally write her.

And I'd give anything to feel that inspired again. God knows I've tried everything else: a writers' group I turned up to every single month, even when it just reminded me of how far I was falling behind; cheap red wine like Bukowski; writing on yellow legal pads like Didion; using a pencil like Morrison and Nabokov and Hemingway (and, it seems, everyone else); writing lying down and smoking cigarettes and drinking sherry like Capote; writing standing up like Woolf; eating apples in the bathtub like Christie; booking into a hotel like Angelou . . . The only author I haven't tried to emulate is Murakami because he wakes early and writes for hours, then spends his days running and swimming, and honestly, I had to draw the line somewhere.

But none of it has worked. Despite it all, I'm still blocked. I'm still blocked because Vee is right; I've done everything except the one thing I need to: let life leave its fingerprints on me again. Let it teach me something worth retelling.

And now I have the chance to change that.

So yes, it *is* worth the risk.

Besides, it'll be different this time.

Because this time I know what I'm getting into, this time I'm *choosing* it, this time *I'm* in control. This time it's for my art—I'm not going to do anything self-destructive like fall in love, or lust, or whatever it was that I fell into with him last time again. Nice as he is, I've learned my lesson there. I'll just be super casual and keep my emotions in check. I'm three years older and a lot wiser—I can do this.

So slowly, intentionally, I type out: *so great seeing you. Let's catch up soon. Z x*

And then I press Send . . .

Eleven

Almost four years ago

It was the middle of July when I first arrived in LA. As the cab pulled away from LAX, I was filled with this narcotic sense of possibility. Because it was all happening.

Fractured hadn't even come out yet and we'd already sold the film option to a big studio. All the buzz created by that million-dollar deal meant everyone was interested. And while I'd heard lots of stories of books being optioned and the adaptation never being greenlit, fuck it, that wouldn't happen to me. I was going to be an executive producer; I was going to help write the script; I was going to learn so much.

This was just the beginning.

But I needed to be here, on the ground, making things happen.

And I know that sounds naive, that dreams are crushed here far more often than they're realized, but something happens when you land here. You believe, with all your heart, that you'll be the exception.

And for me, it seemed justified; my future was assured. All I had to do was rework my book, and I had eight whole months to do it. Easy-peasy.

Except, like I said before, it wasn't.

No matter how hard I tried, the words wouldn't come. I'd never been blocked before, I didn't know what was going on, and so I just sat there, staring at my laptop screen between those same four walls in that same orange light, for days on end, waiting for the block to shift. Around two weeks in, I decided I needed to do something—anything— to get out of my own head.

So that's why I signed up for the dating app.

That summer was a whirlwind of hazy sunsets, fish tacos, the silhouettes of palm trees against power lines, fake grass, frozen margaritas, street art on every corner, crappy motels that belonged in Tarantino movies, billboards on La Brea, *Baywatch* lifeguard towers the same color as the aqua sky, and acute observations I'd note down and never use, like the way the air rippled above hot tar in the distance when I was driving (and I was *always* driving). The men I dated were all more or less the same: lots of overly expensive watches and name-dropping and looking over my shoulder at who was behind me. Very few second dates. But it distracted me from the tyranny of that blinking cursor, and I told myself eventually I'd figure it out. I just needed to give my subconscious time to think.

But soon it was early November. The air had turned cold, the days short, the leaves dry; I'd experienced my first Santa Ana winds—hot, dusty, and wild—and my deadline was even closer. It was a Sunday night and I was planning on staying home and "writing," but then I matched with a guy named "Will" on the app. He was an aspiring screenwriter who tended bar at a place in Santa Monica and claimed to love books. I didn't have my writers' group yet and I reasoned it couldn't hurt to know a screenwriter—maybe he'd give me some tips. So when he said it was his day off but suggested I come down to the place he worked at (free drinks), I said sure.

So there I was, on a late Sunday afternoon three and a half years ago, walking into the Bungalow under an orange sky. It was an old-school surf-style place, with a Ping-Pong table and an open fireplace as I walked in. I moved past a security guy in a black beanie and through to the outside courtyard, looking around for someone who matched Will's photos: tall, sandy-blond hair, good body.

There were couches, low tiled tables, and a couple of trees with lanterns in them, and the bar was at the far end; lots of blue glass suspended by fisherman knots hanging from the ceiling and liquor bottles flashing with the gold of the setting sun. There were two bartenders moving around behind the wooden bar. One of them was wearing aviators, and the other one had the best Afro I'd ever seen. But Will wasn't there yet, not that I could see, and I couldn't just stand there looking awkward, so I moved toward the bar, adjusting one of the spaghetti straps of my dress as I moved. My dress was knee-length and black and I was wearing a leather jacket over it, but the air was colder than I'd expected, and I wished I was wearing jeans and a T-shirt.

I went up and stood at the edge of the bar, and the bartender with the amazing hair smiled at me and leaned forward a little, and I opened my mouth to order a drink. But then someone called out "Hey, Ky?" and he turned to look and went over to them instead. My face flushed; my pulse sped up. I felt small.

So I did what I always do when I'm alone and self-conscious: I reached for the book in my bag. I was halfway through Eve Babitz's *Slow Days, Fast Company*, and so I stood there and pretended to read for a moment, my eyes tracing and retracing the same sentence as I waited for my phone to buzz, thinking: *God, have I been stood up? Did he see me and leave?*

And then I had this feeling.

It was a nervousness that flew through my spine, like I knew something big was about to happen, like I could hear love's footsteps. Feel them.

Then I heard the words "What can I get you?"

And I looked up.

And that was the first time I saw Zach.

He smiled at me, lifted his aviators up, put them on his head, and winked. And something inside me shifted. It was like the earth moved off its axis.

It would be easy to say it was because he was the most beautiful man I'd ever seen, the kind of man you know is destined to be watched on a huge screen by a million eyes, the kind of man whose flaws are somehow luminous. But it was more than that. It was the expression in his eyes that got me. No, something *behind* his eyes. Something familiar.

In that moment all I could think about was that Emily Brontë quote from *Wuthering Heights*: "Whatever our souls are made of, his and mine are the same."

I wouldn't admit that out loud, I know it sounds ridiculous and childish, but if you're not going to tell the absolute truth in fiction, where all truth can be denied, what's the fucking point? So here it is, the truth: In that moment it felt like I'd stumbled upon magic, something that proved life was more than just a chaotic soup of random encounters, stark mornings after and dashed expectations. In that moment that spanned all of three seconds but branded me, everything made sense.

But then I felt a hand on my arm, and a voice said: "Zoe?"

I turned to look. And there stood Will. He looked just like his pictures on the app, and he was . . . fine. But there was no Emily Brontë quote echoing in my mind when I looked into his hazel eyes that first time. My heart was still beating a normal rhythm. That's a roundabout way of saying I was disappointed. And to make it worse, I could feel Zach watching the whole thing unfold.

"Hey, man, can't get enough of this place, huh?" Zach said from behind me, and Will glanced up, toward the bar.

"Pretty much," Will said as he went over and leaned in. I watched as they did some sort of bro-code handshake. Then Will looked over at Ky and nodded, and Ky nodded back. But all I was truly conscious of was Zach.

Stop it, I thought, focusing my eyes squarely on Will. Because I knew Zach was way out of my league, that someone like him would never look at me like that. But I was thinking: *How long do I have to stay before I can say I'm on a deadline and I need to go home?*

That's when Will turned back to me, took in my expression, laughed, and said: "Don't worry, these things are always awkward. I'll win you over. Let me get you a drink." And there was something in that, his ability to read me, to read my discomfort and want to fix it, that softened me.

And he did win me over, at least for a while.

Twelve

Just over three years ago

The best way to characterize my relationship with Will was as a "new-city romance." It wasn't so much that I was attracted to him as it was I needed him—the way a ship needs an anchor and a compass. By the time we met, I'd realized how alone I was here, and I didn't want to be alone. And Will knew things, like what "animal style" was at In-N-Out, which bits of downtown were safe, and how to navigate the traffic. He needed me for the way I looked at him (like he was important), for the way I told him he was talented and could do anything (all the things I needed him to say to me). He was charming as hell when he wanted to be. We loved a lot of the same movies. The sex was fine. Honestly, the worst things I could say about him in the first three and a half months were: (1) he was impatient and moody (but he was an aspiring screen-writer, he lived and breathed heightened stakes, what did I expect?); (2) he had a garish, overly expensive watch just like every other man in this place; and (3) he was always chasing some new moneymaking venture. If it wasn't selling weed gummies or learning about crypto-currency, it was trying to "win at eBay" (his words, not mine). But look, he always had nice things in his apartment, he was generous and took me out to dinner, and nobody is perfect.

But then we had our first fight.

It was Valentine's Day, and I was at home alone writing because Will was working at the bar that night. I hadn't been back there since our first date—Will said he was tired of always hanging out where he worked—but he'd sent me a text earlier in the evening: *Happy V day babe, wish we were together! See you tomorrow xx.*

And by 10 p.m., fueled by wine, a blank page, and a bit of boredom, I thought it seemed like that was a coded message, asking me to come down and surprise him.

So there I was, clutching a red envelope with a card inside and heading up to the bar. I remember feeling so much warmth for him as I drew closer. Excitement. But when he saw me, he didn't look like I expected him to. Not at all. He looked . . . annoyed.

"Surprise, happy Valentine's Day," I said, leaning in to give him a kiss.

"What are you doing here, Zoe? I'm working," he said under his breath. "It doesn't look professional."

My cheeks flushed.

"Oh, sorry," I said—this was not how the scene was meant to run. Not how I'd imagined it on the drive over, at all.

His eyes darted around behind me. "Look, I'm sorry, but I have to do my job. You should go."

"Um, okay," I said.

"I'll see you tomorrow."

And then he turned away from me, and I just backed away from the bar and walked right out again. I was numb, confused, my head nothing but white noise as I headed into the parking lot. That's when I saw two guys coming inside. The two bartenders I recognized from the last time I was here—Zach and Ky.

Shit.

I rushed over to my car with my head down. I'd thought about Zach a few times since that first night, and didn't want him seeing me like this, vulnerable, upset.

That was when I heard: "Hey."

I looked up. And it was him. He was walking toward me.

"Hi," I said, trying to smile.

"Zoe, right?" Zach said.

I nodded and my pulse sped up. Because there it was again, the same feeling I'd had the first time I saw him. I was worried he'd notice, so I looked behind him, to Ky walking inside.

"Are you leaving?" he asked.

"Yeah," I said, my eyes back to him. I was trying to sound upbeat and hugging myself, my fingers clinging to my leather jacket.

"But Will's working tonight," he said, like he was confused. He was close to me now. That was the first time I smelled the cologne I would later struggle to get off my pillowcase: earth and musk.

I swallowed hard. "I know." I looked down at the ground.

"Wait, are you okay?" he asked, moving a millimeter closer to me.

I nodded and forced a smile. "Yes. Fine. Will is just really busy."

Then his eyes moved down to the red envelope in my hands. His mouth opened just a little.

"Oh shit, today is Valentine's Day. Is that for . . .?" His voice trailed off.

My cheeks got warm.

"It doesn't matter; I don't even believe in it. I shouldn't have come. He's working. Busy," I said, trying to shrug it off.

"No . . . it's sweet," Zach said. "Why don't you come back inside? I know what he can be like, but his bark is worse than his bite. Whatever he said, he probably didn't mean it."

But I couldn't forget how he looked at me, like he just didn't want me around. And now that felt even worse when held up against how lovely Zach was being. My lower lip started to quiver and I hugged myself a little harder.

"Hey," he said, taking a step forward, putting his hands on my shoulders, looking me in the eye.

"It's okay. I've got a deadline. I should write anyway," I said. And this was true. My deadline was in two weeks.

"Okay," he said, his eyes still on mine. "If you're sure?"

I nodded.

"I'm Zach, by the way," he said. And that was the first time I heard his name, and it seemed to fit him perfectly. And then he said: "Hey . . . we're both *Z* names . . . how cool is that?"

I laughed and he took his hands from my shoulders and I immediately wanted them back. I knew I shouldn't feel that way, but I did.

"Well, see you around, Z," he said, and then he went inside.

So you see it wasn't really just three days I spent with Zach, not really. It was three days plus the six months he lived rent-free in my mind before that.

Thirteen

Three years ago

The weeks passed, my deadline came and went, and the excitement of my early days in LA was replaced by twenty-four seven self-loathing and anxiety. I got a new deadline, four months away; I assured Barb *this* one was good, *this* one I would meet. But all I did was smoke long, thin menthol cigarettes that made me feel glamorous and stare at that cursor as it taunted me, thinking: *I'm going to fuck this up. I'm going to totally fuck this up.*

Now it was the beginning of May, I was still stuck, and I was close to giving up.

And for the first time since Valentine's Day, I was back at the Bungalow, feeling sorry for myself, waiting for Will to arrive as I stood at the crowded bar. It was Zach and some other guy working that night, and secretly I was hoping Zach would be the one to serve me.

I looked down at my phone as I waited, and then I heard: "Hey, Z, what can I get you?"

I looked up and there Zach was, smiling.

A little jolt ran through me as I said, "Gin and tonic, please?"

His eyes lingered on me, and I was pretty sure he was going to say something else, but then his gaze caught on something behind me, his expression changed, and he said "Sure thing" and went off toward the other side of the bar.

I turned to look just in time to see Will stride up to me. I scanned his face for clues to his mood. Will had been really moody—even by Will standards—for the last couple of weeks. Snapping constantly. Causing fights over nothing. And about a week before, when I was staying over, a woman had called in the middle of the night.

I could hear her crying on the other end of the line. Sobbing and saying things I couldn't quite make out. When he got off the phone and I asked him who she was, he got irritable, said it was a friend whose husband had died, that she was calling for support. He accused me of being jealous. I wanted to believe him, but his lower lip twitched when he said it, and that was always a pretty surefire way of knowing he was lying. And now I was thinking about how seldom I came to this bar with him. How weird he'd been on Valentine's Day when I just turned up. So yes, I was starting to wonder if he was cheating on me.

"Hey," Will said. "Grab us some drinks. I'll get us a table."

"Okay," I said as he hurried off.

Zach was watching me when I turned back. I held up two fingers and mouthed "Two," and he nodded.

I looked over my shoulder. Will was sitting at a table under a tree, one foot crossed over the other, scrolling through his phone, his features lit up by the blue-white screen.

Two minutes later Zach was back, handing over my drinks. The glasses were icy in my hands as I made my way over to the table. My bag was about to fall off my shoulder as I awkwardly put the glasses down. A couple of leaves fell. I remember thinking: *It's spring. Why are leaves falling?* Even nature seemed confused by what was about to happen that night.

"So how was your day?" I asked as I sank into the sofa chair and reached for my drink. He'd been working on a screenplay with a friend nearby.

"Good. I had some really strong ideas. I think this will be the one," he said, picking up his drink and taking a big gulp. By this point I'd learned that Will's need for admiration and praise had nothing to do with a lack of self-esteem and everything to do with ego. He needed to know that I understood 100 percent that he was better than me. And I had to admit that, yes, he probably was. If not talent-wise (everything I'd read of his was a Guy Ritchie knockoff), then definitely confidence-wise. Because while I was staring at my blinking cursor, paralyzed by doubt and fear and overwhelming pressure, he was out there happily hustling, just believing in himself and doing the work.

And why couldn't I be more like him? *How* could I be more like him?

That's when his phone lit up in his hand, and he looked at it and smiled and starting typing again.

"You made progress?" I continued, my voice pitching up at the end.

But he just kept typing, ignoring me—who was he texting?—and I was embarrassed, sitting there, talking to myself.

"Could you do that later?" I asked.

"Fuck," he said. "Fine, you have my attention. Now what?"

His stare bore into me, and I could feel those damned tears brewing again like the weight of everything was just too much. And it wasn't even just about him, about us; it was about the state of my life. Why was it so hard to finish my book? I'd done it once, got to those blessed words "THE END," and rewriting was meant to be the fun part. So what was wrong with me? And why couldn't I admit it to Barb, to Felicity, ask for help?

Why could Will finish, and I couldn't?

Why could *everyone* finish, and I couldn't?

"Don't you dare cry," he said, looking around. "People know me here."

"I can't help it," I said in a low whisper as I tried my best to stop the tears. I took deep breaths and used my fingers to wipe away the couple that had already escaped.

"Fuck, Zoe, why are you like this? Why do you always act like your problems are the worst problems? Like you're the center of the world."

And now the tears came in earnest. I let out a sob. People were looking and my cheeks got hot.

"You know what?" Will said, standing up. "I don't want to do this anymore. You make everything too fucking hard."

"What?" I asked, confused.

Then he leaned forward, and his hazel eyes—eyes I thought I knew—met mine and he said, "I'm done. Get your stuff out of my place before I get home tonight."

My ears rang and I waited for him to take it back, but he didn't. He just stormed out.

And just like that, it was all over.

Everything I'd learned about him in the six months we were together—how he liked to have his back gently scratched as he fell asleep, that his middle name was Harvey and he hated it, that he didn't like almonds—was now wasted. But at least it all made sense now: *That's why he's been so moody and snappy.* He'd been getting ready to dump me. Maybe I was right; maybe he *was* cheating on me. But it didn't matter anymore. It was over. And part of me was relieved.

So no, I didn't go after him.

I sat back in my chair, tried to steady my breath, bit back tears. And then I grabbed my bag and stood up on shaky knees, and just before I headed for the door, I glanced at the bar.

Zach was watching me.

He lifted up a pink drink, smiled, and motioned in a come-over way.

I looked back to the door, to the guy with a beanie, and then back over at Zach again. At the cocktail. And even if I weren't shaking and didn't need a drink to get me through the next couple of hours gathering up my things, there would still have been no choice in the matter. I walked toward him.

He slid the cocktail across the bar to me on a napkin—there was a cherry on the edge. "Tough night?" he asked.

I nodded. People on the other side of the bar were flagging him, so he said, "I'll be back," then went to serve them. I gulped down my pink cocktail—grenadine and gin—mentally cataloging what I had at Will's place, what I needed to get.

We weren't living together, I didn't have my own key, and I was never there without him, but I *did* know where he kept the spare, and I *did* have two drawers full of my things at his place. Just a few bits of clothing, some makeup, toiletries—together with a few books on his bedside table with notes in the margins I didn't want to lose. And in that moment it felt like I didn't know him at all. Like if he'd just break up with me like this, not even want to talk about it, he was the kind of guy who'd set it all on fire.

A couple of minutes later I was chewing on the cherry and Zach was back, leaning toward me on the bar.

"Where did he go?"

I shrugged. "I don't know. We just broke up . . ."

He nodded. "Yeah, I thought it looked like that."

"He's been going through some stressful stuff," I continued, trying to save face. "Anyway, it's probably for the best."

"Well, you'll be okay. It's all material, right? You said you were a writer?"

I nodded.

"Screenplays?"

I shook my head. "No, novels."

"Really? But why LA then? I'd think London was more literary."

I shrugged and tried to think of something cool to say. "LA has Didion and Babitz and Bukowski . . . and, you know, earthquakes." I took another sip. "Living on a fault line has to be inspiring, right?"

"You like to live on the edge then?" he asked, his eyes seeing right through me. Past anything I might say. To my insecure core.

"Not really." I laughed.

"So, what kind of books?" he asked, dropping some lime into a drink.

"Thrillers . . . ," I said, looking up. Our eyes met.

"Interesting." He leaned in a fraction closer. "I would have thought rom-coms or romance, looking at you," he said.

"Really? Why?" And somehow I felt insulted. I wanted to seem interesting and mysterious and alluring and razor-sharp, not light and fluffy.

"You blush. Nobody in this city blushes."

My cheeks got warm.

"See, there you go again. It's cute."

His eyes moved to my glass, which was almost empty. "Another?"

"I can't," I said. "I have some things at his place, so I need to go get them now. Before he gets back."

Zach's eyes darted to his wrist, his watch. "Well, I'm off in half an hour. I could come and help you, if you want?"

"Really?"

"Of course. You shouldn't go alone. Will can be a . . . dick."

And as I looked into his eyes in that moment, I knew he would be my undoing. I knew it like I knew my own name. But I just didn't care.

And now, here I am. Undone.

Fourteen

Just after 1 p.m. I'm about to leave to do the afternoon deliveries, and I head through to ask Vee if she wants me to bring anything back. She's on the phone when I get there, using her super-professional voice, so I know it's someone important.

"Okay," she says. "Uh-huh. Of course. Yes, I know, definitely. Yes." She's nodding big nods and grinning.

Then she says: "Sure, yes, I understand. Thank you. Talk soon."

She hangs up and looks at me, eyes wide. "Oh my god, we just got a Levy event."

"A what?" I ask.

"A Levy event," Vee repeats, but still it means nothing to me. "Bartholomew Levy? Executive producer of *There You Stand*, *Unreasonable*, and *Tell It Again*?"

I've only seen *Tell It Again* and it was great, but I'm assuming from her expression that they're all extremely successful. "That was Holly, the event coordinator for the Everett Hotel. The florist they'd booked fell through. It's next Saturday and, babe, we're invited. We get to go to this thing!"

"Great," I say.

"No, you don't get it. You know who went to the last two? Andreas Murphy."

She waits for my reaction, but I don't know who that is either.

"Andreas Murphy . . . that producer guy I auditioned for last year? The one who gave me the callback?"

I'm frowning, so she continues.

"And then I saw him on Raya? But he didn't match with me? Obviously because it would have been weird after almost casting me . . ."

"Oh, right, yes," I say. It's all coming back now. In Technicolor. Vee was convinced if she could just get in the same room as him again, he'd give her a part. She said they'd had great (and I quote) "creative energy."

"That's cool," I say, but she's not really listening. I can almost see her interior monologue playing out, and I'm pretty sure it involves watching her future self collecting an Oscar.

"Hey, I'm going to do deliveries. Do you want me to grab you something to eat while I'm out?"

"I can't eat now. This is so fucking good—even better than an audition from my agent. Who knows who else will be there. We have to make everything about this event perfect."

"Okay, we'll start working on it when I get back. See you in a bit," I say as I head to the back of the shop and the garage. I pull open the door, flick on the garage light, unlock the van, and get in. But before I turn the key in the ignition, my phone beeps. My heart stutters.

I lurch for it. *Zach, please be Zach.*

But it's not—it's Greta. It's about tonight, my monthly writers' group meetup—we're holding it at her house. And my stomach drops as I read the words.

She's coming.

Fifteen

I pull up outside Greta's house—a little gray-and-white weatherboard number in Culver City, with tiny purple daisies at the edge of the garden—and debate squeezing into the driveway behind three other cars. Too risky. Someone might box me in, and if Sophie is coming tonight, I don't know how long I'll last.

That text message, *She's coming*, that's what it meant.

Sophie. Sophie is coming. Sophie, the one who didn't say *happy birthday*.

My nemesis.

I drive down the street and find an empty spot under a streetlight beside a cactus garden.

Then I take a deep breath—*I can do this*—and get out of my van. Sophie hasn't been to the writers' group in almost four months now and stopped checking in every Wednesday. I'd secretly hoped she'd moved away or found a new career or something else. Something that meant she'd never come back. But no such luck.

I go up to the door, steady my breath, and knock.

Bang. Bang. Bang.

Voices filter through the door, then laughter, then it opens and Greta is grinning at me, holding a glass of red wine.

"Welcome!" she says loudly, hugging me. Then quietly, into my ear, she says: "Deep breaths."

I nod and go inside.

We move to the living room where everyone is sitting on either a sofa or a cushion on the floor around a low, oblong coffee table with guacamole and salsa and chips in the center. Laptops are open. Notepads are out. Wineglasses are full. And pictures of Greta and Candice, her live-in girlfriend, smile back at us from the walls. Candice is the most adult person I know; she's an engineer and owns this house, and she's the reason I know what compound interest is. The reason I know I should have some but don't.

"Hey," I say, sitting down at the one free spot and looking around the table.

"Hey," everyone says in unison, like they're trying to show their invisible support of me in these trying times. There are five of us.

Greta writes women's fiction and is all positivity and light, saying things like "I'm a talented writer" in front of the mirror every morning. That is, until she's a little drunk, then she's the realest person you've ever met and starts using words like "Weltanschauung" in conversation just to confuse people. I like her a little drunk.

Rita is a thrice-published crime writer. She's the realistic one and comes along with statistics of how hard it is to get published and that most novels only sell three thousand copies *ever*. She's also super well-connected and worked in a TV writers' room once straight out of college—her eyes get a little glassy whenever she talks about it.

There's me: the sad one.

There's Tom, who is just the nicest man I've ever met and writes poetry that should be published but isn't.

And then there's fucking Sophie, looking pleased with herself. "Zoe, so nice to see you," she says.

"You too." I smile back as I open my laptop, and something clenches in my stomach. Sophie has been mean to me ever since I joined this group, so now I kind of hate her back. Maybe it's because we're similar ages and write similar things; maybe I just remind her of someone she didn't like in high school. But it's always directed at me and only me. And it's so fucking subtle. Like, it's enough to make everyone notice (so it's humiliating), but she does it in such a way that she could always deny meaning anything bad by it. It could always just be me being "overly sensitive" and her being "helpful."

The least subtle example of what I mean would be: the idea incident.

The idea incident happened six months ago. For the first time in ages I'd had an idea and I'd brought it to the group. It was about a bachelorette weekend in Vegas that goes very, very wrong when the bride wakes up with blood in her hair, a hole in her memory, and a million dollars in her bank account . . . It was only in its early stages, and everyone else was super supportive, they said the twist was really clever, but Sophie's exact words were "Sorry, Zoe, but it's just shit. You can do better. I know you can." See what I mean? Enough to crush your confidence but simultaneously make you think that maybe she has a point. Maybe she's doing you a favor. Maybe she's stopping you from showing yet *another* bad idea to your agent . . .

It was only when poor Greta texted me after the fact to check that I was okay that I realized I wasn't imagining things. It was mean. Sophie was mean. But even so, I shelved that idea and haven't brought anything else to the group since. Honestly, if it hadn't taken me so long to find this writers' group, if I didn't like Greta so much, I might have left after that. But then Sophie stopped coming along, so the problem dealt with itself, until tonight.

Still, maybe none of that matters now, because the idea I have now is way, way better than that one—if my subject matter would just text me back. I stare at my phone and will it to light up.

But: nothing.

And what will I do if he *never* texts back? I don't know any other celebrities.

Still, calm down. You only saw him this morning. He might reply tomorrow . . .

"So, guys, I have news . . . ," Sophie says. Oh good. This must be why she decided to grace us with her presence this week. "I got an agent."

"That's great," everyone says. Greta throws me a look.

"I know, isn't it?" Sophie says.

And it is, I know it is, and I want to be happy for her, but also . . . argh.

Greta pushes a full glass of wine toward me.

I mouth "Thanks" and take a sip.

"Who is it?" Rita asks. Deadpan. Rita doesn't do excited. She knows better.

"I can't say until we make the announcement," Sophie says.

And I remember that feeling. Back when the future was all ahead of me and I didn't reek of failure.

"I'm really happy for you," I say, because I refuse to be the kind of person who holds a grudge, and she flashes me a smile.

"So what are you working on, Zoe?" she asks, and my throat involuntarily closes up like it won't let me speak even if I wanted to. Not after last time.

"Just playing around with an idea," I say.

"Awww," she says, jutting out her lower lip. "You'll get there. Everyone's journey is different. Like, it only took me three months to write the draft of this book. But other people take ten years . . ."

See? Could be bitchy . . . could be encouraging. This is why she gets away with it.

I give her a small, tight smile and stare at my laptop screen, at that blinking cursor, and pretend to read words that aren't on the page.

At our writers' group we write for half an hour at the beginning, and then the group gives twenty minutes of feedback to each of us on whatever we've sent around ahead of time. Or that's how it works for the others. I usually just stare at my screen for half an hour, say I have nothing to share because what I'm working on "isn't ready yet," and then say nice (but hopefully helpful) things about everyone else's work. They usually indulge me. It's kind.

Greta shoves some guacamole on a chip into her mouth and sets the timer on her phone. Everyone puts their phones away—it's a no-phone exercise—and I put mine on the floor beside me. Face up. Everyone stares at their screens.

"Go," Greta says, and the room fills with the sound of keys being tapped.

But my fingers stay static, hovering over the keyboard and doing nothing.

I glance across at Rita, who is frowning at her screen—I can see it reflected in the lenses of her black-framed glasses. I swear she already has half a page there. Then there's Tom, who is scribbling on a notepad. And Sophie, who is smiling at her work.

And then it happens. Something so wonderful it's enough to make you believe in a benevolent god: my phone screen lights up with a message.

My heart flares as I surreptitiously reach for it and glance down at the screen.

It's from a number I don't have in my phone.

It reads: *Yo Z, is this still your number? What are you doing to-night? Z x*

Sixteen

So that's how I end up on the third floor of a parking garage at eight on a Thursday night instead of at my writers' group, reminding myself: *Don't feel too much, Zoe. You're just here for your book. For research. Focus on that.*

But the problem is, there's helium in my veins and a fluttering in my stomach and I need to get myself in check. I really can't afford to end up in the same Zach Hamilton–shaped hole as I did last time—I have too much to do.

I reach for my phone and double-check the text messages Zach sent me: *Level P3, Bay 168, 8 pm.*

That's where I am. I drove past the orange wall with P3 on it when I came in. And I'm sitting in Bay 168. And now it's 8:03 p.m. So where is he?

Zach said we needed to do it this way to protect his privacy (and mine) as we organized tonight from my parked van outside on Greta's street. And I texted back: *Of course.* Like I expected it. Like I'd done it before. But this is the exact sort of information I need for my book, the sort of detail I'd miss without him. The sort of detail that will bring his world to life on the page . . . and it feels like once I understand the world I'm writing about, the story will be clear.

I glance at myself in the rearview mirror. I'm wearing the same dark-blue jeans, white T-shirt, and cardigan that I had on when I went to work this morning, and *shit*, there's a fleck of mascara under one eye. I wet a finger with my tongue and wipe it away. It smudges; I try again.

And then there in my mirror: the white glow of headlights.

Behind me.

They're coming this way.

I turn my head and watch as a big black SUV with tinted windows parks in the bay beside me. *This is it.*

My heart thuds in my chest as the door opens and a sturdy man in his late forties with a shaved head and a black T-shirt gets out. He's peering in at me now with narrow dark eyes that don't blink. I put down the window.

"Zoe?" he asks.

I nod and smile. "Hi."

"I'm Carlos. I'm here for Zach."

I grab my bag and step out into the cool air that smells of exhaust fumes, and under a flickering light, I lock the van up after me.

Carlos is holding the back of the SUV open for me and I get in. He closes the door and gets in too, and I hear the click of locks.

We drive to the exit in silence, then out onto the road. We turn left, then left again. And soon we're heading in the direction of the hills, to Zach's place.

My phone beeps and glows in my hands. A message.

Greta: *Are you okay? xx*

She thinks I left early because Sophie was there. They all do.

I type back: *Am okay. Just needed an early night. See you soon! xx*
Send.

Then I put my phone in my bag and watch the grit of Hollywood—homeless people living out of tents or shopping carts—turn into houses on tree-lined streets, turn into the hills on either side of Outpost Drive, turn into lush greenery and mansions. The tinted windows give everything a filmic effect, and the red of taillights and the white of headlights all blur together in the dark.

As we move, a memory floats back: that night Zach helped me go and get my things from Will's place. I was too shaky, so Zach drove my car, and I remember watching the lights through the window then too. A flash of me in Will's bedroom, collecting my makeup and tampons and clothing and books into a plastic bag I'd found in the kitchen, while Zach waited for me in the front room. Then leaving the key where I found it, on the top of the doorframe, knowing I'd never use it again. We drove back to my place and Zach helped me bring my things inside, and then he looked at me and said, "I could stay, if you wanted me to?" His eyes moved to my lips and something flipped in my chest.

And that was the first time I realized he might actually like me. That it wasn't just me.

I blink hard, pushing the memory away and focusing on the present moment. I glance up at the back of Carlos's head; he's staring at the road, his big hands around the steering wheel. He looks up at the rearview mirror and I do too. Our eyes meet and I smile.

Carlos clears his throat. "Zach says you're old friends?" he says, like he now feels obliged to make conversation.

I nod, a little too hard.

"Yes, we met years ago, when he was still a bartender. I dated someone he worked with for a while." I feel like I need to emphasize this point so he knows I'm safe. I knew Zach *before*.

Before he had people to pick up women in parking garages for him. *Before* he was *People* magazine's sexiest man alive. *Before*.

"Zach was a bartender? Hard to imagine." He gives what I think is supposed to be a smile, but it looks weird on his face.

"Mmmm-hmmmm," I say. "He was pretty good too."

That's when I get paranoid. *Shit, is he testing me?* Because I signed an NDA . . . is he testing what I'd tell people? Did I just fail?

But if I did, he doesn't say anything. And now we're heading up

Zach's street. Carlos presses a button on a small remote and the gate opens, and we drive inside and up the driveway.

Zach's house is looming at the top of the hill. It looks different in the nighttime, bigger somehow. Concrete and creepers and glass against the indigo sky. I can see where I was parked this morning up ahead, by the edge of the cliff, but Carlos drives straight into a garage at the bottom end of the house. I hear the doors unlock and we get out.

"This way," Carlos says, and he opens a door.

Seventeen

We step into the house—a huge painting is in front of me. It's white, just like the wall behind it, but textured, with seemingly random flecks of gold and a single black line running through the center. I can tell it's expensive from the conspicuous raw edges and lack of frame, and it makes me feel small, unimportant. Like this was a bad idea and I'm out of my depth. Genius and Randal rush around the corner, paws and slobber and wagging tails.

"Hello," I say to them, petting them one at a time—wet noses on the palms of my hands—and then I hear Zach's voice: "Hey, stranger."

I look up.

He's wearing jeans and a long-sleeved white crew neck just like he was this morning, but now he's wearing a purple beanie too, and walking toward me. And oh shit, a warmth runs through me.

Don't feel it. Don't feel it. Don't feel it.

Because everything dangerous starts with warmth: fire, hope, love. Even hypothermia feels warm before it kills you.

"Hey," I say as he gets to me. He leans in and kisses my cheek. I can smell his cologne, earth and musk. A flash of my pillowcases from three years ago. Then a flash of him when we woke up together this morning.

"I'm still wrecked from last night. I thought we could stay in?" Zach says casually over his shoulder as I follow him into the kitchen and the dogs run ahead.

"Sure," I say.

He goes to the fridge and I stand by the kitchen counter. It's wide and made out of white marble, with a silver bowl of lemons in the center. All the bottles from drinks last night have been cleared away by now, and in their place lie swatches of fabric—the same ones that assistant was carrying this morning when I left—laid out next to each other.

"Drink?" Zach asks, pulling a bottle of champagne from the fridge.

I still feel a little hungover too, but I need to calm my nerves. "Sure, thanks." I smile.

He pops the champagne and pours two glasses.

"What are these for?" I ask, picking up the pieces of fabric and assessing them in turn like I know anything about upholstery.

"A project. That's what Franz and Mary from this morning are working on. Which one do you like best?"

I flip through them—red velvet, blue denim, some sort of dark-green fabric with a burned-out pattern on it.

"I'm thinking the blue," he continues, handing me a glass.

"The red one," I say.

I say that because I want him to remember me. To see me. And it feels like if I'm too agreeable I'll just melt into every other woman he's had here in the last three years. I also know from *Vanity Fair* that red is his favorite color, so . . .

He bursts out laughing. "See, this is why I like you, Zoe. You're straight with me. Come."

And then his free hand finds mine and he leads me past the two white sofas we all sat on last night, past the coffee table covered in magazines, through the big glass doors, and outside to a terrace decorated with cacti and draping greenery. The house wraps around it in a C shape, and in the center is a pool lined by four well-spaced deck chairs. It's lit up bright blue and steam is rising off it, the city sparkling back at us from the distance. A flash of my tiny apartment, the scratchy towels in my bathroom. How could anybody ever get used to this? Could I?

He pulls two of the deck chairs together and sits down on one of them. And as I take a seat on the other, he scrolls through his phone, then taps, and music starts playing from speakers I can't see.

He picks up his glass again and leans toward me, and we clink.

"To kismet. Bringing us together again," Zach says.

"To kismet," I say, then I take a sip. Our eyes meet and something inside me flips. *Don't feel it, don't feel it, don't feel it.* I look away. My eyes land on the black beads around his wrist.

"You still have these," I say, reaching out to touch them. My fingers touch his skin. Zap.

"Black tourmaline, man. Keeps the bad vibes away." He grins. "So I have an important question."

"What?" I ask.

"Hang on," he says as a new song starts to play. It's hip-hop but with a woman singing a riff in the background. "What do you think of this?"

"I like it," I say, smiling.

"I coproduced it. It's that friend of mine you met last night, Kenneth . . . Man, listen to his voice, his lyrics," he says, putting down his drink. "He's going to be huge."

He reaches beside him and opens a small wooden box. "But that's not my question," he says, pulling out a joint and a small metal lighter. "What's been going on with Zoe Ann Weiss these last three years? I feel like you told me nothing last night." He smiles, his eyes narrowed in a sexy way I recognize from his movies.

"What do you mean?" I ask. He lights the joint and takes a drag and then hands it to me.

He breathes out a cloud of thick smoke. "I want to know all of it, man. A lot can happen in three years."

I shrug. "There's nothing to tell," I say, then take a drag even though

I don't really smoke weed. I cough a little, then hand it back to him and look out at the lights of LA and hope I look mysterious.

He takes a drag. "I don't buy that."

And this is not the plan. The plan is to find out all about *him*. For my book.

"Well, I'm way more interested in you," I say. "What's all this like?" I motion to the house, the pool, the view. "You got everything you wanted."

"Yeah, nobody expected it to blow up like this. You know that callback I was so nervous about the last time we hung out?"

I nod. Every time he talked about it, he got this vulnerable look on his face that made me want to hug him. It was scheduled for two days after he walked out my door.

"That was it. My big break."

"That's amazing." I smile. But something inside me aches. Would he have called me if he hadn't got that role?

"It's been such a wave, but you just have to ride it, right?" He continues, "Still, shit's not perfect."

"Looks pretty perfect."

"No . . . it's not."

He takes another drag and offers it to me, but I wave it away.

"What's so unperfect?"

"Like, I can't go out in public without having to do a face. Either I have to be charming and smile or brooding. I can't just, like, be a fucking human."

"Show me brooding?"

He does a face I've seen in tabloids before and I laugh. "Very good."

"And I have PR people who tell me what to do, and everyone wants something from me now." He gives a small smile. "Except you, it seems."

Guilt pulses through me.

"So why didn't you want to meet that guy I was going to intro you to last night? Steven? He could really help you."

"I did. I just got tired," I say.

"Okay, well, I'm going to try to connect you another time. He's a producer and one of the only people who reads in this town; he's always turning books into movies. What was the name of your book again? I'll send it to him."

"*Fractured*," I say, my voice small. Then I look away.

The option on *Fractured* expired eighteen months after we sold it, and the studio didn't renew. So I should be jumping at this opportunity. But even thinking about it still makes me hurt all over.

"Wait . . . what's that?"

"What?" I ask, my gaze moving back to him.

"You get this weird look on your face every time I bring up your book. What's that about?"

I swallow hard and shrug.

"I don't know . . ."

"Yes you do. What is it?"

I reach for the joint that's almost burned down now and take a deep drag, hold the smoke in my lungs for a moment, then say, "It bombed and broke my heart." And then I breathe out a cloud of smoke.

Silence.

"Fuck, I'm sorry. That sucks," he says, reaching out to touch my hand. *Don't feel it, don't feel it, don't feel it.* "That must have been so hard."

I hand the joint back to him, and he lets go of my hand and stubs it out.

"It's fine," I say, then take a sip of my drink because now my mouth tastes like weed.

"So are you writing anything new?" he asks.

Actually yes, it's about a celebrity I know, a deep dive behind the celebrity curtain . . .

"Not really, just playing with a couple of ideas."

"Cool, just don't write about me, okay?"

I laugh, but my insides clench. "Of course not. You had me sign that NDA, remember?"

"Yeah, sorry about that. Brian insisted. He's so high-strung about everything."

We both look out at the lights for a bit.

"So if you were going to write about me, though, what would you write?" he asks.

"You want it both ways, do you?"

He smiles that perfect smile and gazes out into the distance. "I guess."

"I would write about a movie star who is actually just a regular guy underneath."

"Right . . . I see where this is going . . . and he falls for a regular girl?" he asks. Grin. "Maybe a novelist? Like that movie *Notting Hill*?"

"He was a bookstore owner," I quip. "But if I had a story idea, I'd be writing it."

"It'll come. When you least expect it."

Then he finishes his drink and stands up. "Should we go for a swim?" he asks and pulls off his beanie, then his crew neck.

"Umm," I say. "I don't have a swimsuit. And it's freezing. I mean, you're wearing a beanie."

"It's heated," he says, stripping down to his underwear now. "Don't be a pussy."

He walks toward the pool, and he looks like he's paid to keep in shape, and I'm not. But also, I want to swim right now. Even just for those three days we spent together, he had that effect on me, that vivifying effect that could jolt me out of character. That was what was so intoxicating about him. I was closer to who I *wanted* to be when I was with him. A little reckless. A little bold. So I stand up and quickly unzip my jeans and pull them off.

He gets to the edge of the pool, jumps in, and swims to the center, and I take off my cardigan and pull my T-shirt over my head. Now I'm in just my underwear and bra, and I dive in.

I'm underwater for a moment, the world sounds muffled, and when I come up, he's right there in front of me.

My first instinct, before I think, is to reach out and touch him—it's like there's a magnet drawing me toward him—but *no, no, no.*

So I do the other thing. I splash him.

"What the—?" He grins. "Are you, like, five?" He splashes me back.

And I'm laughing, my eyes half-closed so the water doesn't get into them. Then it happens. His hands are around my waist and he's pulling me to him.

And there's this moment when he hesitates, we both do, but then he reaches for my face and kisses me. A rush moves through me and I kiss him back. He tastes like weed and metal and champagne and salt, and he lifts me up and I wrap my legs around his waist, and he holds me close. I pull away a little, trying to remember everything about this moment. The lights flickering like fallen stars in the distance. The warmth of his chest. His wet hair under my fingertips. His hands on my hips, holding me in place.

"It's so weird, I always knew I'd see you again," he says, his voice husky. "I just knew."

I frown at him now and shake my head. "What a lie." I say that even though I want it to be the truth.

"I did," he says. "I thought about you often."

"I'm sure," I say, my eyes on his chest. Then I look up and our eyes meet. "That must be why you just wouldn't stop calling me . . ."

He grins. "I was wondering how long it would take for this to come up. I listened to your messages, if it makes it better. Twice."

"Asshole." I laugh, pulling away from him and swimming to the steps.

I sit and watch him as he wades toward me.

"I should have called," he says.

"It doesn't matter now," I say, nonchalant.

"No, it does. I really wanted to. I liked you, Zoe; you know I did. I *do*. But everything was just breaking for me and I wanted to avoid any complications. Which is fucking ironic, because all I've had since are complications . . ."

"Poor little Zach." I grin as he gets to me.

He tucks a piece of hair behind my ear. "Well, I've grown up. I'm different." We're standing close again now; I can feel his warmth. And something is tugging in my chest. Because the truth is I *did* think he liked me, I was sure of it—that's why it made no sense when he disappeared.

"Yes, you are different," I say. "I mean, I didn't have to sign an NDA last time."

I'm feeling him out, trying to figure out how upset he'd be if I broke it. How much it matters to him vs. how much it matters to Brian.

He narrows his eyes again. "You're seriously pissed about that, aren't you? I mean, you've mentioned it twice."

"A bit. I didn't sign one last time and I didn't tell anyone that time either. Not even after you became super famous." And I *didn't* tell anyone. I didn't want to be *that* girl. It felt like that would cheapen the memory.

"I know you're not like that," he says, cupping my face in his hands. Then he leans forward and kisses me on the forehead.

And now I feel like a really shitty human being. Because he doesn't know it, but I *am* like that. And I don't want to be, but I also want my book.

"Okay," I whisper.

Now his mouth finds mine and I feel his hands move down my back. My bra unclips and I shrug it off. His hand lands on my breast as he kisses me again. Then he pulls away and looks me in the eye and we're silent for a moment, and then he says, "Should we go inside?"

And that's when the dogs start barking.

Loud barking, just like when I broke that vase yesterday.

And I'm expecting him to say something like *They just love cars, man*, like he did before, but he doesn't.

He frowns and gets out of the pool and says nothing, just strides over to where his phone is, dries off his hands quickly on his clothes, and taps and scrolls. His frown deepens.

"What's wrong?" I ask.

"Nothing," he says.

But he's looking around frantically now, and I'm not sure what's going on.

He stabs something into his phone.

Then the back doors to the house open and Carlos comes outside. Zach looks at him. He looks at Zach. Something I can't read passes between them.

Then Zach says: "Hey, um, I'm so sorry, but there's a security thing I need to deal with. Carlos will take you back. But talk soon."

Eighteen

Forty minutes later I'm back in that parking garage, turning the key in the ignition and driving away from Carlos. My hair is still wet from the pool, my bra is in my bag, and my arms are covered in goose bumps, but I feel more alive, more inspired, than I have in years.

And *oh shit*, I know what those feelings mean. Scary things. Big black-hole things.

Exciting things.

And *oh double shit*: my headlights.

I flick them on, drive toward the exit sign, and put my ticket into the machine, and as the boom lifts, images from tonight flicker in my mind—a black SUV, red velvet, the smell of weed, the lights of LA, Zach's mouth on mine, my legs around his waist, his grin, *I listened to your messages, if it makes it better. Twice*—and that warmth, that dangerous warmth, gets a little hotter.

I turn left into the treacle-black night, a couple of half-empty water bottles rattle on the floor beside me, and the traffic lights ahead glow red just as I get to them.

Headlights zoom past and blur together, and as I wait for the lights to go green, the last part of tonight replays itself in my mind. The dogs barking. Zach rushing for his phone. The look on Carlos's face. Then

Zach's words: *Hey, um, I'm so sorry, but there's a security thing I need to deal with. Carlos will take you back. But talk soon.*

What sort of security thing? Something I can use in my book? Is there a story there?

I glance into my rearview mirror, searching for Carlos's SUV as it leaves. There's a white Prius behind me, and behind that, the parking garage, but I don't see Carlos anywhere. The lights turn green, I put my foot on the gas, and that's when my phone starts ringing from the holder.

Dad . . .

Triple shit. But I can't avoid him forever. He'll get on a plane and come over here.

"Hey," I say, pressing the talk button and trying to sound perky. "Sorry, Dad, I was going to call you. I've just been so busy . . ."

"No problem, sweetheart, I just wanted to say happy birthday."

Guilt pulses through me as my eyes dart to the time: 10:33 p.m. That means it's 6:33 a.m. in the UK.

"Thanks, Dad," I say. "How's everything?"

A billboard with Zach's new movie flashes past, and something ignites in my solar plexus.

"God, you sound so American," he says. He says this every time we talk.

"Do I?" And I always say this back.

"So have you thought about coming home?"

I take a deep breath. Because how do I say *No, I'm too scared to end up like you, with a life like yours. Never really reaching for anything. I'd rather risk gun violence and serial murderers, thanks?*

Even thinking it makes me feel like a terrible person. "I *have* thought about it, Dad, and it's a good idea. I just don't think now is the time," I say.

He lets out an all-too-familiar sigh.

"Sweetheart, be sensible. You can't be chasing some crazy dream forever. And that's not your home. This is."

"Dad, things are going really great over here. I have a new idea. My agent loves it . . ."

A moment passes.

"Well, I just want you to be happy."

"I *am* happy, Dad," I say as I flick on my indicator and go to change lanes. My eyes dart to the rearview mirror.

And—wait.

There. Behind me.

A white Prius.

Is that the same white Prius that was behind me when I left the garage?

It can't be, can it?

My hands grip the steering wheel as I squint at it.

But now all I can think about is Zach's face when his dogs were barking, then *There's a security thing I need to deal with.* My underarms start to sweat.

"Dad, I've got to go. I'll call you back," I say, and hang up before he can object. My eyes are glued to that white car now. I want to see who's driving, but I can't make them out. And I'm being insane, I know I'm being insane, but also . . . what if I'm not being insane? I don't want them to know where I live.

I take a right at Sunset Boulevard and *please don't follow me . . . please don't follow me . . . please don't follow me . . .* but it turns right too. It fucking follows me.

Shit.

I exhale and force myself to breathe normally, but my eyes keep searching the mirror as I get closer and closer to my street. And that little white car just stays there, behind me. What do I do? I can see the Trader Joe's sign looming from the big white building on the corner up ahead, and Chateau Marmont gleaming from the hill, and my road is coming up in just a moment . . .

I'll turn down my street, and if they follow me, I'll just keep driving.

And so I take a deep breath, turn on my indicator, and head down North Laurel. And that white car? Well, it keeps on driving forward.

Relief washes over me. My pulse slows down. Far better I'm going full *Bell Jar* than somebody is *actually* following me.

I find a parking spot under a streetlight, turn off the ignition, get out of the van, and head toward the terra-cotta arch with my keys between my fingers. Just in case. Jake is sitting by the pool having a beer when I get inside, his legs dangling in the water, his face lit up by the blue-white light of his phone.

He looks up. "Hey, beautiful," he says. "Want a drink?"

A flash of him and that other woman just thirty-six hours ago, his jacket over her shoulders. There's probably been another one since then. And there will be another one tomorrow. And the day after that. And my hair is still wet from Zach Hamilton's pool. I don't need this shit.

"I can't," I reply, wrapping my arms around me as I quickly rush up the stairs. Because all I can think about is a certain blank word document. A certain blinking cursor.

I get to the top, turn the key in the lock, and go inside, and the door clicks shut after me.

Then I head over to the sofa, drop my bag on the floor, sit down, and turn on my laptop. I watch as it fires up. I pull up a blank word document. I name it New Book V1.

My fingers hover over the keyboard and I close my eyes.

Images from the last twenty-four hours flicker in my mind, a little zing moves through me, and then, for the first time in two years, I start to write . . .

I write about the tangerine sky and the vase I broke and the dogs and fate; I write about Zach walking out my door in that Nirvana T-shirt three years ago; I write about the party and Kenneth with his red canvas bag and Solange and drinks at Zach's place with actors I've seen on TV, about the sound of his zipper and being bent over his bed, about falling asleep with my head on his chest and waking up to bright light and sheer curtains and a dissolving view, about the way he makes me ache, about us in the pool and him unhooking my bra . . . I write about the dogs barking tonight and Carlos, and that parking garage, and what it feels like to have my hair still wet from his pool, my cheek still raw from his stubble, as I sit here and write about him. And as I do, a jolt runs through me. Because it's back . . . my muse is finally back.

Nineteen

It starts like any other Friday, except I'm grinning. I can't stop grinning. I'm surrounded by empty brown boxes, the smell of trimmed stems and flower food, and bits of cellophane on the floor around me.

We order our blooms from a wholesaler who sources from both local flower farms and overseas suppliers, and they deliver to the store twice a week—Tuesdays and Fridays. They have a key, so everything is always here, waiting on my worktable, when I arrive at 8:30 a.m. It takes around an hour to unpack, clip off excess foliage and put everything in water before I get started on the day's arrangements. That's why I get here at nine thirty on other days while Vee always starts at nine sharp and locks up at night.

Right now, I'm putting some pink roses in a bucket of water—I'll need to reflex the petals for today's orders and that process works best at room temperature, so I leave them there on my worktable and start to unpack the peach tulips. There's a noise in the other room, the front door opens, and then I hear Vee call: "Helloooo." That means it's 9 a.m.

"Hey," I call back as I trim the stems. I can hear her uneven gait make its way down the wooden floorboards.

"Do you like?" she asks when she gets to me, flashing a pink walking boot. Then her eyes land on my face. "Why do you look so fucking happy? What were you doing last night?"

"Writing." I smile even harder. And finally—*finally*—that's the truth.

A flash of my laptop screen, that blinking cursor flying across the page as I filled it with real and lucid words. I mean, obviously I can't use those scenes as is—I'll need to change the names and alter the details significantly, turn them into an actual story—but they were words, *my* words. A research document, if you will.

"That's amazing," she says. "I told you you could do it."

Then she heads back to the front room, and I go over to the sink and fill a bucket with a bit of water (not too much, or the tulips will droop) and a dash of bleach. Vee swears they do better with bleach than with the commercial solutions we generally use. I don't know whether she's right or not, the internet can't decide either, but I know better than to argue with Vee.

I put the tulips in the bucket, take them over to the flower cooler, and set them down amid the buckets of blossom stems, Persian buttercups, lilies, and green cymbidium orchids. Then I go back to my workstation, take off my gloves, sit down, print off today's orders, and glance through them. But I can't focus. My phone is lying there on the table, and I'm watching it in my peripheral vision, willing the screen to light up with Zach's name.

Every time I think about him, I get a little high. And I know this wasn't the plan—I even added his new number to his old *Zach TOTAL DICK DO NOT CALL* contact name in my phone, just to remind myself not to feel everything I'm feeling right now. This dangerous warmth. But the feeling isn't going anywhere.

And there is this little voice inside me whispering: *What if you're wrong?*

What if it *could* work between us? Like, really work. I mean, there was always *something* between us. That elusive "thing" that can't be bottled. And he always had my back.

A flash of three years ago. Us sitting in bed, drinking minibar booze. I can almost taste the rum.

The morning after we got my things from Will's place, Zach had had an idea: we should go somewhere. Get in the car and just drive. He had a couple of days off work, and usually I'd have said no to something like that—I barely knew him—but with him, everything felt possible. Like he'd plugged me into some big power socket in the sky. Like I could do anything if I was with him.

So that's how we ended up in Palm Springs at Hotel California. Then it was 11 p.m., we were playing Truth or Dare, I had kitten whiskers painted on my cheeks (part of a dare), and it was his turn. He chose truth.

I swallowed hard. "Okay . . . so there was this woman that started calling Will in the middle of the night . . . ," I started. I was a little drunk, but I was testing Zach. Yes, he was here with me, so clearly he wasn't *that* close to Will outside of working with him, but I wanted to see if he'd tell me the truth. "Was Will cheating on me?"

The room was so silent I was pretty sure we were both holding our breath.

Then he clenched his jaw and swallowed hard and said: "I'm so fucking sorry, but he was. We fell out over it. I would have said something, Zoe, but I just didn't think telling you would help anything. And then you broke up . . ."

I nodded and tried to smile—he'd passed my little test, I should've been happy—but my eyes filled with tears. I bit down on my lip and forced a smile to stop them, but maybe it was the booze—I couldn't.

"Sorry," I said, looking down and wiping them away. Zach took my glass, put it along with his own on the bedside table, and then held me tight. "That's not about you. That's just who he is."

I nodded into his chest, but I wasn't so sure. I was pretty certain it *was* me, that I was just unlovable.

But then he whispered, "Don't ever change, okay? You're a good person and you have talent. Everything else can be bought if you have enough money."

And sometimes someone says the exact thing a future version of you will need to hear when she looks back, like they instinctively know where life will leave its bullet holes in you. Zach was like that.

Of course, he was *also* the guy who stood at my door and waved me goodbye, saying he'd call. And then . . . nothing.

That could happen again.

But that was three years ago. People change. Especially people who have been in the public eye all that time.

Maybe now he wants something real, with *someone* real . . . and that's what I am: real. I know Zach in a way none of those perfect girls at that party ever can. And he seemed really happy to see me again . . . He didn't *need* to ask me to that party—he chose to. Just like he *chose* to go home when I left. And he *chose* to ask me over the very next night . . .

I can hear Vee in the kitchen getting a cup of coffee from the pot, and I wish I could tell her about last night. Get her thoughts. But I can't. So instead, I reach for one of the pink roses and start to gently peel back the petals, starting from the outside of the bloom and using my thumb to support the base, until the outer petals are fully open and a perfectly formed bud remains in the center.

Still, if it worked between us, how would I publish my book? It wouldn't matter how much I blurred the details; everyone would guess it was about him, including him. But I'll deal with that tricky little detail later . . .

I put down the first rose and reach for the second as I ponder this imaginary problem, and then I hear: "Babe?"

Vee is calling me from the other room. But it doesn't worry me at first; she's always calling for me. And I need to finish reflexing this rose before I go through and help her find her scissors or whatever it is.

"Babe?" she says again, a little frantic this time. Louder too.

"Yes?" I call back.

"Zoe?" She's basically yelling now.

"Huh?" I look up. She's in the doorway, hobbling into the room.

"What did you say you did last night?" she asks, her eyes narrowed.

"Nothing." I shrug. "I mean, I wrote a bit."

"You wrote a bit? That's all?" And what is that expression in her eyes? Is she amused? Angry? I can't tell. My gaze moves from her face to her hand—she's holding her phone.

"Well, you must have a doppelganger then," she says, her voice all singsong as she taps her phone screen. Then she puts it down on the table for me to see.

And as I squint down at it, trying to make sense of what I'm looking at, something explodes inside me.

Twenty

Now, it's not that I've never imagined what my name might look like in an all-caps headline—I have. Of course I have. When *Fractured* came out, when I realized it was failing and panic-downloaded that manifestation app, that's exactly what I was trying to will into being—my name splashed across the *New York Times* or the *Washington Post.* I imagined the exact curve of the font night after night, while the dulcet tones of that app assured me anything I imagined could be real. I did that for a good two months before I gave up. But in all that time, you know where I did *not* try to manifest a headline?

On Page Six.

Yet there it is, screaming from the page: *DOES ZACH HAMILTON HAVE A NEW WOMAN? MEET ZOE ANN WEISS!*

And all I can think is: *How did they get my name?*

Did somebody leak it? Who would do that? Why?

My eyes skip to the pictures beneath it.

In the first two, Zach and I are in the pool. They were taken last night. I'm clearly topless in both, but my nipples are covered by two tiny black squares. The caption reads: *Over Solange already, Zach?*

A flash of Randal and Genius barking.

Well, that makes a lot of sense now. They probably sensed a photographer waiting, focusing . . . Their ultrasonic ears could probably pick up the clicking of the lens.

"How could you have not told me you were fucking Zach Hamilton?" Vee squeaks.

I look up at her. "I'm not. Not really. I just . . . he was there the other night when I went to do that delivery. And I sort of knew him from before."

Her mouth opens a little. Thoughts dance behind her eyes.

"What do you *mean* you knew him from before?"

But I don't answer. I'm too busy looking back down at the screen, staring at the third picture. It's of me in my van, driving out of that parking garage last night. They must have followed us. My face is perfectly visible through the windshield.

"Zoe? What do you mean?" Vee repeats herself.

"We met, like, three years ago," I say, willing this whole thing to disappear. "When he was still a bartender."

"Do you think you can introduce me?"

And I can't believe she's asking this right now, but I bite my tongue. I just want the conversation over. So I say "Maybe" as my eyes scan to the right, to the final image. It's of Zach and Solange at a premiere last year. I've seen this image before. Except someone has taken to Photoshop and created a big tear down the middle of the image, splitting them apart, so her hand is detached from her body.

I scan the text.

Condolences to almost everybody, but Zach Hamilton may be off the market again.

The action franchise star, 32, whose first movie grossed over $800 million and made him a household name, has been recently seen "fawning over" a new flame, Zoe Ann Weiss, according to sources close to the star. "It's heating up fast," says an inside source. "They're spending all their free time together."

Zach Hamilton is one of Hollywood's brightest new stars, and our hearts collectively broke for Solange Grey, 33, when he ended it with her late last year.

Zoe Ann Weiss is an emerging novelist and florist, known for her debut novel Fractured. *"It was a thriller, but perhaps she'll be moving to romance novels next," an inside source says. But not everyone has high hopes for this romance. Zach's PR rep, Geraldine Haigh, commented: "They're just old friends, that's all. They have history."*

And *shit.*

Shit. Shit. Shit.

My pulse speeds up. How the hell did I, of all people, end up half-naked on Page Six? What will Barb think? What will Felicity think if she sees this? How could I have let this happen?

Nobody's going to take me seriously now. I'll always just be that girl that got naked in Zach's pool, and I think that might be even worse than being nobody at all.

"Well, you look really pretty in the photos," Vee says. "And this will be good for you. Better than being a nobody. Maybe you'll sell loads of books?"

And maybe she's right, but this doesn't feel like a good thing. My eyes skip to the comments beneath the text. They're coming in thick and fast, and my stomach clenches.

@Tiffaniiiii999: OMFG the drama!

@RandyRoo: Zoe looks like a hoe, just gonna say it.

@Calista3939: Who is this Zoe person?

@Jannnniiiiee: Just some starf&cker

@MelissaShort: I thought I couldn't make 1000 per week from home too, but I know the secret now, DM me for more info.

@Lovenotwar replying to **@Calista3939:** I just googled her. Her book sounds like crap.

It's as I'm looking at those comments that a new one appears.

@Jannnniiiiee: OMG, GOOGLE HER AUTHOR PIC. She looks sooooo smug. What is Zach thinking?

And I know which picture she's talking about. The serious one from my book cover: a smile with no teeth. And in this context, yes, I do look smug. The room spins around me and a thin layer of sweat forms under my arms.

Then another comment comes in: Zach belongs with someone better.

And another: Like you?

And then the phone rings from the other room, and Vee takes her phone and goes through to it, and my eyes snap back to my own phone.

Has Zach seen this?

Because what if he thinks the same thing Vee did? That I could sell a load of books this way? What if he thinks *I* told someone? What if he thinks *that's* why I kept asking about the NDA last night in the pool?

I need to talk to him.

Twenty-One

I tap through to our last messages—the ones about that garage—take a deep breath, press call, and hold the phone to my ear.

It rings. And rings. And rings.

I need him to pick up. I need him to know I had nothing to do with this, because I didn't. I didn't even tell Vee.

And then a generic voicemail message starts up: "The person you are calling is unavailable. Please leave a message after the tone . . ."

Shit.

My throat tightens and I hang up. *Don't leave another message, Zoe. Remember how that turned out last time . . . you're not good at voice messages.*

But I have to do something. So I type out a frantic text instead: *Hey Zach, just calling because I saw the thing on Page Six. I don't know how that happened. Call me?*

Send.

And then I sit there, chewing on my inner cheek so hard it hurts and staring at my phone screen, willing it to light up with his reply.

But I still have work to do, so I reach for another pink rose and start to peel back its petals. I can hear Vee's voice trickling in from her call in the other room, and I have so much to do, but I can't stop looking at my phone, waiting for a buzz, a flash, anything . . . but nothing comes.

And how did the press even find out about us? Did somebody see us in that parking garage, recognize Carlos, and follow us back to Zach's place, then call them? Or did—

Oh my god.

That white Prius from my drive home last night. Maybe I'm *not* going insane after all. Maybe it *was* following me. Maybe it was the paparazzi who took those photos, or a journalist who was with them, trying to figure out who I was, where I lived . . . That would explain everything. I was driving my van with a big green VENICE FLORISTRY logo on the side. All they'd have to do to figure out my identity is google the florist's shop, go to the website, go to "Our People," and match the pictures they'd taken of me with my face and name. And once they googled my name, they'd know all about *Fractured.*

And then it happens. My phone starts flashing and ringing from the table next to me. I lurch for it—*Zach?*—but I don't recognize the number: best case it's a call center and worst case it's a journalist. So I watch it ring and flash and ring and flash and let it go to voicemail.

The screen flashes with *One new voicemail.*

I reach for it and press Play.

There's background noise, traffic, then an irritated female voice speaks loudly and clearly into the phone. "This is a message for Zoe Weiss. This is Amy, Zach Hamilton's assistant." A flash of the redhead who stood in the doorway judging me yesterday morning. "Zach asked me to contact you and request that you cease all communication with him. I appreciate your compliance."

And then the line goes dead and something under my ribs deflates. Something I didn't even know was there.

And I sit there staring at my phone. I want to cry, but the tears don't come. It's like I can feel every part of my skin but I'm numb at the same time. Because what just happened? Did he fucking ghost me again? He did. But this time he did it through his assistant. And that's so much worse.

"Did he call?" comes Vee's voice, and I look over at her. She's standing in the doorway, holding onto the frame, her face tense. "Zach?"

I shake my head. "No, it was his assistant. She left a message," I say, forcing a smile so I don't cry.

"Well, what did she say?"

"That he doesn't want to talk to me anymore." I smile even harder.

"What an asshole," she says, her voice high-pitched. "Jesus, I always thought he'd be sort of cool. Like the kind of down-to-earth movie star that was just like us. You're better off without him, focusing on your own stuff."

Then the door to the shop creaks as it opens, and she turns and looks up the hallway toward it.

"Shit, my client's here," she says to me under her breath. Then she flashes a big smile and says in her singsong voice, "Hi there, welcome to Venice Floristry," and hobbles back to the front room.

And I swallow hard. Because she's probably right, but all I can think about are his arms tight around me and his breath on my lips and how close we were last night. How close I was to everything I ever wanted.

So, so, so close.

And now here I am, back exactly where I started forty-eight hours ago: no Zach, no access, and no book. Except no, now it's even worse. Because now I have a looming deadline I know I can't meet, and half the internet low-key hates me.

Twenty-Two

I drive past a jacaranda tree, a carpet of purple flowers beneath it, and pull into a car space just down the street from my apartment. Then I sit still for a little while, my eyes burning with tears. I haven't felt this fragile, this unsettled and at odds with fate, since *Fractured* came out. Since I sat refreshing the Amazon bestseller rankings, watching them move in the wrong direction; since I sat on Goodreads, waiting for more people to review it. To read it.

I felt invisible.

But you know what? Right now, I think I'd take invisibility over this.

Because now I feel exposed, self-conscious, watched, like everyone in the world has seen me half-naked on Page Six and wondered what my nipples look like, like everyone agrees with the comments, like everyone is judging me.

I glance over at my birthday cake on the passenger seat beside me. Vee said I couldn't leave it in the shop; she'd eat it all. So I take a deep breath, get out of the van and go around to the passenger side. I open the door, reach for the cake, push the door closed with my shoulder, and head in the direction of my building. I just want to get inside. For today to be over. A delivery van speeds past, I look left and right and take a step into the road to cross. And that's when I see a flicker of movement in my peripheral vision.

It's barely noticeable at first.

And then: a flash of light.

My pulse speeds up as I look in that direction.

Flash. Flash.

Two people are rushing toward me; both have cameras. Did they follow me home from the shop?

"Zoe?" one of them calls out. "Zoe Ann Weiss?"

My pulse explodes, and I'm trying to balance this damned cake as I run across the road and up to my building and punch the code into the security gate. They're closer now. Flash. Flash. Flash. Fuck. A dizziness falls over me and I drop the cake. The door opens and I run inside, banging it shut after me. I can hear them on the other side saying, "Get a shot of the cake . . ."

I move quickly past the hum of the pool and the smell of chlorine and up the stairs to my apartment. My hands shake as I fumble with the key, twist, and push open the door. It's only as it closes behind me that I finally exhale.

I drop my bag and the keys on the kitchen counter—clang—beside Dad's carnations, screw the top off the open bottle of red wine that's sitting there, and fill the biggest glass I have. I take a sip, then a gulp, and as I down the rest and pour another glass, a calm slowly washes over me. I grab my phone from my bag and head to the sofa, open the window, put my head out, and look at the street. There's nobody there now. They're gone. I take another sip of wine, sit down on the sofa, kick off my shoes, and look around.

Everything is exactly where I left it this morning, except now it's flat, gray, and a little fucked up. Dad's carnations look like an *I told you so*; my laptop, charging on the table, now looks a lot like a failure's laptop again; and I'm pretty sure those pencils on the kitchen counter aren't even sharp and I don't have a sharpener—not unless you count my eyeliner sharpener. What kind of writer doesn't have a sharpener?

I was so close. So close to all of it. To Zach, to writing my book, to fixing this shit show I call my life . . . and now . . .

Something aches inside me as I take another gulp of wine and stare down at my phone. And I know I shouldn't do it, but I can't help myself: I scroll through to my voicemails and press Play again.

"This is a message for Zoe Weiss. This is Amy, Zach Hamilton's assistant. Zach asked me to contact you and request that you cease all communication with him. I appreciate your compliance."

Hot shame flushes through me. He couldn't even be bothered to do it himself.

A flash of last night. His scratchy voice when he said *I thought of you. Often.* And me, how I believed it. A heat moves up to my cheeks and my eyes prickle.

How could I have been so naive?

How could I have thought someone like Zach would really be interested in someone like me? Am I totally delusional? Sure, he'll fuck me. But he's embarrassed for the world to know. He's embarrassed to go from Solange to me and, fair, I get it.

This is why I was meant to keep it casual. *This* is why I wasn't meant to feel too much.

I take another gulp of wine, then reach beneath the sofa, feel around for my box of writing cigarettes, take one out, and drop the box on the coffee table. Virginia Slims. Menthol. I grab the lighter, kneel up to the open window behind me and light a cigarette, and as the cherry glows red, I take a deep drag. I breathe out a cloud of menthol smoke, then take another drag. My head gets a little light, and I look at the bookshelf, scanning the spines through a blur of tears. Did any of them ever feel what I feel right now?

Like they're worth nothing? Nothing at all?

My gaze catches on *A Moveable Feast* . . . and was it Hemingway who said *Write hard and clear about what hurts*? It sounds like him. Like I imagine him to be, at least.

Well, everything. Everything hurts, Ernest.

And I can almost hear him whisper back: *Well, use it.*

So I take another drag, leave the cigarette balancing on the window-sill, open my laptop, fire it up, and pull up my work in progress: New Book V1. I scroll down to the bottom of those scenes I wrote last night when I got back from Zach's place, and stare at the blinking cursor, my fingers poised over the keyboard. But nothing comes.

I swallow hard, staring at the blank screen. The same blank screen I've been staring at for two years. And then it hits me.

I can't do this.

I'm *never* going to be able to fucking do this. It doesn't matter how hard I try, how much wine I drink, how many classics I reread or ciga-rettes I smoke or pencils I collect . . . I just can't do this.

A hot tear rolls down my cheek as I sit dead still and stare at my re-flection in the screen now, at the pure desperation in my eyes.

Maybe this is a sign. Maybe Dad is right: maybe I *should* just give up. But what would that look like?

My old bedroom, in a house that's so quiet you can hear the sadness rolling through the halls. All my dreams on the other side of a big ocean. Inertia setting in.

Everything inside me seizes up at the thought.

I can't do it. I just can't.

So fuck it.

Fuck that blinking cursor. Fuck my deadline. Fuck Page Six. And fuck being just another girl infatuated with Zach Hamilton.

This is not how my story goes. I *can* do this. I have to.

I just need to shake myself free of Zach. Regain my focus. Take back control.

And I know exactly how to do that.

So I wipe my tears away with the back of my hand; snap my laptop shut; stub out my cigarette; close the window; grab my keys, phone, and bag; slip on my flip-flops; and rush out the door. I run down the stairs quickly before I can change my mind, past the pool and the smell of chlorine and the hum of the pool pump, forcing myself not to think it through. And now I'm standing at Jake's door. And I know this is a bad idea, but that's exactly what I need right now. Because it's *my* bad idea. It's not something happening to me. It's something I'm choosing.

So I lift my hand and knock.

Tap, tap, tap.

There are footsteps. The door opens, and there he is, tanned and shirtless in a pair of jeans, smelling like a patchouli mistake.

"Zoe, hey," he says, his eyes on mine.

"Are you alone?" I ask, my eyes darting behind him.

"Yeah," he says.

And so I lean in toward him and kiss him and he grabs my waist and pulls me inside and slams the door after me . . .

Twenty-Three

I wake to the sound of snoring and the morning light pouring in through the curtainless bedroom window. I wince, reach for my phone, and squint down at the time: 6:51 a.m. There are a *lot* of new Instagram follower notifications and three texts hanging on the screen. The first is my writers' group thread. I tap on it.

Rita: *Go Zoe!!!!! Saw the press!!!!*

Dread rolls through me as I tap out of it. Who else has seen it? The other two messages are from Barb. On a Saturday. Almost nobody in publishing takes the weekends off.

The first reads: *Is the celebrity you're writing about Zach Hamilton?*

The second is a link. I tap on it and it lands on some celebrity gossip site. There are five pictures there.

I've seen the first two already; they're from Page Six yesterday (pool, little black squares over my nipples). But the three new ones were taken outside my apartment last night. In the first one, I'm standing by my van, getting ready to cross the street and looking straight at the lens. I must have just noticed them. You can see palm trees and the sign for the Laugh Factory in the distance. The next is closer, of me at my gate, fumbling with the code to get in. And the third is of my birthday cake, lying on the ground. You can just make out *Happy Birthday* because we'd eaten the *Zoe* part. I quickly scan the text: *Sources claim the cake was from Zach!*

My eyes snap to the time stamp. It went up at 10 p.m. last night. Do these people never sleep?

Another text flashes on the screen.

Barb Wallace: *This is all excellent. Keep it up. Buzz is good.*

And that's the most enthusiasm Barb has shown me in ages, probably since she signed me. I don't want to ruin it with details like how Zach doesn't want to talk to me ever again so "keeping it up" isn't really an option anymore. So instead, I send back a thumbs-up because that's the only emoji she uses—at least I know for sure she'll understand it. Then I turn off my alarm before it can ring and look back over my shoulder: Jake is lying dead still, wrapped in grayish white covers and facing away from me. I can see my clothes lying on the floor, where we dropped them last night.

Slowly, carefully, I sit up, edge my way out of bed, and creep toward the bathroom, picking up my underwear, T-shirt, and jeans as I go. I close the door and, as I get dressed, I look around. There's a pink G-string hanging on the faucet of his shower and little ball of brown hair is stuck to the wall. My stomach twists. What was I thinking? How was putting myself back on Patchouli Jake's rotation ever going to fix anything? How is *this* me taking back control? It's almost like I want to feel bad, want to self-destruct, and maybe I do. Sometimes I think the only thing worse than feeling bad is feeling nothing at all. Especially for a writer.

I carefully push the bathroom door open and peek outside. Jake is still snoring, so I slip on my flip-flops, quietly grab my bag, tiptoe to the front door, and slowly close it behind me with a gentle click.

The sun is warm on my neck as I rush up the stairs to my apartment, push my key into the lock, and go inside. And as the door closes behind me, I catch sight of myself in the mirror. My hair is a tangled mess, my lips are pale and dry, and my tear troughs are extra deep today from wine, cigarettes, crying, and . . . well . . . life. As I look at my face, all I can think about are those photographs on Page Six, on that celebrity gossip page this morning, and then the comments: *Zoe looks like a hoe, just gonna say it.* Then Zach's assistant on the phone. The traffic in the background. The sterility in her voice. How quickly she spoke. And that's the memory that stings the most. Because I was just another task on her list, something to be crossed off between picking up his dry cleaning and grabbing a protein shake.

How can everything fall apart so quickly?

I swallow hard, go through to the bathroom, shower, brush my teeth, and reach for the tube of lip gloss I keep by the mirror. I slather it on, like maybe lip gloss is the answer to everything. Then I throw on some clean clothes, and two cups of tea later I'm walking out the gate, looking around as I head to my van, flinching every time I see the flash of the sun catching on glass in the distance.

But there's nobody watching me this morning.

No flashing cameras.

No voices calling my name.

Just the sounds of a lawn mower and the beeping of morning traffic. It's okay.

Today is a new day.

Soon, there will be new stories on that site. Soon, nobody will even remember. Soon, nobody will even care. Soon, I'll be back to being a nobody. And if I'm honest, I'm not sure how I feel about that.

I stride down the street, past cactus gardens and jasmine and hedges and the purple jacaranda tree, and there my van is just up ahead, the windshield glittering with the sun. But then my stomach clenches.

What the hell is that?

There, on my windshield.

I squint at it. My pulse speeds up, then my pace. I rush toward it, my eyes glued to the space between the wipers. And I'm telling myself it's an optical illusion, a reflection, anything other than what it looks like.

Because no. It can't be.

But I'm five steps away now and fuck, fuck, fuck. A shiver runs through me.

Because: *it is.*

There, in the middle of the windshield, is a mass. A large, dark reddish-brown mass. Yellowish fat deposits at the bottom. And I know exactly what it is—I thought of it—and I think I'm going to be sick.

Because it's a heart.

A real. Fucking. Heart.

Just like in chapter 3 of *Fractured*.

Twenty-Four

I stand dead still, staring at it, the world spinning fast around me as I hold on to the van so I don't fall over. And I can smell cut grass and gasoline fumes and hear traffic in the distance. *Who would have done this?* My eyes dart from house to house—a neighbor? Did somebody recognize me on Page Six and then google my book and get this awful idea? Did they think it would be funny? Or is it someone I know?

Because whoever did this knows where I live.

Except . . . *Oh shit.*

Anyone could have figured out where I live.

Because that picture from last night. The one on that celebrity gossip site.

The one by my gate with the Laugh Factory sign in the background. If somebody wanted to find me, that would have let them do it.

Now the pieces start falling together.

Because: that same picture had my van in frame. And that Page Six article yesterday said I was a florist. And my van was parked just down the street from my building, with a nice big VENICE FLORISTRY logo on the side. And that same article mentioned my book, *Fractured*, too. And you wouldn't need to read my whole book or even get to chapter 3 to find the heart-on-the-windshield scene; it's right there in the jacket blurb. Right there on Amazon and Barnes & Noble, *heart on her wind-*

shield, right there, for anyone with access to Google and a screw loose to see.

A thin layer of sweat covers my scalp now.

Because: *Oh my god, is it human?*

The heart in *Fractured* was human, but where the hell would anyone get a human heart? Anyone who wasn't a medical student like the stalker in my book or an absolute nutjob, that is.

It's probably not. It's definitely not. It's just someone messing with you. Calm down.

But I can't calm down; my breath is too quick and my heart is racing. I think I'm having a panic attack, and I need to go, get somewhere I can breathe.

In-two-three-four.

Out-two-three-four . . .

But nobody will believe me if I tell them this. I need pictures.

So I get out my phone, angle it toward the van, and take a couple of photographs.

Then I pull some tissues from my bag, cover my hand, and pick up the heart—it's soft and warm from the sun and oh god, I can feel wetness on my fingers. I gag as I throw it to the sidewalk, just behind a tree. It lands with a light thud.

I open the van door and reach down to the passenger-side floor for one of the half-empty bottles of water. But as I twist off the top and rinse my hands, a deep shame moves through me. Shame that I'd be the girl this is happening to. The girl caught half-naked and put on the internet. Shame that I'm this hateable.

I should call the police.

But would they come? Could they do anything?

And I can't stay here waiting—what if whoever did this is still here somewhere, watching? What if I go back inside and they figure out which apartment I go into?

I'll do it from the shop. Where I'm safe.

So I get into the van, turn my key in the ignition, and, with shaking hands, flick on the windshield wipers to wash away the smear. And then, like it's just another day, I drive away.

I decide against the 10. I don't want to be driving at speed right now—what if I have a panic attack or throw up or something?—so I'm on Venice Boulevard when Vee calls for the first time. I let it go to voicemail. She's been organizing a dinner for tomorrow for some acting-class friends (and me)—changing the time, the venue—and it'll be about that.

Instead, I focus on my breathing, on the present moment, on the road, on the haze in the distance and the way the sun cheerfully bounces off car hoods like nothing bad is happening . . . anything to calm me down. But it's not working. I think it might actually be making it worse.

By the time I park in the garage at work and the door rolls down, there's a thin layer of sweat under my arms and the novelist in me is convinced this is it: this is how I die. By the hands of some psycho off the internet.

Because: What if it *was* human? The heart? What then?

This is LA. All sorts of bad things happen here. I know this because Dad is always sending me articles about them. So I sit there in the dark for a little while, listening to my own heart thudding in my ears as images of that burgundy mass flicker in my mind. The reddish-brown gleam. The smear on the glass.

And then I grab my phone and flip through to the pictures of it. I did a lot of research into what a human heart looks like when I wrote *Fractured*—I looked at many, many images so I could describe it—but now, when faced with a real one, I have no idea if it's human or not.

I pull up a browser and type in: *differences between human heart and cow or sheep*.

I tap on Images.

I scan through them, scouring the captions. And finally, my pulse slows down. This heart, the one on my windshield, is too big to be human. It's about double the size and longer—a different shape.

As I stare down at the images, relieved that only a garden-variety psycho has taken a dislike to me, not an actual murderer, my phone starts flashing in my hands and I almost drop it. *Vee* . . .

I take a deep breath, get out of the van, and go inside.

I can hear her voice from the front room—she must already be on the phone with somebody else—so I go straight to my work studio, drop my bag on the table, and sit down. A flash of that heart on my windshield flickers in my mind. The icky smear on the glass . . .

I clench my eyes shut to block it all out, but my heart keeps racing.

"Babe, why didn't you answer my calls?" comes Vee's voice as she heads down the hallway with her uneven gait. "You have to see this," she says, arriving at my door and walking toward me. "Wait, what's wrong?"

I blink hard. Another flash of that heart. My stomach twists like I might be sick.

"Something happened," I say.

"What?"

"I . . ." I reach for my phone and go to my photos, then show her the ones from this morning. "Someone left this on my windshield."

She zooms in on the picture, frowns. I watch her face shift. "Oh my god, what is that?"

"A heart," I whisper.

She looks at me, her mouth in an "ick" formation. "Like in your book?" And as I see the horror on her face, fear creeps up my spine to the base of my neck.

I nod. "It's bad, isn't it?"

And my breath is getting too quick now. Shallow and staccato.

"Let me get you some water," Vee says, and she goes to the kitchen. I can hear the cupboard door open and the faucets turn on and off, and soon she's back and handing me a glass.

"Who do you think did it?" she asks, stroking my arm.

"I have no idea. Some psycho off the internet? Some of those comments were really harsh. Maybe they meant them . . . Do you think I should go to the police?"

"Maybe," she says. "I mean, where's the heart now?"

"I left it on the sidewalk . . . Why?"

"Oh," she says.

My stomach clenches. *I should have taken it. For evidence. What if they could test it for . . . I don't know . . . something? Why did I do that?*

"Well, maybe, I'm not sure what they can do, but it might make you feel better?" She goes silent for a few seconds and her eyes dart to her phone, then back to me. "Shit," she says, then bites down on her lower lip.

"What?" I ask.

She lets out a big breath. "Try not to worry."

"What?" I repeat, a little more frantic.

"You're trending on TikTok. That's why I was calling."

"What do you mean, trending? What are they saying?" My pulse speeds up even further.

"It's not bad," she says, tapping on her phone. "Not from what I've seen, at least."

She holds her phone so I can see it as a video starts playing.

I recognize my book cover straight away. It's there, front and center, long red nails clutching the title, *Fractured*, as a woman of about twenty-five says straight into camera: "Okay, so I couldn't resist. I wanted to see what this woman Zach Hamilton is seeing was all about. So I got her book, I am only a third of the way in, but oh my god, it's great . . . If you read it, hit me up so we can discuss . . ."

"There's loads of them," Vee says. "I mean, I know you're going through something scary, but don't lose sight of the fact that this is also good. You can't buy this kind of publicity."

And she's right. This could be the best thing to happen to me since

I got my book deal. I could sell a million books. I could get on the lists. I could get my future back.

But it could also be the worst thing.

Because the list of potential suspects has just multiplied by . . . I don't even know how many; I'm not good at math. But lots.

Still, I'd be lying if I said I wasn't a little excited. Because Barb said to keep it up, that buzz was good, and here I am, doing just that.

Maybe she'll even be a bit flexible on that three-week deadline we discussed if I stay relevant . . . in the press . . .

"Ummm . . . ," Vee says.

"What?"

"There's one other thing you should see," she says, scrolling and tapping on her phone again. "It's not really that big a deal. But just so you know."

Then she shows me her phone. It's that Page Six article from yesterday. She scrolls down to the comments, and I've seen them all before, but then she points to a new one. And it *is* a big deal. A huge deal. This bit is *definitely* not good.

It's from @anon6969.

And it's my phone number.

Twenty-Five

I don't go to the police. I don't want to have to talk about it, admit it's real, admit any of this is happening to me.

Instead, I tell myself everything is fine, just fine. That @anon6969 is just one of the many people I met when I first moved to LA—I gave my number to almost everyone when I was first trying to network. I remind myself that not everything is bad. I'm trending on TikTok for fuck's sake. This is huge. This is worth it.

And it'll all die down soon enough. I'll be back to being nobody in an instant. So I need to capitalize on it all while it's happening.

I tell myself that story the whole way home, like if I say it over and over again, it'll be true. I do that even after my phone rings with the fifth strange number for the twenty-seventh time. I do that so I don't truly have to consider the alternative, that this is just the beginning of my nightmare.

I park the van, get out, and look around, and even though there's nobody there, I can feel eyes on me. The little hairs on the back of my neck stand on end as I look toward the place I was parked this morning, where I dropped that heart. Because I can still get it, bag it up, take it to the police.

I edge my way over to it and look down to the sidewalk, behind the tree. But it's gone. A dog must have eaten it. Or somebody threw it in the trash.

So that's where I'm standing, the late-afternoon sunshine on the back of my hair, when my phone pings with an email notification.

I glance down at it.

Sender: *Barb Wallace.*

And it's a relief, at first. *She's probably seen all the buzz online.*

But then I tap through to her message and scan the words.

I need whatever you have. URGENT.

White-hot panic flies through me. Because she said three weeks. She said that on Thursday and today is Saturday and that means I'm supposed to still have, what, nineteen days left until deadline . . . And, shit, I don't need this extra pressure right now.

I cross the road and wait until I'm safely inside, behind the security gate, before I pause.

Calm down, maybe she just forgot she said three weeks . . . deep breaths . . . be a normal person, just ask her . . . So as I stand there, I type back: *Hey Barb, I thought we said three weeks? Zoe.*

Then I rush past Jake's apartment and the pool—my hair still smells like patchouli and I want a big cosmic eraser for last night, for this morning, for all of it (except TikTok, I'll keep TikTok, thanks)—and up the stairs to my apartment. I push the key into the lock, the door clicks open, and then: ping.

I close the door after me and drop my bag on the counter, and chewing on my inner cheek, I look down at the screen.

Barb: *That was before. Felicity wants to see what you're working on NOW. This is important, Zoe. She's been waiting over a year. We need to show her something.*

And, well, shit.

Because she's right: it *has* been over a year since my deadline for the second book passed. And Felicity has been so great about waiting. She could easily have canceled my contract by now. But instead, on the few occasions we've spoken, she's said things like "It's just second-book syndrome. You'll get there, I know you will." Of course, she's also said other, less helpful things, like "Remember, your second book needs to be even better than your first." But fair, it does. And now, because I ended up in a few photographs with Zach Hamilton, because TikTok has decided I'm readable for a hot moment, she's remembered I exist and wants to see where I'm at. And I'm not ready.

What do I do?

Because I have nothing. No pages. No words. No title. No synopsis. *Nothing.* I mean, I have those scenes I wrote when I got home from Zach's place, but they're just that: scenes. I expected them to become something more cohesive. They were only ever meant to act as research so I didn't forget anything.

But I can't say no.

"No" would be death. "No" would mean that Barb would realize what I've already realized, that I'm a talentless hack who only had one book in her.

And I don't want that. I need to hold on for as long as I can, so I type back: *sure, it's still rough, but I'll send you the first part soon.*

Because "soon" could mean a week, two weeks . . . three bloody weeks.

And then: ping.

I NEED IT NOW. JUST SEND IT.

My eyes snap to the sofa and my laptop and my box of writing cigarettes sitting on the coffee table from last night. A flash of Jake. But tonight I will not lapse into self-destruction. I will be a grown-up and just do what needs to be done. So I sit down on the sofa, fire up my computer, open up New Book V1, and scroll through all those scenes I've written about me and Zach. And yes, this was only ever meant to be a research document, a starting point, but fuck it. Desperate times . . . I do a quick search and replace for the names—I'll worry about smudging the other details later, when I have time—and attach it to an email. And then I send it to Barb. There. Now she has something. That should buy me a little time.

And then I take a deep breath and stare at that blinking cursor at the bottom and think: *Right, it's okay—tomorrow is Sunday; I have the day off. I can do this. I will just put my head down and focus.* My eyes dart to my bookcase: *Come on, Sylvia, Virginia, Oscar, Charles, and Nora. For the love of god, just channel through me.* But the cursor blinks and blinks and nothing comes.

An hour and a half passes. I smoke two cigarettes. Write three paragraphs. Delete three paragraphs. Boil the kettle. Forget to make tea. Inspect my pores in the mirror. Consider cutting bangs. Take three selfies with the bottom of my hair in fake bangs to see what I would look like. Google *how to write a scene.* Water my plants. Look at the pictures of that heart again. Check the door is locked a few times. Google my name—nothing new has been written. Decide I need dinner. And now I'm halfway through a Pop-Tart, staring at my laptop screen again, but instead of writing, I'm reading Reddit posts from other people who have experienced harassment and intimidation, trying to figure out whether I should tell the police about that heart on my windshield after all. Some posts say yes, just so they have it on record. Others say no, they can't do anything if you don't know who it is. Especially after just one incident. But it sounds like I did the right thing by taking pictures at least . . . It's good to have a strong account of events, just in case it "escalates." These posts use that word a lot: "escalates."

That's when an iMessage flashes up in the top right-hand corner of my laptop screen.

A moment of panic: What if it's something from a troll? Maybe I should change my number . . . but then I register the name. Greta.

It reads: *Just checking on you. Hope you're okay. Xx*

And I assume she's talking about the pictures on Page Six. So I click on it and type back: *Am okay, it was just a shock! xx.*

A moment of nothingness.

Then another iMessage comes in.

Greta: *Of course. She's such a bitch. Why didn't she tell you on Thursday????*

I sit staring at the words, trying to decode what she means. Then . . . another message comes in.

Greta: *I bet that's why she came back to the group this week. And to put it on Instagram before mentioning it?????*

And all I can think is: *Sophie.*

Twenty-Six

Sophie has one of those annoying Instagram pages that are always baiting you with exciting news that never eventuates, so I'm irritated but not that worried when I grab my phone and first tap through to her profile.

It takes a few moments to load, but then there she is, looking all glamorous in the profile picture she had the whole writers' group weigh in on. Thrice. Until we chose the one she'd liked all along.

I scan quickly past her biography to the grid of images, looking for whatever Greta was talking about.

And then: *Oh my fucking god. No.* My ears ring. And everything gets hot.

Really hot.

Because what's going on?

Of everything, why this?

She's just posted a picture. And in that picture, she's grinning at the camera and signing a piece of paper. But she's not alone in that picture—no, no, of course not. There's someone else in there too. A woman of around sixty. And she's giving the camera a thumbs-up.

And of course it's Barb, *my* agent.

Of course.

A deep ache pulses from the center of my chest as I tap on the picture and read the caption: *#bignews. Just signing with the one, the only Barb Wallace. I can't tell you how excited—*

Fuck.

But I will not be jealous. I will not wish her ill. That's not who I am. I don't own Barb, she's allowed to have other clients, and there's enough for everyone, but also . . . I hate Sophie. Because I just saw her on Thursday. Why didn't she tell me?

That feels wrong, right?

And why is everyone else's life rolling along at full speed while here I am, stuck in some weird *Groundhog Day* loop where the words just won't come and the clock won't stop ticking and . . . shit.

An icy fear washes over me.

Because: *Those pages.*

The ones I just sent Barb a moment ago.

The random set of scenes with no synopsis . . .

Shiiiiit. WHAT WAS I THINKING?

My throat tightens with a dark certainty: *She's going to read those and realize how crap I am and I'm going to be replaced by Sophie or somebody else if I don't do something soon.*

And all I can see in my mind's eye is that tarot reader and the Tower card and the Death card, and maybe this is what that meant. This moment right here. Because this is it, the moment of truth.

I grab my cigarettes, lean out the open window, light one, and take a deep drag. I exhale, quickly take another, then blow menthol smoke out into the purple twilight.

And as I stare at the bricks of the building next door, I think, *Fuck this.*

I will not just give up.

I will not wave a white flag.

If I'm going to fail, I'm going to fail spectacularly. None of this half-assed shit. I'm going to write the most insane book ever. The words will be electric and fly off the page and . . . It's at this moment that my eyes sweep across the room and land on Dad's carnations. And fuck, I'm probably delusional. I'm probably bad *and* delusional. Because I might have an idea—high-concept, thriller, celebrity curtain—but those are just words. An idea. They're not a story. And I don't even have Zach anymore. So what the hell am I going to write about? Who is going to coax my muse out? Who's going to tell me things about being a celebrity?

But I need to write something. No matter how.

Twenty-Seven

By the time Sunday night rolls around I need to get drunk. Forget-your-life-is-a-shit-show-and-you-have-no-future drunk. Catch-an-Uber drunk. Because yes, the strange calls have stopped, and yes, a steady trickle of Instagram followers continue to find me, but those are the only two good things that have happened over the last twenty-four hours—aside from, perhaps: I did a load of washing.

Because no matter how much I tell myself it's fine, just fine, I'm still seeing flashes of that heart every time I blink, the veins on the side, the icky smear on my windshield, wondering about the sort of person who'd leave it there. Hoping they get bored easily. Willing them to forget me now that there's been nothing more about me in the press, nothing more on any of those celebrity Instagram pages . . . even TikTok has moved on.

But I can still feel their eyes on me even when I'm in my apartment and I know for sure nobody can see me. And worst of all, I *still* haven't heard back from Barb about my pages. Which might not be such a bad thing if I'd been working while I waited, but I haven't.

Because it turns out Google and AI know *nothing* about being a celebrity, nothing I couldn't figure out by reading a few trashy magazines, so despite all the hours I spent researching and dutifully staring at that blinking cursor, smoking so many cigarettes that now my lungs are tight, I still have nothing new. I still don't know the story I'm writing.

Luckily, tonight is Vee's catch-up dinner, and it's at a Mexican place that doubles as a tequila bar . . .

I walk inside, my nails biting into my palms. The bar is to my right, some brass-edged, yellow-lit stars hang from the ceiling above it, and liquor bottles sparkle from the shelves behind the bartender. The tables are all pale wood and the chairs are upholstered in red leather. As I scan the room and look toward the windows—the orange sun hanging low and Santa Monica Pier across the road—I see a big red wall full of tequila bottles all backlit and calling to me, and then I hear: "Babe, over here."

I turn toward the sound.

Vee is standing up and waving from a round table in the far left-hand corner by the window. In the middle of the table are two metal bowls of chips and salsa, and maybe ten or twelve full tequila glasses, some empty ones too. *Brilliant.*

She rushes over to me and throws her arms around my neck; her perfume smells like peach schnapps.

"If anyone asks you to go to their show, just say no. It'll be fucking improv," she says into my ear, then she grabs my hand tight and grins, and we head back over to the group. There are five others there and I don't know any of them.

"Guys, this is Zoe," Vee says.

"Hey, hi, hey-hey-hey," comes a chorus in slightly off-kilter and disinterested unison. If anyone saw that article on Page Six, they're pretending they didn't, they don't recognize me, or they just don't care.

I sit down on the one free chair and Vee pushes two shots of tequila and a couple of wedges of lime toward me. "Thanks," I say.

I lick the salt off the rim of the first shot, down it, and bite into the lime as flashes of Sophie's smile and Barb's thumbs-up flicker in my mind's eye. I do the same with the second one.

"My kind of girl," says the woman next to me, bringing me back into the present moment. "I'm Adriana." She has this perfect, fine bone structure and thick dark hair to her shoulders, and I know she's half-Japanese because Vee has mentioned her before. She said she got some really cool action role and did I think Vee should try to get an action role?

"Hey." I smile, putting down the glass.

"And this is Shannon," Adriana continues, motioning to the brunette next to her.

"Hi." I smile a little harder, as I sneakily reach for another tequila shot from the middle of the table. I down it, and a blessed calm washes over me. A few more of these and I'll be numb. This is what I need. To stop my thoughts. My feelings. I wonder if anyone would notice if I took another one?

"Isn't it awful?" Adriana says to Shannon, like she's continuing a conversation that started before I arrived.

"I know." Shannon shakes her head. "It makes me feel sick. Like, how didn't I know?"

I frown toward them and lean in a little.

Because: *What's awful?*

Adriana turns to me. "Our friend took a bunch of pills. Tried to end it."

"I'm so sorry," I say.

"She's had a bad run of it. This town can take its toll," Shannon explains.

And I can see how that might happen. That's the serrated edge of dreams nobody wants to talk about. There's so much further to fall when you dare to try.

And it's right then, on cosmic cue, that my phone pings with an email.

My stomach flips as I reach for it.

Sender: *Barb Wallace.*

She will have read my material. *Please love it. Please love it. Please love it.* I squint down at the screen, almost scared to look.

It's only one line and it's in all caps.

GOOD START! WHERE IS THE REST OF IT? NEED ELEVATOR PITCH!

And, well, *fuck.*

Because there is no rest of it. And there is no elevator pitch because I don't know what the story is yet. And how am I meant to tell her that the secret project I pitched her is bogus? Doesn't exist? That I can't write it now because my research won't talk to me?

I look up from my phone to the street outside. The light is a hazy golden tangerine, and it's so heavy with promises—promises I still want to believe—and I'm three tequilas deep, and there's a fourth right in front of me just past the chips. I reach for it, down it—I don't even bother with the stupid lime—and make a choice. The *only* choice.

Because, while a part of me never wants to talk to Zach ever again, there is another part that knows I can't do this without him.

Especially not in eighteen days.

And then I will be left with nothing.

So as Adriana says "Is the new girl coming tonight?" and Vee replies from across the table, "No, she had to work," I'm only half listening. My true focus is on my phone, on scrolling to my last message to Zach and typing: *I think we need to talk.*

My pulse speeds up, a split second of hesitation, and then: Send.

Now I sit staring at the message as the chatter continues, rereading it over and over again, waiting for a reply. For typing bubbles. For anything. But nothing comes. An urgency rises inside me. It's hot and bitter. Because he doesn't get to ignore me. Not this time. It's not fair.

So I go to type again . . .

But then I stop.

No. I need to be strategic here. I need to be calm.

"Zoe, are you okay?" Vee asks, and I look up.

"Fine. I've just got to make a call," I say. "My agent."

Then I take my phone and go outside. And there, in the cool breeze, looking out past tourists feeding squirrels, and palm trees, toward a glimpse of the mountains in the distance, I think of every reason I came to this town. Who I wanted to become. Then I pull up Zach's number and press: Call.

I hold the phone to my ear and let it ring as my pulse bangs in my wrist.

It'll probably go to voicemail.

Don't say anything crazy, Zoe, just be cool and relaxed. Keep it simple and say you'd really like to talk about things . . . Do NOT do what you did last time . . . Just be sweet. He's a good guy. If you're sweet, he'll feel bad.

Ring. Ring. Ring.

"The person you are calling is unavailable. Please leave a message after the tone."

Shit. My mind goes blank. What do I say?

Beeeeep.

"Hi, Zach . . . it's me. Zoe. Look, um . . . I just think we need to talk. If you don't want to see me anymore, that's fine, but you could at least tell me yourself, not hide behind your assistant. I don't even get why you're so upset. I'm the one who was half-naked. I'm the one everyone is throwing hate at. Somebody—" I'm about to tell him about the heart on my windshield, but I stop myself. He said he wanted no complications. And that's a *big* complication. "I mean, this is just like what you did last time . . . ," I say. Then I let out a big breath. "Anyway, call me back?"

And then I hang up and my cheeks get hot and all my cells get heavy, really heavy. Because he's totally not going to call me back. He's totally going to ghost me again. And so much for my steely resolve last night. Because this is it, me waving that white flag . . . I still have eighteen days till deadline, but unless something big changes, and soon, I already know I can't do this.

I'm done.

I look up and Vee waves at me through the window. Adriana joins her. And there's a tequila cart next to the table now, with lots of bottles flashing under the yellow lights. And my original plan of getting totally wasted seems like a pretty strong choice. So I smile, beg the gods to send me a story, any story, and go back inside.

Twenty-Eight

I wake to sequins biting into my cheek, a mouthful of hair, and the sound of bells echoing off the walls. My eyes crack open, and I squint against the morning sun bursting in through the window as I reach for my phone and turn off my alarm.

My head throbs and everything spins as I look around the room. I'm on the sofa—I must have fallen asleep here—and my laptop is still on the coffee table beside me, still open from yesterday when I was researching. The air smells like old menthol cigarettes and the ashtray is full of butts smeared with pink lipstick . . . And then . . .

I sit up. Fast.

Did I call Zach last night?

My cheeks get hot and my stomach clenches and I hate myself. Because yes I did. An echo of my own whiny voice haunts me: *If you don't want to see me anymore, that's fine, but you could at least tell me yourself, not hide behind your assistant . . .*

Fuck.

He's *never* going to call me back now.

And why am I like this? Why can't I just stick to a plan?

Then comes another flash. That email from Barb: *GOOD START. WHERE IS THE REST OF IT? NEED ELEVATOR PITCH!*

Now the room tilts and blind panic floods my veins.

Because I didn't do anything *else* last night, did I? Email Barb back? Tell her how I have nothing?

I can't remember.

I swallow hard as I frantically scroll through my emails. My Sent folder. My texts. My calls.

But there's nothing new there, just that call to Zach.

I leave my phone on the coffee table, stand up, and trudge over to the kitchen, where I fill the kettle and turn it on.

And as I wait for it to boil, and down a glass of water, I do some fuzzy, hungover math—I still have, what, seventeen days to write this book?

It's not going to happen. Unless a story falls from the sky, I'm done.

I grab a tea bag from the cupboard, put it in a cup that's drying by the sink, and pull the milk out of the fridge. The kettle boils and I pour the hot water into the cup, let it sit for a little bit, then put in some milk and take it to the bathroom. I inspect myself in the mirror—knotted hair, dry lips, heavy eyes—take a big gulp of tea, put it down by my tooth-brush, and turn on the shower.

Then I close the door, strip off my clothes, put my hair up in a bun, and step into the bathtub, under the showerhead.

The room fills with steam as the warmth flows over me. I close my eyes for a moment and the room spins a little faster. A flash of that smudge from the heart on my windshield . . . the missed calls . . . But I push the thoughts away. Nothing else has happened. It's over.

I take a deep breath, turn off the water, and reach for my towel, al-most slipping as I step out onto the bathmat.

It's as I'm squeezing the water from my hair that the message comes in. But I don't hear it; my phone is on silent. I'm completely oblivious as I pull on my dressing gown and head back to the kitchen with my tea, open the cupboard, and scan past unopened wine bottles to the boxes—*do I want oatmeal or a Pop-Tart for breakfast?* I decide on a Pop-Tart and take it over to the sofa with my tea. I sit down and fire up my computer, and as I tear open the silver packaging with my teeth, I glance at my phone. And that's when I see the message.

It's right there, in the middle of the screen. From a number I don't have stored.

My insides clench and I hold my breath.

I put the Pop-Tart down, reach for my phone, and tap on it. And as it loads, the walls pulse in toward me.

Because now I'm living out chapter 10.

It reads: *R U willing 2 die 4 Zach?*

I stare down at the screen, willing the words to disappear. Wishing I'd written a different book—a rom-com, maybe. Because this is the first message my protagonist gets from her stalker. Except in *Fractured* it is *R U willing to die for him?*

But a rage rises within me now, and everything gets hot. Because who the hell do they think they are?

I imagine a troll sitting in his mother's attic, grinning as he sends me this shit.

And I know I shouldn't type back, I know I should ignore it, but before I can stop myself I'm stabbing in: *Sod off asshole.*

Send.

Then I sit, staring at my phone in that orange morning light, sipping my tea and chewing my cheek, thinking, *Shit, I shouldn't have done that. I should unsend it.* But before I can unsend anything, there they are: typing bubbles . . .

Crap.

Beep.

I swallow hard as I stare down at my phone and the message loads.

And all I can hear is the roar of the ocean in my ears even though I'm in West fucking Hollywood; my heart is going to bang its way out of my chest.

Because this time it's a picture.

My vision blurs as I glance from corner to corner. The street. The building. The red-and-black signage. It's of the Mexican restaurant. The one I went to last night. I zoom in. And there I am, on the pavement outside. I'm on the phone. Frowning. It was taken last night.

I was leaving that message for Zach.

The floor moves up toward me and I'm struggling to breathe.

Because this—the photograph—happened in my book too. In chapter 14.

This exact scenario.

They've read my book . . . They've definitely read my book.

First they figured out where I lived and left that heart; now they've been following me and taking pictures. And they have my phone number . . . What are they going to do next?

And then my throat tightens a little more and my hands get damp. Because now I'm thinking of everything else that happens to the protagonist in my book, in chapters 19, 24, 30 and 36—and look, none of it is good, but what happens in the final chapter is especially bad.

Because in the final chapter, *she dies.*

Twenty-Nine

I head out past the security gate and look around. *Is somebody watching me right now?* My heart thuds as I rush toward the van, my arms covered in goose bumps even though it's not cold. I get in and lock the doors. Click. Then push the key into the ignition, put my foot on the pedal, and drive.

It's okay. Everything is okay, I think as I scan the sidewalks and drive down my street toward Santa Monica Boulevard, then turn left.

But nothing is okay.

Because the next thing that happens in *Fractured* is the stalker breaks into the protagonist's flat and steals all her light bulbs. What am I going to do if that happens to me?

I need to calm down.

That *won't* happen. It can't. There's a security gate at my apartment block. Nobody can get in without a code . . .

But who would even do something like this?

My gaze snaps from the man in the Lamborghini in front of me, who is looking in his rearview mirror, to the woman pushing a stroller up the street, to a dogwalker with six or seven dogs, to a cyclist . . . but then I think of TikTok and those articles about me and all those shitty comments, and honestly, it could be anyone.

Absolutely anyone.

But why?

I turn right onto Fairfax, the options spinning around in my mind.

In *Fractured*, the stalker turns out to be a woman in love with the protagonist's boyfriend . . . Oh god, is that what's going on here?

Has some troll or one of Zach's superfans developed a crush, seen us together, and decided they want me gone?

Because it's definitely about Zach: *R U willing 2 die 4 Zach?*

But this is so unfair, because I *am* gone. He never wants to talk to me again.

Maybe I should text them back? Tell them we're not together. Maybe that will end it . . .

But also, maybe it will make it worse. Maybe they won't believe me. Maybe it'll piss them off.

I just don't know.

And look what happened last time I replied. They got cross and sent a photo. But *oh god*, all those times I felt watched over the weekend, there was a reason. They were there at that restaurant. Where else have they been? When have they been watching?

My thoughts blur together as I drive past billboards and homeless tents and a guy juggling on the side of the road, then I'm on Venice Boulevard and somehow—eventually—I get to the alleyway behind work.

I swallow hard as I reach for the clicker and press the button for the garage door, and it opens slowly. Clickety, clickety, click. I glance in the rearview mirror, making sure nobody is waiting behind me, ready to follow me in, then I drive inside, park, and press the button to close the door again. Only once it has closed completely, only once I'm shut into that dark space with a single light flickering from the ceiling, do I get out of the van.

I rush to the back door of the shop and go inside.

"Why didn't you text me when you got home last night? I was worried!" Vee calls to me as I close the door after me.

"Sorry, I was pretty drunk," I call back, my voice cracking as I wander into the kitchen. And I don't know why I don't tell her immediately. I just don't. I guess I don't want to hear the words out loud. I want this all to be some terrible misunderstanding. The messages. The heart. All of it. I want to be overreacting.

The coffeepot is full and I pour some into my favorite cup, then go to my work studio.

I sit down and place my phone on the table and stare at it as the room spins beneath me. What am I going to do if it beeps again? If they send something else? Something worse? My head throbs, my breath still smells of booze, and I need a pill. Maybe a couple. I reach into my bag and rifle around for some ibuprofen. I find a bottle, take two out, and swallow them with a gulp of coffee.

And then, midswallow, I think: *Instagram.*

Because: *All those new followers I've gotten since the story broke . . .*

What if whoever is doing this is one of them? What if they're watching me online too? What if—

My throat closes up as I frantically go to Instagram and tap on my follower list. I scan down through the little circular profile pictures—colors and smiles and jawlines. What if whoever is doing this is one of them? I bet it is. But I have 4,481 followers, so which is the right fucking one?

I can't just start randomly deleting people. Barb is always pushing me to get more followers as it is . . .

Besides, there's nothing personal on my page—just pictures of books I've read and loved—and I hardly ever update it.

So I do nothing.

I just put my phone down on my worktable and sit there. Still. Stress-sweating and sipping bad coffee, staring at the *Find what you love and let it kill you* quote, and that hits a little different today.

"So an update on the Levy event on Saturday," says Vee from the doorway. "They want a shitload of Mrs. Dalloway's Roses, but they want them to float in two swimming pools." She comes inside. "I thought we could do the same thing we did for the Garcia engagement party?"

"Sure," I say, trying to smile and look right at her, but that's hard because no matter how much I try not to, I can't stop looking at my phone. Just waiting for the next beep.

"Are you okay?" she asks. "You still seem a little jumpy."

My lower lip quivers first, then my eyes prick with tears.

"Babe . . . ," she says, coming around to my side of the table and putting her arm around me. "It's okay. People are the worst. It'll pass."

I swallow hard.

"I got this really messed-up text," I say. "This morning. Two of them."

The room rings with silence. I can tell she's trying not to panic. "What? What did they say?"

I reach for my phone, go through to my texts, and show her.

"Are you willing to die for . . . ," she reads out loud. "Oh my god, that's like your book too." She frowns down at the picture, zooming in. "Babe, this was taken last night." She looks up at me as I wipe my tears away.

"I know," I say.

"They must have followed you," she says, eyes wide. "Did you call the police?"

"Not yet," I say.

"You should. Just so they have it all on file in case . . . you know . . . it escalates." And there's that word again. "Escalates." She's squinting at my phone now.

"Wait, what's this? Did you write back?" She looks up at me.

Sod off . . .

I nod.

"Babe, you never reply. Ever. It just encourages them."

Vee pulls out her own phone and starts typing into it, looking at my phone, then hers, my phone, then hers.

"What are you doing?" I ask, taking another sip of coffee.

"Googling the number . . ."

She squints. Frowns.

"Shit, there's nothing," she says. "Maybe the police can track it. Are you going to block the number?"

I shake my head. "I'm too scared. Then I won't know what's happening. If they're trying to send me something else. I won't know if it's getting worse. I think it's better to know, right?"

"True," she says. "You know, this is good, babe, in a fucked-up kind of way. You have a bona fide stalker now. That basically means you're famous." Then her eyes move to her phone. "Damn, I have to go; I've got a venue visit. But go to the police. I can courier the deliveries this afternoon. And . . . maybe you should tell Zach? Or his people or whatever? His name was in that message—someone should know."

But I don't want to tell Zach. He's going to think it's some desperate damsel-in-distress plea to get him back. Especially after that voice message I left last night. He'll probably think I staged it, sent it to myself. That *I'm* the psycho.

And even if he *does* believe me, what the hell could he do about it anyway? No, I'll deal with this myself. I'll go to the police. That's what people do in these situations. Though, people like me aren't meant to be in these situations. But Vee's right: I need to do something.

So as she goes to the other room, I reach for my phone and type in: *West Hollywood how to report a crime.*

Thirty

The metallic letters of SHERIFF, WEST HOLLYWOOD STATION glint in the sunshine from a red brick wall as I make my way over to the front door. I've driven past here a couple of times before, but I never once envisioned myself going inside. But now here I am. I could have called, but I wanted to come in and show somebody the messages, the photographs I took, in person. I didn't want my case to get lost at the bottom of a pile, and I certainly didn't want to wait for an appointment.

Almost an hour later, when "Zoe Weiss" is finally called, I've learned four new stats off various internet sites:

1. In the US, more than three million people are stalked each year.
2. One in three women and one in six men will be stalked in their lifetime.
3. Weapons are used to harm or threaten victims in one out of five cases.
4. And less than a third of victims report it to the police. So at least I'm normal for waiting a bit.

But the stat I was really looking for, the important one for me—how many victims of stalking actually end up getting killed—well, I couldn't find it. So I still don't know how scared I should be. I could, however, find a number of celebrity gossip Instagram accounts, so I followed all of them and set up a Google alert for my name. If anything else is posted about me, anything at all, I want to know about it. Of course, then I realized whoever is doing this probably set up the same Google alert, so now I feel sick.

"I'm Deputy Barnes," the man standing in front of me says, shaking my hand. He's at least six foot two, he has dark-brown skin and thick dark hair, and he looks like the kind of man who can help me.

I nod and follow him out of the waiting room. But hang on, where are we going? All the people I've been waiting with have disappeared down the long corridor in front of me and into what I assume are small inter-view rooms, so why are we heading into a brightly lit office area instead?

Why are we weaving through desks with people staring at computer screens and chatting, and over to what I assume is his desk? *Shit.* I know they deal with murders and rapes and drive-by shootings, but are they not taking this seriously?

Barnes sits down heavily on one side of his desk, jiggling the mouse so his computer lights up, and I sit down on the other, put my bag on my lap, and scan the contents of his desk. It's messy, and there's a pho-tograph of a woman with red hair in a silver frame to one side. She's holding a small golden-brown terrier in her arms.

I've already given the guy at the front desk a rundown of why I'm here, and he said I needed to file a police report.

"So, you received some concerning text messages this morning?" Barnes asks, looking at me, then back down at his notes. "And a . . . wait, a heart was left on your windshield?" He looks up at me, frowning.

"Yes," I say through a tight throat.

"A human heart?" There is slight panic in his voice.

"No," I say. "I don't think so. I think it was bovine. At least from the images on Google. Here, I took some pictures." I scroll through my phone to one of the photographs of the heart. I hand it over the desk.

He looks down at it, zooming in. "When did this happen?"

"Saturday morning," I say.

"And where is this heart now?"

"I don't know. I threw it on the sidewalk and drove away."

He turns to his computer and types for a bit, and I sit there, anxiously watching him, willing him to fix this for me.

"Can I see the messages from this morning?"

I nod and tap through to them and hand them across the desk.

He frowns down at the screen, scrolls up and down, and frowns some more.

"That's me, talking on the phone," I say. "It was taken last night when I was out with friends. Whoever took it must have followed me there . . . Ummm." He looks up at me. "There's something else. I'm a novelist, and both these things happened in my first book. I think whoever did them is getting the ideas from that."

"Hmm," he says. "What was the book called?"

"*Fractured*," I say. He puts my phone down and starts typing on his computer.

"And this message was written exactly like that in your book? 'Are you willing to die for Zach?'" he asks, turning back to me.

I nod. "Except, instead of 'Zach,' it said 'him' in my book. 'Zach' refers to a real person. Someone I know."

"What is Zach's full name?" he asks.

Shit. NDA, NDA, NDA.

My face gets hot. But this is a police investigation—surely I can tell them? And also, screw it: Zach doesn't get to fuck me, ghost me, put me in harm's way, and then muzzle me too when I'm in danger. Besides, it's all over the internet, 100 percent in the public domain, not exactly a secret anymore. "Zach Hamilton," I say.

His eyebrows raise just a millimeter, if that.

"The movie star?"

His lips turn up just a little at the edges like maybe he's going to laugh or smile—he thinks I'm making it up, and I feel like I have to defend myself.

"I was in the press with him," I say. "Here, I'll show you." I reach out for my phone and he hands it back to me; I pull up a search window and go to that Page Six article, to that picture of me with those little black squares over my nipples. Then I hand it back to him. "That came out on Friday."

My cheeks get hot as I watch him frown at my screen, scroll a bit, then glance back up at me. "So you think it was because of this, then?"

I nod. "Some of the comments were awful, and it's the only thing that makes any sense. Somebody posted my phone number up there as well. So I'm guessing that's where they found that. And there was another article too," I say, reaching out for my phone again. He hands it back to me, and I navigate to Barb's message and the link with those pictures of me outside my building. I pass it back over the desk. "It came out late Friday night. I'm pretty sure this picture is how they knew where I lived."

He looks down at it and takes a big breath. "Yes, if somebody wanted to find you, this would help them do it."

He taps a couple of times and I can see him back in my messages now.

"And this 'Sod off' is you? You replied?" he asks, looking up at me. I nod.

He says nothing but puts down my phone and turns to his computer and types out some more notes. Clickety-tap-tap.

His eyes move to the handwritten notes given to him by the guy at the front desk. "You live in an apartment?" he asks. I nod. "Good. What kind of security do you have?"

"A locked gate. There's a code," I say, my throat tightening. Because the security light is still broken, and who knows when it will finally be fixed?

"Are there any cameras?" he asks, his eyes narrowing.

"No," I say, shaking my head. "But maybe the neighbors saw something?"

He turns to his computer and types again.

"Okay, aside from those articles, anyone else you can think of who might be doing this?"

"No, I don't think so," I say. "And it all started after that first article, so it *must* be about that."

He nods. Tap, tap, tap.

He turns back to me.

"So the story came out on Friday morning, the phone number was put up there by someone on Saturday . . ."

"Yes, also I have been getting calls from unknown numbers," I add, just so he has all the information.

"You found the heart on your windshield on Saturday morning," he continues, ignoring my interruption. "The text messages came through today, Monday, and they must have followed you last night, Sunday. So this has been going on for four days?"

I nod. It feels *a lot* longer than four days.

He turns back to his keyboard, makes a few more notes, then takes my phone and gets up and walks away. And I sit there for a little while, listening in on keyboards being tapped and low conversations and a bout of laughter.

A few minutes later, he's back on his side of the desk, passing my phone and a few pieces of paper to me. "Can I get you to read this over, check your details, and sign here," he says, sitting down again.

I look down at copies of the messages, some brief notes about what I've told him, and my name, address, and phone number, and is this it? Panic moves through me.

Are they not going to do anything to help me?

He hands me a pen and I sign it.

"So what now?" I ask, my insides twisting. "Can't you trace the messages or something? Figure out who's doing this?"

He gives a big sigh. "We'll look into it. And it's good that you came in, that it's on record now. But keep in mind, we don't know for sure that it's all the same person."

"But they're following the exact sequence of things that happen in my book. Surely more than one person wouldn't have thought of that?"

He gives me a small nod. "Maybe, but we can't be certain."

"So what do I do? If something else happens? Because there are some pretty scary things that happen in my book."

"The first thing you need to do is tell them very clearly to stop."

"But I did. I wrote 'Sod off.'"

"You need to be absolutely clear. Then if it continues, if it escalates . . ." *There's that word again. "Escalates."* "We might have more to go on."

Dread rolls through me.

"So, what? I have to wait until someone breaks in or hurts me before you can help me?"

His expression shifts, hardens. Probably because yes, according to one post I read on Reddit, that's exactly what he's waiting for. "The best thing you can do is alter your routines, your routes to work, and take notes if anything else happens. I know it's scary, but if this is just because of an article in the press, it will most likely fade away. It has only been four days. They're probably just trying to scare you. Get some attention. So keep a low profile and report it if anything else happens."

I can feel tears burning in my eyes and grit my teeth to stop them.

He stands up, which means it's time for me to leave.

"In the meantime I'll file this and"—he hands me a small white business card—"here's my card, just in case."

Five minutes later I'm walking back outside to the parking lot, and now I feel even more vulnerable than when I got here because at least then I believed they could help me.

I open the van and get inside and reach for my phone. I'm thinking about what Deputy Barnes said—should I text the number back and tell them to stop? But won't that make it even worse? If they're looking for attention, that might prolong it. Maybe I should wait and see what they do. If they do nothing, then I do nothing. If they text me again, *then* I'll tell them to stop.

And I want to call Dad and hear his voice. But if I tell him what's going on, I'll never hear the end of it.

He'll beg me to come home. Now. And I might just do it after today.

And if I leave now, I'll never write this book. Any book. I'll have to pay back the advance and move in with him. I feel sick.

But now I'm thinking of the last time I spoke to him, on my way home from Zach's house. And how, if it wasn't for Zach, I wouldn't have been in the press; I wouldn't be in this situation right now. And he can't even be bothered to call me back.

It's all so wrong. And he doesn't get to treat me this way.

Brush me off like I never even happened. Maybe Vee's right: maybe I *should* tell him what has happened, make it his problem too.

And so, as a heat simmers beneath my skin, I don't think. I just take screenshots of the messages from this morning, go to the last message I sent him last night, and start to send texts.

First, I send him the picture of the heart on my windshield. Then, I send him the two screenshots.

And then I stab in: *Great catching up again. Definitely worked out well for me. At police station. Fun times.*

Send.

I turn the key in the ignition and look behind me while waiting for a gap in the traffic, and I'm just about to back out when my phone starts ringing.

My eyes snap to the screen. My pulse flares.

What if it's the psycho?

But the screen reads: *Zach TOTAL DICK DO NOT CALL*

I stare at it for a moment. My heart bangs against my ribs. Because what's he going to say?

I answer the call and say, "Hello?"

"Zoe, hey . . ."

"Hey," I say.

"Are you okay? What the fuck were those messages? What's that thing on the windshield?"

"It's a heart," I say, my voice flat and cold. "A present from one of your fans."

"Shit. What did the police say?"

"They can't do anything," I reply. "I just have to wait and see if anything else happens." My voice cracks here but *I will not cry*.

"Well, are you okay? Where are you now?"

"Just leaving the station."

And he doesn't even hesitate. "Come here. I might be able to help you," he says.

My thoughts slur. This is not what I was expecting. I'm ready to yell at him, tell him how awful he is, but he's being . . . nice. A horn beeps from behind me.

"Zoe?" he says.

"But what about the press?" I ask, wary. "What if they see me?" There's an edge to my voice. An edge that says: *Are you going ditch me yet again? Asshole.*

"Who cares? They can't break a story twice. Just come."

Thirty-One

I roll down my window as I approach Zach's intercom, and I press the buzzer. The screen glitches for a moment, then the gate opens and I head up the driveway beneath a bright-blue sky, a tight knot in my solar plexus. Because what am I doing coming back here?

I park the van and look out at the smoggy view, and then comes the barking. Genius and Randal run up to my door. I get out and pat them, wet noses nuzzle into my hand, and then I hear: "Hey."

I look up. There Zach is, walking out of his open front door. He's wearing jeans, a black T-shirt, and no shoes, and he's coming toward me. My stomach flips. Because I'm thinking of that message his assistant left on my voicemail.

I give a small, tight smile, but when he gets to me, he cups my face in his hands, looks me deep in the eyes, and says, "Fuck me, it's never dull . . ." Then he kisses me on the forehead. And he's acting like nothing has changed between us. Like he still cares. I don't understand; I don't know how to be.

But when he reaches for my hand, I let him. He leads me inside, and the dogs follow us in. It smells of incense or maybe room spray in here, and we go through to the kitchen. Carlos is sitting at the white marble counter in front of the big silver bowl of lemons. I look around, expecting Amy to be hovering somewhere—I'm not looking forward to seeing her at all—but she's not here. It's just the three of us.

"You remember Carlos?" Zach says, pouring me some water out of a jug.

"Yes, hi," I say.

Carlos motions to the empty seat next to him and I sit down, folding my hands on my lap.

"Zach tells me you've had some trouble?"

"I showed him what you sent me," Zach says, putting the glass on the counter beside me.

"Can I see the messages on your phone?" Carlos asks.

"Sure," I say, unlocking my phone and handing it to him.

I take a sip of water and watch him scroll through the messages.

"When did the heart happen?" he continues, looking up at me.

"I saw it on Saturday morning," I say. "So maybe in the night?" A flash of me waking up that morning in Jake's bed. "There were pictures of my building and street posted in an article the night before. So it's possible that's how whoever did this found me. But . . . that would make them . . ."

My voice trails off. Insane. The word I don't say is "insane." Because I thought about it the whole way over here from the police station. Whoever did this either has my name as a Google alert, as feared, or would have had to be googling me and googling me and googling me to see that article the moment it went up, and that might be even worse. They would have had to already have read at least the blurb for my book; already had the idea, gone to a butcher, and found that heart. Known what they were going to do once they figured out where I was. That shows incredible commitment. Scary-level commitment.

And why would anyone hate me that much?

"These messages came in this morning?" Carlos asks, interrupting my downward spiral.

I nod.

"When was this picture taken?"

"Last night," I say. My throat tightens. Because: that voicemail I left Zach. I can feel him watching me. "I went out for drinks and dinner with friends." I emphasize "drinks" so I have an excuse for the message he never replied to.

"Zach says you went to the police? What did they say?" Carlos continues.

"To let them know if anything else happens."

"The police have too much other shit going on," he says, waving them off. "I can help you. But first, do you have any idea at all who might be doing this?"

I shake my head. "It could be anyone. Anyone who's read my book. Because all of this happened in my book. The heart on the windshield and both those messages. It's like they're reenacting what I wrote, against me."

I can see a flicker behind Carlos's eyes, and please, dear god, don't let that be fear.

"Fuck," Zach says under his breath, touching my arm. And I know I should pull it away, but I don't.

"But it all started after that Page Six article, and the message I got this morning mentions Zach. So I'm guessing it's someone who saw me there or on TikTok and googled me. Probably one of Zach's superfans, or maybe a troll? The police said it might just be for attention."

"Where did they get your phone number?" Carlos frowns.

"It was posted in a comment on that first article. But loads of people have it."

He nods. "Is there anything else you can think of? Anything at all that might help?"

And then comes a flash of memory. *Should I say it? Does it make me sound paranoid?*

"Ummm . . ."

They both look at me.

"I don't know whether it's something or not, but the other night when I came over here, it felt like this white car was following me home.

They didn't come down my street, but they saw which street I turned onto. I mean, it could be them. I just don't know. That was before any of the press, though. So I kind of presumed that was the journalist—"

"What kind of white car?"

"It was a Prius."

"Did you catch the license plate?" Carlos asks slowly. "Or who was driving?"

"No."

Carlos makes a note.

"And there's nothing else? You haven't spoken to anyone unusual lately? Seen anything strange?"

"No . . . everything's been normal. I mean, there were the people that came over that night, after that party, but you know them, right?" I say to Zach.

"It wouldn't be them," Zach says. "Zero chance."

"What about the party then?" Carlos says. "Did you talk to anyone there? Did anyone ask you about yourself? About Zach? Even if it seems small, it might be helpful."

"I wasn't there long," I begin, but then I remember something. "Wait, there was one woman. But I only spoke to her for a couple of minutes. She gave me a cigarette as I was waiting for my van."

"What did you talk about?"

"She just said she'd seen me arrive with Zach . . . I told her we were old friends, and she said Zach had a lot of old friends."

"Did she tell you her name? What she did for a living?"

I shake my head. "She said she did this and that. But she seemed nice enough. So it's probably nothing."

"Okay, what did she looked like?" Carlos asks.

"Blonde. Maybe midthirties."

Carlos turns to Zach. "Did you see her?"

Zach shakes his head. "No . . . and it's unlikely she had anything to do with this." He's frowning, like he's weighing it up. "Everyone there knew someone. And you needed a password to get in. If she saw us leave together, she might have been the one to leak that to the press, though. That shit happens. That's why Kenneth took everyone's phones, to try to contain how much can get out there. We've had that before."

And that's true. She *was* probing about me and Zach and she definitely saw the logo on my van. She could easily have looked that up and figured out who I was if she wanted to sell the information to the press.

"I'll look into it anyway," Carlos says, giving me a reassuring nod. "Is there anything else?" he asks.

I think for a moment, but I've given them everything I have. "No, sorry," I say.

"Can I keep this for a moment? See what I can find out about the number that sent those messages?"

I do a forensic scan of what's on there: some questionable selfies, a text thread to Jake I should have deleted, but nothing too embarrassing. And I want him to find this person. So I say, "Sure."

Then Carlos heads off and Zach comes and puts his arms around me and I let him. I'm enveloped in warmth and musk and the smell of laundry detergent.

"I know it's scary," he says into the top of my head. "But this shit comes with the territory. Sometimes attention can be a bad thing. I've had it happen a lot. Sometimes fans take it too far. Or get really personally invested. But Carlos is the best. He has a load of contacts at the police. He'll figure this out. The shit he has sorted out for me is endless. So don't worry, he'll be watching out for you, making sure you're okay." Then he pulls away and looks me in the eye. And I'm searching his for answers, for how he really feels. "You look like you need a drink . . . come. I want to show you something."

He leads me down a series of hallways, then down a set of stairs. Now we're standing at a door. There is a keypad on the side of the wall.

"Welcome to the safest place in the world," he says as he punches in a code.

A lock clicks. He pushes the door open, we go inside, and he flicks on the light.

I look around. The first thing I notice is there are no windows. There's just a cinema screen that takes up one full wall, six old-school red velvet theater chairs facing it, a fully stocked bar against another wall, a fridge, and another door on the third wall that is closed.

"You were right. I went with the red."

The red velvet. On the chairs. This is what it was for.

"Looks good," I say.

He picks up a remote control, points it at the ceiling, and presses a button. There's a whirring and the ceiling seems to peel itself back, and above us are blue lights and ripples of water.

It's the pool.

He's built it under the pool.

"It's calming, huh? This is one of the projects I've been working on with Franz and Mary," he says, pouring us each a whiskey. "For when the world is just too damned crazy. Now we're doing a music studio." He hands me a drink, then sits down and pats the chair next to him.

I sit down and take a sip. Then another. It's strong and burns my throat a little. But I can feel that knot inside me slowly start to uncoil.

He lets out a big sigh. "So . . . I got your message." His eyes meet mine.

"Oh," I say. Swallow. "I was upset."

"No, you were right. It was weak as fuck getting Amy to call you. I just didn't know what to say. My next movie is out so soon, and Geraldine, my main PR rep, is all over me not to be in the press unless she puts me there. She flipped out. I didn't really have a choice."

A flash of that article: *Zach's PR rep, Geraldine Haigh, commented: "They're just old friends, that's all. They have history."*

I nod and take another big sip of my drink.

"That must be hard. Always having to live your life like that?" I say.

He shrugs. "It's sure as hell not what I expected. I mean, I'm not complaining. I have a great team. Brian is on top of every opportunity. That's why he brought in Carlos, to make sure I didn't have to worry about anything other than my career. And Carlos is seriously the best in the business. Just gets shit done. My agency works hard. Geraldine and my whole PR team know their stuff. And man, they've turned me into a movie star. That shit doesn't happen anymore. Not with streaming. So yeah, I'm grateful. But it's stressful. Now I need pills to sleep and this to unwind," he says, lifting up his glass to the ceiling. "And like, sometimes, when I really sit and think about it, it just seems so fucking pointless. All of it."

"Scary, rather."

"No. I mean, have you actually thought about it? Like, in two hundred years, nobody is going to even know what we did or didn't do."

"They'll remember you," I say.

"No they won't. Maybe some descendant decades from now will take a photograph of me to school, or like a hologram or some shit, and tell her friends about how her great-great-great-uncle was a star of some medium that won't even exist anymore. And they'll be like, 'Cool,' and that will be that. That's if we haven't gone extinct."

He downs his drink and goes and pours another.

"That's depressing," I say.

"It's true. And yet we have to fight so fucking hard to keep it all." He takes another sip and walks back over to me to sit down again.

"Well, it's easy for you to say, because you've realized your dream. You don't remember what it feels like when you haven't."

"That's true. I'm grateful and I love it all; I'm not saying it's not great. It just seems petty sometimes. Like, why does it matter if I want to hang out with you? Or why did everyone care if I broke up with Solange?" He pauses for a moment. "It was a fake relationship anyway. Geraldine set it up."

"Really?"

"Really. God, it's so good to be able to talk about this stuff," he says. "It's so tiring having to put on a show the whole time."

"It sounds like it," I say.

He sighs and takes a sip of his drink. "Anyway, I don't mean to complain. It's just tougher than I thought it would be. And in ways I didn't expect. But I signed up for that. You didn't. So I'm sorry I put you in the firing line. Truly."

A muscle on the side of his jaw twitches a little, and something in my chest aches. I want to reach out and hug him. I want to make it okay for both of us.

"See, this is why we had you sign that contract," he says, standing up. "I couldn't talk to you like this without it." A pang of guilt rolls through me. Because if I'd thought of a story, I know I would have written it.

And then he reaches out his hand and says, "Why don't you stay the night? Let's try this thing again . . . third time lucky."

Thirty-Two

When I wake up, I'm wearing one of Zach's T-shirts, my arm is hanging off the edge of the bed, and the blinds are already up. My eyes flick open to pink clouds, palm trees, white flimsy curtains. A sharp inhale. *Wait . . . where am I?*

"Hey," comes a voice. Gentle.

I turn to look. *Zach.*

He's wrapped in a white towel, coming out of the bathroom. We stayed up until after midnight, drinking whiskey and talking about everything. And then we came upstairs and he got me a spare toothbrush and I assumed we'd have sex, but he said, "Are you sure you want to? We can just sleep next to each other."

And I didn't want to. Not really. Not after yesterday. So instead, I fell asleep in his arms.

"I've got training," he says, moving around to my side of the bed and sitting down and gazing at me. "But Amy can make you coffee and something for breakfast. Also, I'm having some people around tomorrow night. Steven, that producer I wanted you to meet, will be here."

"Oh," I say, still hazy with sleep.

"You should come. I'll introduce you."

"Okay," I say, sitting up and touching his face. My fingers trace the stubble.

"I'm going to text you Carlos's number, okay?" he says. "If anything happens, just call him."

"Thanks." I smile, my cheeks getting warm. He leans forward and kisses me gently on the lips. I can smell the toothpaste on his breath, and I don't want him to go. Not yet. So I reach my hand into his hair and kiss him back, and he wraps his arms around me.

"Is this okay?" he asks, pulling away a little, his eyes soft. Like he's unsure.

"Yeah," I say, breathless. Then I lift my arms up and he smiles.

"You're going to get me into trouble," he says, reaching for my T-shirt and pulling it up over my head.

Then he drops his towel to the ground and lies down on top of me. He's propped up on his elbows, his face close to mine. "This is nice, right?" he says, brushing my hair out of my eyes.

I nod, and he leans in, and his lips hover just above mine. And then he kisses me again, softly, and I swear I can feel his heart beating.

His mouth moves to my ear, then my neck, and something flips in my lower abdomen as he tugs at the corners of my underwear. I lift up my hips and try to wriggle out of them, but they get stuck at my knees. And he's sitting up now, pulling at them, laughing, and I'm laughing too, and something aches beneath my ribs because right now it's like he's just Zach again, not "Zach Hamilton." Like it's just me and him in this big house. He lies back down and his chest is hot against mine. His eyes look straight into me, and he slowly moves my legs apart with his knee. And I know this wasn't the plan, I wasn't going to feel any of the things I'm feeling right now, but there is no part of this moment I want to change. Because then he's inside me. His hips melting into mine. And everything feels okay.

We're lying in bed now, on our backs, looking up at the ceiling.

"Is this the real reason you needed an NDA?" I ask, glancing over at him. "So nobody knows you're actually into missionary?"

"Pretty much." He laughs and lifts his wrist up, looks at his watch, and says, "My trainer is going to kill me." He sits up. "I really have to go."

I watch as he rushes over to his clothes and pulls them on: gray tracksuit pants, a white T-shirt, and a navy hoodie half-zipped-down at the front.

"See you tomorrow night," he says, and then he blows me a kiss and walks out the room, and as I listen to his feet pad down the hallway, I reach for my phone. And I'm scared to look at it. I almost wish Carlos had kept it, instead of delivering it back to me an hour later with no news at all about the number that had sent those scary messages.

So as I squint down at it, my stomach is tight: What if something else has come in?

Another picture? Another threat?

But there are no new notifications.

I roll onto my back and stare at the ceiling. But now that it's just me in here, yesterday is quickly filtering back: *R U willing 2 die 4 Zach*, the picture of me outside that restaurant, the pictures on my phone of that heart. How Deputy Barnes could do nothing.

I turn onto my side, let out a big breath, and scan the room for the rest of my clothes. They're on the chair. And I should go home right now and change into new clothes, clean clothes, I know that, but I really don't want to go back there. I can't. Not yet. I'll do that tonight. After work. Once I've had a bit of space from it.

I sit up, I look out at the hazy view, a window flashes with the sun in the distance, and I'm thinking of those paparazzi outside my building. Then sound bites from last night trickle in. Everything Zach told me about the realities of being a celebrity. And then . . . *it* happens.

Out of the blue.

The way *it* always happens.

The thought.

Because *hang on* . . .

Frantically I tap through to my mail app. I need to get this down before I forget it. It's like I'm hanging on to the corner of butterfly's wing, trying not to crush it, trying not to let it fly away. I pull up a new email and type in my elevator pitch:

A thriller writer who starts dating a celebrity has to deal with a psycho fan who uses everything in her first book against her. The police can't help her, nobody can help her . . . except maybe the man she loves . . .

And then I save it to Drafts.

Because this is it. What I've been looking for. I can feel it in my gut.

I should make it autobiographical.

That's perfect. Absolutely perfect.

Then I don't even need to make up a story, because I'm living it.

I mean, sure, I'll have to fictionalize it, sensationalize it, maybe even recontextualize it, to get around that NDA. But I could do it . . .

And then: beep.

A message flashes on my phone screen.

Zach: *Here's Carlos's number. Hope today is better. Xxx*

And with it comes a contact card.

And as I stare down at it, guilt settles over me and reality rolls in, fucking things up the way it always does.

Because he trusts me. He's been so open with me. So how could I do that to him? Now? When he's the only one who is helping me? The only one who is there for me? And last night, this morning . . . none of that was casual. It was vulnerable and real. Things are different now. Complicated.

And even if I recontextualized the shit out of this story, even if I got away with it with everyone else, Zach knows what's going on right now; he'd know I'd used him and his superfan or whatever to write it. He'd hear his own voice in the dialogue, I know he would—I won't be able to help myself.

And what kind of person would I be if I betrayed him like that? Not a good one, I know that much.

And I *am* a good person. I really like him. I think there might actually be a future for us . . . if I don't write this book.

Because I also know this: I can't have both. I have to choose.

So, well, *fuck.*

Amy, Zach's assistant, is standing in the kitchen when I get downstairs, frowning down at her phone and typing something at lightning speed. I can hear a vacuum cleaner going in another room, and there's a woman in a light-gray uniform with white cuffs carrying a bucket of cleaning supplies through the kitchen and down one of the many hallways.

"Hi," I say.

Amy keeps typing. "Morning," she says cheerfully, like she didn't leave that message on my phone. "Just a second."

Her eyes move back and forth, and her lips move a little like she's reading what she's just written, and then she stabs the screen one last time with her finger and looks up at me.

"Coffee? Breakfast?"

"Just coffee," I say, sitting down at the counter. She must have seen the article. Must have seen me half-naked. But she fakes it well.

"How do you take it?"

"Black," I say.

She nods and puts a cup under the nozzle of a machine, presses a button, and looks down at her phone again, now buzzing, as the coffee machine whirs.

"Shit," she says under her breath as she answers. "Brian, hi, no . . . Not yet, he'll look at it this afternoon. I promise. It's with all the other scripts on his desk, waiting."

The coffee machine stops whirring and she brings the cup over to me.

"Thanks," I say, and she nods, then gets back to the phone call.

"Yes, I know he said this afternoon . . . No, she hasn't called yet . . ." She pulls her phone away from her ear and looks down at the screen, then talks into it again. "She's calling now."

She stabs the phone and answers what I think is probably a new call. "Geraldine, hi," she says.

Geraldine. The PR rep who freaked out when Zach was in the press with me; the reason Zach couldn't see me anymore.

I take a sip of coffee and watch Amy's expressions. Could I live like this? With all these people around all the time, weighing in, the way they do with Zach?

"I don't know," Amy says, and then she looks at me in this way that makes me think maybe they're talking about me. "I know he agreed, but yes, that is accurate."

She heads out of the room, and I'm not sure if I'm paranoid or not, but I swear she says, "She's still here."

So they *are* talking about me.

Geraldine is pissed off that I'm here and Zach is helping me anyway.

The cleaner with the bucket of supplies is back and I can't just sit here and watch her wipe things down while I sip coffee. I'll feel too bad, like I should help her. So I leave my cup in the sink, grab my bag, and go to the front door. Amy is still talking on the phone when I get there so I call out "Bye" to not be rude, then head out into the bright sunshine and get into my van.

As I drive down toward the gate and press the button that will let me out, the last of the safety I felt in Zach's arms fades away and the horror of the last few days is back with full force. The message. The picture. Then that smear on my windshield from Saturday. Because there's still some psycho out there with my name in her head. A psycho who probably knows where I live. Who knows what van I drive. And how much danger am I actually in?

Thirty-Three

An hour and a half later I'm in the shop, surrounded by brown boxes, cut stems and buckets of flowers I need to be putting in the flower cooler. But instead, my gloves are off and I'm staring at my phone screen, typing in *Z-o-e A-n-n W-e-i-s-s*.

Because I have a plan. I'm going to figure out exactly what he or she, whoever they are, knows about me. What they can do to me. Because even if they *want* to do everything in *Fractured*, they won't be able to without the right information. In *Fractured*, the protagonist lives in the same on-campus residence building as her stalker, which provides ample opportunity for terror. But that's different for me. I live in a secure apartment building, with a security gate that requires a code for entry.

Which cuts down their options considerably.

I press Go and the results load.

There, at the top, is the photograph of me from the back of my book. The semi-smug one. Then the brief bio that's on everything from Goodreads to my publisher's website to my own website. Three book covers: the one from here in the US, then two more from Poland and Germany—the only two international territories we sold into.

I scan the links.

Past the Venice Floristry website—yes, that has my name and photograph on it, but that's already out there—then past the reviews of *Frac-

tured. Past a couple of stories I had published in journals before I got my book deal. I come to a mention of the manuscript prize I won back in London, the prize that had me sign with Barb, the one that felt like the beginning of my career but was really signaling the end. And then *there my Instagram account is . . .* But like I said before, my whole grid is just pictures of books.

What I need is to get into their head . . .

So if they're following the sequence of events that happens in my book, then I should be able to guess what's coming next.

After taking my protagonist's light bulbs in chapter 19, the stalker in *Fractured* breaks in and trashes the protagonist's place of work. That happens in chapter 24. So, I'm guessing that would be the shop in my case.

I mentally scan it for vulnerabilities. The only people who have keys are me, Vee, the owner, and our flower supplier, but Vee has been using him for years. Vee locks up every evening, and the front of the shop is on a main street and monitored by CCTV. The back, not so much. But while there's no surveillance back there, it's completely secure. The only entrance is through the garage, and you'd need a remote for that. So that's not a risk. The worst they could do would be to trash the outside at the back.

The next scary incident happens in chapter 30, when the stalker writes *SEE U SOON* in steam on the protagonist's mirror. But if whoever is doing this can't even get into my apartment complex, they sure as hell can't get into my apartment, so that one is out. Next, in chapter 36 the stalker cuts up all the protagonist's clothes and leaves them scattered on her bed. And then, in chapter 40, the final chapter, she shatters a mirror and slits the protagonist's wrists in the bathtub, making it look like a suicide. Like my protagonist made the whole thing up. That was the new ending Felicity and I finally agreed on, and, god, I wish we'd settled on something else. Because it was scary enough when I wrote it, but it's even scarier now.

It makes me want to be sick.

But *nobody can get into my apartment, nobody can get into my apartment, nobody can get into my apartment.*

They really, really can't. I mean, they may know which street I live on, maybe even which building I'm in, but I could live in any one of the six apartments in my block. And I'm on the second floor, so even if they figured it out, it's not like they could break in through a window.

I'm fine.

Except, what if they improvise?

Do something that's *not* in my book? That'll be even worse. Then I won't know what's coming next. What else could they do?

I stare at the screen, scrolling, scrolling, searching for vulnerabilities, and then my pulse speeds up: the shop's Instagram page.

Could they somehow use that? Is there information on there about me? Something they could manipulate?

How?

I go to Instagram and pull up Venice Floristry.

I look down through the pictures first. They're just of arrangements and events, nothing about me. Next, I scan the bio. But there's nothing about me there either. Just a link to Vee's page, directing people there with event enquiries. I tap on her profile and up it comes.

Again, nothing about me. It's mainly about her acting career, selfies outside auditions, pictures of her acting class. A couple of headshots.

I go back to my Google search and keep scrolling. It's more of the same, though the reviews are from Bookstagrammer blogs now, not literary review sites.

A calm washes over me; my pulse slows down.

Because there is nothing else. Nothing else they could use. *I'm going to be okay . . .*

The front door opens and Vee is here.

"Hey," she calls. I can hear her limping around in her walking boot. I put down my phone and pick up some calla lilies and take them to the flower cooler.

"What did the police say?" she asks, popping her head in the doorway and coming inside.

"I need to alter my route to and from work and let them know if anything else happens."

"Like what? Get assaulted?" she asks, going to the shelves behind me.

"I don't know," I say. *Basically.*

"Weren't you wearing that yesterday?" She frowns, her gaze moving over me.

"I stayed at a friend's place."

I say this because (1) the NDA and (2) even if there were no NDA, she'd think it's a bad idea that I'm still seeing Zach after that phone message from his assistant—even if it *was* so he could help me. She'd say that was just an excuse I was making, that I'd end up getting hurt again. And I love Vee, but she can be sort of judgy and unyielding in her opinions. It's not her fault; she has baggage from her ex. One strike and they're out now: that's how she protects herself. But if Zach can back me against Geraldine, I can back him against Vee. Just . . . silently.

"Good for you." She smiles at me before rummaging through a box on the bottom shelf.

"What are you looking for?" I ask.

"A spare laptop charger. I have a client meeting this morning and mine's broken. I swear I saw one in here," she muses before pulling it out. "Thank god." She stands up and heads out.

As the morning passes, I tidy away the cardboard boxes from our most recent delivery, flattening them down and taking them to the recycling bin in the garage. I wipe down my workspace. I print out today's orders, and I'm about to start on the first one when my phone beeps.

It's a text. From Greta.

And it reads: *Are you coming tonight?*

I frown at the message, then tap through to my calendar. Have I forgotten something? Do we have a writers' group social thing? Does someone have a book launch? But there, beneath today's date, is nothing. It's wide open.

I text back: *Coming to what, babe?*

A call flashes up on my screen: *Greta.*

"Hey," I say.

"Don't be upset," Greta starts. My insides drop and the line buzzes a little. "Sophie is having drinks tonight to celebrate something secret. You know what she's like. I'm sure she meant to ask you. She messaged everyone on Instagram . . . are you sure you didn't miss it?"

"Oh, right," I say, but I can hear my pulse in my ears now. A flash of her and Barb in my mind's eye. "Maybe . . ." But I know for certain I didn't miss any message. She didn't ask me on purpose. And I'm filled with this sense of impending doom. I bet she has a book deal. Probably a multibook deal. What else could it be?

"You should come," Greta says, her voice light.

Now, if it were this time last week, I'd probably bow out. Say I had plans and go home and read, but I'm scared to go home. Really scared. It feels like the longer I can put it off, the better.

Also, I need to know what Sophie's news is. I need to know how far I'm falling behind.

So I say: "Okay, sure. Where is it?"

"I'll send you the details," Greta says.

Then we hang up.

And as I sit in my work studio, surrounded by the life I never chose, I'm gripped by panic. Filled with this certainty that if I don't do something big, and soon, I'm going to live and die and it will be like I was never here, while people like Sophie and Zach zoom off into their futures.

And I really, really like Zach, I don't want to break his trust—I don't want to end up with a lawsuit on my hands either—but I can't sacrifice my whole future for him. And the moment he got his big break, he grabbed it with both hands, and everything else, every other "complication," just had to fall away. That's what I need to do.

I need to choose my dreams over everything else. Because Vee is right. That's the only way people like us ever make it. If we go all in.

So goodbye, soul, I guess.

I go to my email, navigate to Drafts, and scan the elevator pitch I noted down this morning in Zach's bed. Then I put Barb's name in the To field. In the Subject field I type: *Elevator Pitch*. And even though I kind of hate myself as I do it, even though I feel a little sick, in the message body I write:

Hey Barb,

Elevator pitch: A thriller writer who starts dating a celebrity has to deal with a psycho fan who uses everything in her first book against her. The police can't help her, nobody can help her . . . except maybe the man she loves . . .

Chat soon, Zoe.

And then, before I can change my mind, I press Send.

Thirty-Four

I hold it together all day, but as night falls, the fear begins to creep back in. I can't help it; it's the dark. And I've been thinking. Just because they can't figure out how to get into my apartment, just because they can't learn more about me online, doesn't mean I'm safe. Like right now, I'm walking from my van to the bar where we're meeting. I'm on a side street and semi-lit, but what if they hurt me now? There's barely anyone around.

I clench my keys between my fingers and rush toward the main road ahead.

I turn left and exhale as I move into the crowds of people spilling in and out of bars and restaurants, as I take in the cars driving slowly, their headlights and taillights puncturing the night. But the truth is, I still feel watched. The little hairs on the back of my neck standing on end. I look behind me and scan the street, but nobody's there.

Then there it is, the bar. It's just up ahead—red ropes at the door, a bouncer—so I quickly text Greta: *I'm here.*

The bouncer checks my ID and nods at me, then I go in through the wooden door and look around.

It's dark in here, with distressed mirrors all over the wooden walls, plants dangling their foliage from shelves up high, and a lot of expensive white T-shirts, blazers, puffy sleeves, and Converse sneakers filling the room. I walk through a cloud of smoke that smells like weed but could be a vape, my ears adjusting to the loud conversations and music.

My phone lights up and buzzes in my hand.

Greta: *back corner xx*

I look up toward it and see Greta, waving at me. They're in a cordoned-off section of the bar with a couple of red sofas. I see Rita too, just behind her, sitting on one of those sofas. Tom and his wife are standing against a wall, holding hands and talking to Candice. There are a few other people I've never seen before. Mainly women with long, glossy hair. And me. The one person who wasn't invited.

"Hey." Greta smiles as she gets to me. Her cheeks are bright pink from champagne, the glass in her hand.

"Hey," I reply.

"The bitch is over there," Greta says, still smiling as she nods toward the group in the corner. This is why I prefer drunk Greta. I look in the direction she's pointing and there Sophie is, in a low-cut red top, her head thrown back as she laughs. It's performative. And sometimes I think my life would be better if I was performative too. If I could fake it the way others can.

We head to the group.

Sophie sees me and flinches, then rushes straight over. "Zoe, I'm so sorry, I thought I'd invited you!" she says, moving in for a hug.

"No problem," I say, hugging her back. "What's the news?"

"Argh, I'm not allowed to talk about it until Friday, but I'm away then. Let's just say it's fab and worthy of champagne!"

I give a small smile and *I will not be bitter, I will not be bitter, I will not be bitter*. "Well, congrats on whatever it is. And I saw your post. Barb is amazing. I hope she does wonderful things for you."

"Thanks," she says. "She's sooo excited about me. It feels great."

I nod and smile again. Because it *is* great.

"She says I'm a *true* talent. The kind that *never* comes along."

I grit my teeth.

"How are you doing? Still struggling?" Her face does this pitying thing where she juts out her lower lip. "Poor thing. You'll get there eventually." Then she spots someone over my shoulder and goes to them, and I turn to Greta and raise my eyebrows.

"I know," she says, putting her hand on my arm. "Let's get you a drink."

We head to a sofa and sit down next to Rita, who is checking her phone.

"Here," Greta says, pouring me some champagne.

"Thanks," I say, then take a big gulp.

"Zoe, hey, what the actual fuck? Zach Hamilton?" Rita asks, turning to us and leaning in. She's a bit drunk, slurring and spitting a bit when she speaks. "I saw the pictures on Page Six. Like wow. *Wow.* You must have a magic vagina." She lets out a really loud laugh.

Greta rolls her eyes at me, and I can see Sophie looking in our direction now. Listening in on the conversation. And for a split second I think: *Would she do this to me?* And the answer is: maybe. If it were easy.

But not if it meant touching a raw heart with those perfectly manicured hands of hers. Not if it meant she had to spend her evenings following me around taking pictures. She might have put my number on the internet, though. I wouldn't put *that* past her.

"What's he like? At sex?" Rita asks, and I look back to her.

"I can't really talk about it. I signed an NDA," I say, louder than I need to. It's bad, I know, but Sophie is listening and I like how that sounds and I want to irritate her. I like how it makes me sound important even though I'm not. Not at all.

She nods. "Fair."

"Are you okay about all those . . . comments?" Greta asks me quietly. "I saw them. Didn't want to bring it up and upset you."

"It was awful," I half whisper back. "And—"

I'm about to tell her about the heart on my windshield and show her the scary messages—tell her that, actually, it's all for the best because

I've been writing. It's given me a story idea. A great one. But before I can say anything, Sophie comes over.

"What're you talking about?" she asks, sitting down on the other side of the sofa and crossing her ridiculously long legs.

And . . . um . . . no. There's no way I'm saying it now. Because the last thing I need is her saying something that makes me think this idea is shit too. And she will; I can see it in her eyes. They're mean. And so I just say: "Not much."

Because I need to protect this story of mine.

I need to protect it even if I haven't heard back from Barb yet, even though I haven't even written it. Even though I'll lose Zach if I write it and there's that NDA to worry about . . . But that's how I know it's the right one. I feel the need to protect it like a little flame that could be blown out at any moment.

I feel the need to write it, no matter what it costs me.

Thirty-Five

It's as I turn onto my street that I know why I felt watched tonight. I notice the headlights first, close behind me, then the familiar shape of an SUV. It's Carlos. I park and he drives past me, pulls into a free space ahead, then sits with his engine still running, his lights on, as I get out.

I'm safe. He's watching out for me. Just like Zach said he would be.

I slam the door of the van, hurry to the security gate, and punch the number into the keypad. The gate opens, and as I go to shut it after me, I see him drive off.

I cross the courtyard. It's dark, but I can make out where everything is from the ambient light of streetlights filtering in. I move past the hum of the pool and Jake's apartment, which is dark—he must be out—and up the stairs to my apartment.

My fingertips feel around in my bag for my key. I find it, push it into the lock, and go inside. There's a click as the door shuts behind me, and I reach for the wall, my fingers tracing over the familiar rough old paint as I search for the light switch.

There it is.

Flick.

But the room stays black. Inky black.

My pulse speeds up.

I flick it again. Nothing.

Then again. And again.

My ears roar.

Because: *CHAPTER NINETEEN!*

I step backward, pull open the door, and rush back outside, my heart banging against my ribs as I stare into the darkened interior of my flat.

But they're not meant to be able to do this . . . How did they get in?

And then: *Are they still here?*

A shiver runs through me as I swivel around and scan the courtyard for movement.

But there's no movement at all, just the hum of the pool pump and the sounds of traffic in the distance.

Maybe I should text Carlos. Get him to come back here . . .

Frantically, I go to his contact info and type in: *Hi, it's Zoe, I think they've been here.*

But the moment before I press Send, I stop myself.

Because: *Hang on . . . am I being ridiculous?*

The door was locked when I got here. There was no sign of forced entry. And I have a security gate. You need a code to get past it.

So maybe I just tripped a circuit breaker.

That's a logical explanation, and it'll be the first thing Carlos asks me. Whether I've checked that. And this *has* happened before. When I'd just moved in.

I mean, *that* time I was using the lights, the kettle, and a hair dryer simultaneously, but it's possible . . .

I look down into the darkness where the breaker box is.

All I need to do is go down there, into the corner by the laundry, and turn the little switch back on. That's all.

I can do this.

So I reach into my bag, pull out my phone, and creep back down those stairs. I turn on my phone's flashlight and shine the light into the inky corner. And I can see the box right there on the wall outside the laundry, partially obscured by a large potted palm. I hold my breath as I move the light left and right, searching for movement in the shadows.

I'm looking for eyes shining back at me. Maybe the glint of a weapon.

But there's nothing there. Nobody. So I take a deep breath and walk quickly toward it, lighting my way with my phone until I'm standing in front of the metal box.

I focus my phone's flashlight on it, reach past a couple of cobwebs, grab the latch at the bottom, and pull open the metal casing, then scan for my apartment number. It's been a while since I've done this, but there it is, number five. Upper, middle. I lift up the plastic covering and glance across the electrical panel, looking for the breaker that's turned itself off . . .

But now my breath catches and I get a little dizzy.

Because: . . . *What?*

It's not just one little circuit breaker that's tripped—it's all of them. The *main* breaker has turned off.

And I'm not so sure that happens by itself. Not when nobody is at home. And nothing is turned on.

I spin around to look behind me: the courtyard, the gate, the steps up to my apartment. They're all empty. My ears strain as I listen for the crunch of gravel, the shutting of curtains, or footsteps retreating. But all I can hear is the sound of my heart thudding in my ears and a car horn sounding in the distance. I could probably hear a star shooting, I'm straining so hard.

This is insane. Calm down. It was probably just a power surge.

Because there's nobody else here.

I look at the gate again, reminding myself: *To get inside, they'd have to have the code, and how would they get that?*

But even so, terror rolls through me. Because: What if they did? Somehow?

I flick the main breaker back on, close the metal door with a clang, and run quickly back upstairs.

I go inside, feel along that rough wall, find the light switch, and: flick.

The room is flooded with light.

And that should calm me down, but it doesn't.

As I close the front door, my heart bangs a little harder in my chest, and I look around, from the sofa to the kitchen, to the spindly little latch holding the kitchen window shut.

My stomach clenches, and all I can think is: *What if they're in here somewhere?*

And I know that makes me sound paranoid and crazy, I really do, but I'm also the person finding organs on her windshield and getting text messages with the word "die" in them. I'm scared.

I need to check. It's the only way I'll feel safe.

So I hold my breath and creep toward the kitchen. There's a rack full of plates and cutlery drying beside the sink and the gleam of a blade. A big knife. I grab it, then gently tiptoe over to the bathroom.

I take a deep breath, and my heart hammers in my chest as I get ready to push open the door.

But what am I going to do if someone *is* in there?

Still, I can't just stand here all night either. So I push.

The door flings open and my eyes dart across the tiles to the shower, the bath, the mirror . . . but nobody's there.

Adrenaline pulses through me as I turn to the bedroom behind me now. And I don't even pause this time—I want this over—I just rush inside, knife out in front of me.

But there's nobody here either. I roughly pull open the closet doors and, again, nothing but my clothes.

So I go back to the living room, put the knife down on the coffee table, and flop onto the sofa.

And I cry. Big, heavy tears. I push the heels of my palms into my eyes, trying to make them stop. But they won't. And I know there's nobody here now, and there was nobody outside either, and I'm safe, so why can't I stop my heart from beating so fast? Why can't I breathe normally?

Hot tears drip down my cheeks as Hemingway and Didion and Ephron and Capote and Dostoyevsky watch on. I stay like that for a good half hour. Until, eventually, the tears dry up and a numbness descends.

Then I get up, check that all the windows are secure one by one, make sure the chain is on the door, and push a chair up against it. I take a shower, brush my teeth, and put on Zach's shirt.

And then I turn the lights off and try to sleep.

Thirty-Six

At 7:06 the next morning, I'm pouring boiling water over three heaping spoonfuls of instant coffee. Tea won't cut it this morning—I'm exhausted. I barely slept last night; every sound in the distance woke me, every siren sounded like it was coming for me. So I lay there, drifting in and out of sleep, making and remaking two mental lists, trying to figure out how crazy I am.

Reasons to be scared about the lights:

1. My power has never gone out like that before, not when I wasn't home.
2. In *Fractured*, light bulbs are removed. And if someone couldn't get into my apartment, turning off the power is the next best thing.
3. The circuit breakers are easy to get to because the panel is in a communal area.
4. There *is* some psycho out there using the plot points of my book to terrorize me; my fears are not entirely unfounded.
5. Honestly, it's just my fucking luck.

Reasons *not* to be scared:

1. I googled and it could have been a power surge or an overload.
2. My emotions are extremely heightened at the moment and I could be reading too much into it.
3. In order to get to the circuit breakers, you'd have to get past the security gate.
4. In order to get past the security gate, you'd have to have the code, and how the hell would some random person off the internet have the code? It's mildly possible they could have piggybacked their way in with Jake, but we're the only two residents who live here right now. So if he didn't recognize them and they couldn't explain being there for me, I'm pretty sure he'd clock it. It's not a big building.
5. And finally, if some psycho broke into the property last night, surely they would have broken into my apartment, done something more? Surely the light bulbs would, in fact, have been removed? Surely I'd be lying here in a pool of blood right now, not making a strong cup of coffee and craving a cigarette? Surely.

It's point number five that wins me over.

And then I think: *Unless they were just showing they could get to me . . .*

I need to stop thinking.

And I need to eat something, but I'm not hungry. So I add two sugars to my coffee, take a big gulp, grab my phone, head over to the sofa, and open my laptop. As it fires up, I open the window behind me, pull out a cigarette, light it, take a long drag, and check my phone.

It's 7:09 now, and still no more crazed messages. No more photographs.

Maybe it's over.

Maybe Deputy Barnes was right and they just wanted attention.

Maybe last night was just a terrible coincidence. Something I wouldn't have even noticed under normal circumstances.

I tap through to my emails now, take another sip of coffee, and scroll down, down, down, looking for *Barb Wallace*—maybe I missed her email. But there's nothing. No reply about my elevator pitch. But that's okay: it gives me more time to work on the book before she asks to see more pages.

So I turn to my laptop and pull up that research document. The one I started on Thursday night, the night I came home from Zach's place still wet from his swimming pool, the night before I ended up in the press and this whole nightmare started, and scroll to the bottom. I scan the last paragraph, finish my cigarette, and start to type.

I write about the smudge on my windshield, the beep of the messages on Monday morning, the policeman's messy desk, his card in my bag, how they could do nothing, Carlos, Zach, his cinema room, the whiskey, and everything he told me about the press and fame and him and Solange . . . how I feel bad about writing this book. I don't press the Backspace button once. I don't edit myself. That bitchy voice in my head can't keep up with the words that fly from my fingers. And every time I hear her clear her throat, I type a little faster. Because I don't have time for her. I need words on the page, to get it all down.

Do I feel guilty writing about Zach? Yes. I do.

But I may never get another idea like this. I have to see it through. And maybe he'll forgive me if he comes out looking good in the edit.

My eyes move to the top right of the screen. It's 7:41 a.m. now. I need to get ready for work. For tonight. So I gulp down the rest of my coffee, close my laptop, go to my bedroom, and open my closet.

I only own one dressy dress, a silver sequined number I bought when I first moved to LA, back when I had visions of attending the sorts of parties you might wear something like this to. It's been jeans and a T-shirt ever since. But there it is, shimmering from the far left-hand side like a forgotten dream, and tonight—well, tonight is the kind of night when I can wear sequins. I pull it out and lay it down on my bed to air it out. And as I do that, a little jolt runs through me; a swarm of bees fills my stomach.

Because no matter what else is going on in my life, it's not *all* bad. Right now I'm wearing Zach Hamilton's shirt. Tonight, I'm going to his house. I'm going to meet a producer who can maybe turn *Fractured* into a movie. *And* I have a second book idea, a great one. So maybe the good makes all the bad worth it; there's nothing for nothing in this world after all. And as I stand there, in my little orange apartment, in the version of my life that's held me prisoner for the last two years, ever since my book bombed, I think: *It's happening. It's finally happening.*

My life is *finally* back on track.

Thirty-Seven

The lights of LA wink back at me as I park my van outside Zach's house and pull the hand brake. I slip on my shoes—I can't drive in heels—and glance at myself in the rearview mirror. Am I wearing too much sparkly eyeshadow? Probably. Am I still a little anxious after last night? Yes. I am. But I push it down. Because nights like tonight, when dreams are made, are exactly what drew me to LA to begin with. The pure possibility of it.

And I don't want to miss a moment of it.

I edge the door open, trying not to bang the car beside me as I slink out. The sky is a darkening blue and the moon nothing more than a sliver tonight. There are around fifteen cars all parked in a perfect line, and behind me is a man with white gloves. He's the one who directed me to this tiny car space; I think he underestimated the girth of the van.

I move past him to the front door. It's open and I go inside, through the kitchen, and past five people wearing all white with trays of hors d'oeuvres and champagne. A young woman is standing next to a blender, chopping up mint and lemons. I look to the big glass doors that lead out to the terrace. About fifty people are out there, milling around the bright-blue pool. The steam from the heat makes it look ethereal, like a stage, like somebody hired a smoke machine.

I scan the faces for Zach. I'm nervous. I don't want to be walking around randomly, looking for him; I need to know which direction to head in. And as I do, I wish I'd worn a different dress. Nobody else is as . . . sparkly. I'm going to stick out like a disco ball. My gaze latches onto a man with light-brown hair—he's a musician, I think. A flash of him on the TV with a guitar. And the woman beside him—short jet-black hair and almost a head taller than him—is from a perfume ad.

And all I can think is: *How the hell did little Zoe Ann Weiss end up here?*

My gaze moves a bit to the right. There's Zach's assistant, Amy, wearing a long black dress, talking to Franz and Mary. Their backs are angled toward me, so I can see Franz's hand as it briefly moves to Mary's lower lower back, then brushes her butt. *Isn't he married? Are they having an affair?*

My eyes shift to just beside them now, to a guy I've seen in a few TV shows. A couple of other people I sort of recognize. Then there's Zach, in a pair of jeans and a white shirt. He's smiling and talking to a man with gray hair. He laughs, his perfect smile making me smile. I take a deep breath and a step toward the door and almost bump into a guy with a tray of champagne.

Shit.

"Sorry," I say, and he nods at me and heads outside.

That's when my phone starts ringing from my bag.

I step sideways, out of the way and against the wall, and pull it into view. The screen reads: *Barb Wallace.*

My elevator pitch.

I fumble to answer it.

"Hello?" I say.

"Zoe, hi, I have good news. Can you talk?"

The blender starts up in the kitchen, and I press a finger against my ear so I can hear her.

"Just a second," I say as I look around—I need somewhere quiet. My eyes move to the spiral glass stairs that lead up to the second floor and Zach's bedroom and then to the hallway right in front of me. I head down it.

"I sent what you have to Felicity and she loves it," Barb continues as the noise of chatter fades behind me. "Loves the premise, loves the voice. Loves the elevator pitch. She wants to take it to her team to discuss the next steps."

"That's amazing," I say, leaning against the wall behind me and closing my eyes for a moment. Just to feel the pure relief.

"She wants to see the rest."

My eyes snap open. *Shit.*

"It's taking longer than I thought," I say, my voice coming out a little strained.

Silence rings down the line.

"I told her we were pretty close to having the full manuscript. I thought you said you'd been working on it for a while?"

"I have," I lie, crinkling my face up. "It's just not ready."

"Zoe, it's okay if it's rough. We just need to get her something more. She can work with you on it."

And this is true. Felicity is a brilliant editor, but you can't edit a blank page, and I just don't have a whole story yet. Who am I kidding: all I have are some scenes, a few notes, and an elevator pitch. I have no idea where it goes from here. No idea how it ends.

"I'm going to need another month. Two, tops."

Silence. I think I hear her swallow. Or clench her jaw. Hard to tell.

"I'll talk to Felicity and see what I can do. But, Zoe, focus. This needs to get written. Just get it on the page, then we can worry about making it great."

I nod, reflexively. "Will do." And then we hang up and I think *Fuck* and go to stare at the wall in front of me, but I'm right in front of a room with an open door. And inside that room, I can see a set of photographs on the wall. There is an older woman in one of them—*is that Zach's mother?*

I look around me. Nobody is here. And I know it's bad to go inside, to snoop, but . . . *I can just look quickly*. Because I need as much inspiration as I can get for this book, and I need it soon. So I go inside and walk up to that picture, scanning it for all the pieces of Zach he's never shown to me, to *Vanity Fair*, to audiences. I lean in a little closer and trace her features with my gaze.

Would she like me if we met? What kind of upbringing did Zach have?

I glance at the next picture. Zach is standing with two men; one is older—his father, maybe—and the other one is a little younger. *Maybe that's his brother*. They look similar, with almost identical features that somehow hang differently. This other man has the face of a sales manager, not a movie star. Beauty, like fate, is a matter of millimeters, it seems.

I look around behind me. There's a computer, a desk with a stack of scripts on it, and a table at the far side of the room. This must be his study.

And there on the back wall are more pictures. I move toward them, peering at a group shot. It looks like it was taken when he was maybe fifteen years old. He's holding a tennis racket and standing with five other people. And then—

A voice.

I hear a voice outside in the hallway. *Shit. I shouldn't be in here.* I take a step toward the door, my pulse banging in my throat.

But that voice is getting louder now. It's coming this way, with heavy footsteps.

And it belongs to the very last person I want knowing I'm in here, snooping.

The voice belongs to Carlos.

Thirty-Eight

Fuck.

Fuck. Fuck. Fuck.

How the hell am I going to explain being in here to Carlos? Or Zach? I look around. Should I hide?

His voice is even louder now. It's really close.

"I'm checking now," he says.

I have a split second to make a choice: go outside and face him, or hide. I panic and hide behind the door.

Carlos comes into the room and strides over to Zach's computer, the phone held up to his ear.

And all I can do is try not to breathe too loudly as I watch him. But what the hell am I thinking? What am I going to say if he looks back and sees me? There is no innocent reason to be hiding here.

He leans down and stabs a password into the keyboard with one finger, still holding the phone with the other hand. An email inbox fills the screen, and then click-click-click, up comes what I assume is Zach's iMessage. Lots of gray and blue bubbles.

"No, I'm looking at it right now . . . there's nothing there," he says in a low whisper into the phone as he scrolls through. He pauses. "I know what happened last time, but I'm sure. There's no contact."

Then he turns around and heads back out the door and into the hallway but hovers at the entrance. He's right on the other side of this door. So all I can do is stand still and wait for him to go away.

But he doesn't. He just stands there listening to whoever is on the other end of the line.

I can hear the faint buzz of them speaking.

"Brian, just let me do my job," he says. "Huh? No, Zach is fine. He's too busy playing the hero to get in the way . . . No, the girl doesn't know anything. She thinks it's some superfan or troll . . . For fuck's sake, I know what studios are like . . . this isn't my first rodeo." His whispers are getting louder. Angrier. "Nobody loses their career on my watch. It'll be fine. It's always fucking fine. That's what I do—I make shit fine . . . Look, she's already in danger. We might as well just use her to end this, otherwise it'll never stop . . ."

More buzzing on the other end of the line.

"Yes, of course I called the press. You get that I've done this before, right?" he hisses into the phone. More buzzing. "Well, fuck Geraldine. Look, Brian, I'm doing what you asked, so just back off, okay? Fine. Sure."

And then I hear his footsteps fade as he heads down the hallway, and I'm left there in my sparkly silver dress with my pulse wild and my breath burning in my lungs.

Thinking *What did I just hear?*

I stand there for a little while, telling myself I must have misunderstood, as Carlos's words ring in my ears. *No, the girl doesn't know anything. She thinks it's some superfan or troll . . .*

And I don't want to be melodramatic.

I don't want to jump to conclusions.

I know I could only hear half of the conversation. But if Carlos is so sure that it's *not* a superfan or troll, does that mean he knows who *is* doing this?

And if he does know, then why the hell aren't we going to the police with that information?

And what did he mean by *She's already in danger. We might as well just use her to end this, otherwise it'll never stop*?

End what? And use me—how?

Of course I called the press.

Why would Carlos call the—

Oh god.

Time stutters.

The only reason Carlos would call the press is if he *wanted* me in the press.

But why the hell would he want me in the press?

I need to talk to Zach.

And so I smooth down my dress and go to the other side of the door. I peek around the corner and can't see anybody, so I try to walk casually back down toward the kitchen area. I pass a bathroom, and a man and woman are coming out, laughing, the man rubbing his nose like maybe they've just done coke. I head straight outside onto the terrace and look around for Zach.

The sky is a deep indigo now and the pool is bright blue, the steam still coming off it, and everyone has teeth that are inhumanly white and skin that is clear and pale or perfectly tanned, and they're all smiling, all the time. Laughing. Swaying with the booze. What the hell is there to smile about? And it feels like the world is spinning around me double time, like someone has pressed the Fast Forward button.

Where is he?

The guy I almost bumped into earlier walks past me with a silver tray of champagne flutes. I grab one. Down it. Then I grab another.

It's okay. It's okay. It's okay.

It's probably not as bad as it sounds. There's probably an explanation for it all. A very logical, sane explanation.

I spot Franz and Mary. They're on the other side of the pool now;

he's standing so close to her and her arms are crossed. And there is Amy. But where the hell is Zach?

And then I see him.

He's sitting on a deck chair, smoking something; I think it's a joint. The end glows in the dark. He's talking to a woman . . . sitting close to her. And something inside me twinges.

I down the rest of my drink and go over to them.

"Heya," I say as I get to them.

"Zoe." Zach grins up at me. "I was wondering where you were." The sweet smell of weed is all around him.

"Can we talk?" I ask.

He nods. Relaxed. "Sure. This is Charlie. She's also from London."

"Hi there. Charlie Buchanan." She smiles. She looks like the kind of woman who has a perfect life. The kind of life I was supposed to have. But instead I have . . . this one.

"Hi," I say, then I turn back to Zach. "It's important. *Really* important."

He frowns, but we head toward the kitchen. Then he suddenly waves at someone and comes to a stop, and I stop too.

He turns to me and cups my face in his hands. "Babe, Steven is over there. He's the producer I was telling you about. Let me introduce you; then we can talk." He takes my hand again and starts to lead me back to the crowd.

"Zach, please," I say, pulling him to a stop. "You're really not going to want me to talk to you about this out here."

Thirty-Nine

We go into his cinema room and he closes the door after us.

"What's going on?" he asks. He's looking right at me.

"I just . . . ummm . . . overheard something." My hands are shaking and I clasp them together to stop them. "I didn't mean to. I was taking a call and . . . I heard Carlos on the phone, and it sounds like . . . like maybe he knows who sent me that message, who left the heart on my windshield. Like he knows for sure it *wasn't* a troll. Like . . ." I bite my lip and stare him in the eye. "Like maybe he knows who is doing this, like it's happened before and he wants to use me to stop it somehow. He said he's the one who called the press. Why would he do that?"

The room rings with silence and I swallow hard. Because what I'm saying sounds insane. I know it does.

And he's frowning at me now, like he's confused. "Wait, what? That's not true. Carlos is protecting you."

"That's not what it sounded like," I say, shaking my head.

"Zoe, I have a whole load of people out there. I don't have time for this right now. We can talk about it later," he says. "Come." And then he starts to walk to the door.

"Zach?" I say. "Please."

He turns back to me. "I don't know what you think you heard, but you're wrong. Plain wrong," he says. "Carlos wouldn't do that. Any of it. Are you coming?"

But I don't budge. "I know what I heard, Zach. Brian asked him to do it."

My words hang in the air. The energy around him shifts. His face gets a little pale.

"What makes you say that?" he asks. His voice sounds different now, less sure. "About Brian?"

"Carlos said so," I reply slowly. "I *heard* him."

His frown deepens and he goes over to those red chairs, sits down and pulls his hands through his hair.

I sit down on the one next to him.

"What *exactly* did he say?" he asks slowly, his eyes on mine. "Like, word for word?"

I think back to hiding behind the door, watching Carlos go through Zach's emails, and I don't want to mention that part—the snooping—so I start at the next bit.

"First he said something about how I didn't know anything, that I thought it was some superfan or troll. Then he said, 'Nobody loses their career on my watch.' And then 'She's already in danger. We might as well just use her to end this, otherwise it'll never stop.' And then he said the thing about how he'd called the press."

"What were his exact words, about the press?"

"Um, like: 'Yes, of course I called the press.' Then he said, 'Fuck Geraldine. I'm doing what you asked.'"

Zach just sits there, staring at me. Then he sinks back into the chair, hands behind his head, his eyes clenched tight, and says: "Fuck."

He takes a deep breath. Then another. "Fucking Brian."

"Zach, what's going on?"

He lets out a big breath and leans forward now, elbows on his knees, his eyes looking deep into mine. "If this is true, and I'm not saying it is, but if it is, it's because my movie is coming out."

"What, like a PR stunt?"

"No," he says, shaking his head and looking down. "If he did this, he was trying to protect me. Get in front of things before . . ." He reaches forward and takes my hand; there's something in his eyes that is scaring me. "Zoe, please don't freak out."

I swallow hard. "About what?"

"I . . . ," he starts.

"You what?"

"Fuck, this is hard to say." The little muscle on the side of his jaw twitches, and then his words come out as little more than a whisper. "You were sort of right about what's been going on. But it's not just some random superfan or internet troll. I have a stalker."

My breath catches and the walls pulse toward me. Because a troll or superfan was scary enough, but a proper, bona fide stalker?

This feels . . . worse.

"How long?" That's all I can manage.

"A couple of years," he says slowly. "And yes, we think she's the one who sent you those messages. Put the heart on your windshield. She threatened Solange back when we were dating. Sent me notes saying she'd target her next. She even left a note at Solange's place. That's why I broke up with her. That's why I was so freaked out when you and I were in the press. I was worried something like this would happen."

"But, Zach, Carlos is the one who put me in the press. He did this to me. He put me in danger. Him and Brian."

"Man, I just find it so hard to believe that they'd go so far. But, I mean, in this business, anything is possible." He reaches for my hand now. "And if it's true, Zoe, I'm so, so sorry."

And then it all starts to make horrible, horrible sense.

That's why Carlos called the press, how he's planning on using me to "end this."

He needed Zach's stalker to know I existed so that she'd target me.

And then, if he followed me closely enough, maybe he could finally find her.

I'm bait.

A flash of my empty orange apartment. How safe I was just last week. When nobody knew who I was. When nobody cared enough to hate me. To use me.

"So, what? He's using me to catch her?" I'm staring at him now.

"No . . . I mean, I don't know," Zach says. "Shit."

"You should have told me about her," I say, my voice jumping an octave. "When I sent you those messages, when I showed you that heart. How could you have just pretended you didn't know who it was?"

"I'm so sorry, Zoe. I wanted to tell you. But I wasn't allowed to. I'm still not allowed to. But I *don't* know who she is. That's the problem—if we knew that, we could deal with it. And you only told me everything that was happening on Monday. Today is only Wednesday. I'm not that bad."

My mind swirls. I'm struggling to figure this out. To feel safe. Scanning through every face I've seen on the street, in cars beside me, in the shop. "How can you be so certain you've never met her?" I ask him.

"Well, I'm not *certain*," he says. "I can't be. I know a lot of women, Zoe; how can I be absolutely sure? But it definitely wouldn't have been recently. Carlos and Brian vet everyone."

Now I'm thinking of Sophie's drinks-thing, whether anyone suspicious was there, and the party I went to with Zach.

"It's *possible* I could have met her years ago, maybe gone on a date or something . . . ," he continues. And as he speaks, a sound bite floats back: *Zach has a lot of old friends* . . . "Like before any of this happened for me, but—"

"Zach," I say, cutting him off. "You know that woman, the one I told Carlos about—did he ever look into her?"

"What woman?"

"The blonde woman at the party we went to. The one who was talking to me? Because everything started happening after I spoke to her. And why was she even paying attention to me? Nobody else at that party did. They all pretended I didn't exist. *And* she wandered off really quickly as soon as my van came . . . that seems suspicious, right?"

Now I'm vibrating with certainty. I'm either going insane or onto something. I can't tell which.

"And there were all those big groups of people wandering in together from the parked cars outside," I say, my pulse speeding up. "She could have easily blended in with them . . . snuck inside . . ."

"Fuck," Zach says slowly, his expression changing. "Hang on, I think Carlos did check. He said he was going to. Said he was going to ask to see the CCTV and figure out who she was. But I'll make sure."

Frustration bubbles up within me. I shouldn't be having to sit around, waiting for Zach to make sure Carlos is doing his job. I'm in danger.

"This is crazy. We should just go to the police. When I went, there was nothing they could do. But if it's been going on for a while and she threatened Solange, you must have evidence of that, right? One of the notes? They can help us. Then we don't have to wait for Carlos to do anything."

He shifts in his chair, clenches his jaw. And he's looking down at my hand now, stroking it with his thumb.

"We can't," he says, his voice small.

"Of course we can," I say.

"No," he says, eyes to me. "It's not that simple. Especially right now. She has it in her head that we were in a relationship and I . . . did things to her. Look, she keeps saying she'll tell the press 'everything.'"

"Well, *did* you have a relationship with her?"

"No, of course not. I've never met her. She's insane. Look, a couple of years ago she started sending me nude DMs on Instagram. There would always be a rose over her stomach, so I knew it was her even though I couldn't see her face. We'd block her account, but then she'd just open another one and do it again. Then it changed. She started writing to me about all of these imaginary memories she had with me. Some of them were loving, but some of them were . . . She said I'd hurt her. Physically." He pauses and let out a big, shuddering sigh.

"Then a little over six months ago it all got even worse. I'd started dating Solange, and the messages the stalker was sending became really scary. The things she said she was going to do to Solange were terrifying. And then she left a note for Solange at her place, and I knew she meant it. I wanted to go to the police then, but in every message to me, she said if I did that, she'd tell the press everything I had done to her. She'd wait until my new movie came out and ruin everything for me. I wanted to call her bluff, but then . . . then she sent this video of me. Some deepfake, and it wasn't me, but it looked just like me, Zoe. You couldn't tell it was fake. And I was . . . I was doing terrible things. And that stuff, even when it's not true, it sticks. It tarnishes you. I was so scared of losing everything. I didn't know what to do. That's when Brian brought in Carlos. He said it was a better way of dealing with it. But I ended things with Solange so she was out of it. And the stalker hasn't been in touch since." He lets out another deep breath. "Fuck, I really hoped this was over. But Carlos warned me it wouldn't be. That she'd be back. He's been trying to find her ever since."

"So you never told the police?"

He shakes his head. "It's too much of a risk. Because what if she does what she threatened? If something like this came out now, it could ruin everything. If she went public, accusing me of whatever she makes up, it'd make the studios too nervous. And I have a reputation clause in my contract. They can terminate for something like this. I'm not established enough to weather it, Zoe. I'd lose everything. My career, my reputation, this house. I mean, I have such a big fucking mortgage on this house . . . Brian had to cosign. I'd definitely lose the third movie. So no, I can't go to the police. She's insane and too unpredictable. But that's the only reason Brian and Carlos would have done something like this. Trying to find her before she could do permanent damage."

My mouth dries up, and my pulse gets quick. Because great, just great. Just what I need: an insane person sending me *R U willing 2 die 4 Zach* . . .

"I'm so sorry," he says, his eyes welling with tears. "I should never have hooked up with you again. I knew there were risks, but I thought we could be careful. That she wouldn't know. And I was just so fucking happy to see you again. But I shouldn't have taken the risk."

Something aches beneath my ribs. And I was happy to see him too, so I see how it happened. And the moment he found out about the messages, about the heart, he tried to help me.

He could have just turned away, shut me out. Saved himself.

But now I'm thinking of my light switch. Of how it didn't work last night. Then of the electrical panel and the main breaker switched off, and my pulse is going wild.

Because that probably *was* her . . .

"Zach, I think she's been in my apartment block. My power went out last night. And when I went to check it, it was like somebody had turned it off on purpose." My voice comes out hoarse, almost a whisper. The gravity of everything weighing heavily, muffling me.

He sits and looks at me, frowning.

"Are you sure?"

And I'm not sure. But I nod anyway.

"Maybe *I* should go to the police then. Tell them about the lights in my apartment. Not tell them anything about you . . ."

He reaches for my other hand now, and he grabs tight, like he's pleading.

"Zoe, please don't. They won't be able to do shit unless you tell them about my stuff, and if anything about this comes out, I'll never recover. She'll say whatever she wants and I'll be judged and there will be nothing I can do about it."

"But what about me?" I say, my voice small and childlike. "I'm in danger."

"Why don't you stay here? I've got plenty of space. Just until we find her and it's over. Carlos will be watching you the rest of the time. And he really is the best. I know this is a shitty situation, but if anyone can sort it out, it's him."

I nod slowly. Mainly because what other choice do I have? I'm already bait now, whether I cooperate or not. "Okay."

"Thank you," he says, squeezing my hand. "Well, you know it all now, my deepest, darkest secret. Do you want to run?"

I look up into his eyes and shake my head, and he smiles. And something passes between us; it feels like we're bonded now, in this secret. But the truth is, I *do* kind of want to run.

"We'd better get back," he says. And then he stands up and takes me by the hand, through the house and all those hallways and back out onto the terrace, into the cool night air again.

"There's Steven," he says. "Let me introduce you." And we walk toward a short man of about fifty. "This is Zoe; she's a novelist," Zach says, letting go of my hand to grab a glass of champagne from a passing waiter. I have to clench my fists so my hands don't shake. "She wrote a brilliant book called *Fractured*," he continues.

"Great. Tell me about it," Steven says, then flashes a perfect smile.

And I can hear my voice reeling off the well-rehearsed elevator pitch I haven't said out loud in two years now, but all I'm thinking is: *I wanted this.* To see behind the celebrity curtain. To be close to Zach. To have a story to write. But now that I'm here, is it worth it?

Because here in my silver sequined dress beneath that sliver of moon, it occurs to me that there's a dark side to everything that sparkles: sequins, the moon, love, ambition, the Hollywood sign. Every Hollywood day turns to Hollywood night, eventually.

And every single one of us is lured here by that magic-hour light.

Forty

I can feel it. Even before my alarm rings, before I realize the bed is empty, before my eyes open to the flimsy white curtains waltzing in the breeze and the hazy view of palm trees outside, before I remember any of it, I can feel it: dread.

Hot and heavy, lying over me like a thin and weighty veil. Making it hard to breathe.

I reach for my alarm and turn it off and check my phone. No new texts. No new messages. Just one new stalker. *Brill.*

The blinds are up and Zach is gone; he must be working out. I sit up slowly, sound bites from last night playing at a low volume in my mind. First comes Carlos: *The girl doesn't know anything. She thinks it's some superfan or troll . . .*

And then Zach's voice chimes in: *I have a stalker . . . She's insane . . . No, we can't go to the police.*

And how the hell did I end up here?

In *this*?

And okay, yes, I know *how* I got here—the book. Zach. That magic-hour light—but why am I *still* here?

Part of me wants to get in my van right now, drive away, and never come back. But then what? And I don't just mean: What will the stalker do to me? I mean, beyond that, once all this is over, what about my life?

Because this is exactly what I wanted.

I'm dating Zach Hamilton. Felicity loves my pages and my pitch and wants to see more. Steven, that producer from last night, said he would email Barb for my manuscript. And if I had a story to tell before, I *really* have a story now. Because last night delivered a plot twist I did *not* see coming.

How can I walk away from all that?

Besides, would the other version of my life really be so much better? So much safer? I'd go back to my apartment, miss my deadline, lose my second book deal and have to pay it back, and start sleeping with Patchouli Jake downstairs again? Or sign up to a dating app and meet someone even worse? Or someone better and end up in the Valley with a white picket fence and a husband I don't really love that much? Or one I do love, who cheats on me with his secretary or our neighbor or my best friend? Or back in the UK, telling everyone about that one time I *almost* did something big, I almost *was* somebody? Because every story takes a dark turn eventually. At least I already know what this story is; I already know the dark turn.

And sometimes you just have to *play it as it lays.*

I sit up and scan the room. There my silver dress is over the armchair, winking in the morning light. And I'm going to have to put that on again. Because with everything that's been going on, I'm forgetting things now—I didn't bring any clothes for today.

I'm naked and the air has a chill to it, so I get up and quickly grab a hair tie from my bag, then rush to the bathroom as I put my hair up in a bun. I catch sight of myself in the mirror. I look tired, thin. I turn on the shower and check the temperature, then get under the water.

As I reach for the shower gel, I think: *Am I crazy to not just go back to the police?*

I mean, if this stalker is the one who turned off my power, then that means she can get past my security gate. A shiver runs down my neck.

A sharp inhalation of breath. Maybe I should go in and tell Barnes everything.

There's nothing stopping me.

Even that NDA had a line under exceptions that read: *Any information that could be considered illegal, a threat of harm, or an emergency.*

Surely this would be counted as all three? Surely this means I could tell.

Except, what could I say?

Nothing solid has actually happened since those messages on Monday, and the police already know about those. The rest of my story is full of "buts." I think she turned off my power, *but* I have no proof. I overheard Carlos saying some things, *but* he'll never admit to them. Zach could corroborate my story, *but* he won't; he has too much to lose. And what would I say about that blonde woman at the party? She was suspiciously nice to me when I looked upset; she dared ask how I knew Zach? Dared look at the logo on my van? They're not going to go and question her over that. I'll end up looking like some nervy, melodramatic woman who is reading too much into everything. And I'll alienate Zach.

I almost wish she *had* taken my light bulbs like in *Fractured*. At least then I'd be sure. I'd have something solid to tell Deputy Barnes.

Except now I'm thinking of Zach's voice: *I have a reputation clause in my contract. They can terminate for something like this. I'm not established enough to weather it, Zoe. I'd lose everything. My career, my reputation, this house.*

So maybe I'm lying to myself—maybe I wouldn't go to the police anyway. No matter what evidence I had.

Because I don't want to do that to him. Especially if there's nothing Barnes could do for me right now . . . especially since Zach will already hate me when he finds out I'm writing about him. So if I can just give him this, my silence, it might soften the blow. And it's not forever, just until his movie has come out. Besides, soon Carlos will find her and it will be safe.

I turn off the shower, get out, and wrap a towel around me. Then I head back into the room.

I dry myself off, reach for my dress, step into it, and pull the spaghetti straps over my shoulders. And as I reach around for the zip and pull it up, as I look out at the smoggy view, I scan my memory banks, searching for that blonde woman in another setting. Because if I'm right, if it *is* her who's doing this, if she's been watching me, surely I would have seen her again?

At least once or twice. In my peripheral vision?

Has she stood behind me in a line for coffee? Or at a food truck? Has she come into the shop? Has she walked past me on the street and I didn't even notice? And then gone home and pored over *Fractured*, planning her next move?

Now a chill rolls through me. Because I know exactly what her next move is.

She's going to trash the florist's shop.

Forty-One

Five minutes later I'm dressed in last night's silver dress, trying not to trip, as I head down that spiral glass staircase to the ground floor. I can see the kitchen and living area from here and I scan them for Zach. But he's not there.

Instead, Franz and Mary are both poring over some papers and a laptop at the kitchen counter. He's leaning over her, touching her arm as she leans her head away from him. Like he's wearing too much cologne. Amy is talking to a young man in a gray tracksuit, saying: "His foot is still sore." Genius and Randal are on leashes and panting beside her, so I assume she's talking about one of them. She hands over the dogs, the man leaves, and as I get to the base of the stairs, she glances over at me: "Morning."

Franz and Mary follow her gaze and look me up and down.

My cheeks get warm. They've noticed the dress. And just what I need this morning: an audience.

"Hi, where's Zach?" I ask Amy, pretending not to notice.

"Working out. He shouldn't be long," Amy says. "He asked that you wait for him."

And I need to get home, get changed, and get to work. I can't hang around here all morning. I look around, trying to figure out where to sit.

Franz gathers up some papers and moves over to the other side of Mary, making space for me at the counter.

"Thanks," I say, sitting down, and I tap intently on my phone. Trying to look busy and not like a woman in last night's dress in Zach's kitchen. But really, I'm on Instagram, thinking of all the new followers I've accrued in the last five days. And how *she's* probably one of them.

And there's a part of me that wants to just take control of this whole situation. Do something before she can. Post a bunch of stories and see who watches them first. Try to find her that way. But I'm too scared— what if I make it worse?—so I don't. Instead, I tap on my follower list again and scan it, searching the profile pictures for somebody blonde, somebody I might recognize. But it's useless. If she's watching me, she's using a fake account.

I tap through to my feed now, my phone hot in my hands as I scroll past baby announcements and book announcements and holidays in places with turquoise seas. A woman whose debut came out a month after mine has just released her sophomore novel. I like the post and keep scrolling, and then with absolutely no warning at all: there *I* am.

In two pictures.

I stop dead and stare down at the screen, my pulse speeding up.

In picture number one, I'm standing with Zach by the doorway, right before we went inside and I told him what I'd overheard Carlos say. But in the picture, you can't tell I'm scared. No, he's cupping my face in his hands and we're looking deep into each other's eyes like we're auditioning for *Romeo and Juliet*. In picture number two, I'm standing by myself in my silver dress, in the middle of the party, looking wistful.

Who posted these?

I glance up at the account—it's one of the celebrity gossip pages I followed while waiting at the police station. And: fuck.

Where else are these pictures posted?

I open my emails and skim past the junk and advertising and newsletters, and there it is: a Google alert.

Fuck.

So who knows how many places these pictures will end up at.

The stalker will see them. My stomach twists. What will *she* do?

And how did anyone even take these?

Although, I have a pretty good idea: Carlos.

He must have called the paparazzi last night too, to really hammer home that we're a couple and I'm a superb target.

I tap through to the account, then onto the picture and read the caption. It starts with: *Is Zach Hamilton finally in LOVE?*

Brilliant.

If she's obsessed with him, she's *really* going to hate that. I grimace as I quickly scan the rest.

Zach Hamilton and new flame Zoe Ann Weiss, who penned the book Fractured, *looked completely in love as they entertained friends at Zach's home . . . Zoe wore a silver dress . . . Rumor has it that the couple are planning a holiday following the release of Zach's new film. "It's moving quickly, but it's been going on for a while, behind the scenes. I've never seen Zach like this before," says a source close to the star. More as we know it . . .*

"Source close to the star," my ass. That's Carlos again.

I tap on the comments.

@Jent_82: She is such a social climber

@Jannnniiiiee: OMG Cringe. Nobody else is sparkling, what does she think this is?

@Dudette9090: It's just a matter of time before that ends

@KimlovesDave4: THAT WILL BE SO BRUTAL LOL!

And as I watch the comments flood in before my eyes, it's like they're talking about somebody else altogether. Like I'm not a person, like I'm just entertainment.

And is the stalker there, among them? Is she reading these? Is she one of the people commenting? Is she walking right into Carlos's trap? *Please be walking into his trap. Please do it quickly.*

"Coffee?" Amy asks, and I look up from my phone, my palms getting damp.

I nod. "Thanks."

"Black, right?"

"Yes, thanks. Can I get two sugars too?"

She nods and presses a button on the coffee machine and it whirs, then there's a buzz from a box on the wall—the intercom—and Amy goes over to it and presses a button. A little screen lights up and I can see a car. A face.

"It's Geraldine," comes a voice that has smoked too many cigarettes for too many years. Maybe yelled at too many people.

"Hi, buzzing," Amy says and presses the buzzer and then goes back to the machine to get my coffee.

She passes it across the counter to me and I take a sip. Mary keeps typing next to me, pretending Franz isn't bothering her; Amy is texting someone, pretending she likes her job; Franz is pawing at Mary, pretending his wedding ring isn't glinting in the light; and here I am pretending everything is fine. Like there's not some psycho after me. Like Carlos didn't put a bull's-eye on my back. Like I'm not secretly taking mental notes for a book I know I shouldn't write but absolutely will write. And it all feels so fake, so dirty. Like the sheen, the glamour, of Zach's world is fading fast. Like a layer of dust settled over everything in the night, muting the sparkle, revealing cracks I couldn't see before. Like everything anyone has ever told me about this town is true: it glitters, sure, but if you scratch the surface, just a little, there's a second story running beneath it, and that one is rancid.

And Zach is a good person, he doesn't belong in a world like this, but this *is* his world now. Now he accepts things like Brian and Carlos going behind his back as being part of business; he makes excuses for them. He makes excuses because god forbid the world think badly of him, even for a moment. And that's not who he is.

So maybe *this* is what my book is about, deep, deep down, below the plot and the drama: the invisible decay of the human soul when it's always on display.

But who am I to judge? Because I'm here too, in this world. Choosing to stay. And I didn't get here out of a lack of self-interest.

"Hello?" comes the same smoky voice, calling from the direction of the front door.

"In here," Amy calls back, and a short woman with black hair to her shoulders arrives in the doorway.

"Fuck LA traffic," she says as she comes over and sits near me. She doesn't seem to notice I exist.

"Coffee?" Amy asks her. "Zach is still working out. He shouldn't be long."

She looks at her watch. "Sure, thanks." That's when she sees me. A moment of recognition.

"This is Zoe," Amy says.

"Oh. Hi," Geraldine says. Icy. I'm going to guess she saw those pictures too. I'm going to guess that's why she's here. She's upset about it. I guess Carlos didn't check with her before he did his thing.

"Geraldine does Zach's PR," Amy says.

I nod and smile, like I don't already know that, like I don't know she's the reason Zach got Amy to call me and cut things off, like I know nothing. Then I sit in silence and sip my coffee quietly.

"There he is," Amy says, and Geraldine looks outside, past the pool, and I look too.

Zach is walking toward us. He's shirtless and sweaty and accompanied by a guy with a man bun. From the muscles on his arms, I'd say it's his trainer.

He slides open the door, says a general "Hi" to the room, then comes over to me and kisses me on the forehead. "Morning," he says. "How did you sleep?"

"Okay," I say.

"Can we chat quickly?" he asks.

"Zach?" Geraldine says. "A word?"

"Just a second," he says, and we go down the hallway in the direction of his study.

"Hey, so I have to go away until Saturday. But stay here if you want? I have a fuck-off security system and the dogs will be here," he says as we move.

My ears ring a little. Because no, I don't want to stay here, rattling around in this huge house without Zach. I'd be a sitting duck. Now that I know what Carlos has done, who knows what else he'll do if I'm here alone? I'm better off going home, where it's small and I can search the rooms in less than a minute.

"I'll go home," I say. "I can come over when you're back."

"Are you sure?"

I nod.

"Okay," he says, kissing me on the head.

And then Geraldine yells out, "Zach . . ."

"There are more photos of us," I say, my voice low. "All over Instagram."

"Fuck," he replies. "Coming . . ." And then he turns back to me. "I'll see you when I'm back then."

I nod. "But, Zach, are you going to ask Carlos about that blonde woman? At the party?"

"Of course, I've already texted him to say we need to speak. Don't worry, we'll get this sorted out."

Forty-Two

As I pull up outside my building, my gaze snaps from the pink bougain-villea to the street and the parked cars, searching for a woman watching my building, waiting for me. But there's nobody suspicious, just people leaving for work or walking their dogs, or striding up and down the street in activewear.

A flicker of movement in my rearview mirror—my heart speeds up as I look toward it.

But it's just Carlos, pulling over a few cars behind me. And as I watch him watch me, something blisters within me. Because this is bullshit. I shouldn't be in this situation. I shouldn't be scanning the street for a stalker right now. I shouldn't be scared to go home. I shouldn't be thinking: *Has she seen the pictures from last night yet? Has she read the caption? Is she angry? How angry? What's she going to do next?* And I certainly shouldn't have to be followed around by the guy who put me in this situation because, ironically, it's safer.

But here I am and there is nothing I can do about it. I turn off the ignition, take a deep breath, put my heels on again, and get out of the van. Then I stride across the road.

I punch the code into the security gate and go inside, past the pool, up the stairs, and into my apartment.

The door closes behind me and I look around. It smells musty, like carnations and menthol cigarettes; I need to open a window. But everything is exactly where it was when I left here last night in the same sparkly silver dress I'm wearing right now. But that's the *only* thing that feels the same today as yesterday.

I move through the clitter-clatter of door beads into my bedroom and unzip my silver dress, leave it on the bed, then pull on a pair of jeans, some sneakers, and a white T-shirt.

And as I go into the bathroom and look in the mirror to brush my teeth, I imagine Carlos outside. How he'll turn up to my work next. Always hovering, always at a bit of a distance. Just out of sight so he can see if *she*'s around. And as I put on lip gloss, I think back to what Zach told me about him: he has contacts in the police, he does security . . . But what else? Because Zach might trust him, but I don't.

Three hours later I'm in my work studio, surrounded by a printout of today's orders and some peeled-back roses I really need to arrange. But instead, I'm frowning at a page of pictures on my phone. Pictures of Carlos. Because I want to know everything about him; I *need* to know everything about him. This man who so casually put me in danger, this man I'm trusting to get me out. I mean, is he up to the job?

So far, I'm not sure.

First, I had to figure out what his last name was. I found it through a Google search: "Zach Hamilton, Carlos, security." It took a bit of scrolling but eventually up came an article with a picture of Zach and Carlos together at what looked like a black-tie event. The caption read: *Zach Hamilton with associate Carlos Santiago.*

So I typed that into Google:

C-a-r-l-o-s S-a-n-t-i-a-g-o, L-o-s A-n-g-e-l-e-s

I flipped to Images.

That's what I'm currently looking at. It took forever to load, but now here I am, sipping coffee that tastes like an ashtray, scanning through the images.

Clearly there are quite a few Carlos Santiagos in Los Angeles because I have to scroll and scroll and scroll before I find a picture of the Carlos I know. He's standing next to a celebrity I recognize from a sitcom. I scan down a little further. There he is again, in the middle of the page with an older man who's large and balding. I tap on that image and scan the caption: *Executive producer of* The Other Raven *with Los Angeles private investigator Carlos Santiago.*

Private investigator?

Shit. I think I'd feel better if he were a sniper.

I go back to the search results and keep looking. Up comes another picture of Carlos now, and from the color grading and the hairstyles and how young Carlos looks, I'd say it was taken in the late nineties. He's standing with two people I don't recognize, but I can tell from the caption I'm supposed to. They're almost-celebrities. Forgotten celebrities. I wonder where they are now?

Right, so clearly, he's well connected.

Clearly, he's experienced.

Clearly, he's been doing this for a while.

But doing what, exactly? Saving celebrities from stalkers by setting up unsuspecting women like me?

I go to the top of the page, click back to All, and change my search terms to *Carlos Santiago, Los Angeles, private investigator.*

Go.

Up comes a page of links, a few sponsored adverts for PI companies and workplace investigators . . . but nothing that helps me. No link to a PI agency *he* works for or owns. I scroll and I scroll and I scroll and I scroll . . . I scroll so long I have to press More Search Results.

And then finally—*finally*—I find something useful.

A link to a press article.

Click.

It's dated 2006.

The headline reads: *Carlos Santiago, LA Private Investigator, Acquitted.*

My pulse speeds up.

Carlos Santiago, 30, was today acquitted of allegations of intimidation and unlawful surveillance. Mr. Santiago had been accused of acquiring damaging information illegally as a means of gaining leverage for his clients, as well as ongoing intimidation of a journalist . . .

A chill moves through me. It starts at my mid back and rises to the base of my skull. Because he did it. I bet he did it.

A flash of his dark eyes as he helped me into the back of the SUV in that parking garage. The flicker of lighting above us. The practiced way he asked me all those questions in Zach's kitchen. The way he went through Zach's emails last night while I watched from behind the door. How Zach said Brian brought Carlos in to help with the stalker.

Then Carlos's own words on the phone last night: *For fuck's sake, I know what studios are like . . . this isn't my first rodeo.* And as I'm staring at the text, my mind whirs. What exactly is Carlos's job? This doesn't sound like standard PI stuff. Protecting careers? Intimidating journalists? Unlawful surveillance? Neither does putting me in the press so some stalker will show herself. It all seems illegal . . . covert. And then my breath catches and gravity gets a little stronger, because now another sound bite is floating back: *Nobody loses their career on my watch. It'll be fine. It's always fucking fine. That's what I do—I make shit fine.*

And *oh my fucking god,* is Carlos . . . a fixer?

One of those people who go in and make potential celebrity scandals disappear—by any means necessary?

And if he is, what does that make me? Collateral damage? How much other collateral damage is there out there?

My stomach clenches, but a little zing moves through me.

Because this *definitely* needs to go in my book.

So I go to my Notes app and I'm about to start typing when I hear: "Zoe?"

It's Vee; she's been at a client visit all morning, the BACK IN FIFTEEN MINUTES sign lying to everyone from the door. She must be back. As I listen to her footsteps come toward me, I close down the app, put my phone face down, and start working on an arrangement, like she'd be able to tell what I was googling if she caught me. And then there she is, at the door in her walking boot.

She frowns and comes inside. "Babe, are you still seeing Zach Hamilton?" she asks. She must have seen those pictures. But this is not what she's like; she usually gets judgy and prickly. Right now she looks . . . worried.

"Not really, I just went to a party last night," I say. "It was to meet some people. He's trying to help me. There's this guy who—"

"I have a really bad feeling about this. That psycho is still out there, right?"

I swallow hard as I take in her tense expression. Because Vee doesn't even know about my lights going off on Tuesday night. In part, I didn't tell her because I wasn't sure it was real. But if I'm honest, really honest, it was *mainly* because I knew if I kept seeing Zach she'd find out eventually, and I didn't want to have this exact conversation. But the fact that she's so scared for me right now, even without the lights situation, without knowing about Zach having a proper long-term stalker who is now after me, without knowing Carlos is using me to catch her, makes my insides clench.

Makes me realize the true gravity of my situation.

"Like, it's fine for him; he's not vulnerable like you are. But you could really get hurt. Are you sure you want to risk that?"

And no, I'm not sure. Not at all. But I don't really see a way out of it now. Or even if I do, deep down, I don't want to take it.

"It's all under control," I lie. "Nothing else has happened since Monday. I think whoever sent those messages lost interest."

"Okay, but, babe, he's not worth it, even if the psycho *has* disappeared. They never are."

And then her eyes fill with tears.

"Are you okay?" I ask, reaching out to touch her arm.

She sits down, nods, and lets out a big breath. "Joel is having another baby." That's when the tears start in earnest.

Joel, the married guy she dated for four years. He already has four kids, two of whom were conceived during his affair with Vee.

"How do you know?" I ask, stroking her arm.

"Instagram."

"I thought you blocked him?"

"Please. There are ways."

She lets out a massive sigh and wipes the tears away, forcing a smile. "Fuck, I'm supposed to be over this. I'm supposed to not care. I think if something happened in my career, I'd be okay, you know? But nothing ever fucking happens. I just work and work and work and for what?"

And I know that feeling too well. I had it for two long years. That sense that no matter how hard I fought, how often I stared at that cursor, I was destined to fade out into Plath's feared "indifferent middle age." I think that's why it's so impossible for me to just walk away right now, no matter how much it looks like I should. I don't want to walk away from this book. I don't want to walk away from Zach. I don't want some psycho stalker to ruin my life.

No, if I'm going to ruin my life, I want to do it myself, thank you very much.

"It only takes one break," I say, my voice small.

She smiles and her whole face brightens. "You are *so* right. And that could happen on Saturday. Everything can change in an instant, right?" Then she glances around the studio. "Do we have everything we need for Saturday?"

I nod and say, "Mmm-hmm," but *oh god. No we don't.*

Because these are the sorts of things you forget when you're being stalked. When your focus is scattered.

I remembered to call in the flower order. And we have enough large Lomey dishes and floral foam here. I think we even still have the fishing wire and little weights from the Garcia engagement. We definitely still have the right adhesive. But I totally forgot to get polystyrene wreaths, and nothing is going to float without those. Nothing.

Still, today is only Thursday; I have time. I'll go and get some this afternoon during my deliveries.

"Is your ankle going to be okay?" I ask. I want to change the subject before she asks to see anything.

"I'll be fine. It's almost better, and there is no way I'm missing Saturday. Besides, you'll be there." She winks and heads for the door. And I get back to googling Carlos.

Forty-Three

The air is cool and smells of gasoline and jasmine from a neighbor's hedge, and the sky is the color of rust as I pop the back of the van. I'm on my street now, not far from my building. I reach for the polystyrene wreaths first and loop them over my arms—I had to go to two places to find the right size. Then I pick up the stack of Lomey dishes, slam the van shut with my shoulder, and cross the road.

Usually, I'd make these up at the store, but I didn't want to be there alone after dark for obvious reasons. I look around when I get to the security gate, and I can see Carlos parked down the street in that SUV, watching me.

I awkwardly punch in the code with a single outstretched finger and let myself in. As I close the gate, Carlos drives off, and I carry everything past the pool and Jake's apartment. I can hear a woman giggling through the window, sense their silhouettes right behind my reflection in the glass. And that was me last Friday night. The night before this all started in earnest. Back when the only place hearts were left on windshields was in my book.

I set the dishes down at the bottom of the stairs and take the wreaths up first.

I fumble around in my bag for my key, push it into the lock, and twist. The door flings open. I go inside and drop them by the coffee table, then my bag on the sofa. Then I go back down for the dishes. I grab them, head back up the stairs, and close the door after me. I put them down by the wreaths, then run back to the door and put on the chain, then slowly look around.

Nothing has moved. Everything is exactly as it was when I left. Nobody has been in here.

So why won't my heart listen? It's still banging double time in my chest like there's danger all around me, danger I can't see, so I go to the bedroom, through the whoosh and clitter-clatter of those plastic door beads, and check that the windows are secure in there. Then I check the bathroom. The small window is closed, and nobody could fit through it anyway. I head to the kitchen. Again, the window is latched shut.

It's as secure as I can make it in here. And yet, I'm still scared.

So I pull a pint glass out of the cupboard and fill it with wine. I take a big gulp and go over to the sofa, and then I just stare at the little chain on the door for a moment as it glimmers under the light. But how strong is it? Could someone break it? Cut it? I take another gulp of wine and reach for my phone.

But shit, it's almost dead. And every time I look at it, I think of her. Of those messages she sent. Of my Instagram follower list. Of what she might do next. I just want one night of peace. So I take it to my bedroom and plug it in to charge next to my bed, then head back to the sofa.

From my bag I pull out the glue, fishing line, and the super-sharp scissors I brought from work, set them up on the coffee table, then grab the first wreath. I cut off three pieces of twine and knot each one so there's a loop in the middle. Then I tie those loops to the wreath, dividing it into thirds. I'll need them in order to attach the fishing weights—those help to anchor the arrangements in the pool, otherwise they float and won't stay put.

Once I've done three, I reach for a bowl, put some glue around the edges, then position it in the middle of the polystyrene wreath. The back of the tube says it takes ten to twenty minutes to dry, but I like to leave them overnight. And then I'm on to the next one.

An hour or so later it's dark outside, I'm a little drunk, the air reeks of glue, my apartment floor is covered in polystyrene wreaths and Lomey dishes, and all the windows are wide open so I don't asphyxiate. So much for security. I didn't think this through. I'm going to have to stay up until I can close them.

And now I'm thinking about that Google search today and those pictures of Carlos and how I haven't written about that yet. Haven't written about last night. Haven't written about any of it.

So I grab my laptop, fire it up, pull up my work in progress, scroll down to the bottom, and begin to type.

I write about last night, the sliver of moon, the party, the people, me hiding behind that door, what I overheard Carlos say. I write about Zach, about what he told me. About the stalker and why we can't go to the police. I write about this morning in his kitchen, about my cheeks flushing in my silver dress and those photos on Instagram, and I write about tonight, about my pulse speeding up and how my mind won't stop seeing threats in everything. I write about my Carlos Santiago Google search and all those celebrities he knows and how I'm pretty sure I know what he does for a living and that he set me up and used me as bait ... And I still don't know how I'm going to get around that NDA or how I'll cope with Zach's reaction, but I write anyway.

I write until my eyes are heavy, my laptop is closed, and I'm falling asleep on the sofa. It's my phone that wakes me, ringing from the bedroom.

My throat tightens. What if it's her?

I get up, my heart banging against my ribs as I stumble into the darkened room, the only light coming from the screen. But as I peer down at it, it reads: *Zach TOTAL DICK DO NOT CALL.*

Relief rolls through me.

"Hello?" I answer, sitting down on my bed. "Zach?"

"Zoe, hey, are you okay?"

"Yes, just at home."

"I can't talk for long, but I spoke to Carlos."

The blonde woman.

"What did he say? Who was she?"

"Oh, that woman you were talking to was nobody, a dead end. But, I mean, I talked to him about the other thing too. The press."

My insides twist: *Is he angry?*

"What did he say?" I ask, and the line breaks up a little, crackling. "Are you there?"

"Yes, sorry," he says. "I think I have bad reception. He said he *did* call the press, but it was to tell them to lay off you. To stop photographing you. He was trying to protect you. Stop the situation from inflaming. Geraldine was pissed about it because the press is her domain. She didn't want him alienating her contacts."

A flash of that news article I found today, how Carlos was accused of intimidating a journalist. So maybe this is true . . .

"See? I told you he was a good guy. And I knew Brian wouldn't go this far."

"But what about the other stuff?" I ask as the rest of the conversation comes floating back. "The bit about him using me to end this?"

Zach lets out a big breath. "Yeah, he did admit saying that. He said he was trying to calm Brian down, trying to reassure him that it would be over before my movie came out. And that he has been watching to see if *she* shows up around you, so . . . yeah. You weren't all wrong."

"Oh," I say, weighing it all up. This doesn't sound as sinister as my version. And it all makes sense. Maybe I *did* misunderstand.

"I just wanted to call so you didn't worry about it. Carlos is a good guy, and he's watching you all the time. And now that you know about the stalker, he can be more transparent with you. Anyway, I have to go, but see you when I'm back?"

And what Zach is saying makes sense, but also, I'm just not sure.

"Zach, do you believe him?" I ask.

The line rings with silence.

"Because the press was right there, taking pictures at your party. Does that not feel like Carlos called them again?" I continue.

I can hear him sigh. "I really don't know, but I can't see any value in not believing him. I mean, I have a movie coming out and we've been pictured together lately; the press might have been watching for more of a story anyway, with or without somebody calling them. But we're in it now. Let's just hope he finds her."

Forty-Four

At 7:13 the next morning, I stand exhausted, waiting for the kettle to boil, trying my hardest not to look at my phone. I've been up for around ten minutes and already I've checked my emails five times, and I know that's not healthy. But I can't help it.

I couldn't sleep after my conversation with Zach. I kept thinking about Carlos and what I overheard and what he'd said it really meant, and, well, I don't know what to believe. My mind couldn't let it go. Wine didn't help. Cigarettes didn't help. All I could do with the anxiety was write. So at around 2 a.m. I did a quick search and replace, changed the names, and sent some of my new material to Barb. And now I wish I hadn't. It was raw, needed a good edit—but she said she needed *something, anything*, that Felicity could work on it with me, and so I sent it. Because the only way any of this is worth it is if I get my book at the end.

The kettle boils and I make a strong cup of instant coffee, add too much sugar, then wade through white wreaths and air that still smells of glue and old cigarettes over to the sofa.

I sit down, open my computer, pull up the email I sent Barb last night, and stare at the words: *Hey Barb, here's so e mire material. Zoe.*

And no, that's not a typo here—I'm being true to reality now; I genuinely wrote it like that and I want to die.

But instead, I do the next best thing. I take a sip of coffee, sit back on the sofa, open Instagram, and scroll through the relentless good news: Books have been signed. Covers, revealed. There's a celebrity book club pick. A starred review (I never got a starred review). A couple of Bookstagram giveaways. A few of those celebrity gossip sites have been dropping fun little grenades into other people's lives, and at least there's nothing new about me. And then I see a post from my old flatmate in London. She hasn't posted for ages. She's holding a bump on her belly. She wasn't even dating anyone when I left; we were both living on biscuits and dating off apps. Comparing matches on the sofa after work. Texting any men we had in common the exact same message to see if they noticed.

I press the like button and tap through to her profile.

She's living in Crouch End now—there's a picture of her and a man standing on a street with rows of red-brick buildings and green trees and middle-class cars parked bumper to bumper behind them. I zoom in on her face, and something aches inside me because she looks so happy. Now I'm thinking of those nights we spent crying on the sofa, drinking cheap wine and wondering if it would ever get better. Our old flat is still in Greenwich, probably with the same shower door that got stuck, the same mold problem, but with new people living in it now, new dreams between those walls, like we were never there.

And it occurs to me how much has changed since I've been here. How much I have changed. And I'm not sure if it's for the better.

And then, with no warning at all, I see *her*.

No, not my ex-roommate. The other her.

Sophie.

She's right there on my phone screen. Grinning at the camera with the kind of smile that doesn't reach her eyes.

And of course she is. It's Friday—her big news day.

I squint down at my screen, telling myself to just scroll past, not engage, not read the caption, not this morning, not while there is still a stalker out there who probably has my face on a corkboard with a box of darts beside her, not while I'm fragile, but I can't help it.

My finger taps on it anyway and my eyes scan the caption. Quickly. Like if I do it with speed it won't count.

It starts with: *EXCITING NEWS ALERT! DEBUT SOLD!*

My stomach drops and either my hand or my phone gets hot. Really hot.

I can finally share the exciting news that my debut novel will be released in summer next year! It's a thriller about a bachelorette weekend in the Hamptons that goes very, very wrong when . . . And then the words all start blurring into one another as I read *the bride wakes up with blood in her hair, a hole in her memory, and a million dollars in her bank account . . .* and now I can't breathe properly.

Because it's *my* idea.

The one she said was "sorry, but just shit." She's simply tweaked it a bit. Like, mine was set in Vegas. But that's it. The solitary change.

What the actual fuck? How could she do this? How could anybody be so awful? Is she an ACTUAL SOCIOPATH? These are my thoughts as I shower and dress and speed into work this morning. I'm fucking furious. My skin is hot and sort of itchy and I want to cry but also scream, and I can't tell if this is all because of fucking Sophie or if it's just that I've been living off adrenaline, caffeine, and nicotine for a week and I'm tired and sick of everything.

I'm sick of being the victim.

Of her, of the stalker, of the public's perception of me, of Brian and Carlos's plan to use me, of the whims of my fickle muse and the pressure, the fucking pressure to write something great.

So I'm frowning, violently putting some orange-and-pink snapdragons into buckets of water, surrounded by the usual Friday brown boxes, while the printer whirs with today's orders and I hear Vee arrive. She stomps past me to the kitchen.

The cupboards open and slam closed again. The fridge opens. The tap turns on. I hear her banging around with the coffee machine. She's pissed off too. Why? I glance at the wreaths for tomorrow, stacked in a neat white pile to my left. *Does she know I forgot?*

"Morning," I call, my anger sidelined for a moment, in case I'm in trouble.

"Hi," she says as she goes past again and through to the front room. This is very un-Vee. What's wrong?

"Are you okay?" I ask, following her. She's staring down at her phone, stabbing in what looks like an angry text message when I get there.

"No." She lets out a big breath. "My scene partner blew off class last night. Adriana had to step in, and she didn't know any of the lines. It totally sucked and we had a fight," she says.

"A big fight or a little fight?"

"A big one," she says, firing up her computer, then looking at me. "She called me a bitch. Am I a bitch?"

"No," I say. "I just found out the girl in my writers' group who told me my idea was shit stole it for herself and signed with my agent, and now she has a book deal. She's a bitch. Not you."

Silence.

"What?" she says.

"I know."

"What the fuck is wrong with people in this town?" Vee turns back to her computer, reaches for the cup on her desk, and takes a sip of coffee, then says, "Everything arrive for tomorrow?"

"Yep."

"Thank god, one good thing," she says. "Now I just need Andreas to be there, and everything will be okay." I'm confused for a moment, but *ahh, Andreas Murphy, yes, the producer from Raya.* "I'm going to totally lose my shit if he's not."

She taps through to her emails and squints at the screen.

"Wait, there's something from Holly," she says. "The event coordinator. Apparently there's a loading zone out the back where we should park . . . You'll need to drive, obviously." She scrolls through the email. "She says it's dressy . . ." She looks over at me. "What are you going to wear?"

"I don't know . . . ," I say. But I know exactly what I'll wear: the only dressy dress I own. My silver dress. "What about you?"

"Something fucking extraordinary . . ." She winks. "Oh, and bring your swimsuit—look what happened last time."

Last time, at the Garcia engagement party, I had to get into the pool and physically walk the arrangements over to their rightful positions.

I nod.

Then the phone rings and Vee rolls her eyes, and as I hear her say "Venice Floristry, this is Vee" in her singsong voice, I head back to my work studio and start on today's orders. There's one for a Hemingway's Last Letter, so I go to the cooler and get out some irises, sweet peas, delphinium, lavender, and anything else in a shade of blue or purple. Then it's my tools and some brown paper. But before I do anything healthy and constructive, I reach for my phone. Still no reply from Barb. So I go to Instagram, tap on Sophie's profile, and stare at the comments under her most recent post, and my pulse speeds up.

Congrats Lady! Xx
You deserve it all and more
Woohoo!

And this deep self-loathing moves through me now. I shouldn't have listened to her. I should have just written that book. Then I wouldn't have needed to write this one and wouldn't be in the mess I'm in. Why am I like this? Why am I so fucking hopeless?

Then my phone beeps and lights up with a message.

Greta: *Babe, did you see?*

Forty-Five

I'm still texting Greta six hours later when I drive up a small street in Santa Monica to do my last delivery for the day, the last delivery before the big event tomorrow. The sky is bruised and overcast, May gray and June gloom finally setting in, and thank god for that. I couldn't stomach sunshine right now. I check the number on a mailbox as I pass, I'm looking for 727, but I'm only at 702.

My phone beeps and flashes with a message.

Greta: *I still think you should tell your agent.*

Greta is totally on my side. So are Rita and Tom, although Rita was quick to point out that while Sophie is definitely a "c-word," you can't copyright an idea. That did *not* help.

And maybe Greta is right. Maybe I should tell Barb. But how would that even go? I imagine the email.

Hi Barb, just heads up, your new star author who you're actually making money off stole my idea. Please unsell her book. Please drop her. My writers' group can attest to the fact that it was MY idea, not hers.

Maybe it would feel good, standing up for myself. But I just can't see it working out in my favor. I'm scared Barb will side with her, tell me to focus on the current book I'm supposed to have written by now instead. Remind me that everyone in this town has a great idea, but that's a far cry from a full manuscript.

So (and yes, I know it's bad to text and drive, but I'm going slowly, and honestly, this is not the most dangerous thing in my life right now), I write back: *I'll think about it.*

Then I press Send and search for a house number again.

There's a big brass 723 sparkling from a mailbox, then 725, and now I'm outside a pale-yellow Californian bungalow with a porch that has a sofa on it by a window, squinting at the front door . . . It reads 727. I look around. There's nowhere to park on the street, but there's a driveway attached to the house, and I'm right about to turn into it, but then I stop. My breath catches and ice rolls through me.

Because *NO.*

NO, NO, NO.

There, parked in the driveway, is a car.

A white one.

A Prius.

A flash of that night, after Zach's place. Me, talking to Dad on the phone, that white Prius behind me . . . Is it the same one? Now, I live in LA and there are a lot of white Priuses here, so maybe not, probably not, but also there's something about this one that feels dangerous. Familiar. Like maybe something deep within me is recognizing the license plate, like maybe that was the first sign of the stalker and I just didn't know it yet. I swallow hard and the little hairs on the back of my neck stand on end.

So I keep driving instead, my throat tight.

But what am I going to do? I can't just *not* deliver the arrangement *in case* it's the stalker because I saw a white Prius. That's ridiculous. I have a job to do.

So I pull into the first free car space and sit for a moment, trying to calm my breath.

Right, I'm just going to deal with this.

I grab my phone and the delivery note, put them in my pocket, and go to the back of the van. I'm hit by a cloud of lavender as I pop the doors and reach inside for the arrangement, then slam them shut again. I clutch the brown paper to my chest as I move down the street, but I feel sick.

What if it's her?

I get to the driveway, to the Prius. I look at the door. I take a step toward it.

But my heart speeds up and my hands start to shake and *fuck I can't do this*. It doesn't matter if it's crazy—I just can't.

I can hear my pulse banging in my ears, and there's a thin layer of sweat on my forehead now and another under my arms.

What do I do?

I look around.

There aren't that many people on the street, just a few walking their dogs in the distance. Nobody would see if I went up to the door and it *was* her and she did something to me.

I stand there for a little while, in the middle of the pavement, stress-sweating and clutching that arrangement a little too tightly now, the brown paper crinkling in my arms as I scan the street for Carlos. Where the fuck is he when I actually need him?

Nowhere. That's where.

I should just leave it on the stairs and run away. But what if I'm right? What if it's her? I *still* won't know who it is. But how will I know if it's her, even if I see her?

Except . . . maybe I'll recognize her. From the street. The florist's. Trader Joe's. Somewhere.

And so I creep up to the front porch, gently place the arrangement on the floor at the top of the stairs, and then run across the road and hide behind a red car.

I pull my phone and the delivery note from my pocket and text the phone number.

Hi there, this is Venice Floristry, I can't come in, parking issues, leaving the arrangement out the front.

And then I sit and wait. My mouth is dry and my eyes are scared to blink and, fuck it all, I'm almost out of battery again, and now is not the time to need a new phone. And honestly, how did I become this person? Hiding behind a car, watching for someone to come out? And how long do I wait? I can't sit here all day.

And then . . . movement.

The door opens. Quickly.

I see a flash of blonde hair first. Then the side of her face. My vision tunnels and I hold on to the car so I don't topple over.

Because it's *her*.

It's really her.

It's the blonde woman from the party.

She steps out onto the porch, looks down at the arrangement, and then runs out onto the lawn, looking around in both directions.

She's looking for me.

My pulse flares in my chest as I take her in. She's blonde: tick. Midthirties: tick. She's just like I remember her. Tick. Tick. Tick. I fumble with my phone, angle it toward her, and start taking pictures.

It's her. That's Zach's stalker. Just like I told him it was.

She goes back up to the porch, takes the arrangement inside, and slams the door after her.

I point my phone toward that Prius now, zoom in on the license plate, and take a picture of that too.

Then I edge my way out of view, cross over to the other side of the street, and run back to my van.

Adrenaline swirls through my veins as I press the unlock button, get inside, and slam the door after me.

I start up the engine, put my foot on the gas, and pull out of that car space. This is good. We know it's her now. And I have pictures. I can show Zach and Carlos and he can end this. I even have her address . . . I should call Carlos. Tell him to come here.

And it's then that I finally see him.

He's parked just down the street. Was he watching me the whole time? Was he even paying attention? His lights turn on as he goes to pull out, but I pull over instead. Because he's right here. He can go and deal with this right now.

Relief pulses through me.

It's all over . . .

I get out, take my phone and keys, slam the door to the van, and run toward him.

He rolls down his window, looking around.

"Zoe, what are you doing?"

My mouth is dry as I scroll to the pictures of the woman and hand it to him.

"That's her. The woman I just went to deliver to—she's there, number 727," I say, pointing at the yellow bungalow down the street. "That's her Prius. I think it's the one that followed me. I got a picture of the license plate, if you can use that?"

My heart is beating so fast I can feel it in my throat.

I watch as he swipes through the pictures. Frowns. Looks up at me.

"Zoe, this is not the same woman who was at the party."

My ears roar.

"It is. I promise it is." I need him to believe me. I need him to help me.

"No," he says, his voice almost . . . gentle. "I've seen images of her. CCTV. It's not the same woman." He hands me back my phone and reaches for his own. He taps and scrolls and I hug myself, looking around in case she's somehow figured out I'm here, in case she's coming to find me. Then he shows me his phone.

"This is a still from the CCTV," he says. "From that party."

And as I look down at it, time slurs. Because the woman on the phone is *not* the same woman I just saw.

"No, that's not her. The woman I was talking to is in that house."

He looks at me now with—what is that? Pity?—and says, "Zoe, I know for sure this is who you were talking to because there were people who saw you. And I went to ask her about it."

I look back down at the picture on his phone. And they do look *similar*, but I'm certain it was the woman in that house who I spoke to. Who offered me that cigarette.

"I promise you, she's right there."

"I can go and knock on the door if you want, but, Zoe, I'm telling you, *this* is who you spoke to at the party. Her name is Kaylee and she's a makeup artist. Like I said, there were a handful of people who saw you talking, including the valet."

And as I stare down at his picture, I'm suddenly *not* quite as sure. Because she's also blonde and also midthirties.

Now the image in my memory is melting, shifting, and oh god, I just don't know anymore.

"Why don't you go home and get some rest," Carlos says. "I'll deal with this. But you've been under a lot of stress; it's normal for it to get to you. You need to find a way to calm down."

My throat tightens and I take my phone from him and my eyes burn with tears because I don't want to be wrong about this. I want it to be over. But what if I *am* wrong?

So I nod and go back to my van and get inside, and as I put on my seat belt, the world speeds up again. I turn the key in the ignition and flick on my blinker, and as I go to pull out, her face flashes before my eyes again. But it's sort of distorted now. It's half the memory I thought I had and half the woman on Carlos's phone. *How could I be so wrong?* And I can see Carlos there behind me getting smaller in my rearview mirror, and I'm thinking about *all* of it. The breaker box. Me wandering through my apartment with that knife. My certainty that Carlos called the press to use me no matter what he said . . . no matter how much sense his version of events made—what if I really was wrong about that too? Because I've just been hiding behind a car taking pictures of a woman simply because she's got a white fucking Prius. That's crazy behavior.

And now I'm thinking: What if Zach's stalker isn't even coming after me? Nothing solid, nothing I can prove, has happened since those text messages on Monday. What if it really *was* just some troll off the internet, someone who *did* just want attention and now it *has* passed, just like Deputy Barnes said it would?

As for the rest—the lights in my apartment, me always feeling watched, the woman I've just been photographing—what if I've been so desperate to write this story that I've been living in my imagination? Letting my novelist brain go wild? Making it all up in my head?

And that's when I have the scariest thought of all: *Am I the unreliable narrator of my own life?*

Forty-Six

I tap ash onto the windowsill with one hand as I swipe through the photographs I took this afternoon with the other. I'm kneeling on the sofa, smoking out the window, my phone plugged in to charge, and this is the fourth time I've looked at them. I take another drag and zoom in a little closer, assessing the woman's features. Overlaying them with my memory of the woman I spoke to at the party that night. And I know what Carlos said, I know what he showed me on his phone, but no matter which photograph I look at, no matter which angle, no matter how many times I look at them, the woman in that house *still* looks familiar. I can see her in my mind's eye, right there in front of me, smiling, offering me a cigarette. But then, I can sort of see the woman in Carlos's photograph too now.

How can I be so certain and so uncertain at the same time?

But I need to stop this; I've been looking through the photos for so long, my phone is burning hot. I exhale and stub out my cigarette, then close the window behind me and look to the door. It's locked. The chain is on. So why is my breath still quick? It feels like I can sense her in here. Like there is something wrong, really fucking wrong, but I'm not seeing it . . .

My pulse thuds in my ears as I clench my eyes shut. Is this what going crazy feels like?

Maybe. So I do the only thing I can. I flick open my eyes, reach for my laptop, fire it up, and do what the mad and the damned have done for generations before me. Write.

I write about what happened this afternoon. About how certain I was. About how wrong I was. About everything . . . I write with so much ferocity and so many tears that the voice in my head doesn't even try to stop me. I start with thirty-seven thousand words, and by the time 11 p.m. comes around, I have forty-nine thousand.

That's when my phone pings with an email. It's from Barb, and my first thought is: *Finally*.

She's *finally* read my new scenes . . . maybe she's heard from Steven too.

Barb Wallace: *Zoe—I need a book. Not random scenes. Are you okay over there? The writing seems garbled. Where is the through line?*

And honestly, I don't know—where *is* the through line, Barb? So I give up. Go to my bedroom, put on Zach's shirt, get under the covers, and cry myself to sleep.

I wake with a jolt, adrenaline shooting through me, and sit up right away. The sun is bathing the room in orange, my teeth are furry because I forgot to brush them, and my heart is pounding in my chest. I reach for my phone and it's already lit up, waiting for me. There are five missed calls on the screen and one voicemail. All from Dad.

I roll onto my back and squint at my phone through sleepy eyes as I turn off my alarm before it can ring, and then I tap through to voicemail.

I press Play.

"Ummm . . . Zoe, it's me. I . . ." He swallows hard and his voice gets wobbly. "I saw something on the internet. Some pictures of you with a man in a pool. I'm really worried about you, darling. Can you call me, please?"

My face flushes.

My dad has seen me topless. He's read those comments underneath. I get a little dizzy.

This is even worse than Barb's email last night.

I'm fucked. My life is fucked. EVERYTHING IS FUCKED.

I get up and take my phone into the kitchen. The air smells of stale menthol cigarettes, and my laptop is still open from writing last night. But now that all seems so pointless. Like it's taunting me. I go over to the stove and turn on the kettle, then pull my fingers through knotted hair, and as I glance over at Dad's carnations, my old friend Shame is back. Because what am I going to tell him? How am I ever going to face him again?

God, he was probably googling for bad LA news and dear lord did he find it.

Maybe he's right after all; maybe nothing is going to be great and I should just go home.

I reach for his flowers and change the water in the vase as the kettle starts to hum.

And maybe I should reply to Barb. That's something I *can* do.

Explain to her why I'm so frazzled. Why the work is "garbled." Maybe she'll understand.

Because I haven't even told her about the heart on my windshield or that message *R U willing 2 die 4 Zach* yet. And I know why. It's because the moment I tell her that, she'll know what I'm writing isn't fiction. And she's been in this business for forty years; she knows about celebrities and NDAs. She'll ask if I signed one. And what if she and Felicity run scared from this book? I don't want that. Because I don't have a backup idea. And maybe if I can just make it good enough, when they read it they'll know it's worth fighting for . . . maybe we can work on it together to blur the lines to the point where we no longer have a problem . . .

I have to believe that. Because if I don't get this book out of everything, it will all have been for nothing.

The kettle boils and I make a strong cup of instant coffee, take a sip, leave my phone on the counter, and go into the bathroom.

I turn on the shower and strip off Zach's shirt, and as I get under the water, all I can see in my mind's eye is me, crouching behind that red car, taking pictures of some poor woman who happens to own a white Prius.

Why am I like this?

Honestly, I'm the psycho here. No wonder Carlos was looking at me with such pity. And what is Zach going to think when he tells him?

I let the water flow over my face, my hair, my back. I wash my hair and try to slow my thoughts. I take a deep breath and exhale slowly as I step out onto the bath mat and reach for my towel. I dry off my legs, my arms, my face and am squeezing the water out of my hair when it happens.

I turn to look at myself in the steamy mirror, thinking, *I bet my tear troughs are extra bad today*, and time folds over on itself.

Reality stutters and I take a step back.

And I swear I can hear my blood pump through my veins.

Because the mirror is covered in steam.

And etched in the middle of it, staring back at me, are three all-caps words. Three words I know too well.

They come from the end of chapter 30 in *Fractured.*

And they read: *SEE U SOON.*

Forty-Seven

I stare at the letters as the ground ripples beneath me. Because *SHE'S HERE*.

In my apartment.

That's the only way she could have done this.

I hold the towel tight around me, my hair dripping down my back as I tiptoe toward the door. What am I going to do if I find her? Confront her?

Will she hurt me?

I pull the door open, fling myself out into the living room, and look around. But it's empty. I run to the kitchen and grab a knife. Then I burst into my bedroom and pull open the closet—there's nothing but clothes and shoes.

So where? Where is she?

I run to the front door, pull it open, and scan the courtyard.

And then I stand there, holding my breath, watching for movement as my heart hammers against my ribs. But there's nobody here either; it's just me and my shaky hands and the knife reflecting the morning sun.

Even Jake's flat is quiet.

So where the hell did she go?

And will anyone believe me if I tell them this?

Especially after yesterday, after me getting it all so wrong. Carlos already thinks I'm losing it. And oh god, the steam will be disappearing right now . . . and along with it, the words. All proof.

I need evidence. Pictures.

I run back inside, leave the knife on the kitchen counter, grab my phone, and head back into the bathroom. The steam has cleared a little with the open door, but *SEE U SOON* is still there, still visible.

So as I hold the towel up with my elbows and goose bumps cover my arms, I take a picture.

I clean steam off the lens and quickly snap another.

Then another. Just in case.

I swipe through them quickly, and as I do, a shiver runs up my spine. Because I can imagine her here. Doing this.

I lean in a little closer to the mirror now and go to take another one.

But hang on . . . there's something sticky on the glass.

Like this *wasn't* written in steam, the way it was in *Fractured*; like it's been written in something else. Something clear and viscous.

That means she could have done it any time between now and the last time I showered, which was . . . ummm . . . Friday morning.

She would have known that as soon as the bathroom filled with steam, it would show up.

That's really, really smart.

And, fuck. I don't want a smart stalker.

That's when my gaze dips down . . . and I see it.

My lip gloss tube.

It's sitting right there by my toothbrush under the mirror where it always is.

Oh my god, is that what she used?

I lean in toward it. Go to pick it up.

But no, it might have her fingerprints on it. Or DNA. I mustn't touch it.

So I leave my phone on the edge of the sink, run back to the kitchen, and pull open the drawers, looking for a plastic baggie. That's when my breath catches in my throat and I notice the kitchen window. It's pulled closed, but not latched. Did I leave it unlatched the other night when I was airing out the smell of glue? Or did she open it?

That's how she got in.

Fuck.

I find the box, grab a plastic baggie, and run back to the bathroom. I turn the baggie inside out, put my hand inside, then scoop up the lip gloss. And as I zip it shut, my mind races through the plot of *Fractured*, trying to remember what comes next . . .

But then my ears ring and my breath catches.

And all I can think is: *What the hell happened to chapter twenty-four?* Where the stalker messes up her place of work?

Because this—the mirror—isn't meant to happen yet.

Now nausea rolls through me.

She's skipping steps.

And *SEE U SOON* is just two steps from the ending . . . the ending where the stalker smashes a mirror, slits the protagonist's wrists in the bathtub, and makes it look like a suicide. Makes it look like she made the whole thing up. Like it was all in her head.

And is that what's going to happen to me?

FUCK THIS.

I'm not willing to sit around and find out.

I care about Zach, I really do, but enough is enough. Carlos isn't doing his job properly—I mean, where the hell was he when she broke in and did this? I'm in real danger. So I need to tell the police. Now. Before it gets any worse. I can call Deputy Barnes—I still have his card in my bag. Maybe he'll finally come around . . .

Or maybe he won't. Maybe he'll just fob me off like last time. It's better that I go in person, I decide—show him the pictures, give him the tube of lip gloss. I'm going to tell him about the lights going off too.

Hell, maybe I'll just tell him everything.

So I run back through the plastic door beads into my bedroom. I dress quickly in jeans and a T-shirt and squish everything I'll need for tonight—my silver dress, swimsuit, spare underwear, and makeup bag—and the lip gloss in that baggie into my bag. Then I head for the front door. I run down the stairs and out the security gate and look around for Carlos, but he's nowhere to be seen. Great protection, he is.

And my van is right there, just up ahead, so I rush toward it, get inside, and put the key in the ignition, and with veins full of adrenaline, I drive.

I can't say what happens between leaving my flat and getting to the West Hollywood Sheriff's Station; it's a manic blur. All I know is that, as I park, I'm practicing what I'm going to say to Deputy Barnes, trying to figure out how to put it in such a way that I don't have to mention Zach.

I turn off the engine and close my eyes. And then I just sit there for a little while, trying to calm my breath. Recenter myself. I can't seem erratic when I go in there. I need to make them take me seriously. But all I can see is Zach's face in the dark.

In-two-three-four.

Out-two-three-four.

And I can hear his voice now too:

I'd lose everything. My career, my reputation, this house.

In-two-three-four.

Out-two-three-four.

I'd definitely lose the third movie.

And I don't want that.

But she's been in my apartment now and that's serious, and I'm too scared to do nothing anymore. I have to do this. I have no choice. So my eyes flick open, I click the button on my seat belt and reach for my bag, and then: tap, tap, tap.

Somebody is knocking on my window.

I look toward the noise, and a jolt shoots through me.

It's Carlos.

He's peering in through the window, the sun bouncing off his shaved head.

How the hell did he find me here? He wasn't at my place . . .

I put the window down, my pulse loud in my ears. "Hi," I say.

"What are you doing, Zoe?" he asks, looking over at the police station then back to me.

"Something else happened. She left a message for me inside my apartment, on the mirror. I took photos," I say, scrolling through my phone, then handing it to him. "And I have this." I reach into my bag and pull out the baggie with the lip gloss. "I think this is what she used . . . maybe she left fingerprints or DNA? Maybe the police can use it to figure out who she is? I need to report it, but don't worry, I won't mention Zach or any of the other things," I blurt as I push open the door to get out.

"Zoe, get back into the vehicle," he says, his voice calm but firm.

My breath catches.

I can hear my heartbeat. What if I say no? What if I insist? His dark eyes bore into me; the man barely blinks. A flash of that article I found: unlawful surveillance . . . intimidation.

Is he threatening me?

"But . . . I . . ."

"Go to work, Zoe. I have this under control," he says and hands me my phone back through the window.

I swallow hard, my stomach churning, and start to put up the window, but then he leans in. "Give me that, though. I'll do some digging."

He's motioning to the lip gloss, and I don't want to give it to him—

it's my one bit of evidence—but how do I say no? What excuse can I use other than "I don't trust you"? Then what would happen?

And he could easily reach for it himself, so with a shaky hand I hand it over.

"Zach says you'll be staying with him tonight?" he says.

I nod. "Mmm-hmmm."

"Great," he says, standing straight. "Have a good day."

And then he watches as I turn the key in the ignition and drive away.

Forty-Eight

I'm sitting in the garage at work now, watching the door slowly close behind me, my hands gripping the steering wheel as I think: *What the hell happened this morning?*

Because that wasn't normal.

I know Zach said he couldn't go to the police because of the stalker, I know he has loads to lose, that she might lie about him, but fuck that.

She was in *my* apartment. She wrote a message on *my* mirror. I'm in danger.

And I even said I wouldn't mention Zach.

So why couldn't *I* go?

And I mean, yes, Carlos was probably worried the police would look into it and find her and she'd spin her lies . . . I can see that. But would that really be such a bad thing in the end? If she's breaking in and writing *SEE U SOON* on my mirror, she's clearly not the best witness. She's clearly pathological. The police wouldn't listen to anything she said. Surely. And if they found her, all this would be over.

So what am I missing?

And how did Carlos even find me? He wasn't outside my apartment this morning, so he didn't follow me from there. Now that I think about it, how does he *ever* find me? He doesn't follow me twenty-four seven . . . and yet he's always somehow around.

And then all the air leaves the van.

Because: fuck.

Is he somehow tracking me?

I bet he is.

My ears ring as I scan the van around me: the steering wheel, the gear stick . . . My phone lights up, like it's about to ring, and I stare at it, but nothing happens. Then my gaze moves to the copy of *The Great Gatsby*, just beneath it—it's still half-read. How different everything would be right now if I'd just gone home the night I saw Zach again. Just gone home and read that book and said no to that party. I wouldn't have been in Zach's pool the next night, my bra wouldn't have been off, I wouldn't have ended up in the press with little black squares over my nipples, and Carlos would be using some other girl to lure out this psycho right now. And then my gaze lands on my bag.

Did he put something in there?

I grab for it and feel around inside, in the front pocket, the inside pocket . . . fuck it. I tip it out on the seat beside me and scrabble through my wallet and old receipts and a nail file and some crumpled-up pieces of paper I made notes on and never used, my portable battery that I really need to recharge, tampons, and a lipstick, but there's nothing suspicious in here. So where then?

Is it in the van somewhere?

I look up to the sunshade, the one above the steering wheel, and pull it down.

Nothing.

I check the other one.

Nothing again.

I feel behind the rearview mirror, then reach for the glove compartment and look inside, but it's empty aside from a user's manual. I flip through the pages, but nothing falls out; I feel around on the black plastic interior of the glove compartment, but there's nothing there either.

Maybe it's underneath.

I get out of the van and take my phone, turn on the flashlight, and look beneath it. And I'm not really sure what I'm looking for—what does a tracker look like?—but I'm guessing I'd see it . . .

But I can't see anything at all. Nothing suspicious, at least. It just looks like the bottom of a van should: lots of metal and the smell of grease and a warmth pulsing off the whole thing.

I stand up again, looking around, thinking.

Is it under the seats?

But then my eyes move to the phone in my hands and memories flicker in my mind.

That night I went over there, after that *R U willing 2 die 4 Zach* message . . . Carlos took my phone. I even unlocked it for him. Did he put something on there? Something to track me?

My stomach gets tight. *That's it.*

It's on my phone.

I scroll through it, staring at app after app after app, and what am I even looking for? What does a tracking app look like? There's nothing there that I don't recognize.

"Zoe?" comes Vee's voice. I can hear her on the other side of the door just before it opens. "Is that you?"

"Hi," I say, looking straight at her and doing my best to appear calm. Because if I look stressed, she'll ask what's wrong, and that would be bad. If I tell her about the mirror, she'll tell me to go to the police, and if I tell her I can't, she'll ask why, and if I tell her about Carlos this morning, she'll probe, and I can't tell her about Zach or his stalker because yes, I signed an NDA, but more than that, I'm scared to. I'm scared of Carlos. Of what he'd do if he found out. There was something in his eyes this morning, something dangerous. Something that tells me he did everything he was accused of and probably more. That he's not the kind of man you fuck with.

So I say nothing.

"What are you doing out here?" she asks, frowning. "We have so much to get done."

"I couldn't find my phone, but here it is," I say, giving a sheepish smile.

"Great," she says, and I reach into the van, put everything back into my bag, and follow her in.

We both go into my work studio and I can see floral foam soaking in water. All the roses and greenery are already out on the worktable, a palette of deep reds, oranges, and pinks.

I put my bag down. But I can feel my underarms getting damp with sweat, and I need to calm down. So I go to the kitchen and stand there for a little while by the sink, my eyes prickling with tears as *SEE U SOON* flashes in my mind's eye.

What do I do?

I'm clearly not safe at home, but I'm scared to go to Zach's place tonight, or ever again, for that matter. Because: Carlos.

I reach for a cup—but *find what you love and let it kill you* got me into this mess, so I grab the one that reads *Stay calm and carry on* instead and pour some coffee. Then I head to my work studio, sit down, reach for a rose, and start peeling back the petals like everything is normal.

"You okay?" Vee asks. "You seem weird?"

Fuck.

"I'm fine." I grin a little harder. "Just deep in this story I'm writing."

"That's great, babe. You can do it."

"Made up with Adriana?" I ask. I need to change the subject. Think about something else.

"Yes, we both hate the new girl now."

I reach for another rose and start working on its petals.

And what will Zach say when I tell him about this morning? Will Carlos tell him first? Will he be angry because he begged me not to go to the police? Or will he understand once I show him the picture of the mirror?

The phone rings from the other room and Vee goes through to it. And as soon as I hear her answer, I wipe my hands dry on my jeans and reach for my phone. I need to be quick. I type in: *how to find a tracker on your phone.*

Up come the results and I tap on a link.

The first few paragraphs are full of information on what sorts of spyware are available. It seems it's not just GPS tracking they do; they can do other things too. I pick up a few phrases like *read the text messages on a target device* and *listen in on phone calls* and *turn on the microphones* . . . but I don't have time for this. It's way too long and comprehensive, and it's stressing me out. All I really want to know is how to delete the damn thing before Vee gets back. So I quickly scroll past most of it, searching only for two words: "delete" or "remove."

And there it is. Right at the bottom.

How to remove spyware from your device.

Perfect.

I read slower now, carefully following the directions.

It tells me to do a search on the home screen for two terms: *SB-Settings* and *Cydia*.

Seems simple enough. So I pull up the search bar and type in *SB-S-e-t-t-i-n-g-s* . . .

But nothing comes up.

Fuck.

Next I type in: *C-y-d-i-a.*

Again, nothing comes up. Maybe I'm wrong. Maybe he's *not* tracking me on my phone.

I tap out of the article and type *can spyware be hidden* into the browser.

Two seconds later I'm scanning through the first link.

It turns out yes, it *can* be hidden. In many, many ways, apparently. Though I don't know enough about clever tech things to understand anything this article is saying or to know how I'd find it *once* it's hidden.

So I tap back out of it and go into the next link in case that's any clearer. And that's when my blood really speeds up.

Because this article starts with signs your phone is being monitored even if you can't find an app. There's even a neat little numbered list. It reads as follows.

1. Short battery life.

Fuck.

2. Your phone is hot a lot.

Fuck-fuck.

3. Slow run speed.

Fuck-fuck-fuck.

4. Phone screen lights up when locked.

Fuck-fuck-fuck-fuck.

5. Strange background noises when you're making a phone call.

Fuck-fuckety-fuckety-fuckety-fuck.

There are others too, but I don't need to read them. He's tracking me. He's definitely fucking tracking me. I'm pretty sure he's listening in on my calls too . . . a flash of that crackle while I was talking to Zach . . . probably reading my texts and god knows what else. And I have no idea how to stop it. How to delete this thing.

"Oh my god," comes Vee's voice. I close the search window and put my phone face down on the table. "Some guy just called to complain because his flowers were dead after two weeks. What the hell did he think they were? Plastic?" She looks at me now. "Babe, are you sure you're okay? You don't look right?"

I nod aggressively. "I'm just really tired. It's been a big week."

But inside I'm thinking: *I was right.* If Carlos would do all this— track me against my will, threaten me outside the police station—he would *also* turn me into bait. I heard exactly what I thought I did. But how am I going to get Zach to believe me about any of this? I have no proof of any of it, and Carlos has him totally fooled.

Forty-Nine

"She said there was a loading zone . . . ," Vee says, frowning as she looks around the parking lot from the passenger side of the van. "I think that's it." She points to a pale beige wall in front of us, a free car space, and a couple of pigeons wandering around in the sunshine.

I nod and slowly pull into it and the pigeons fly away.

Vee reaches for the door handle and gets out, and I take my phone from the charging port, grab my bag, and get out too. Carlos is pulling up by the entrance, and even looking at his tinted windows makes my stomach clench. I'm not sure whether I'm more anxious about him or the stalker at this point.

He followed us here, sat right behind us in traffic, me watching him in the rearview mirror as he watched me.

I follow Vee around a couple of corners and now we're at a grand entrance. A valet is taking car keys from hotel guests, and a man in a top hat opens the door for us. We go inside and over to the reception desk. A line of people stand waiting to check in while three very busy receptionists echo "Welcome to the Everett" and tap names into computer keyboards.

"I'll call her," Vee says. She scrolls through her phone, taps the screen, and holds it up to her ear as I scan the faces for danger. But there's nobody I recognize, nobody I've seen before. Nobody watching me.

"Holly," Vee says from beside me in her professional voice. "It's Vee . . . We're here. In the lobby . . ." She looks around and starts waving. "There she is," Vee says, hanging up, as a woman in long white pants and big hoop earrings walks up to us.

"So great to see you," Vee says, air-kissing her. "This is Zoe." Holly smiles back and shakes our hands.

"Are you okay?" She frowns down at Vee's foot. She's still in a walking boot.

"It's fine," Vee says, waving it away. "Almost healed."

We follow Holly to an outside area. It's paved in beige with two rectangular turquoise pools cut out in the middle, cabanas to the left, a bar with tables and chairs to the right, and a series of palms on the periphery. "That door opens out onto the parking lot. Here," she says, handing Vee a key card. "Just keep it closed. Oh, and we've turned off the pool pumps like you asked." Pool pumps create currents, and currents move floating arrangements around, even with fishing weights holding them in place. "Everyone will be here in three hours." She glances at her phone. "I have a meeting now, but call me if you need anything. Otherwise, see you later."

"Thanks," Vee says, and Holly wanders off.

Then it's just me and Vee.

"We need to take a *before* photo," Vee says. "So everyone can see how amazing we are. Do you want to be in it?"

And no, all things considered, I do not.

"No, I'll take it of you," I say. She goes over to the pool and poses. I snap a few pictures and hand her phone back to her.

She swipes through them, tapping and typing, and I know what she's doing, she's posting one to Instagram, and my stomach is clenching.

"Should we unload?" she asks, looking up.

"Sure," I say, and we go over to the door. By "we" she means "me." She swipes the card and waits with her sore ankle as I go over to the van.

I pop the back doors and look inside. The arrangements are all tightly packed in and strapped down. I grab the little bag of fishing weights, twine, and scissors and put them in my bag, then I reach for the first arrangement with both arms and take it through that door again.

I do that over and over until the van is almost empty. Then as I grab the last one, I look around. Carlos's SUV fires up—he's been watching, like I'm his prisoner under house arrest—and he drives off, heading toward the ocean.

Two hours later we're in the bathroom. I'm coming out of a stall, carrying a towel from the pool and dressed in my silver dress again. I put it by the sinks and take my hair out of the bun on top of my head and glance over at Vee, who is inspecting herself in the mirror. I had to get into the pool and walk the arrangements over to their positions as predicted—it was the only way we could get them to balance—so my skin is a little itchy from the chlorine and my wet bathing suit is in a plastic bag in my bag. I reach past it for my makeup and pull out my eyeshadow first.

"Do I look okay?" Vee asks. She's wearing a red dress that comes in at the waist.

"You look amazing." I smile and put on some bronze eyeshadow with my finger.

She inspects herself in the mirror some more, and my phone beeps with a message. My stomach tightens as I read the screen.

Zach TOTAL DICK DO NOT CALL: *Hey Z, I'm back, see you later on tonight. x*

I swallow hard, trying to decode his tone. Has Carlos mentioned me going to the police yet? Will Zach believe me about anything? Or has Carlos told him all about yesterday; has he already been priming him, making me seem unstable and irrational, so anything I say will simply make me look even more paranoid and neurotic? I bet he has.

"Who's that?" Vee asks, watching me in the mirror, and I look up at her.

And this is it. My chance to just tell her everything. To have somebody else in on this secret with me. Know what I'm going through. But when I open my mouth to say it, my throat closes up. And all I can see are Carlos's dark eyes boring into me this morning, and the words won't come. Because now I'm thinking of a couple of phrases I read earlier: *read the text messages on a target device . . . listen in on phone calls . . . turn on the microphones . . .* So it's no longer an if-I-told-her-and-he-found-out situation. Because if I'm right and he has one of those apps on my phone, he could be listening in right now. He probably is.

So I lie. "Greta. From writers' group."

Her eyes linger on me a little longer as she primps her hair in the mirror and frowns.

"I'm getting worried about you. You don't seem like yourself," she says.

"I'm just really tired. The troll thing was stressful and I've been writing a lot this week," I say, attempting a smile as I pull out my mascara. "I'll be okay."

"Well, you can sleep all tomorrow . . . but tonight. Tonight we sparkle." She grins.

"Agreed," I say as I put on my mascara. But I don't think I've ever felt less sparkly. I put on some lipstick, pack my makeup back into my bag, and take a deep breath.

"Okay, you ready?" Vee says, pouting into the mirror. "Let's go."

We head out of the bathroom toward the event room. There are photographers all around, snapping pictures. Flash. Flash. Flash. And now I'm remembering that night outside my apartment. Me: rushing to get inside, dropping my cake, trying not to cry. Them: running toward me. And the next morning: that heart on my windshield.

A shudder rolls through me as I move past them to a hostess standing at the door with an iPad, marking off names.

"Veronica Santos and Zoe Ann Weiss," Vee says from beside me as I scan for anyone watching me. Then the hostess nods and we head outside to the pools.

The sky is glowing a deep blue, and it looks like a fairyland in here. There are low yellow lights strung up overhead, our roses are in the pools, and the palm trees cast silhouettes against the sky. It looks like the sort of place where nothing bad should ever happen.

Vee pulls out her phone, "And now for the *after* shot."

She snaps a picture, types out a caption, and posts it to Instagram then says, "I need a drink." So we head over to the bar and stand at the back of the line.

Vee scans the faces around us as we wait.

"Do you see him?" she asks me.

"Who?"

"Andreas," she says. She shows me her phone. It's an IMDb page. There's a picture of a man with glasses, thick sandy-colored hair, and deep lines on his forehead. He's wearing a tuxedo—a black jacket, a stark white shirt, and a little black bow tie—and giving a smug smile. Above his face is the name Andreas Murphy.

I look around too. "I don't think so," I say.

Then her hand grabs my forearm.

"Wait . . . is that him?" she whispers into my ear. "Over there by the pool. Talking to the short guy? Don't be too obvious."

I follow her gaze and *maybe?* It does look a bit like the guy in the picture.

"I think it is . . . ," she answers for me.

We're at the front of the line now, and the bartender hands us each a glass of champagne, then we turn to face the party. "I'll be right back. I'm just going to do a lap," Vee says with a wink.

I watch as she walks in his direction, looking at her phone. If I didn't know she was going over there to talk to him, I'd think she was texting somebody. Like she was too busy to notice him.

Everyone is moving around me—chatter, laugher, elbows—so I walk over to the cabanas to get out of the way and stand there trying to be invisible. I don't want to talk to anyone right now. I just want to be still and breathe.

All around me swirls a sea of blazers and cologne and Rolexes and heels and long low-cut dresses and perfectly placed hair. At least I'm not the only one in sequins tonight. But after a lifetime of never being in rooms like this, I think I've had enough of them after just a week and a half. Everyone grinning at each other, their teeth bared, nodding so enthusiastically their heads might fall off, desperate for something. Terrified of going unnoticed. I'm tired.

And then a voice starts up beside me.

"Oh my god, are you Zoe Ann Weiss?" comes a voice, and I turn to look.

It's a group of three women. The one in the middle is speaking. "You are! I read your book, *Fractured*. It was sooooo good." She grins. "I saw it on TikTok," she tells her friend. "Are you writing anything else?"

"I'm working on something right now." I smile and push away Barb's comments.

"I can't wait—I'm such a fan."

"Thanks so much," I say as a little thrill rolls through me. I can feel myself standing just a little taller for a moment. But then they wander off without a goodbye, and I slump back into reality. My gaze moves to Vee, and she's talking to him now. Andreas Murphy.

She's grinning at him and he's grinning back, and I'm happy for her—this is everything she wanted—but then she looks down at her phone. She smiles up at him, says something. And then he nods and smiles back and takes her glass. She looks down at her phone again and taps and scrolls and then . . . she flinches. Her shoulders tense. Her entire energy shifts. And then she looks up and around, like she's searching for someone. And her expression is . . . distraught.

She sees me. Turns back to Andreas and says something, takes her glass, and strides over to me. Fast.

And all I can think is *Oh shit, what now?*

Because why does she look like that? And *oh god, the shop. The stalker has finally somehow broken in and trashed the shop. I bet that's it.* I'm imagining graffiti with slurs like *ZOE THE HOE* all over the walls . . . Or something worse.

What has she done?

Vee walks the line of tiles between the two pools and gets to me, and her hands are shaking.

"What's going on?" I ask, my voice wary.

Her amber eyes are wide and her lip is quivering and she's letting out short, sharp breaths, shaking her head.

"Vee?" I say, touching her arm.

And then she whispers, "She's dead. My acting partner is dead. I'm such a bad person for saying so many horrible things about her. I should have been nicer." Her eyes start to fill with tears.

"What?" I ask, leading her away from the crowd, out of earshot.

"My acting partner who didn't turn up to class," she whispers loudly. "I just got a text about it, from Christian, the acting coach. The police went in to see him and ask for all our contact information. They want to ask us questions. Why do you think they want to talk to us? Fuck, do you think she was murdered? Do you think they think one of us did it?"

"They probably just want to see if you know anything that will help," I offer, but something about this is making me nauseated. It's like I know something but I don't know what it is that I know.

She nods.

"It's just all so weird. Like, apparently her name isn't even Ruby. It's Jodie fucking Spencer. Why would she lie about that? Do you think she had an abusive ex? And he found her? I bet that's what happened . . ." She bites her lower lip. "God, she only got to one class, poor girl. I should have known there was a reason she didn't turn up on Thursday . . . I wonder if she was already dead?"

She's tapping and scrolling on her phone now.

"But I will say this: I *did* think there was something about her. Something broken. Like, I said that to Adriana. She'd be the girl they cast to play the dead girl. Look at her eyes. They look like something bad would happen to her, right?"

She shows me a picture. It's of a small stage. There are two people holding scripts. And as she zooms in on the blonde one, it feels like the ground beneath me gives way.

A flash of that woman at the party who gave me a cigarette. The one on her lawn on Friday as I hid behind that red car, taking pictures. The one Carlos assured me I'd never seen before.

Because it's *her*.

They're all the same. The woman from the party. The one I saw on Friday. The one on Vee's phone.

It's *definitely* her.

And now *I'm* the one who is shaking, and I'm dizzy, so dizzy.

"God, I feel so bad. I thought she was nosy and annoying, but she was probably just calling out for help . . . trying to make a friend."

Vee is biting her lower lip again.

And I want to help her feel better, but I can't. I need to get somewhere quiet, where I can breathe and I can think and I can figure this out.

And so I say, "I'll be right back." And before Vee can say anything to stop me, I turn around and rush back inside. To the bathroom. Because there is bile burning my throat and I think I'm going to be sick.

Fifty

I push open the bathroom door and rush inside. It's empty, aside from one woman standing in a long backless dress by the sinks, drying her hands. I rush past her and into the stall by the far wall, lock the door, fall to my knees, and vomit into the bowl.

I stay still for a little while, listening to the clicking of heels and then the bathroom door opening and closing as she leaves, trying to calm my breath. In-two-three-four, out-two-three-four. I reach for the toilet roll and blow my nose, drop the paper into the bowl, and flush. Then I put down the lid, sit down, fumble for my phone in my bag and frantically scroll through to the pictures I took the other day. The photos of that blonde woman. The woman I swore I recognized. The one Carlos swore to me wasn't the same one I met at that party with Zach.

Maybe I'm wrong. I need to be wrong. Please let me be wrong.

But as I flick through them, my throat tightens with each swipe.

Because I'm not wrong. This is *definitely* the same woman Vee just showed me.

Definitely the one in the picture from her acting class.

But why would she be there?

Looking for information on me? Trying to figure out how to get into the store? Vee said she was "nosy," so maybe . . .

So, what? She *was* my stalker then?

I struggle to put together a timeline. She saw me with Zach on the Wednesday night of the party. She would have seen the VENICE FLORISTRY logo on the side of the van as I drove off. It wouldn't have been hard to google it the next morning.

She would have found the Venice Floristry Instagram page, then Vee's page and all those posts about acting class. And then she turned up that night. Just once. Just to ask some questions. That's why she wasn't there the next week, not because she was dead like Vee thinks— hell, I saw her yesterday. She wasn't there because she didn't need to be. She'd figured out I did the deliveries and had placed an order with the shop so I'd bring myself straight to her.

But how is she dead *now*?

I need to know everything.

How she died. When she died. Where she died.

What did Vee say her name was? It wasn't Ruby; it was . . . *Jodie Spencer*?

So I pull up a browser window, set the search parameters to the last twenty-four hours, type *J-o-d-i-e S-p-e-n-c-e-r* into the search box, and press Go.

But nothing comes up.

Absolutely nothing. Which I guess makes sense—this is LA; not every death gets into the press. Not unless it's a slow news week, you're famous, or it's particularly clickbait-able.

I change the search parameters back to "Any time" and try again.

Go.

Now I have the opposite problem. Now there's too much. I hit Images at the top and frantically scan through the pictures.

No. No. No. No. No.

No. No. No.

No. No.

And then: yes.

There she is. Staring back at me from my screen.

It's her.

That's 100 percent her. That's the woman from the party.

But now every part of me is vibrating because she's not alone in the picture. There's a man in it too, their hands interlocked, cheeks squished together. And I recognize him too.

It's Ky, that bartender who worked with Zach and Will all that time ago. A flash of Zach and Ky coming inside from the parking lot that Valentine's Day I went down there . . . They were friends.

And now it's all making so much sense. That must be how Jodie met Zach. At that bar. She was with Ky. Maybe she used to hang out there. Maybe that's when she developed her obsession . . . I scan my memory—do I remember seeing her there?

No. But I only went to that bar three times.

The door to the bathroom opens, and three voices move inside and hover around the sinks.

"I mean, she's pretty, but not *that* pretty," says voice number one. "She's, what, like an LA six? A seven, tops."

"Maybe he gets into that tired smart-girl look. Some guys do." Voice number two.

"Or maybe she's, like, into weird sex stuff," says voice number one again, laughing.

"Well, it's definitely not her writing. I read her book. It was terrible." Voice number two again.

"I thought you said you liked it?" comes voice number three.

"I was being polite. And that's the same dress she was wearing at his house on Wednesday. I saw the photos . . ."

Then the other stall doors open and close, and I just sit there staring at my phone. Because now I'm thinking of that photograph Carlos showed me when I was freaking out. The one he assured me was of the woman I was talking to at the party, like I was losing my mind . . . but no.

Carlos lied to me.

He knew I was right, it *was* her, and he lied.

Why would he do that?

Why would he show me a picture of a different woman altogether? And why would he have the picture right there on his phone, ready to lie?

Unless . . . he knew he'd have to lie. He was ready to lie. He planned on it . . . He didn't want me to know it was her.

Oh god. Fuck.

Did he do this?

Did he kill her?

My breath gets quick and shallow now.

He did. I bet he did.

Did he *always* know he was going to kill her when he found her?

Probably.

And now I'm thinking about Carlos this morning, how threatening he was. How he wouldn't let me walk into that police station.

This is why.

If my gut is right about this—*is it right?*—he killed Jodie yesterday after I showed him where she lived. So he *knew* she was dead. He *knew* the police had probably already found her body, that they'd fingerprint her during the autopsy. So how could he let me wander into that police station with a tube of lip gloss that might have her fingerprints or DNA on it? He couldn't be sure of what I'd say. Would I *only* say that she'd been stalking me? Or would I buckle and tell them that she'd also been stalking Zach for years? That I'd overheard Carlos say he was going to "end it" on the phone to Brian? Because if I did that, they might put two and two together. They might start asking inconvenient questions of him. Maybe ask more of me . . . show me Jodie's picture and ask if I recognized her . . . then I'd show them the pictures I'd taken of her outside her house. Tell them Carlos had been right there on the day she died. Everything could come crashing down.

And how would he get out of that one?

It was too big a risk; it could go too wrong.

But *oh god, all the questions I've been asking.*

How I walked right up to him and told him I was certain it was *her* I saw at the party. I was right, but now Carlos knows I recognized her. I could pick her out of a group of pictures again . . . My stomach twists.

Because if he killed this woman, Jodie, would he hurt me too? Probably.

If he saw me as a threat.

Now all the blood drains from my head and I start to sweat. Because I'm thinking of that long article about all the things spy apps can do. And . . . I don't even want to think it . . . really I don't, but can it see my search history?

Can he see that I googled him?

That I googled *Jodie Spencer*?

That I googled *how to find a tracker on your phone*? Is that possible? My heart speeds up. *Fuck.* What if it is?

The three women are outside now, faucets going, then hand dryers. They're talking about some TV show I haven't seen. And I'm staring at my phone, chewing on my inner cheek. How do I go to the police now and tell them what I suspect? Because I *have* to tell them. Someone is dead. And it's my fault.

I'm the one who told him where to find her. I pointed out her house. *Oh god.*

The door opens and closes, and now it's just me in here.

How do I do this?

My heart beats loud in my ears as I formulate a loose plan. All I need is a window of time when nobody knows where I am.

So first, I go to my text messages, find Zach's last message, and reply with: *Can't wait, see you soon! Xxx.*

I don't want to lie to him, I want to tell him everything, but Carlos may well be reading my messages.

Send.

Next, I go to text Vee, to tell her I'm leaving, but I stop myself. I can't. It's too risky.

Instead, I pull up a draft email and attach the photographs of the heart, the messages, the *SEE U SOON* message on my mirror, and the ones I took of Jodie and her Prius yesterday. I'll need them to show the police.

Save.

And then, I text Dad. I text him because when all this is over, it's time for me to make a change. A big one. That's the promise I make to myself.

Hi dad, I've thought about what you said, maybe you're right. It's time to come home. Let's chat soon. Love you so much. Zoe xxx

I look around. There's a sanitary bin right beside me, so I hide my phone behind it. I can come back later tonight or tomorrow and get it with a nice, safe police escort. But that means if Carlos is watching me with his tracker, he won't know where I'm going, because he won't even know that I've left. And then I stand up and open that stall door.

Fifty-One

I edge past the mirror, pull open the door, and scan the lobby. Carlos isn't there. The photographers have all dispersed. And I can see a green EXIT sign glowing to my right.

I stand up straight and quickly walk toward it. I can hear the party outside, imagine Vee there, talking to people, networking, wondering where I am, but at least she's safe, and I need to get out of here so I'm safe too.

I push through a door, and now it looks like I'm in a staff area. People in white uniforms are looking at me in my sparkly dress. But I just keep following the signs, walking past them. I get confused looks, but none of them are paid enough to care. I turn down a long hallway, following the exit signs, and a young guy in a white uniform is walking toward me, frowning. "You're not meant to be in here," he says.

"Sorry, I'm lost. I need to find my car. It's parked in the loading zone outside the pools?"

"You need to go back that way," he says, pointing to where I came from.

My breath catches. "Is there another way?" I ask. And he must see the desperation in my eyes because something shifts behind his and he nods, slowly.

"Sure, keep going that way and you'll come to a big metal door. Go out and past the dumpsters and turn right. Then circle back."

I nod and rush in the direction he pointed, and he keeps walking down that hallway.

And then I'm there, at the big metal door, and I know it leads outside, and what if I'm wrong—what if Carlos is out there? Waiting?

I hold my breath and slowly push it open, my pulse quick as I scan for danger. What would he do if he realized I was onto him? If he realized what I was doing right now?

But there's no movement out there aside from headlights and beeping from a street in the distance, behind the hedge. I step out into the parking lot and let the door bang behind me. The air is cool on my bare arms as I rush past the dumpsters—the stench of rubbish, a few rats scuttling—and turn right like the guy told me to. But where am I? Where's my van? I look left, right, my heart beating faster and faster, and then I see it. Parked right where I left it. I run toward it, grabbing for my keys in my bag, holding them between my fingers.

Everything will be fine. I'll go to the police and tell them what I know and they will help me . . .

My hands shake as I press the unlock button and get inside and re-lock the doors after me. Click.

I quickly take off my heels, put my foot on the brake pedal, push the key into the ignition and turn. I switch on my headlights and take off the hand brake. And then I shift the gear stick into reverse, practicing what I'm going to say to the police. But as I glance into the rearview mirror to back out, time warps and stretches. My ears ring. And I can't see anything other than a dark silhouette behind me.

A blinding panic rolls through me.

I reach for the door handle, open my mouth to scream.

But a hand comes forward now, grabs me over the mouth, and pulls me backward. Hard.

My head hits the headrest.

What's happening?

Something comes around my neck—is that a belt?—and I hear it fasten behind me. The clinking of the metal buckle. I want to scream. But I can't. That hand is too tight around my mouth . . . I can't breathe.

My eyes dart back to the rearview mirror, searching for a face. Carlos. This has to be Carlos.

But all I can see is the outline of a head. The faint gleam of two eyes. And then I hear, "Don't."

One word. Whispered.

That's when I feel the other thing. Something small, hard, and circular pushing into my skull. It twirls around my hair a little and makes the little hairs on the back of my neck stand on end.

Because *oh god* . . .

Is that a gun?

Fifty-Two

I always thought I'd be good in a crisis like this, that I'd somehow know what to do. But all I can say about that is: I was wrong. It feels like I'm frozen. I can hear everything at volume: my own breathing, the sound of the van idling, the blood moving through my veins. And my vision has snapped to such high definition I can make out the texture of the paint on the wall in front of me, lit up by my headlights. But I'm struggling to even inhale.

"Keep your eyes forward and back out of here," comes that dark whisper again as the gun presses a little harder into my skull and nausea rolls through me.

And my instinct is to reach for the door handle. To escape. But there is a belt around my neck, holding me to the seat, and that gun is still pressing into my skull, and I don't want to die. I don't want this beige wall in front of me to be the last thing I see.

So I do nothing. Absolutely nothing. I just grip the steering wheel, my knuckles white and my breath so quick now I'm getting dizzy.

Maybe someone will come outside.

See us.

Call somebody.

"Drive," he hisses from behind me. "Now."

And I can't think straight and I'm scared to look back again and piss him off, so I ease my foot off the brake and hit the gas, and the van jolts backward as I turn the wheel.

I hit the brakes, shift gears, turn the wheel toward the road, and start to drive.

And now I'm heading for the exit and I don't want to be and *don't you dare have a panic attack right now, Zoe.*

Just breathe. In-two-three-four, out-two-three-four, in-two-three-four . . .

My hands shake as I get to the exit.

"Turn left," comes that whisper again, and I do as he says, glancing quickly back at him, then back to the road.

It's not Carlos. His shape is different—his shoulders aren't as wide.

It must be someone he hired.

This is because I asked so many questions about Jodie Spencer. Because I took those photos. Because I googled him. Because I pushed it. Why couldn't I just shut the fuck up?

Now he thinks I know too much, and now that she's dead he wants me gone too in case I tell somebody. *He's hired someone to kill me.*

I shouldn't have gone to the police this morning. That was my other mistake.

I should have just played along. Done what he told me to.

Fuck.

Fuck. Fuck. Fuck.

But Brian wouldn't have okayed this. Zach wouldn't let him hurt me . . . unless Carlos has gone rogue. Decided to deal with things his way. *End* things his way. He didn't tell Zach about using me as bait; maybe he hasn't told him about this either.

"Go right on Fourth," comes the voice again.

I can see the turn up ahead, and I take it.

And as the streetlights whoosh past, I have a flash of the life I was meant to have. The books. The book tours. The . . . I don't know . . .

joy. A flash of me pitching my book to Barb. The book that got me here. But all that fades away, and now all I can think about is Dad's face, and I have to get back to him. I have to hug him again. My eyes prick with tears as I think of his name flashing up on my phone. I bite down on my lip. I don't want to cry; it might make things worse. I need to be strong. But my breath starts to shudder and my cheeks are wet with tears and—

What's he doing?

He's reaching forward and grabbing my bag; I can see it in my peripheral vision. I can hear him riffling through it behind me now. What's he looking for?

"Where's your phone?" he asks, and the gun nudges into my skull a little harder.

Ice rolls through me. "I left it at the hotel," I say, choking on my tears.

He doesn't want the police to be able to track me . . . or maybe Carlos told him to get it so they could take the tracker off . . .

"You'd better not fucking lie to me," he hisses. "I have no problem killing you." A shiver runs up my spine—he's telling the truth, I can feel it.

"I promise," I say.

And then he drops my bag back onto the seat beside me.

Now everything is blurring into everything else, panic rolling through me. Maybe I should start beeping my horn. Then someone will see and we'll have to stop. But this is LA; they'll think I'm high and probably clap, and there's a gun pressing against my skull. Maybe I should crash into a shop. Stop us that way. They're all closed. I wouldn't hurt anybody. But I have a belt around my neck; the impact will probably strangle me or break my neck.

"Where are we going?" I ask. Maybe if I make conversation with him, I can calm him down. Make him not kill me. Remind him that I'm a person.

But he doesn't reply. And all I can do is watch houses and palm trees swirl by, that belt biting into my neck every time I try to pull away and *hang on . . . why are we heading back here?* Because now we're at Electric Avenue and I recognize everything.

And then I hear: "Drive to the alleyway behind the florist's."

Everything inside me clenches and my skin gets cold.

Because I don't want to. There's no CCTV there. There's nothing, aside from dumpsters and darkness.

But I do what he says. And now we're crossing Abbott Kinney and I'm willing someone to see us, stop us, but nobody does. Now there's the turn and my hands start to shake as I take it. Because *oh god, I know why he's bringing me here.* It's quiet. Dark. Empty.

There's a juice bar that closes at 6 p.m. on one side and an empty store on the other.

And then I hear: "Open the garage."

But I can't. I'm frozen. And I can't breathe.

I'm going to end up in one of those dumpsters.

The gun presses harder into my skull, and I don't want to die right here, right now. Every breath matters.

So I reach for the button and press it, and the garage door slowly rolls up.

"Drive inside."

My breath is so shallow I'm pretty sure I'm going to pass out, but I do what he says. And the moment we're in there, I think: *I was wrong.* I should have smashed the van into something. Beeped the horn. I should have done *anything* but come here.

Because now I'm going to die. I'm going to die just like the character in my book.

Fifty-Three

My mouth gets sour and the van warps around me. *Oh god, I'm going to throw up again.* A hand reaches forward and takes the keys from the ignition and I can see it clearly now.

It's wearing a glove. A leather one. And a long black sleeve.

And I'm cataloging details like that because maybe they will help the police identify him. When I get out of here.

Please let me get out of here.

I hear the doors click as they unlock. And then the clickety-click-click sound of the garage door coming down. I've heard that sound a thousand times before, but right now it sounds eerie, sinister.

Then that hand comes forward again, and it's holding a mask this time—a sleeping mask. "Put this on."

I do what he says and the world goes dark. All I can see are thin fragments of light seeping in from the edges.

The gun moves away and I hear the belt around my neck being unbuckled; pressure releases from my throat as he takes it off me. But then the gun is back, pressed against the side of my head.

I hear the back doors of the van open and then . . . footsteps. But the gun is still there.

There are two of them.

My van door opens now. A hand reaches in and helps me get out.

And as we walk to the back door and I try not to trip, I'm thinking, *It is Saturday night and the shop is closed until Monday morning.* Vee gets in at nine. That means nobody will be here to help me for, what, twelve . . . twenty-four . . . thirty-six hours.

That's if they let me live for thirty-six hours.

The keys jangle and the door opens and we go inside and I'm met with the familiar smell of white vinegar, the earthiness of the greenery, and the sweet smell of freshly cut roses. The same roses that are floating in pools at the hotel where I should be . . . I should never have left. A flash of Vee out by the pools, networking. Oblivious. Then my phone in that bathroom stall.

Will someone find it? Wonder what happened to me?

We walk a little and I know the layout well, so I know that right now we're entering my work studio. And this is good. If they leave me in here, I can find a weapon. There are drawers full of pruning shears and knives and snips and scissors. There's bleach and white vinegar and other cleaning supplies in the cupboard under the sink. There are heavy vases I can swing. A laptop I could use to email for help. I just need them to leave me alone.

Above the roar of blood in my ears, I can hear them whispering quietly to one another, but I can't make out what they're saying.

Someone grabs my hands and holds them in front of me; I hear the screech of tape being pulled off a roll and my insides freeze.

But there's nothing I can do. They have a gun, and there are walls upon walls around us now. If I screamed, nobody would hear. I just have to stand there, whimpering, as my wrists are taped together.

Another screech. Tape is put over my mouth.

And then they walk me to the far side of the room, past the sink, and I want to run because I can see it in my mind's eye. I know where we're going.

I hear a door open and I'm hit by the combined smell of cut flowers and preservatives; I feel the chilled air on my cheeks. The humidity clinging to my skin.

The flower cooler.

They push me in and close the door after me.

And then click, I'm locked inside.

Fifty-Four

So I guess this is it. What happens behind the celebrity curtain. The exact story I pitched to Barb, the story I was looking for. It ends in this cold room that's eight feet high and six feet wide, with me sharing the oxygen supply with peonies and roses and snapdragons and everything else I was planning on using on Monday for orders I'll never get to deliver now.

Goose bumps cover my bare arms as I mentally scan for an escape. Because there has to be one.

But the door is locked.

There are no windows.

And there's a fan in here, but no ventilation. Or if there is ventilation, there's very little, and certainly nothing I can climb through. Even if my hands weren't taped together. I know this because it's better for keeping the flowers fresh, but not so great for keeping me alive if I'm in here for too long.

I move slowly, carefully, trying not to trip over my dress as I use shelves to feel my way around. I sit on the cold concrete floor in the corner, my hands in my lap, as I shake and the last ten days fill my mind in the darkness. The night I saw Zach again, that magic-hour light, the party, Solange, the hazy view of palm trees from his window, his hands on me in the pool, that article, the trolls, my book on TikTok, the night with Jake, that heart on my windshield . . . and then it starts speeding up, the flashcards flipping forward: overhearing Carlos, the blonde woman on her lawn, my photographs, the police station, Carlos at my window, tap-tap-tap, the party, my bathing suit wet in my bag, Jodie Spencer dead, the sanitary bin, my phone still behind it, the gun against my skull, the screech of duct tape, then all the way back. To the morning it all started.

My birthday. And that tarot card reading.

Death. The Tower. The Five of Cups.

This is what that was predicting. My throat tightens and tears form under the mask, but I can't let them fall.

In-two-three-four, out-two-three-four, in-two-three-four.

But it's not working because *oh god. I'm going to die in here.*

I'm going to take my last breath and I won't even get to write a line about how dreams are cold and smell sweet and medicinal when they die, the way García Márquez likened unrequited love to the smell of bitter almonds, or how Eve Babitz likened the stench of fame to burnt cloth and rancid gardenias . . . All of this has been for nothing . . .

In-two-three-four, out-two-three-four, in-two-three-four.

Because don't you dare cry, Zoe. Not now. I can't. If I cry, my nose will get blocked with tears and I need to be able to breathe and there's duct tape over my mouth and I need to not think about not being able to breathe because now there's a tightness in my lungs.

In-two-three-four, out-two-three-four.

I have to get out of here.

I slowly move my hands back and forth, seeing if I can loosen the tape around my wrists. But the skin keeps getting stuck, the tape biting into it, and I think I might be making it worse.

And then I hear the click of the lock being undone and my shoulders tighten. *They're back.*

The flower cooler light flicks on—I can see it coming in through the edges of my mask—then there's a creak as the door handle moves.

I hold my breath as two sets of footsteps come inside and *what are they going to do to me?*

But I need to stay calm. I need to not cause any problems. I need to be placid and not give them a reason to kill me quickly . . .

But they're right near me now—I can feel their heat, smell sour sweat and deodorant—they're doing something behind me, and there's a scream trapped in my throat, held there by duct tape. Something is moved behind me. I can hear it being pushed to the side. Then I feel the cool whoosh of air and hear that duct tape being peeled off the roll again.

My ears ring. Then somebody reaches for my mask and yanks it off, and I'm blinded as the light streams in.

Fifty-Five

I squint and struggle to focus, my eyes readjusting to the light. There are three of us now in this cramped space. My kidnappers are both wearing black jeans, black sweaters, and black ski masks. The kind of masks they sell on Venice Beach. The kind I always thought nobody bought. From their sizes, their shapes, I'd say one of them is a man and the other is a woman. And what are they doing?

Panic floods through me now—*this is happening, this is really happening*—and survival instinct kicks in.

I scream.

As loud as I can, my eyes wide. Even though I'm in a room within a room and nobody can hear me. But my lips are taped together, so it comes out muffled. Small.

And they just look over at me, barely flinch, and keep going about their business.

The woman steps outside the cooler now, and the man stands in the doorway. He's holding a phone, angling it toward me. He taps, then glances down at the screen, looks up behind me, points the lens at me again, then tap-tap-tap.

He's taking pictures of me.

He moves his hands a little to the left, looks down at the screen, and takes another.

And I look around, searching for a weapon even though my hands are taped and I wouldn't be able to use it.

That's when I first notice the swathe of black fabric.

To my left. It's like a big black sheet has been taped to the shelves behind me. I look to the right; it's there too.

Dread washes over me.

Because what the fuck is that sheet for?

Am I about to be live streamed to the dark web, some sort of real-time snuff movie?

And I want to beg, to ask them to please let me go and not hurt me, but it comes out like a whimper.

The man looks over at me, then back down at his phone, as the woman watches the screen from behind him. He's swiping now, like he's showing her the pictures he's just taken, flipping through them as I trace the lines of his body with my gaze. Of the two of them, he's definitely in charge. I can see it in their body language. And there's something vaguely familiar about him too . . . It's like I've seen him before. Met him. I can't put my finger on it.

Then he nods and taps again, types something, looks at it for a bit, then taps a couple more times. He looks at her, nods once more, and puts his phone in his pocket.

Like he's done . . .

And now my ears ring and my heart stops midbeat and in an instant I understand. I know what's going on. Because there's only one reason I can think of why they'd bring me here and put a black sheet behind me and take photographs. He just sent one to someone. The black sheet is so nobody knows where I am. And no, it's not as bad as being live streamed to the dark web, but the truth isn't so great either.

Because: I'm being ransomed.

•　•　•

All I can do is focus on breathing, on not choking, as I stare at them and think: *Zach*. That photograph must have been for Zach. He's the only person I know who has enough money to pay a ransom.

The man is whispering something to the woman now, and she's nodding. He looks over to me and a jolt runs down my spine. There it is again, recognition. Like I have a name on the tip of my tongue but I just can't say it. Like I know him.

And then I make out one of the whispers: "If he doesn't pay, we'll have to show him we mean it." Then he turns and leaves the room.

My blood speeds up and I can feel my underarms getting wet. Terror rolls through me.

What the fuck does that mean?

I need to calm down.

But I can't.

The fear is everywhere: my hands, beneath my ribs, my head.

The woman comes toward me now and reaches for my mask to put it back on, and I have a split second to make a choice.

I hurl my body at her, knock her over, push myself up, and run for the door. I'm outside the cooler now and she's inside . . . I hear my dress rip . . . but the man is back. He grabs me by the hair—ow—and his face is so close to mine and his eyes are hazel and they're looking at me in this horrible way I recognize and . . .

And *OH MY GOD.*

Oh my god, oh my god, oh my god.

My ears roar.

My vision blurs.

Because *I know those eyes.*

I know that gaze.

I look away, down to the floor, because I can't let him see that I know. Can't let him see that I've figured it out. That would be worse. And he always did have a knack for reading me. So I just let him frog-march me back into the cooler, and the woman helps sit me down. He's staring at me now, a hot gaze I can feel on my skin, but I refuse to look back.

And then he seethes, "Fuck," grabs her by the arm, and walks out of the cooler. He locks me inside with a sinister click and I watch through the glass door as they both go out into the hallway.

And then I realize: he left my mask off.

And that's when I know for certain: he knows.

He definitely knows.

Fifty-Six

I sit dead still, holding my breath, as a scene from three years ago flickers in my mind.

A leaf falls in slow motion from the tree above us . . . a gin and tonic, icy in my hands . . . Zach watching from the bar . . . And then the words "I'm done. Get your stuff out of my place before I get home tonight."

That's the last time I saw those hazel eyes.

Because it's Will.

The guy I broke up with the night Zach and I got together.

I couldn't be more certain.

I can see the whole thing playing out on the cinema screen of my mind. All those press quotes Carlos meant for Jodie: *DOES ZACH HAMILTON HAVE A NEW WOMAN?* or *They have history . . .* or *Is Zach Hamilton in LOVE . . .*

Will saw them.

He knew I'd met Zach three and a half years ago. I don't know if he ever found out about our three days together, but he might well have assumed we'd been in touch all this time, because there I was, pictured half-naked in Zach's pool. There the article was, saying we had "history." That meant I was important to him. That Zach would pay to get me back safely if somebody took me.

And the worst part is this actually makes sense to me. Will wasn't a good person in the end. And he always *was* looking for a way to make a quick buck. That's what I am now. A human side hustle.

My stomach twists.

How the fuck am I going to get out of here?

But then: a noise.

My eyes snap to the glass door, to my work studio, to the door that's slowly opening.

It's him. He's back.

I hold my breath, wondering what he'll do, say. My eyes are glued to the door.

But when somebody walks in, it's not him. It's the woman. She stumbles inside like she's being pushed. And she's not wearing her ski mask anymore; he must have decided that if I know who *he* is, she should be in jeopardy too. Typical Will.

She's blonde . . . and . . . *wait* . . .

I blink a couple of times, my eyes refocusing.

HER.

Mary. Zach's architect's assistant.

A flash of the morning we first met. Me standing at Zach's door, squinting into the sunlight . . . Then the morning after Zach's party, sitting at his kitchen counter . . . How the hell does she even know Will?

I can't think. It's like my head is filled with white noise.

She walks over to the cooler, unlocks the door, and comes inside. She's crying. "I'm so sorry," she whispers, sniffing back tears as she helps me up. "I tried to warn you."

I'm barely breathing now. A deep fatigue washes over me. All I can do is let her lead me out of the flower cooler, over to a chair by the table, and help me sit down.

Then the door opens again and there he is. Will.

Except now his mask is off too.

He shuts the door and moves toward me and I look to his arms. He's carrying a laptop, his gun, and . . . duct tape.

He puts the laptop and gun down on the table, pulls a long piece of duct tape off the roll, and wraps it around my shoulders, taping me to the chair. Then he does it again and again. And I don't even try to run. There's no point.

I just sit here and let it happen. He pulls up a chair next to me, opens the laptop, and flips up the screen.

He says nothing, Mary says nothing, and an eerie silence swirls around us as he reaches forward and clicks a few times on the keyboard. On the touch pad.

I watch as he pulls up a browser window.

"We might as well all watch together, Zoe. I want you to see that I'm not the bad guy here," Will says in a tone I recognize—a self-satisfied tone—and a shiver runs down my spine. Because *of course* he's the bad guy. He's the one with the gun.

But all I can do is watch as he logs into something else now. And it's like we're all holding our breath, like the tapping from his keyboard is the only audible sound.

He presses Enter.

The screen glitches, like it's trying to load an image but failing. And I watch, waiting. And then, from that dark little screen, I hear a voice.

"What the fuck do we do now?" it says.

I flinch.

That was Zach's voice.

And then the picture loads and I scan from corner to corner. It's Zach's living room.

I recognize the kitchen counter, the bowl of lemons. The space where that blender was positioned at his party . . . And there Zach is, on one of the white sofas. There are two other people in there too. One of them is Carlos and the other looks a lot like Brian, who is pacing around the room.

Will and Mary have somehow accessed his CCTV cameras.

"Let's just all take a breath," Brian says, and I stare at the screen.

"Fuck taking a breath," says Zach, pushing the magazines clear off the coffee table.

And good, this is so good. *Zach's going to do something.*

But then he looks up at Carlos and says, "You said you had it under control."

Fifty-Seven

There's a silence, on both our side of the screen and theirs. Then Brian says, "None of this can be linked to you, Zach. To any of us. We just need to take a breath and regroup."

"Stop telling me to take a fucking breath!" Zach yells at Brian before turning back to Carlos. "And which part, huh? Which part is under control?"

"Well, I dealt with the Spencer girl," Carlos says, his words coming out like bullets.

"But that just makes it worse. What if someone looks into her history and can somehow link her to me? What if she wrote a fucking diary or something? What then?"

"That won't happen. I took care of everything," Carlos says. "And we couldn't just leave her out there. The way she was behaving, she must have known, Zach. She was too big of a risk."

"This is all so fucked. We could have ended this six months ago. You should have let me pay Will like I wanted to. Then he'd be gone by now and none of this would be happening."

My breath catches in my throat as I watch his little figure on the screen.

What is going on? Why would Zach want to pay Will off?

"And how exactly would you have explained that away if he still went to the press or the police?" Brian asks, in a tone that tells me they've had this conversation a few times before. "Innocent people don't pay people for silence."

"Will wouldn't have told anyone; he was part of it all too. He would have been fucking himself over if he did that. We just needed to calm him down and pay him to make him go away."

"You really think paying him would have been the end of it?" Carlos asks. "It would just have been the beginning. Remember, it's not the same for him as it is for you. The police would just love to bring a movie star down for what you've done. They'd give him a deal in an instant if he testified against you."

"Fuck," Zach says. "Everything is so fucked up. It's all going to come out, I can feel it."

He sits down and pulls his hands through his hair the same way I've seen him do before in movies, in his cinema room.

Brian talks now, his voice calm and measured. He's sitting on the other sofa, his hands clasped, forefingers together. "As far as the world knows, Zoe had some stalker, who then kidnapped her. There's even a police report, right? Nothing to do with us. We were helping her. If something happens to her, we're not going down for it. And as long as she doesn't figure out it's Will who took her, she'll think it's that stalker you fabricated."

"I still think that stalker story was a mistake. It just overcomplicates things," says Carlos.

"Well, then you shouldn't have let her overhear you. It was the only thing I could think of on the spur of the moment—because it's almost the truth, isn't it? Somebody *was* threatening to ruin my career; somebody *was* threatening Solange and stalking and terrorizing Zoe. It just wasn't some psycho woman. It was *him*. Maybe Jodie too . . . I don't think either of you understand how stressful this has been for me. I'm the one on the firing line."

Will shifts his weight beside me and nudges me, and I tear my gaze from the screen to look at him.

"They're wrong about that, Zoe. It wasn't me sending that shit to you. Or Jodie. She wasn't involved in any of this. But they killed her anyway. Monsters."

Now the room spins around me and my mouth gets dry. Because if it wasn't Will who was stalking me and it wasn't Jodie, and it wasn't some fabricated stalker, then who was it?

And then all I can feel is Mary's presence on the other side of me. *HER . . .*

But would she do this? Without Will knowing about it?

Why?

Zach stands up and starts pacing, and the other two just watch him.

"And who are you to criticize me, anyway?" Zach says to Carlos. "You're the one who let him take her. Now we're really screwed." He glares at Carlos, then Brian.

"Oh, fuck off," Carlos says, half laughing. "Stop acting like some innocent bystander, Zach; the cameras aren't rolling. You're the one who told me she knew Will—we came up with this plan together, remember? This is just as much your fault as it is ours."

All four walls move in toward me; I struggle to breathe.

"Well, you didn't say any of *this* would happen," Zach seethes. "You said we'd just put her in the press and it'd help us lure him out. That Will would leave notes for her like he did with Solange. Maybe get in contact because he had her number. That this was our chance to shut this down. You didn't say anything about him leaving a fucking heart on her windshield, or that she'd get the police involved. And where were you when that happened, huh? You had your chance to get him, and you blew it. Now here we are . . ." He's staring at Carlos now and Carlos is staring back at him.

And I just stare at the screen.

It feels like a bomb has gone off. My ears ring, my pulse thuds, and something beneath my ribs aches, radiating out to my hands. And I can feel my breath speed up. A flash of what Zach's cologne smells like, what his stubble feels like beneath my fingertips, the way he looked me so deeply in the eyes and promised me everything would be okay. But that version of him is fading to black. Being replaced by another version.

Will nudges me again, leaning in close enough that I can smell his deodorant, and I want to pull away but I can't.

"That plan to catch me was never going to work, Zoe. I could see and hear everything they were planning. Zach never did understand that I was smarter than him."

Then Carlos starts to talk again, and we both look at the screen.

"None of us expected this, Zach. But just remember, this was your mess. Everything that has happened since was us trying to fix what *you* did." He glares at Zach and Zach turns away.

"Look, we have three choices here," Brian says, taking control. "The first is that we pay him and hope he gives her back and that she doesn't know anything about why she was taken, that he says nothing to anyone and he just disappears. Which is risky . . . because like I said, paying him makes you look guilty, and there's no guarantee he won't be back for more."

"Also, we don't know what Zoe knows," Carlos pipes up. "She dated Will. We don't know what he told her back then. And she's smart. She's been asking a shitload of questions. She's a risk . . ."

"What's the second option?" Zach snaps.

"We go to the police and let them deal with it," Brian continues, "but I don't think that's a good option either. Who knows what he'll say to them if they find him. Even if we deny it all, we can't predict how that will bounce back on us. Best case, he looks like a crazed ex who saw her in the press with you and decided to cash in; worst case . . ."

"It all comes out," Zach finishes his sentence for him. "What's the third option?"

"We do nothing."

"So, what, we just leave her?"

"He might let her go once he realizes we're not going to pay. He must have cared about her once. He probably doesn't want to hurt her."

No. Don't just leave me. Please.

"I don't know what to do," Zach says. "I need to think." And then he walks out of the room, and now it's only Carlos and Brian left on-screen.

"Do you really have no idea at all where he is?" Brian says quietly to Carlos. So quietly I can just make it out.

"No, none. He hasn't been near Zach's place in six months—since last time—hasn't tried to contact him directly to get past us again, and none of my contacts have been able to find him. *And* he hasn't gone near the girl even once. I don't get it."

"Where is her phone now?"

"It looks like it's still at the hotel. I'll go find it." Then he adds: "He'd better be acting alone. If he's told someone else about all this, we're in real trouble."

That's when I see movement in my peripheral vision and look at Will. He's over by that white set of drawers labeled *Knives*, *Scissors*, and *Pruning Shears* now. He's pulling open the drawers one by one, taking a look.

And then he closes them up and walks back over to us and says, "Mary, come. We might need to up the stakes."

The door clicks shut as they go outside, and I can hear them talking on the other side of the wall, but I can't hear what they're saying. It's just muffled voices. And nothing is happening on the laptop screen aside from Brian sitting on the sofa alone, drinking what looks like whiskey and staring at the floor.

I'm numb. Like none of this is really happening to me. Like I'm reading a book but I'm the main character, and I'm really fucking sick of all the plot twists.

Because now I'm seeing things like: *This* is why Amy called me to end things after that article on Page Six. It wasn't to keep me safe. Zach had what he wanted. I was in the press. The trap was set. Why keep me around when they could just watch me from a safe distance? Why risk his precious movie deal if something went wrong?

This is why Zach suddenly backtracked on not seeing me anymore when I told him that I was at the police station, why he was so keen for me to come over and have Carlos help me instead. It wasn't because he wanted to save me, protect me. It was because while they wanted to use me to draw Will out, they certainly didn't want the police involved. They hadn't anticipated that. What if the police figured out Will was behind it all and talked to him . . . what if they found out Zach's secret, whatever it is?

Because there is something Will knows about him, something he's desperate to keep quiet. Something that matters so much that he'd put me in danger to find him.

My eyes burn with tears and they start to fall.

A flash of Zach's hands around my waist. His voice saying *I always knew I'd see you again . . . I just knew.* How could I have fallen for it? Been so gullible?

Because I meant nothing to him. I was just a pawn, a role he was playing, a fake relationship like the one he had with Solange.

No wonder he was so happy to see me again at Brian's house that first day. He thought he'd finally find Will. That I'd help him.

And all those eyes at that party we went to. The invisible question: *Why her? She's not that great . . .*

At least now I have my answer.

It wasn't *me* he wanted.

But then, if I'm honest, hand-to-my-heart honest, was it really *him* I wanted either?

Or am I almost as bad as he is?

Because he wanted to use me to find Will, and I wanted to use him to write a book . . . true Hollywood romance, right there.

So maybe we really were perfect for each other in the end.

And if I didn't think I might die here, it'd almost be poetic. Ironic. I wanted so badly to peek behind the celebrity curtain. From a distance it was all applause and glory and red velvet. I never expected it to be so inky black back here.

And then the door opens and Mary comes back in. And she looks like she's going to be sick.

Fifty-Eight

She moves quickly, running over to me. My eyes snap to her hands—she's holding a knife—*WHAT THE FUCK?* My breath speeds up. Then my pulse. A flash of *SEE U SOON* on my mirror . . .

SHE'S GOING TO KILL ME!

I try to scream again, but it comes out muffled . . . and she's behind me now and I'm trying to pull away from her but I can't.

Fuck.

"Be quiet," she whispers, holding on to the chair to stop it moving. "He'll hear us. I'm trying to help you."

My ears roar.

Then ziiip. I hear the first bit of duct tape being cut.

She's cutting me free.

Ziiiip. There goes another bit. I stare at the door. *Please don't let him find us* . . .

Ziiiiip.

"We need to get out of here," she whispers. "Before he gets back. He wants to really hurt you, to show he's serious. And he wants me to take a fucking video! I can't do that . . ."

Ziiiiip . . .

She peels the duct tape back so it's still stuck to my front but not holding me to the chair anymore. Then she comes around and cuts the tape from my hands, and I rip the piece from my lips—*ow*. She looks toward the door and she's shaking.

"We need to be quick," she whispers.

I stand up and follow her, ripping the tape from my dress, from the bare skin of my arms.

"Where is he?" I ask, dropping the tape on the ground.

"Went to get bandages. He'll be back soon," she whispers as we creep to the door. We pause for a second and listen for movement outside, but there isn't any.

"Here," she says, handing me the keys to my van. I take them and stand behind her, holding them between my fingers.

And that's when the door handle rattles and twists, and my stomach drops. We both stand dead still, just watching it turn in slow motion, and the door flings opens.

And there stands Will.

He's holding a small white paper bag, probably from the pharmacy, and I know he has a gun, but I can't see it right now.

He sees us—one, then the other—and moves like a hurricane. The pharmacy bag drops to the floor and he punches Mary in the stomach. She falls to the ground and I hear her knife clatter as it drops. I look to the door and run, but then all the wind leaves my lungs. His arms are tight around me now, pulling me back inside. He pushes me hard toward the far wall and the keys fall from my hand.

"Fucking hell," he says, panting and staring at us, and then he reaches into his waistband and pulls out his gun. He points it at us in turn. Then motions to the flower cooler. "Get in there," he says. "Both of you. Now."

My stomach clenches as we head over to it. "Hurry up," he says.

We go inside, and the moment before he closes the door, he says, "Shut the fuck up, both of you. Nobody will hear you if you scream, except me. And I'm done with this shit." He holds up his gun again as a warning. Then he locks the door. And through the glass of the cooler door, I watch him pick the keys up off the floor and put them in his pocket. Then he takes the laptop and leaves us in here.

Mary stares at the cooler door. She crawls toward it and grabs the handle.

"It won't open," I say, watching her from the corner I'm sitting in. "It's locked." My voice comes out matter of fact. Calm. The voice of resignation.

"Fuck," she whispers under her breath, crawling back to her corner, her eyes full of tears. She looks up at the fan whirring above us.

"It's so cold in here," she says, hugging herself and pulling her knees in tight.

And I hope she didn't do well in biology because if she did she'll realize that the cold is just one of our problems. Without ventilation there's maybe a few hours of life in here for us. A day if we're lucky. I actually don't know how long. I didn't do well in biology either. I just know soon the cold will turn to dizziness, which will then turn to tiredness . . . and then we'll probably pass out.

"I didn't want to do this," she says to me, her voice a low whisper. "I need you to know that. I really didn't. He made me. If we get out of here, will you tell the police that?"

I don't answer. I just look at her. Because if I get out of here, there's no way I am going to tell the police anything good about her. She's the reason I'm stuck in here.

"I'm serious." Her voice jumps an octave. "It wasn't about any of this at the beginning. I never would have agreed. God, I wish I'd never met Will." Her eyes implore me to believe her.

"How *did* you meet him?" I ask.

She swallows hard. "He played me, Zoe," she says in a small voice. "I thought he was some charming big-shot movie producer I'd met at yoga six months ago. He said he was moving out to the suburbs while he built his dream home. That he was looking forward to the quiet so he could focus on a big work project. And I believed him." Her lower lip quivers. "I mean, he seemed legit. He had me sign an NDA, wore a Rolex, drove a Porsche . . . he even had a production company website . . ." She stares straight in front of her and clenches her jaw. "But the truth was he'd been watching Zach's place, seen me working there, followed me, and targeted me. He fake-dated me to get to Zach. The website was a shell, and the Porsche . . . it was a rental." She starts to cry and looks back over to me. "But by the time I realized all that, I was already in it. I couldn't get out. I know you understand what that's like . . ."

She wipes the tears away with the heel of her palm, smearing her mascara down her cheeks. She shakes her head like she's saying no a little late.

I look away, down at my bare feet.

"We are nothing alike," I say, wiggling my toes, trying to warm them up.

"Yes we are. Will played me in the exact same way that Zach played you."

Anger chokes me now. Because she doesn't get to kidnap me at gunpoint and then call *herself* a victim.

"You didn't have to go through with any of this, Mary," I say through my teeth.

I can feel the heat of her eyes on me, but I don't look up. I just stare at the concrete floor.

"No, you don't understand," she says, sniffing back tears. "He set me up from the beginning. He'd ask my opinion on architecture ideas. He'd send me texts asking about what we were working on for Zach, what his place was like, whether he should do anything similar himself." She lets out a big sigh. "And I'd signed an NDA for Zach too—I knew I *shouldn't* send him anything—but he was this great guy who was giving me all this attention, and he was saying things like maybe we'd live together. And . . . honestly . . . having that going on made Franz coming on to me all the time a little more bearable." Her voice shifts, gets more fragile. "So I sent him everything he asked for, and then . . ."

I look toward her now; her eyes plead with me to understand.

I frown at her as if to say: Then *what?*

"Two months ago, he sat me down and said he needed my help. He told me this long story about how he knew Zach from before. How Zach was an awful person who had done something terrible. There was evidence of it in Zach's place somewhere. And he needed me to help him access Zach's CCTV to figure out where it was. Once he found it, he'd steal it and blackmail Zach with it. He said if I helped him, he'd give me half the money."

The room spins—*she did this for money?*

"I couldn't believe it. And I said no, of course," she says, wiping tears from her cheeks as her eyes dart around the cooler like she's reliving it. "I tried to break up with him. I realized he'd targeted me, that he was probably lying about *everything*, that he probably wasn't even a producer. That he was just some criminal, a con man." She clenches her jaw again. "That's when he threatened me. Said I couldn't leave. Because he had four months' worth of texts and pictures I'd sent to him about Zach's place: floor plans, information on that underground cinema room we'd been building, how to reset the keypad, even stuff about the gate. He said if I didn't help him, he'd send it all to Zach, to the police, to Carlos. And honestly, anyone who saw those would think *I* was the one planning a robbery, that I was totally in on it. Never mind the NDA I'd signed for Zach. I didn't want to lose my job; I'd never get another one like that." She closes her eyes and pulls her hands through her hair. And now her voice gets softer. "So I gave him what he wanted."

"What was the evidence?" I ask, goose bumps forming on my arms.

"It doesn't matter," she says. "We didn't end up taking it, because ten days ago *you* came along."

My throat tightens.

"What do you mean, I came along?" I ask, my voice shaky.

She opens her eyes and looks right at me. There's a disturbing calm about her now.

"As soon as Will saw you on Zach's CCTV he became convinced that you were a far better option than a robbery. We could ransom you; we didn't even have to break in. I tried to talk him out of it," she says, letting out a big sigh. "But then he saw you on Page Six and there was no changing his mind. Now that you were a public couple, Zach would *have* to pay to get you back. He said it was foolproof. And every new piece of press just made him more certain."

She wipes away the last of her tears with the backs of her hands.

"And I tried to make you walk away. To keep you safe. I tried to stop this happening. I really tried. Why the hell didn't you walk away? Because now . . . now that you know it's him, now that you've seen him, I don't know what he's going to do."

And that's when I understand.

It *was* her who was stalking me. But *this* was why.

"It was me. All that stuff. The messages. The heart. It was all I could think of. The only way I could make you stop seeing Zach so this wouldn't happen. I didn't want any of this." Something shifts behind her eyes. "If we get out, will you at least tell the police I tried to help you escape? Then they mi—"

"How the hell did you get into my apartment block?" I ask, cutting her off as my mind whirs.

She hesitates, then says, "Your neighbor. Jake. I followed him to Trader Joe's and came on to him . . ."

And of course it was bloody Jake. Him and his constant rotation of women.

"He asked me back to his place, and I knew you weren't there—it was Monday and you were with Zach, Will told me—so I went. When he punched in the code, I remembered it . . . and turning off your power was easy." She lets out a big breath. "I thought I'd have to break a window when I came back to write that thing on your mirror, but your kitchen window was easy to shake open. I'm really sorry, Zoe. I know how scared you must have been."

I scan my memory banks now, trying to piece it together. She must have written *SEE U SOON* while I was at work on Friday . . . *That's why Carlos didn't see her. He was too busy following me around. Taking care of Jodie.*

"But how did you find my phone number?" I ask. "To put it online?"

"Will had it in his phone. I was worried he would figure out it was me. This way it could have been anyone on the internet . . . I'm not a bad person, Zoe. I just didn't want to end up here," she continues. "I knew it wouldn't work out the way he said it would; I could feel it." She looks up to the ceiling. "Fuck, where is he? I can't breathe." And of course she can't breathe—it's 90 percent humidity in here. She looks straight at me now. "Do you think we'll die in here before he comes back?"

"I hope not," I say. But my mind is preoccupied with everything she's just said, everything I overheard Carlos and Brian and Zach talking about . . .

Because what exactly does Will know about Zach?

Fifty-Nine

It's about an hour later. I'm numb from sitting on the cold concrete floor, and Mary is shivering, her lips turning blue. Her eyes are closed, tears dried on her cheeks. And we both might die here, I know that, but there's a part of me that needs to believe we won't. That I still have a future. That I still have a book to write. I need to act like I'll survive this. So I ask the final question. The missing part of the story.

"What exactly did Zach do?"

Silence rings out.

"I don't know," she says, staring at the door like she can will it to open. But her voice quivers.

"I think you do," I say, watching her. "And I deserve to know why this is happening to me."

"You are better off not knowing," she says.

"If you tell me everything you know, I'll tell the police you tried to help me escape. That he coerced you into everything," I say.

She turns to look at me, her eyes flickering as she weighs up the options.

Then she lets out a big breath. "Do you promise?"

I nod. "Promise. But I want to know *all* of it. Every last detail."

I can hear her swallow. She looks unsure.

"Mary, I already know some of it," I say. "Like I know Will and Zach used to work together. That's how Will met Zach . . . But I don't know other things, like how Jodie was involved."

Her eyes well up. She glances quickly at the door again, then back to me.

"They used to do robberies," she starts, her voice shuddering, like she knows she shouldn't be telling me. "The three of them—Zach, Will, and Ky. Out of that bar."

I nod and work to keep my voice calm and steady. I want her to keep going. "Did Jodie do them too? I never saw her there."

She shakes her head. "No, but she knew about them. She was engaged to Ky," she says, quickly glancing at the door again, then back to me. "They had a system. There were loads of different cliques who came in regularly—they'd find the best cars and follow them home to get their addresses. Once they found a suitable target, they'd watch the house, get a sense of their habits, and wait for them to come back in. One person would be working behind the bar and the other two would do the job."

I can picture that bar as she speaks. The low sofas and the blue glass suspended by fisherman knots hanging above it . . . Zach in his aviators.

"The person working would make sure they had eyes on the target and let the others know if they left so they could get out in time," she continues. "And none of the victims knew each other, so nobody ever put it together. But then on the fifth job, it all went wrong."

Dread rolls through me now. Like I don't want to know, but I *need* to know.

"They were all doing this big job together because they knew the owner was out of town. But halfway through, the alarm went off and they had to run. Ky was on the street outside, keeping watch, and Zach was driving . . . he fucked up and hit him. But instead of stopping, he just kept on driving. Ky died right there on the street." She looks at me.

My throat tightens.

"Jodie knew Ky was doing a robbery that night," Mary continues, "but Will told her he was killed in a freak hit-and-run while they were inside. That nobody had seen anything. The police didn't do much to investigate; they had bigger concerns. And Will kept Zach's secret. But he had dashcam footage proving it all—at least at the beginning . . . Then one day he went to look for it and it was gone. He said Zach had somehow come in and stolen it. That was the evidence he wanted to steal back."

My ears ring; my heart thuds. *Oh my god.* That's why Zach came to help me get my things from Will's place the night we broke up. He wanted to find that memory card. He's been using me right from the beginning.

"But wouldn't Zach have destroyed it? If it implicated him?"

"I thought so," Mary says. "But Will was certain he still had it. He said Zach had told him."

"Why? Why would Zach do that?" My mind struggles to make sense of it. What exactly was on that memory card?

"I don't know. Will wouldn't tell me that. But the rest made sense. Like Jodie was one of the only people who knew where Will was. She was always coming around, calling him up at all hours crying . . . Now I got it. It was because of Ky."

"Fuck," I say, and I feel sick.

"It gets worse, Zoe. Much worse. After I gave Will Zach's CCTV log-in information, I started listening in too, like that would somehow ease my anxiety. That's how I learned Will had already tried to extort Zach a few times before, he'd threatened Solange, and Carlos was looking for him—he'd kill him if he found him. And then other things started adding up too, like the real reason Will had moved out to the suburbs six months ago, around the time we met—it wasn't because he was building a house or wanted to focus on a project. It was to hide from Carlos. I looked in his wallet and saw he had two IDs. I realized he only drove rental cars because he didn't want Carlos to track him down . . . he was doing everything he could to hide; he was terrified.

And that made me terrified too. Because what would Carlos do to *me* if he figured out I'd helped Will?"

My stomach clenches and I hug my knees a little tighter. Because Mary was right to be scared; I wouldn't put anything past Carlos at this point.

"I panicked. I wanted out, before Carlos started looking for me too," she continues, swallowing hard. "And the only way out I could think of that wouldn't involve me confessing what I'd done was telling Jodie everything. What really happened to Ky. About that dashcam footage. All of it. I'd seen how much she wanted answers. I thought she'd go to the police. That they'd search Zach's place or take him and Will in for questioning, and then the whole thing would be off. Nobody would ever know what I'd done.

"So three weeks ago I told her everything. She promised not to tell Will I'd mentioned it. But she didn't go to the police like I'd hoped. Instead she started watching Zach, trying to figure out what to do, whether to confront him. And then ten days ago she saw you driving him to that party, and she got an idea: maybe you could help her."

A flash of Jodie offering me a cigarette.

"How the hell could I help?"

"You had access to Zach's place. She thought that if she got you alone and told you what he'd done, you'd look for that memory card for her. Then she'd have hard evidence and Zach couldn't just deny it."

That's why she ordered flowers from the shop . . . so she could talk to me.

Mary clenches her jaw. "But then Will got his idea to take you instead." She lets out a big breath and her words speed up. "Trying to steal back that memory card was bad enough, you know? But kidnapping . . . I definitely couldn't do that. I just couldn't. I panicked. And I should have just gone to the police . . . but I had no proof whatsoever of what he was planning. He could just deny it." She swallows hard. "So that's when I came up with the idea of scaring you into breaking up with Zach. So then you were no longer a good target."

A flash of that heart on my windshield. Of my lights not turning on. Of *SEE U SOON* on my mirror.

"But then everything just blew up," Mary says, her lower lip shaking. "On Friday night Jodie wouldn't answer Will's calls, and he got me to go past her place to check on her. There was police tape all over the outside, police going in and out. She was dead. Will was convinced Carlos was responsible, said he was picking off anyone connected to Zach's big secret and he'd be next."

A flash of me on Jodie's road, pointing out her bungalow to Carlos . . . Guilt rolls through me. How could I have believed Zach when he said she was some psycho? I should have asked more questions. I hate myself for believing him.

"Will was certain he would be found," Mary continues. "Frantic. I mean, Jodie knew where he was; Carlos might have got it out of her before he killed her. He said he needed the money now so he could leave town, threatened to kill me if I didn't help him. So we weren't planning on taking you for a couple of weeks, but when that happened, he insisted we do it now. He said we'd run out of time."

I swallow hard. Nod.

But internally I'm a hurricane.

Because how in the holy mother of fuck did I wander into this poisonous web? I was never in control of it, not for a single moment. Even back when I was dating Will, I was being lied to.

And now I'm thinking of Will's fancy watch, all the nice things in his apartment . . . this was how he paid for all that. Not eBay or crypto or selling weed gummies—robberies. He probably stole that watch. Then that night I went to surprise him on Valentine's Day. How edgy he was. And how I saw Zach and Ky in the parking lot—this is what they were doing that night. And how snappy Will was those two weeks before our breakup. It was because of Ky. And of that female voice calling Will in the middle of the night and his excuse that her husband had died and she was taking it badly . . . It was Jodie.

But Zach . . . a flash of that hotel room and me telling him about those calls, asking if Will was cheating on me. And he said yes. But of course he said yes. Best to cover his tracks.

Now a flash of the three days Zach spent with me, that night in Palm Springs playing Truth or Dare, talking to me about everything. I'd said Will was going through some "stressful stuff" when he asked about the breakup; he was trying to figure out exactly what I knew. What Will had told me. That's why he'd ghosted me . . . He didn't need me anymore.

Whatever this thing between us was, it was all in my head, right from the very beginning. A beautiful illusion, like everything else in this town.

"But all of this happened years ago . . . why is Will doing all this now?" I ask.

She lets out a big sigh. "He's been trying to extort Zach ever since he hit it big. But until he found me, he didn't have any way of getting the evidence he needed to prove it. And then there was you. He was certain Zach would pay a lot to get you back. Besides, he can't back down now—even if he stopped everything, Carlos would still look for him and kill him. Or someone else would. Carlos isn't the only person he's hiding from. He has some pretty scary debts, if you know what I mean."

And then Mary's eyes dart to the door of my work studio. Her shoulders stiffen and she says, "Shhh."

I hold my breath as it swings open.

Will comes in. He puts the laptop and keys to my van on the table, but *where's his gun?* Then he strides toward us and Mary whispers, "Just play along."

Sixty

He peers in at us through the glass door and I physically recoil. "Have you decided to behave?" he asks, his eyes on Mary. She nods and gives me a swift kick in the shins and smiles. And I wince and buckle forward, my shoulders slumped.

But I'm not just playing along. It really hurt.

His hand moves down to the lock and then I hear a click. The door opens and I swear I can feel the oxygen, the warmth from outside, roll in like a wave.

"I'm really sorry, Will. I was just so scared," Mary says, standing up and scampering over to him.

He nods as she kisses his cheek. "Are you ready to take the video now?"

My pulse explodes.

Because: the video. The one to show Zach he's serious. That he absolutely *will* hurt me. The one that might require bandages.

She nods and heads past him, out into the work studio, and Will stares at me. "Don't fuck around, Zoe," he says. "Hurry up."

And what did Mary mean, "play along"?

Just let him hurt me?

I stand up and move out of the cooler and look to the door—I could run, scream. But then I see Mary.

She's holding one of the big white vases up over her head.

And I guess my expression changes just a little; my mouth opens or my eyes widen—something that makes Will turn to look. His grip loosens on me just a little and then—smash.

The vase comes down over his head with a loud crash.

He stumbles into me—I lose my footing, he's heavy, and I hit the floor—and Mary goes to run. I watch, helplessly, as he lurches forward and grabs her by the hair. He pulls her backward, then pushes her hard with both hands across the room. A crack rings out as her head hits the table; she falls to the ground and my heart flares in my chest. The door to the studio is right there. The keys to my van, sparkling from the table . . . It's now or never. I stand up and reach for them and run toward the door, but he grabs *my* hair now.

He yanks me back and throws me to the ground. My wrists crack; my chin hits the floor. My teeth. The keys go flying.

Ow.

The taste of blood—metallic and warm—a sharp pain moves through my skull, a throb behind my eyes. And he's coming at me again.

Adrenaline spurts through me and I kick, hard; I get him in the side of the knee. I have to get out of here. I go to crawl away, but then I hear the click of his safety catch. I hold my breath and turn to look at him, squinting against the bright light above us. And he's standing above me now, pointing his gun right at my head.

"Stop," he seethes. "Just stop. I don't want to hurt you."

And I'm looking into his eyes and he's looking into mine and then something flickers behind his and he turns to look at Mary. Just for a millisecond.

Then his whole body goes slack and I follow his gaze.

Mary is just lying there.

Not moving.

And there's blood around her head. Pooling like a little burgundy lagoon.

"Fuck," Will says, his breath as quick as mine. "Fuck, fuck, fuck." He moves over to her. "Don't fucking move or make a sound," he spits through his teeth as he leans down.

I edge forward.

"Get over there," he orders, pointing to the corner by the printer. So I crawl over and crouch down and shake as I watch him check for Mary's pulse. And I'm looking at the door, then back at him and Mary, and I could try to run for it again, but look what he did to her.

Because she's dead. I know it. Her eyes are still open and staring straight through me like a doll. And there's so much blood. My breath is getting quicker and quicker, and no kind of breathing exercise is going to fix this.

"Fuck, fuck, fuck," he repeats.

And then there, in the silence, comes the sound of a voice.

It's Zach's voice. From the laptop on the table.

"Okay, I've thought about it," he says, and both Will and I sit dead still, waiting. I hold my breath. *Please go to the police; tell them nothing is worth someone dying because of you . . .* "You're right—we don't really have a choice here."

My pulse speeds up. *Say it. Say it. Say it.* Maybe if Will thinks the police are involved, he'll just leave me here and catch a flight to Mexico . . . He won't care that I know he kidnapped me. He won't care that I know he killed Mary. He'll just flee . . .

"We're not bad people, but we're in an impossible situation. We need to sit tight and do nothing. Pretend we never got that ransom note. Let's just hope he panics and makes a mistake. Because we have to find him. My movie comes out in two months. We can't have this shit going on then."

"Agreed," says Brian.

"I'll take care of the ransom message," Carlos says next.

"Great," Brian continues. "Let's all get some sleep."

My ears ring and my breath gets short and shallow and how could

Zach just leave me here? A flash of him in bed with me, his bronzed shoulder under that stark white sheet. His hands in my hair. His stubble on my cheek. The way he winked at me. His aviators on his head. That fucking Emily Brontë quote. Everything that got me here.

Here, where nobody is coming for me and I'm all alone.

And all I want to do is scream, but I know how that ends. With me lying there, next to Mary. I'm not going to get out of this with brute force; he's just too strong. Too strong, with too much to lose.

No, the only way I'll get out of this is if I *think* my way out.

I need to somehow make him believe I'm on his side.

Sixty-One

I sit silently in that corner and watch him. He's looking around the room. His eyes dart from the laptop to the drawers with words like *Pruning Shears* and *Knives* on them to the plastic wrap catching the light right there beside me.

He comes over, pulls down a full roll, and lays it on the floor near Mary. Then he's back, at that white set of plastic drawers, opening the one labeled *Scissors*. He pulls out a pair, goes back to the plastic wrap, and begins to unravel it. He cuts a long piece.

Oh god, what's he going to do with that?

He leans over, tilting his head slightly, like he's trying to figure something out. Then he places the plastic over her face, lifts up her head, and pulls it under and over again. Nausea moves through me as he covers her mouth and she doesn't fight. There's no mist coming from her lips. She's gone.

He wraps her head again and again, his forehead shiny with sweat.

"Fuck," he mutters under his breath, glancing up at me quickly, then back down again. "Don't look at me like that. I didn't want to hurt her—you know that, right?"

I nod. Violently. "Of course I know that. It was an accident," I say.

He wraps the plastic around her head again. "This will all be over soon," he says, shooting me a quick smile, then getting back to work.

And I give a small smile back like I'm reassured, but what I'm really thinking is *how* will it be over? Because I saw him do it. Kill her. And now I'm watching him wrap her in plastic. I could send him to prison. So is he really going to just let me go?

He's going around her neck now and moving to her shoulders. And I can still see my keys, on the table. I imagine grabbing them, running to the back door, pulling it open, opening the van. Getting in. Opening the garage door . . . My throat tightens. There's no way I'd make it. Especially in this dress.

He tightens the plastic against her head, her neck, the top of her torso. "Do you have any bleach here?" he asks, looking up again.

"Under the sink," I say, nodding toward it and trying to keep my voice steady. I want to be helpful. Not give him any reason to wrap me in plastic too.

He goes over to it, pulls open the cupboard, and grabs the bleach we use for tulips, and some rags too. Then he pulls out two plastic garbage bags, looks at them, and returns to Mary.

He puts one of the bags over her head and secures it around her neck with duct tape.

Then he pushes her to the side and stares down at the blood.

And I just sit there, watching him clean it up. Watching him put the blood-soaked rags in the plastic bag as the room begins to smell of bleach. Watching him pick up those bits of duct tape that were holding me to the chair when Mary tried to help me escape; watching him putting them in the bag with the rags. Doing everything I can to look anywhere but at Mary. To notice anything other than her hands changing color, getting dull red patches. Forcing myself not to think of that blood under her head or picture her face pressed up against the plastic.

A flash of Dad's face. The comfort of his voice. The one person I can count on. And, god, I'd give anything to hear him say "I told you so" one last time.

"We have to go. But, Zoe, if I die, you're coming with me. So just do what I say. Then we can both walk away from this. But right now, we need to get her to the van."

I glance at the space beside Mary, where the blood was.

I hope there is some left. Some hiding in the crevices of the floor-boards. Some sort of trail for the police.

But who am I kidding? The police aren't coming to save me. They won't be turning up here with their UV lights looking for blood. They don't even know I'm missing.

None of this will ever come to light.

Zach will never be linked to Will and Ky and Jodie. And even if he is, the deep, dark truth will be covered up by Brain, by Carlos, the way they've always covered it before. As will the truth about Jodie's death. Mary will never be linked to Will. Or if she is, nobody will figure out the real reason. And if Will kills me tonight, it'll look like some crazed stalker did it.

Which is why I need to do exactly what Will says.

"Okay," I say.

He nods and picks up my keys, threading his forefinger through the keyring.

He puts a roll of duct tape around his wrist and we go over to Mary, and still holding the bag of bloody rags and tape, he grabs her shoulders and I grab her legs.

We head to the back door. And I'm pretty sure I'm committing a crime right now, but I don't know what it is or how not to.

He holds her with one forearm and uses his free arm to open the back door. *He's so strong. I wish he wasn't so strong.* The garage light flicks on as we move toward the back of the van. Then he presses a button on the keys and the van opens with a click.

He pulls open the back doors and we push her inside. He throws the rags and old tape in after her.

And then he says, "Turn around."

My jaw drops a bit. Is he going to kill me? Shoot me in the back of the head? I shiver and my eyes burn with tears.

"I'm going to tie you up now. Just until we get there. So you don't do anything stupid."

Then I hear the screech of duct tape, and he tapes my hands behind my back. He helps me into the back of the van with Mary. Then he tapes my feet up too, pulls a cap from the waistband of his jeans, and puts it on—presumably so no traffic camera can recognize him.

"Relax. It'll all be fine."

But as he looks at me and tries to smile, his lower lip shakes. The way it always does when he's lying.

And that's when I know nothing will be fine.

He's going to kill me too.

Sixty-Two

I can see the outline of Will's head in the driver's seat, but I'm on the floor, too low to see the road ahead. We've been driving for half an hour, maybe more, and I really need to pee. I don't know where we're going, but I'm guessing it's somewhere you could dump a body wrapped in plastic without anybody noticing.

We're going up a hill now. And every time any light streams in through the windshield, I can see Mary's outline lying there. Every time we turn a corner I can hear the thud of her moving, the rustle of the plastic bag around her head. And I've been thinking and thinking and thinking the whole time, but there's nothing back here I could use as a weapon, even if my hands weren't taped behind my back.

And I want to stay positive, but I keep thinking dark things like: *This is my fault. I should have just walked away.* But instead, I stayed, for my book, for some imaginary connection with Zach, for a future I could almost touch. It's like I kept stepping closer to the edge of that cliff, thinking maybe if I just tried a little more, edged a little closer, risked a little bigger, I could do it. I could achieve what so many others haven't. I went all in; I went too far. And I want to blame Hollywood; I want to say it's this place that brought it out in me. Did it to me. But the truth is, Hollywood will still be standing long after I'm gone, the magic-hour light promising others exactly what it promised me. And it's not Hollywood that did it to me; it was the thing inside me that drew me here. The same thing that kept me alive at times. Hope. So yes, there's a dark side to everything that sparkles, if you look close enough.

But now I'm here and I'm going to die and nobody will ever know what happened.

And I'm thinking about how on that first night, the one where I went with Zach to that party, I thought: *What have I got to lose?*

Everything, it seems. I had everything to lose.

All I want is for it to go back to how it was. I just want to go home to my orange apartment and work as a florist and whine and moan about being blocked to my writers' group.

We go over a big bump, then a few smaller ones, and my stomach clenches, because if we were still on asphalt there wouldn't be bumps . . . and then we pull to a stop and my heart flares in my chest. I can hear Will getting out of the driver's seat. He bangs the door closed.

I imagine him coming around to the back of the van. He pops the back doors, and as I look at his hands, my insides turn to oil. Because he's carrying a knife, yes, but there's something else too. He just put his gun back in the waistband of his jeans, and it has a silencer on it now.

I look past him, to the lights of LA flickering in the distance—we must be somewhere on Mulholland Drive—and I can smell grass and gasoline fumes. Hear cicadas. The sound of spring. A looming summer I'll never see.

"I'm not going to hurt you," he says to me. "We just need to leave her body, and then we'll go our separate ways. I really need you not to run, though. Or I'll have to."

I nod. Like I believe him. But I start to shake.

Because I know he's lying. I know, because there it is: the mouth twitch again.

He gets into the van and undoes my hands. The tape bites into my skin as it moves and he peels it off. Next he cuts it from my feet. And I could try to run right now, but he has a gun and could shoot me out here and nobody would even hear him. So I don't. Not yet. I need to pick my moment.

I help him roll Mary to the edge of the van. Then we get out and he takes her shoulders and I take her legs, and we carry her into the darkness. We're on a hiking trail going downhill, away from the van and the road. There are the trees all around us, and I can smell dirt. Rocks bite into the soles of my feet and my dress makes it hard to move properly. And with each step we take away from the van, my heart beats a little faster because I'm running out of time.

I need to do something, but I'm too scared. What if it goes wrong? But now I'm thinking of all the other times I should have done something but didn't. I should have driven into a wall if I had to, anything other than driving back to the florist's. I should have told Barb about Sophie stealing my idea. I should have run the moment Zach spun his story about the stalker. I should have pushed past Carlos and gone into the police station.

I should have done *everything* differently.

And now I'm thinking of how all of this started. How if Vee hadn't slipped on that wet greenery that first afternoon, I wouldn't have seen Zach again and I probably wouldn't be here right now.

I do a quick calculation. He needs me to help him carry Mary. Or at least, he'd prefer it. It would take much, much longer alone. And so I trip.

Or: fake-trip.

I drop Mary and hear Will wince with the deadweight as I fall to my stomach.

"Sorry, Will," I say, fake-scrambling to my knees. I whimper a little, fall again. I'm on my hands and knees now.

"Get up, quickly," he says as he lets go of Mary's shoulders and comes over to force me up. And this is it. My chance.

I swing my head up with everything I have and headbutt him in the face. I hear a crack and he falls backward. My head throbs as I turn to face him. He's coming toward me now. I knee him in the groin. He buckles a little, but not like I'd expect him to. And now he's reaching for his gun and *fuck, fuck, fuck.* I punch him in the throat as hard as I can, and he holds his neck and stumbles a little. But the gun is in his hand and he's waving it around . . . His wrist. I grab on to it and I bite. Hard. He tastes like salt. He lets out a yell and the gun drops to the ground, but he pulls my hair and my head goes back. But I have nothing to lose now. Nothing at all.

So I make my hand into a claw and scratch at his face. Wetness. Gross. I think I get his eye.

He releases my hair. His gun is lying there on the ground somewhere, but I can't see it. I feel around for it, frantic. And then: something hard and cold. *Is that it?*

I scramble for it. I've got it; my hands wrap around the handle; I search for the trigger. But he grabs my waist and pushes me to the ground. I hit my head and my vision blurs; adrenaline pulses through me. I can barely see it's so dark. But he's on top of me—I know that much, because he's so fucking heavy, and he's saying, "I'm going to fucking kill you," and he is, I know he is. And I'm holding the gun to my chest but he's grabbing for it and I can't let him get it and—

Bang.

Nobody ever warns you how loud a gun going off will be, even with a silencer. The backward pressure winds me and my ears ring and I'm gasping for breath. But I just keep holding the gun, ready to shoot again if I need to.

He falls limp. Heavy. Really fucking heavy.

And then he just lies there. Deadweight on top of me as my ears ring and ache.

I wait for him to get up again, but he doesn't. And I can feel the warmth, the wetness, of his blood seeping over my clothes. Bile rises in my throat and I start to shake.

I push him off me, whimpering. And Mary is lying there in the darkness, still wrapped in plastic, right where we dropped her, and I'm covered in blood. I look around for the van. It's there behind me. But where the fuck are the keys?

I look down at Will's body, a big gray mass in the shadows, and I don't know if he's dead or just injured, unconscious, but either way I need help. And I'm too scared to touch him, to go through his pockets in case that makes this worse. So I drop the gun and run toward where I think Mulholland is.

Soon I can see it. There up ahead. But there are no cars, just darkness and me and the ringing in my ears. I wrap my arms around me, looking over my shoulder. What if he's not dead? What if he's coming?

But then there, in the distance, are headlights. They snake toward me.

I lift my hands up and step out onto the road. The car slows down. Stops. Pulls over.

It's a black SUV, and for a horrible moment I think it's Carlos.

But then a couple get out—she's in heels, he's in jeans—and come over to me, and I keep looking back to where I left Will. Mary.

And I hear the man's voice. "Hi, we need an ambulance and the police. We've found a girl and she's covered in blood . . . I think she's been assaulted . . ."

And now all I can hear is the beat of my heart and the sound of my own breathing. And then, in time, somewhere out there, I hear sirens . . .

Sixty-Three

I stand with the paramedic, wrapped in a blanket, shivering, a flashlight shining into my eyes.

He turns the flashlight off and I refocus in the dark. The couple that stopped to help me are giving statements a little to my left. The lights from the ambulance are still going, even though there's no sound, bathing the scene in red and blue. My van is there, parked where Will left it on the side of the small road. On the front seat will be that copy of *The Great Gatsby*, the bookmark in the same spot it was that first night I saw Zach again. In my bag, on the front seat of my van, is my wet swimsuit. The bag full of bloody rags and old duct tape is still in the back. And here I sit, in my ripped and sparkly silver dress, covered in blood.

I can't see Mary's body from here, or Will's, but I know where they are because the whole area is being quickly cordoned off with yellow tape; lights have been erected and there are people in white protective suits wandering around, taking pictures and notes. Every time I blink, I can see Mary's face pressed up against the plastic in my mind's eye. My teeth chatter from shock or cold or both; my wrists are red and raw from the duct tape. I'm shaking despite the blanket and the lukewarm air around me.

A man in dark trousers and a blue shirt comes over to me. "Hi, Zoe,

I'm Detective Guerrero," he says. "I need to take a preliminary statement."

I nod.

I haven't seen my reflection yet, but I can tell from the way he's looking at me, the way it hurts to talk, that the bruises on my face must be bad.

"Your name is Zoe Ann Weiss, correct?"

I nod, my throat thick with everything I know, my ears still pulsing from the gunshot.

"In your own words, can you tell me briefly what happened here?" he asks, his eyes moving to the red welts on my wrists.

"I was kidnapped," I say, my voice shuddering as I speak. Flashes from those first moments, the dark outline of a head, the gunmetal against my head, flicker in my mind. "They took me from my van and made me drive to the florist's shop where I work." My eyes prick with tears.

"They? So there was more than one assailant?"

I nod. "The woman took me too, but I think he forced her."

He makes a note on his pad.

"And did you know the assailants?" he asks, flipping back a page in his notebook. "William Simmons was one of them?"

I nod and the first tear falls.

"I used to date him," I say. "The other one's name is Mary. She worked for the guy I've been seeing. Zach Hamilton."

He looks at me now: forehead, eyes, mouth. Like he's sizing up whether I'm telling the truth about Zach.

But I don't even flinch.

"I don't know her last name," I continue. And then I repeat: "I think he forced her to do it."

He frowns. "Do you know why they took you?"

"They wanted Zach to pay a ransom for me."

"What happened to the woman?"

A flash of her face in the flower cooler. The fear in her eyes. Then another flash, of her face being covered in plastic.

"She tried to help me escape," my breath speeds up. "And then Will killed her. He made me help him bring her here with him." My voice is getting faster and faster; I'm falling over my words, trying to get them out. "He was going to kill me too . . . ," I say, and I can feel the heat of tears on my cheeks; I'm struggling to speak. I wipe them away with the back of my hand.

"Whose firearm was it that was discharged?"

"His," I say, my voice cracking.

"Zoe, tell me exactly how Mr. Simmons was killed."

A wave of nausea hits me. *He's dead. And I did this. Oh god.*

"He was sitting on top of me," I start, my breath catches as I remember his weight on top of me. "He told me he was going to kill me and we were fighting for the gun"—my stomach clenches—"and it just went off." A flash of the heat. The wetness. "Then he was dead . . ." I'm sobbing now. Understanding the gravity of what's happened. Trying to catch my breath. And a panic rises in me now as I think of everything else I know.

I want to tell them everything. But if I say it all, right now, what happens then? I can't think straight, can't clearly see how this will play out. I have no proof. It's just my word against theirs. Every other witness is dead—Will, Ky, Jodie, Mary. I'm the only one still standing who knows everything that happened. And who knows what lengths Carlos might go to if he thinks I know what I do and wants to silence me? Zach said he had loads of contacts in the police—what if Detective Guerrero is one of them?

What if he tells Carlos?

I can hear my own blood pumping, my thoughts are wild, and my mouth gets sour. I vomit on the ground by our feet and gasp for breath.

"She's sustained a bad head injury. We need to get her to the hospital to be checked out," says the ambulance attendant.

The detective nods and hands me a card. It has the LAPD Robbery-Homicide Division address on it. "I'll need you to come in on Monday morning, to give a detailed statement. But don't go anywhere in the meantime."

And I nod. That's better. If I'm going to risk telling them everything, it's better I do it in the safety of a police station. With multiple witnesses to hear it and a recording device taking it all down. Where it will be indelibly "on the record."

What can I say about the next few hours? It's a blur of sterile hospital smells and bright lights and people asking if I'd been sexually assaulted and my underwear and clothes being taken as evidence and my wounds, my face, my wrists, my feet being photographed. Cataloged. Waves of fatigue, surges of adrenaline. Fears like *What if I have Mary's blood on my clothes? Even a little bit? Will they believe that I didn't hurt her?* And thoughts like *What's going to happen to me?*

And then on Sunday morning, a police officer drives me home and walks me through my gate.

Sixty-Four

We head through the terra-cotta archway, toward the smell of chlorine and the hum of the pool pump, past Jake's apartment. His lights are all off like he's still sleeping or maybe out. I imagine Mary in there with him. I look over to the breaker box, to the potted palm in front of it, and I can almost see myself there, in the middle of the night. Shaking as my phone lit the way. And even though I know it's over, the little hairs on the back of my neck stand on end. I still feel watched.

But the sun is up now, and it's warm on my neck as we head in silence up the stairs to my apartment. I put the key in the lock, and as the sun glitters off the metal, I twist the door knob, and we go inside.

The police officer moves through the apartment, checking the bedroom, the bathroom, just like I asked him to.

"It's all clear," he says. "Nobody is going to hurt you anymore, Ms. Weiss. I'll be right outside until tonight, then my partner will take over. But I'll be back tomorrow morning. We'll go to the station around ten, okay?"

And then he heads outside and I close the door and put the chain on. Because Will might be dead, but Zach and Carlos are still out there. And right now, the police are probably over there asking Zach about Mary and how he knew her, if he knew Will too, and about the ransom—why he didn't report it. What he *did* do. Carlos is probably wondering what I know, what I'll say to the police.

But even if he wanted to shut me up, I'm safe.

Police will be parked right outside the gate until I go to the station tomorrow. And I know it's only because they don't want me going anywhere—two people are dead, what if I'm lying, what if I did it all? They need to keep an eye on me while they gather their evidence to question me. To make sure I'm telling the truth. But they'll still be there. Carlos can't get to me.

And after I tell the police everything tomorrow, he'll be arrested.

I move to the middle of the room and look around. Everything looks exactly the same as when I left it. My books are still watching me from the bookshelf, my cigarettes are right there where I left them by my laptop, the sequined cushions are still on the sofa, and those pencils are still on the kitchen counter. And everything is still glowing orange. But everything is different now, too. More weathered. Even me, staring back from that mirror with my bruised face. But at least I'm here. Still breathing. *Maybe I can finally be cool and jaded now,* I think as I go over to the sink, pour myself some water, and down it.

Dad's carnations are dying on the counter, giving the whole apartment a sweet and deadly scent. So I reach for the kitchen window and push it open to get some air, but now all I can think about is Mary climbing through it, writing *SEE U SOON* on my mirror.

I clench my eyes shut to push it away.

If I went to shower right now, it would still be there, etched in lip gloss.

Her last warning to me.

Her last-ditch attempt to scare the shit out of me. So I'd walk *out* of that mess, instead of sinking deeper into it.

A flash of her eyes, her tear-streaked face. Then a flash of Zach's fucking smile . . .

I rush to my bedroom and grab Zach's shirt from under my pillow, the same shirt that used to mean safety, rush back to the kitchen, and throw it in the trash, my eyes prickling with angry tears.

And all I can think is: *FUCK HIM.*

Now the last eleven days are flickering in my mind. Playing in a nonstop loop. And I want to scream, I want to break something . . . but then my gaze snaps to my laptop.

It's right there, on the coffee table, beckoning to me.

And yes, I know I should probably sleep right now, I need to be at the police station in just over twenty-four hours, and I've just witnessed two people die. One of them right on top of me. But I'm too wired to sleep, and that story is still inside me, clawing to get out. Blistering my insides. Promising me *this* could be the one.

And I need to get it out. Now.

Before I forget any of the details, before I think it through, before I lose my nerve. Who knows what will happen when I talk to the police . . .

And if I *don't* write it, what will all this have been for?

So I rush over to the sofa, fire up my laptop, open the window, and reach for my cigarettes. As the screen loads, I light one and take a deep drag of menthol smoke, and then I log in.

That's when I see the little red *4* bubble on my iMessage.

I tap on it.

There's one message from Dad at the top: *Can't wait to talk. Love you. Xoxo*

Something twinges in my chest.

Then just beneath that is a thread from Greta. The top message reads: *Hope my post was okay. Do you want me to delete? xxx*

I scroll down. There are two screenshots of an Instagram post beneath it.

It looks like Greta has reposted Sophie's book announcement . . . but then she's also posted our group-chat message thread . . .

All of us talking about how Sophie stole my idea. She's tagged me,

Tom, Rita, Sophie, and Barb. The caption reads: *not cool Sophie.* And there are 1,219 likes.

I write back to Greta: *thanks for having my back babe. Love you xx*

Then I press Send.

But the truth is, the story I have now is so much better than the one Sophie stole could ever have been. It's the kind of story that happens to you only once in a lifetime.

And I get to write it.

So I take another drag of my cigarette, reach forward, and open up New Book V1, then scan the scenes through a haze of cigarette smoke.

I have forty-nine thousand words already written—that's only twenty-five thousand shy of a lean first draft. And while Barb was right—they *are* garbled, no clear through line connecting them—it's not the material that's the problem. I have everything I need here; I can use every single one of these scenes. It's that I didn't know exactly *what* I was writing yet. I didn't know what I was trying to say: That sometimes when you see your dreams close-up, they look more like nightmares.

But now that I know how this story ends, I fully understand the beginning. So I glance up once more at Angelou, Plath, Babitz, and Didion, and all the others staring back at me from my bookshelf. I think of that tarot card reading. Of that magic-hour light. Of Zach's face, the way he shimmered . . .

I pull up a blank word document, that little cursor blinks, and I type: *The Close-Up, by Zoe Ann Weiss.*

And then, on the next page, I type: *One.*

Epilogue

Zoe Ann Weiss, Rumored Girlfriend of Zach Hamilton, Found Dead

Zoe Ann Weiss, 30, was found dead at her apartment complex in West Hollywood on Monday, Page Six can confirm.

Ms. Weiss, a young novelist whose first book, *Fractured*, gained attention recently after her relationship with Zach Hamilton became public, was discovered by a police officer in the pool.

"Zoe was recently a victim of stalking and a kidnapping," a source close to the novelist stated. While an official cause of death has not yet been revealed, the LAPD has confirmed it appears to be an accident.

"Ms. Weiss sustained head injuries during her abduction and it is believed they were more severe than initially thought," Detective Guerrero says. "However, we will be following all lines of inquiry."

"It's so very sad," says her agent, Barb Wallace. "She was such a literary talent and so young. I always believed in her."

"She was a cool girl," Jake Morris, one of Ms. Weiss's neighbors, says.

Zach Hamilton's representatives issued a statement saying, "Zach is inconsolable. He and Ms. Weiss had a friendship that spanned years and he asks for privacy at this tragic time."

Comments:

@Softgirl111: God, that's so sad

@Lovenotwar: Poor Zach! I loved them together! This is so unfair!

@Jannnniiiiee: Honestly good riddance

@HayleyGrand0101 replying to @Jannnniiiiee: She was kidnapped and stalked too you fuck. Can't you read?

@Jent_82: Who kidnapped her?

@RandyRoo: Well I'm going to read her book *Fractured* now

@Softgirl111 replying to @RandyRoo: You should it's so creepy because the girl in her book is stalked and dies too! Like Life imitating art!

@HayleyGrand0101 replying to @RandyRoo: Agreed, read it, I loved it

Manuscript Sheds Light on Author's Death, Carlos Santiago Arrested

Carlos Santiago, 49, private investigator and security consultant to Hollywood actor Zach Hamilton, was arrested today in connection with the alleged murder of the novelist Zoe Ann Weiss. Ms. Weiss was found unresponsive in the pool of the apartment complex where she resided two months ago.

The arrest comes as a result of information provided by a manuscript penned by the deceased. Ms. Weiss's second novel, *The Close-Up*, written in the week and a half before she died, was handed over to law enforcement by her agent, Barb Wallace, soon after her death. Ms. Wallace received the manuscript by email just two hours before the author was found dead.

LAPD commented, with "Our investigators have been working tirelessly to piece this together, along with other crimes detailed in Ms. Weiss's manuscript. We are confident that justice will be served on all counts."

Zach Hamilton issued a statement saying: "I am horrified that somebody so close to me, that I trusted, could have done something like this. I loved Zoe. I miss her every day."

Investigations into other allegations made in the novel, against Mr. Santiago and others, are ongoing.

Comments:

@KimlovesDave4: OMG.

@Truecrimejunkie00000003: WHAT????!!!? What other crimes??? I need to know what's in that book!

@Lovenotwar: Ummm . . . did you see Zach already has a new girlfriend? Looks like he's really, really missing her.

@KimlovesDave4 replying to **@Lovenotwar:** Asshole.

@Centuryheart000: Is it going to be published? Hope so.

Zach Hamilton Pleads Guilty to Hit-and-Run

Zach Hamilton has today pled guilty to a hit-and-run after being brought in for questioning yesterday afternoon. Mr. Hamilton worked with the victim, Ky Walker, at a Santa Monica bar before landing the role that made him famous.

"Mr. Hamilton has been very cooperative," says a police source. Also being questioned is Brian Rollingston, his long-time manager.

Inside sources have confirmed that following these revelations, Mr. Hamilton's upcoming movie, due to shoot later in the year and the third in the action trilogy that shot him to fame, has been pulled. It is unclear whether it will be recast.

Mr. Hamilton will face sentencing later this week and his representatives were unavailable for comment.

Comments:

@Truecrimejunkie00000003: We should have guessed. He just looks like the kind of guy you can't trust.

@Softgirl111: I'd trust him tho.

@Jent_82: Same.

@Lovenotwar: watch him get off with community service or something lame like that. #everytime.

@Jim8080: This is messed up! I loved those movies! Why do I have to suffer?

@Truecrimejunkie00000003 replying to **@Jim8080:** Fuck off Jim.

The Close-Up, a Tell-All Novel by Zoe Ann Weiss, Expected to Drop Next Summer

The sophomore novel of Zoe Ann Weiss, the late girlfriend of Zach Hamilton, will be published next summer by the same imprint that published her first. Ms. Weiss was allegedly murdered earlier this year by Carlos Santiago, Zach Hamilton's security consultant, who is awaiting trial.

Publishing insiders reveal that the book follows the exact sequence of events that marked Ms. Weiss's last days, detailing the stalking incidents, her declining mental health, and her eventual escape from kidnap. "It's like stepping into the mind of a woman you know is going to die—like a train crash you can't look away from," a member of the editorial team has said.

When asked to comment, Zoe's father, Leonard Weiss, said, "She was everything to me. She had such a bright future ahead of her. I told her not to go to that place."

The option has been sold to Andreas Murphy and a screenplay is currently in production. It is rumored Veronica Santos, Zoe Ann Weiss's friend, will play her real-life role of best friend, "Vee." "I miss Zoe every day. I wish she could see all this," she says.

There is a confirmed first print run of 500,000 copies.

Comments:

@RandyRoo: I'm THERE. Read her first one already. So fucking creepy.

@Jent_82: Guys! Who kidnapped her?

@Calista3939 replying to **@Jent_82:** I read online it was some ex of hers. William Simmons. He was a screenwriter. Trust.

@Jent_82: Argh screenwriters are only second to drummers when it comes to shitty dating.

@woowoowoo2: He had an accomplice, Mary Hagel. But he killed her. And apparently he also had these really scary debts to criminals. I listened to this podcast all about him!

@Jent_82 replying to **@woowoowoo2:** I need to listen to that podcast.

@Centuryheart000: I can't wait for this.

@Jim8080: Great. I don't want to read another book about a woman complaining.

@Truecrimejunkie00000003 replying to **@Jim8080:** Umm the Incel forums are elsewhere

@anybodysbaby992: I heard that Zach Hamilton was trying to block the book. Just makes me want to read it more!

WATCH: Leaked Footage from Zach Hamilton Hit-and-Run

Footage has emerged from inside the vehicle Zach Hamilton was driving that hit and killed Ky Walker, a former work colleague. Mr. Hamilton is currently serving a probationary sentence.

While the footage confirms that Zach Hamilton was driving, he was not alone in the vehicle. William Simmons, his former co-worker and the man accused of kidnapping author Zoe Ann Weiss, whose bestselling novel *The Close-Up* was released last week and details the ordeal, was in the passenger seat. The audio provides new details about what actually happened that night, causing fans to jump to his defense. Below is a transcript following the collision.

Zach Hamilton: *Fuck, we need to get him to a hospital. Help me get him into the car.*

William Simmons: *No way, man, look at him—he'll never make it. Look at all that blood. And what the fuck would we tell them? The police will be here any moment. We need to leave.*

Zach Hamilton: *I don't know. I think—*

William Simmons: *Just fucking drive. We're going to get caught.*

This footage puts an end to months of speculation as to what evidence caused Zach Hamilton to confess and provides context to the judge's lenient sentencing. Watch the full footage below.

Comments:

@Truecrimejunkie00000003: Well this explains a lot. Have you guys read the book yet?

@Lovenotwar replying to **@Truecrimejunkie00000003:** I'm just starting!

@Jim8080: See Zach's not that bad!?! He wanted to stop.

@Truecrimejunkie00000003 replying to **@Jim8080:** Someone is dead. And Zach still killed him. And he didn't exactly stop anyway.

@Jent_82: Maybe that Sophie girl can steal this story too.

@Truecrimejunkie00000003 replying to **@Jim8080:** Also he hid it for years! He only told the truth because they arrested him and found evidence at his place! If she hadn't written that book he would have got away with it.

Carlos Santiago Convicted of Zoe Ann Weiss Murder

Carlos Santiago, private investigator and security consultant to Zach Hamilton, was today found guilty of the murder of Zoe Ann Weiss. Ms. Weiss died last year in May in a pool drowning.

Ms. Weiss's global bestselling novel, *The Close-Up*, written in the week and a half before she died, contained information that allowed law enforcement to make the arrest.

Mr. Santiago claims that he acted alone and will face sentencing later this week. Investigation into other allegations made by the novel remain ongoing.

Comments:

@KimlovesDave4: Argh. What the hell were the police doing? They were supposed to be watching her!

@Truecrimejunkie00000003: I bet the Carlos guy snuck in between the watch shifts. That, or he figured out another way in. But at least justice prevailed in the end.

@woowoowoo2: I hope they get answers about Jodie Spencer too. Did you guys read the book?

@Lovenotwar replying to **@woowoowoo2:** Yes I LOVED it. I hope so too. That Carlos guy is everything that's wrong with everything.

@Truecrimejunkie00000003 replying to **@Lovenotwar:** I'm getting Ray Donovan fixer vibes from him. Like I bet that Brian guy knew everything but the Carlos guy is taking the fall. That's what Ray would do.

@KimlovesDave4: How f*&Cked is Zach tho? Action hero? Ummm no. He totally ignored the ransom note. WTAF???????!

@Softgirl111 replying to **@KimlovesDave4:** I agree. He should have saved her.

@Centuryheart000: Have you guys seen the latest about a certain other celebrity? Do you guys believe her?

@Lovenotwar replying to **@Centuryheart000:** Ohhh . . . which one?

@Centuryheart000 replying to **@Lovenotwar:** let me find a link. I'll post it.

@Softgirl111: Exciting!

• • •

Zach Hamilton Comeback

Zach Hamilton, who took a five-year break from his acting career, is back. "Zach needed the time to process his trauma and kick some bad habits. He's been to rehab, served his probation, and started working with a spiritual advisor. I'm excited for this next stage in his career," his manager, Brian Rollingston, shared in a statement.

As yet, details of Zach's film are still under wraps, but it is rumored to be hitting the screens next year.

Comments:

@JessicaM9797 I remember him, didn't he used to play some action guy?

@Calley222 Yeah, his girlfriend died, poor guy

@Lovelove111 Still hot.

THE END

Acknowledgments

Thank you so much to my brilliant editors, Molly Gregory, Roberta Ivers, Brittany Lavery, and Adrienne Kerr. Without you, this book wouldn't be half of what it is (and I absolutely loved working with you!).

To my wonderful agent, Mollie Glick, who is the best ever and always in my corner.

To Berni Vann and Dana Spector at CAA for taking this and all of my other books into the world of film and TV.

To my writer friends, who sent me funny memes and "you can do it" messages late at night, and my non-writer friends, who forced me to think about something other than this world I was living in.

To my mum . . . for way too many reasons to list here.

To my sister, whose belief in me makes me believe in myself. I don't know what I'd do without you.

To Mickey—for all of the hilarious notes you left me around the house to keep me going when it was hard, for helping me keep everything in perspective, and for loving me.

To my dad, hope you're watching. I love you.

To the whole Gallery Books, HarperCollins Australia, and S&S Canada teams for making this book possible. And to Megan Beatie, Laura Benson, Sydney Morris, and Alyssa Boyden for yelling about it from the rooftops.

To my readers, for being on this journey with me. I can't tell you how much your messages and posts mean to me. Please never stop sending them.

To all the booksellers and bookstagrammers who tell people about my books, understand what I'm trying to do, and show me parts of my work I didn't even notice myself the first time around.

And to LA—may I always succumb to your magic-hour light.

About the Author

Pip Drysdale is an author, musician, and actor. She grew up in Africa, Canada, and Australia, became an adult in New York and London, and lives on a steady diet of coffee, dreams, and literature. Connect with Pip at PipDrysdale.com or on Facebook and Instagram @PipDrysdale.